# HOMEWORLD

# OTHER TITLES BY EVAN CURRIE

**Odyssey One series**
Into the Black
Heart of Matter
BOOK 4 (forthcoming)

**Warrior's Wings series**
On Silver Wings
Valkyrie Rising
Valkyrie Burning
The Valhalla Call (forthcoming)

**Other Works**
SEAL Team 13
Steam Legion
Thermals

# HOMEWORLD

## o d y s s e y  o n e

(Book3)

# E V A N   C U R R I E

47N⬦RTH

**Text copyright © 2013 Evan Currie**
All rights reserved.

Printed in the United States of America.

Published by 47North
P.O. Box 400818
Las Vegas, NV 89140

ISBN-13: 9781477808832
ISBN-10: 1477808833
Library of Congress Control Number: 2013940226

To Wynn Currie, my mother, who never doubted that I would eventually succeed in my writing endeavors. Without her support, I would never have made it as far as I have. Thanks, Wynn.

# PROLOGUE

## Star Gliese 581

▶ THE STARSHIP BARRELED into the system, rapidly losing speed and attempting to catch the gravity of the red dwarf star in an additional breaking maneuver. The retro-rockets erupting from nearly every forward surface of the ship strained against the inertia it had built on its voyage. With the help of the localized CM or countermass fields, they slowly succeeded in bleeding away the rest of the relativistic velocities until the ship was under positive control.

The People's Liberation Army Space Force vessel *Weifang* was one of only a half dozen *Mao Tse* class ships that had been reconfigured with fourth-generation counter-mass generators in order to permit faster-than-light travel. Since the success of the North American Confederacy with their much vaunted *Odyssey*, the pressure was on the Eastern Block to show the flag in this new space race, and the *Weifang* was the ship selected to do just that.

Captain Sun Ang Wen unstrapped himself from the acceleration bolster and drifted slightly as he pushed himself out of the chair.

Thanks to the effects of CM, they weren't being crushed by the massive deceleration forces the ship was technically experiencing. But the system wasn't perfect, so some of the impulse of negative gravity was still felt.

"Chart plotted, Captain," the navigator said, turning his head but not clearing his own restraints. "We're precisely on course."

"Excellent. Locate Gliese 581 D," Sun ordered. "That is our primary goal."

"Yes, Captain."

The Eastern Block Alliance had chosen Gliese 581 specifically because it was the home of one of the closest Earth-type worlds ever to be located. Why the Confederation had chosen to fly off in an entirely different direction with their first test, Sun didn't know. It was possible that their transition system used principals different enough from the more conventional designs the Block used that their choice of destinations would somehow make sense.

The Gliese system wasn't particularly likely to have any sort of life that would interest the Block, but the propaganda value of claiming some of the Earth-type planets closest to Earth itself would be of inestimable worth.

Sun thumbed open a comm to the lower decks. "Have the lander craft prepared and all maintenance checked. We will be orbiting our target shortly."

"Of course, Captain."

The *Weifang* continued to let off speed as they circled the red dwarf sun in a blindingly fast orbit. The relatively low energy output of the star let them cut in far closer to the corona than they'd dare in the Sol System. The tight corkscrew path used in extending their braking time was sufficient to bring them into an orbital insertion path for Gliese 581 D.

"Target planet ahead, Captain. We're approaching on an overtake orbit now."

Sun nodded. "Have we slowed enough to allow D's gravity to capture us?"

"Yes, Captain."

"Excellent," Sun said, satisfied as he looked at the display screen that showed the slowly growing orb in the distance.

"We're detecting objects in orbit, Captain."

"Moons?"

"No, Sir, too small. Possibly smaller asteroids captured by the world. There are several," the instrument specialist said, sounding puzzled as he spoke. "That is strange."

"What is it?"

There was silence as the man leaned into his console, glaring intently at the numbers flying past his screens. His eyes widened suddenly and he pushed back, head snapping around. "Captain! They're under power!"

"What?" Sun hooked a hand grip on the ceiling, pulling himself across the command deck to the instrument station. "Are you certain?"

"Yes, Captain. Objects are accelerating out of orbit, counter to the local gravity well."

"Course plot?"

The man hesitated briefly, then looked over. "Intercept plot, Captain."

Sun swore violently, knowing even as he did that it was a foolish thing to do. Thoughts of professionalism, however, were the furthest things from his mind as he kicked off, glided back to his own bolster seat and pulled himself down.

*We chose another direction entirely from where the Confederation sent their blasted Odyssey! Are those aliens they found here as well?*

The thought chilled him, just on the remote possibility that what they'd gleaned from the confidential reports they'd lifted from the Confederation's files were, in fact, accurate. Few people in the upper hierarchy of the Block believed it entirely, though it was obvious that the Confeds had run into something that didn't much like them in the depths of space. The existence of non-Terran life, intelligent life at that, was beyond debate now, but the idea of some apocalyptic horde of space Mongols seemed rather unlikely.

If it were true, however, the *Weifang* now had a distinct problem. More than that, it seemed that maybe the Earth was in more trouble than anyone at home seemed to believe.

*If these are the same, then not only are they closer to Earth than we believed…they appear to have surrounded us.*

"Sound combat alarms," Sun ordered. "All stations to level two."

"Yes, Captain. Level two alert, all stations."

The alarms sounded in the distance, blocked by the airlock doors that sealed off the command deck as the *Weifang* prepared for war.

▶▶▶

The drone ships reacted the instant they detected the approach of the red band. It was a reflex action over which they had no control. Fully ninety percent of their forces drew themselves from orbiting the world they were in the process of cleansing, taking a direct interception course towards the source of the irritation before they even finished analyzing the information.

They were almost within extreme strike range when they recognized that the figures were not what they were expecting.

It was a ship of the band, but not one of the immediate targets. The power curve being registered was even lower than the unknown ship that had so decimated their fleets in previous encounters. Brief consultations were made, probabilities debated, and it was decided that the ship in question had a high probability of belonging to the same source as the unknown ship now classified as *Drakr Yngat.*

The fleet went to high alert and spread their formation as they approached, weapons charged to full power, drives flaring brightly as they accelerated hard.

▶▶▶

"Incoming fast, interception courses, Captain!"

"I see," Sun said sternly. "Initiate evasive maneuvers. Are the CM capacitors fully charged?"

"Yes, Captain!"

"Direct full power to primary laser array capacitors. Maintain charging on all banks," Sun ordered, eyes intently trying to burn a hole in the tactical display.

"Power diverted, full charging."

"Lock in solutions for the lead elements," Sun ordered, highlighting the closest half-dozen ships. "Clear the cannons, wait for orders."

"Waiting."

Sun didn't want to start a confrontation. It was bad enough that the Confederation had gone out like American cowboys and started a damn war with these aliens. The last thing that Sun wanted was to give them any further reason to assault Earth.

*Hopefully they won't realize we're even from the same world. The* Weifang *has practically no similarity to the* Odyssey, Sun thought hopefully. Though as he watched the alien actions on the plot, he became more and more convinced that whether they recognized the *Weifang's* origin or not, they were spoiling for a fight.

Even so, Sun refused to initiate the encounter.

"Helm, hard to starboard," he ordered. "Turn us into the star, full counter-mass."

"Yes, Captain. Full counter-mass to starboard!"

The *Weifang* leaned into a sun dive, showing her flank to the incoming ships as she accelerated to starboard. Sun watched the plot, counting off the seconds it would take for their signal to reach the aliens and return. Almost to the second, his instrumentations officer twisted with a report.

"They've altered their course to intercept, Captain. Speed increasing."

*Damn. They intend to force a conflict, and no matter what else, they have us well outnumbered.*

He counted up the plot again, noting that there was an even dozen of the enemy ships and they all massed just under the tonnage of the *Weifang* herself. Optimistically, he knew that there was just no way he was fighting his way out of this.

"Main thrusters, flank power!"

"Flank. Yes, Captain!"

"Helm, Navigation, give us a best speed exit from the star's gravity. Cut us as close to the corona as you can!"

"Yes, Captain! Plotting new course."

The trick was going to be getting his ship slung around the star before the alien ships could get a solid lock on him. From the briefings he'd been given, he knew that the *Weifang* wouldn't stand a chance against a direct strike from their lasers, not if the reported power levels were accurate. Unlike the Confederation, the Eastern Block Alliance hadn't sunk nearly so much capital into laser resistant armor.

It was odd, to his mind, to be honest. The *Weifang* and other ships of the Type 99S class, indeed the majority of the Block space force, didn't rely on lasers nearly as much as the NAC did. The much vaunted adaptive armor of the NAC was far more effective against their own ships than against the Block.

*That, and apparently against these monsters,* Sun supposed grimly as he watched the plots.

"They're splitting apart, Captain!"

"What?" Sun snapped, refocusing on the alien icons.

They were indeed splitting off into two groups, one accelerating away on a reciprocal course even as the second group continued to close with the *Weifang.*

He stared for a moment, lips turning up slightly as he cocked his head and furrowed his brow. It wasn't until he glanced at the *Weifang's* own projected plot that he got it.

Sun swore again, this time as softly as he could.

*They move to intercept us as we break from the star. Clever.*

Whatever they were up to, they had also split their forces, and that meant that he now had to worry about six less enemy vessels in the immediate encounter.

*Cut the odds in half, though six to one is still hardly what I would call favorable.*

"Captain, pursuing group is closing to under one light minute."

"Begin evasive actions," Sun ordered. "Keep our bow to the corona. Seal all heat shields and prepare for damage control."

"Yes, Captain!"

Sun tested his straps, knowing that there was a good chance he was going to be relying upon them for real quite shortly. Satisfied that they were secure, he thumbed open the ship-wide intercom.

"All crew, prepare for emergency maneuvers," Sun said as calmly as he could manage. "Secure all items. Report to acceleration stations. Prepare for combat damage control."

With her bow angled as deep into the red dwarf star as they dared, the *Weifang* was accelerating faster than the ship had ever quite managed in the past. They weren't breaking any speed records; they'd already done that on the trip to Gliese 581. But they were certainly building speed faster than they ever had before.

"External temperature climbing. We're beginning to see internal spikes," Sun's man at Damage Control reported. "Permission to adapt armor for heat reflection?"

"Granted. Forward armor only."

The Block had managed to reverse engineer (or possibly outright steal) first-generation adaptive armor from the Confederation. Sun wasn't certain which, but it was useful enough for some things. Heat reflection was one of the default settings, along with best general deflection and a few basic camouflage modes. Certainly not in the league of the latest Confederacy toys, but useful.

"Yes, sir. Forward armor adapted," the man said, pausing for a moment. "Internal heat is dropping."

"They're still closing, Captain. Fifty light-sec—" The instrument officer's report was cut off when he suddenly started swearing wildly.

"Shi Ang Fa!" Sun snapped, eyes wide.

"Apologies, Captain. They have fired on us," Shi said, his voice a little shaky.

"And that was cause for your outburst?"

"Captain, you've read the reports on these aliens? The power levels of their weapons?" Shi asked.

"Of course."

"They underestimated."

"What?" Sun snapped his head around to stare at the man.

"The instrument reading on the energy of that laser is at least twice the reported numbers," Shi said. "Probably more. It's difficult to be precise because I'm relying on the reaction of already ionized particles as it passed through space this close to the star. Captain, we can't survive a single strike."

Now it was the Captain's turn to swear, though he did it under his breath as he considered his options. *Running hardly seems a palatable option. They've accurately predicted my plan, and taken steps to intercept me from two separate angles.*

The second group was relying on the first to drive him like cattle. Sun eyed the plot as the light seconds closed slowly, about one second every two minutes and opening. The *Weifang* was building Delta-V faster than their pursuers, but it wouldn't be enough to entirely evade contact since the enemy was already within extreme engagement range and still closing.

"Even armor, best heat deflection!" Sun ordered sharply.

"Armor evened, Captain!"

"Take us into the corona!" he told the helmsman. "Navigation, plot a high speed close orbit with breakaway that takes us clear of both groups."

"Plotting, Captain."

He could feel the unease on the Command deck from his last order, and didn't blame them, but Sun was gratified to find that no one questioned the order. Certainly it would be suicide to take the *Weifang* into the corona of Sol. She'd survive considerably longer sitting on the surface of the sun itself than trying to plow through the corona, in fact.

This wasn't Sol, however, and he just hoped that meant they might have a decent toss of the tiles here. Gliese 581 was a red dwarf, a star that expended considerably less of its energy as radiant heat, and that lower energy level might just give them a chance.

"Penetrating the corona, Captain. Internal temperatures climbing!"

*Gods, that was fast.*

"More laser flares, all around us!"

"Navigation!" Sun called. "We need those plots!"

"Done. Sent to Helm, Captain!"

"Helm!"

"Locking them in!"

"Engage the new course. Maximum thrust, minimum counter-mass!" he ordered. *Let the star do the work for us now.*

▶▶▶

The *Weifang* dipped its bow deeper into the blistering corona of the red dwarf sun, her armor glittering blindingly to any instruments in the system. Since the only ones that could see them both belonged to the enemy and were already locked onto them, her Captain and crew considered it to be a fair trade for their steadily increasing speed as the tidal force of the star's gravity snagged them.

Incandescent beams of light erupted around them as laser strikes spiked through the already excited plasma of the corona. The *Weifang* continued its minimal evasive actions, alternating between corkscrew patterns of varying tightness and a flying figure eight.

Behind them, their pursuers relentlessly continued without hesitation, plunging into the superheated corona themselves.

▶▶▶

On the Command deck of the *Weifang*, it was becoming obvious that while the maneuver might have been marginally successful in extending their lead on the pursuing ships, it had other significant drawbacks.

Sweat was pouring down the faces of every person on the deck, and Sun had no doubt that the entire crew was in a similar state. A few droplets of sweat floating in the micro-gravity environment struck the metal floor and sizzled into vapor, much to his shock and horror.

"Are the heat shields holding?" Sun demanded, eyes narrowed.

The damage control officer nodded wildly. "Yes, Captain. Temperature up, but within operating parameters."

Sun swore, something that was fast becoming a bad habit.

If the heat shields were reporting elevated yet still operating temperatures, there was only one reason for the ship to have gotten as hot as it was. The massive electromagnetic interference they were plunging through was actually turning every ferromagnetic surface of the ship into an induction-based heating element.

*We're a flying oven, in other words.*

"Ready to break out!" he called.

"Captain, we're not in optimal position for break out," the helmsman told him.

"Optimum position is on the other side of the star. We'll be broiled alive before we get there," Sun said, shaking his head. "We have no choice. Prepare for counter-mass pulse!"

"Yes, Captain. All capacitors stand ready for full power pulse to the counter-mass generators."

"Predictive course plot to my screens."

"On your screens, Captain."

The displays directly accessible to his eyes lit up, showing their current course in the tight orbit of the star along with a prediction of where they'd go if he initiated break out at that specific moment.

Sun licked his lips as he considered the timing, knowing that he wasn't going to get a clean escape vector. To achieve that he'd have to stay in the inductive range of the corona for far too long when even just minutes might be enough to literally cook his crew where they sat.

"Break on my command," he ordered.

The escape line would bring them within range of the second squadron's potential strike zone, but if he timed it right they would be able to limit the engagement time. That really just left him with one question remaining.

*They've fired on us. That's effectively an act of war. If I return fire, however, it will potentially escalate the situation. If I do not, there's a much higher chance that we won't survive this encounter.*

There wasn't really much of a choice, in all honesty. So far these ships perfectly matched the stolen intelligence on the *Odyssey* mission, even the line items that most of the Block's military capacity believed to be propaganda.

"Tactical," he called.

"Yes, Captain?"

"Arm aft tubes. Ready them to fire."

Behind the *Weifang*, the alien squadron was beginning to lose their overtake velocity. They were still gaining slowly, but time was now working in the *Weifang's* favor. Sun looked at the numbers, glad to note that at least the alien ships wouldn't be able to close in beyond long range. He didn't want to be on the wrong side of laser cannons that size if they were fired within ten light-seconds.

"Captain, we're showing unusual interference across all our high band instrumentation...," Shi spoke up, scowling at his displays.

"That's probably from the magnetic fields of the corona," Sun offered.

"No Captain," Shi shook his head. "These are hardened systems. The interference has to be in the system, but I can't seem to...."

A building hum took that moment to increase beyond all sense, drowning out the officer's words as a crackling sound joined in. Everyone looked around with growing nervousness, trying to identify the sound suddenly surrounding them.

"What is it?" Sun asked, eyes slowly moving around the Command deck as he looked for whatever it was he was hearing.

"Unknown. We've got interference across all high band instruments, internal and external," Shi said, his voice pitched high enough to hear yet still sounding hushed as he too looked slowly around.

"Enemy weapon?" Sun asked, remembering that the reports mentioned some kind of close-range weapon that the *Odyssey* listed as "unknown, extremely dangerous." He would have thought they were well out of range of any "close-range" weapon.

"Unknown," Shi said again, sounding helpless and irritated by the fact.

Sun didn't blame him. The idea of something happening on his ship that he didn't recognize and couldn't quantify annoyed the ever-living hell out of him. There was something about it that was niggling just at the edge of his brain, something of which he felt he should be aware.

"Aft tubes ready to fire, Captain."

He shook his head, trying to ignore the feeling as best he could. He had things to do at which he didn't have to guess.

"Do we have a firing solution for the pursuing ships?"

"Yes, Captain. Solution has been locked and updated continuously."

He nodded, checking the numbers briefly himself. As promised, the squadron had been locked in and tracked since he'd given the order. At the range they were dealing with, getting a solid lock was out of the question, but it was firm enough.

*And there's every chance that the corona is interfering with them as well.*

"Very well. All tubes go to rapid fire," he ordered.

"Yes, Captain. Rapid fire on all tubes!"

The ship didn't shake or rattle as the tubes belched their lethal payloads into space. The *Weifang* was too massive for that by far, but a chime sounded with every shot to let the crew know that things were running according to plan.

"Stand by to go to full counter-mass and break out," Sun ordered, eyes on the projective plot he was watching.

He barely noticed the acknowledgment, focused as he was on the plot while a portion of his mind was still being distracted by the crackling sound that reminded him of a live wire continuously shorting out. There were no reported drains on any of their trunk power leads, however, so he knew that it couldn't be that.

A grinding of metal on metal caught his attention, and he turned to see the Command deck airlock slide open. Beyond it his first officer, Kong Sha Tu, was waiting for the door to clear.

"Captain," he called as the door lock opened fully and he pushed off. "There is unusual electrical interference through the entire ship."

The word "electrical" clicked something in his mind, oddly perhaps since he'd been thinking it many times once the humming sounds began. Sun's eyes widened. He wrenched around, fighting his restraint straps, and glared back over his shoulder.

"Kong! Freeze! Do *not* move!"

His warning came a moment too late, however, as the first officer glided through the airlock door and thus between two separate metal poles.

The bolt of lightning that intersected his position was blinding, and in an instant Sun could taste ozone in the air as he released his straps and pushed out of the chair. He lifted his arms, hands out to stop anyone from moving past him.

"Everyone, halt where you are!" he ordered, eyes not moving from the lifeless form of his second in command.

"Wh...what happened?" a rather stunned junior officer managed to mumble out despite his shock.

"The magnetic induction field created a charge in the metal hull of the ship," Sun said, a bad taste in his mouth. "The entire hull and many of the internal components of the ship have been turned into live electrical capacitors."

He thumbed open the ship-wide communications. "All crewmembers, this is the Captain. Remain in your acceleration bolsters and do *not* move through the ship until further notice. These are your orders."

He closed the channel, then flipped over to the engineering channel. "Pan, this is the Captain."

"Yes, Captain?" the head engineer came back quickly.

"The ship's hull has become electrified. I need you to work out how to safely discharge the energy," Sun said. "Be aware that the first officer has been killed by a discharge."

"Electrified? How?"

"Most likely"—Sun sighed—"via the magnetic fields we've been flying through."

"Ah, same as an induction oven. Yes, I see. I'll begin immediately, Captain. Will not be possible to finish until we're clear of the corona, however," the engineer warned.

"Understood. That will not be a problem. Captain out." Sun broke the connection and drifted over to the body of his officer.

He couldn't ask someone from medical to come up for the corpse, so Sun had no choice but to pull the body over to Kong's station and strap him down into his bolster.

"Well, Kong," he said softly, "one last mission between us, shall we?"

He patted the dead man on the shoulder and drifted back to his own seat, strapping himself back into place as he quickly examined the displays around him to familiarize himself with the current situation once more.

He thumbed the ship-wide, signaling everyone again.

"This is the Captain. All crew are to stand ready for maneuvering," he said sternly, masking the ice that had sunk to the pit of his stomach. "Helm, go to maximum counter-mass, all flank thrust, on my mark."

A glance at the tactical display caused him to glance in another direction. "Status on the missiles?"

"Impact with targets in twenty seconds."

Sun nodded, examining the plot. *Twenty seconds. Not quite ideal, but close. Yes, that will do.*

"Initiate break away in fifteen seconds!" he ordered, eyes on the weapon plot.

The *Weifang's* missiles were CM-enhanced sub-nuclear guided weapons, a little old school compared to the toys the NAC played with, but very nearly as effective, just the same. They were slower than the speed captured intelligence indicated that the NAC's "pulse torpedoes" were listed as and were unfortunately vulnerable to interception, but the shaped charges within were far safer to handle and packed a punch that was nearly as potent.

At ten seconds to impact, Sun knew that the weapons would have entered terminal guidance, locking onto the specific target and accelerating in a last boost phase that burned up the remainder of their propellant. They would strike at a little under point-one lights, a speed that literally boggled Sun's mind, but his current worry was that it would be slow and they'd be picked off by point defense.

Given the distance between the *Weifang* and its pursuers, however, he would only learn that long after he had already been committed to his maneuver for some time.

The clock ticked down, the last ten seconds passing in an interminably slow fashion until they were gone.

"Break away! Break away!" the helmsman called as he initiated the maneuver. "All flank to thrust, maximum counter-mass engaged!"

Like a ball that had been spinning on a string and had just been cut free, the *Weifang* erupted outward from the star at high speed. The Chinese ship's counter-mass generators powered to full actually extended slightly beyond the ship's hull. So as they exploded out of the corona, they brought some of the plasma with them in a spectacular eruption on par with the most energetic of coronal mass ejections ever recorded by Earth instruments.

"Arm all forward tubes!" Sun called. "Get me a targeting solution for the squadron ahead of us."

"Calculating."

Sun nodded, though he knew that his officers were too busy looking to their own instruments to notice, and returned to the tactical displays focused on the closer pursuit group. "Status on our pursuers?"

"We lost contact when we exited the corona, Captain," Shi said. "Interference is keeping us from monitoring the telemetry of our missiles. We did register detonations, however, so they successfully entered terminal guidance."

"Understood. Thank you," Sun said, shifting his display forward to the second squadron that was now accelerating away from the star on a parallel course to their own.

The *Weifang* had a current time-speed advantage, but they'd lose a lot of that with the enemy now accelerating to keep them in range as long as possible. In open space, there were far fewer tricks they could use to lose or outrun the enemy; either they had the engines to muscle through or they didn't.

Unfortunately, from what he knew of the alien capabilities from captured NAC telemetry data, the *Weifang* simply didn't.

"Ships emerging from the corona, Captain!"

Sun flipped his displays to the rear, eyes on the data as it poured in.

"Four in pursuit, wait…five. Fifth ship appears badly damaged and burning in space, Captain. No sign of a sixth."

*One kill, one crippled. Not as bad as I expected,* Sun considered as he flipped forward again and analyzed the squadron ahead. *They seem as vulnerable to conventional weapons as they are to the Confederacy's latest toys.*

That was a touchy subject in the Eastern Block military, actually. Despite an early tech advantage in the last war, the NAC had outstripped them massively when the economy flip-flopped. Initially, China's massive economy and industrial base gave the Block what seemed an insurmountable advantage over the failing infrastructure of the United States.

For decades, the U.S. and most western nations had let their infrastructure crumble and rot away while China and other Asian nations had invested in the best technology of the day. The U.S. in particular was literally beggared by a point-by-point comparison. As early as 2010, places like Korea and Hong Kong had had Internet and information network access that made the United States look like a third-world country. Initially during the war, the Eastern Block seemed to have an insurmountable lead in industrial and scientific capacity.

The Eastern Block was more socialist in nature, with governments seeing the need for advancement even in the absence of immediate profit. That investment across the board gave the Block a massive advantage over the U.S. in the early days of the Third World War, but what no one in the Block had foreseen was the Second Industrial Revolution.

What started as hobbyist toys turned into a technical revolution that destroyed the Eastern Block as a relevant industrial superpower.

Microfactories, home replication systems, the ability to airdrop a box anywhere on the planet and have it start producing weapons, medicines, vehicles...within five years the Block economy was effectively crippled, and the war began to balance out. The United States had only held on as long as they did because supply logistics to invade the U.S. mainland were a nightmare. The Confederacy Pact bought them a couple years as the full resources of Canada and the worker population of Mexico were swung into the war effort, but it was simple home fabrication units that most people credited with winning the war.

Most people with an education, Sun amended to himself. Publically, the stars of the Confederate War effort were their Archangels of course. Built with captured CM technology stolen from Block aircraft, the Archangels had been effective, but were only a drop in the bucket against the war effort.

"Captain," Shi called, breaking him from his reverie. "The forward squadron is slowing."

*Slowing?* Sun scowled, examining the information. *That doesn't make sense. They'll lose several minutes of engagement time with their current changes.*

Sun didn't like it when the enemy seemingly handed him gifts from the gods. It usually meant that there was a curse hidden within waiting to be sprung.

*What are they up to?*

Sun's eyes narrowed and he flipped his displays back, checking the state of the pursuing squadron. He bared his teeth when he noted that they were still accelerating, and quickly plotted their future course against the *Weifang* and the forward squadron.

*They're going to catch us in crossfire. It'll be a shorter engagement, true, but there's no way the Weifang's defenses will hold up to that kind of firestorm.*

"Navigation, begin plotting alternative vectors," he ordered. "They want us in a trap. I would prefer to not indulge them."

"Yes, Captain!"

*They're better tacticians than the Confederate reports indicated,* Sun thought, annoyed. The captured NAC reports indicated what they actually called "giants swinging clubs about"— dangerous certainly, but also stupid. What he was seeing here, however, didn't agree with that assessment in the slightest.

"Captain, we have no clean escape vectors."

"I guessed as much already. I want a minimum contact vector."

"Plotted. Sent to your station, sir."

Sun nodded tersely, taking a moment to continue his previous thought while it was fresh in his mind. One thing space war had over the terrestrial kind was that decisions were made in leisure. There were limits to functioning within a stellar gravity well, and light-speed was one of those. *Are the Confederacy reports faulty, or are they just now beginning to learn from previous mistakes?*

Either was possible, as was the more remote possibility of intentionally bad intelligence being leaked to the Block's spies. Certainly the reports indicated that the *Odyssey* left few survivors to report back on tactical failures, so perhaps the aliens were simply slow due to poor or no intelligence of their own.

*Whatever it is, they could have picked a better time to learn new tricks.*

"Alternatives to your station, Captain."

"I have them," Sun affirmed, eyes falling on the alternative plots navigation had sent him.

It was all academic, really, just mathematical equations run through the *Weifang*'s network of supercomputers. Three options presented, only one of which offered better than a fifteen percent improvement over their current course. He picked that one.

"Course plot accepted, Captain. Engaging on your command."

"Set sail, Helm," Sun said. "Keep the star at our back, tell all stations to clear the guns, and stand by for combat."

"Yes, Captain. Issuing alert now."

War in space, Sun was learning, did not progress like terrestrial battles. On Earth, even with satellites and advanced instruments, you didn't see your enemy until they were already within striking distance. Over the horizon capabilities of many weapon systems meant that by the time an attack was visible, it had often already landed and it was all over save for the dying.

In space you could see your enemy literally so far off that engaging them would take days, weeks, or even longer. Even at relativistic speeds, as was currently the limit within solar gravity wells, launching weapons at extreme ranges could take hours or more before the payload arrived. Even lasers took minutes or longer, and with those time frames, accuracy was a bad joke at best.

You had to get close, within a few light-seconds ideally, to be considered truly lethal.

Oh, one could get lucky. A stray hit by those alien lasers, even at extreme ranges, might be enough to eliminate the *Weifang* to be sure. Still, no laser was perfectly collimated, and over distances measured in light-seconds, even the best would begin to lose power.

Judging from the initial engagements and from captured intelligence files, Sun was confident that the enemy relied primarily on lasers as their go-to weapon in a clinch. This was both good and bad for the *Weifang*, as a laser travelled at light-speed and was effectively impossible to detect until it was too late. But it was also unguided, and thus incapable of adjusting course after being fired.

The *Weifang*'s missiles were slower, to be sure, but they were self-guided and didn't lose their punch over distance.

*I suppose we'll see if the Block's old-styled weaponry is as effective against these aliens as the Confederacy's high-tech toys.*

"Pursuing ships are closing the distance, Captain. They're entering extreme range again."

Sun grimaced, eyes on the plot. *Damn, they're fast.*

The Block still had an edge over the Confederacy in counter-mass technology, roughly a generation or so ahead of the best the North Americans could manage. It was a struggle to stay ahead of them, but one that had been worth the effort in the local space race. It was also that lead which let the Block develop a FTL drive system separate from the ultra-classified transition technology of the Confederation.

The normally slack security of the NAC had tightened to unreal levels surrounding their transition technology. Anything even having to do with the theory behind the T-Drive was secured off world at a Confederation base on Mars.

In order for the Block to stay competitive, researchers had been forced to push CM technical development well past the bleeding edge and into unknown territory. That meant that the *Weifang* was considerably faster than the *Odyssey*, yet it was clear that the alien squadron was still able to get inside their orbit and would have at least a passing shot at engaging them.

"Shift armor to best deflection. All damage control teams to full alert," Sun ordered. "All weapons to full automatic fire. Engage as the targets bear."

There wasn't really a lot more he could do or say. From this point forward it was all down to the math.

"Yes, Captain!"

The *Weifang* barreled along its escape vector, warping space time all to hell and back as it went, six ships ahead of them angled in to engage from the side while to the aft five more would be opening fire anytime. Evasive course changes began as the closest ships approached within a light-minute, vectored thrust putting the ship into a pattern-eight cone with random interval changes.

Sun hoped it would be enough, but there was a definite limit on what kind of evasive action they could take if they wanted to keep putting distance between them and the enemy. If they spread their course changes out too much, they'd lose ground. Too little, however, and the enemy lasers would have an easy shot and they'd be fried.

*Of course, with luck on the wrong side of these equations, we'll fry anyway. Welcome to the war.*

"We just picked up stray photons from a laser, sir. Missed by at least a light-second."

"Understood. Do we know which ship?" Sun asked.

"Yes, Captain. The corona burn was clear."

"Direct the computers to engage the offender."

"Yes, Captain!"

The target lit up on his plot, and Sun noted that it was one of the ships off their port side bow that had engaged them. The *Weifang's* computers would have to wait until their evasive maneuvers brought them back to port before they could launch against the target.

"More photons, second laser source, Captain."

"Lock in the source, target and engage as the guns clear."

"Yes, Captain."

"Aft tubes one through five firing."

Sun nodded, checking the plot. The missiles were live in space, heading down well under full CM. As the distance between them and the *Weifang* increased, the telemetry feeds became more dated, but he kept one eye on them as they flew anyway.

Sun wanted hard data on the enemy point defense systems, and he wanted it yesterday.

"Forward tubes one through eight, firing."

New lights snapped into being on the plot, this time racing away to the port side forward. Those telemetry tracks quickly degraded as relativity and light-speed limitations took over as well, but he had the aft feeds to distract him from the annoyance.

The telemetry from aft reported the missiles entering terminal guidance, which meant that they'd already struck the enemy ship almost a minute earlier but he had to wait for that data. For the moment Sun contented himself with the limited feed coming from the instrument packages tucked into the missile's noses.

The enemy squadron opened fire with point defense lasers, or he assumed that they were PD lasers at least. It was possible they were using the main guns to swat the inbound weapons, but that seemed to be overkill of the highest order. Telemetry lights blinked out on the missiles one by one as they hit terminal guidance, warheads exploding from the main thrusters.

*Three missiles down before terminal mode. Can they catch the warheads in terminal?*

The answer, he was pleased to note, was clearly no. In terminal mode the warheads accelerated massively, propelled by an explosion that separated them from their thrust modules. They were already close to the target and the last second change of course and speed made them the devil itself to track and kill.

From the last two missiles, eight of the MIRV warheads slammed into the target. He had to wait a few more seconds from the end of the telemetry feed to get decent visual images from the *Weifang*'s scopes, but when they finally were processed he was rewarded with large gouts of fire erupting from the enemy ship and an almost instant loss of acceleration from same.

He flipped to the forward plot, the telemetry from those missiles having already gone terminal. Three of the missiles had survived that far, terminal guidance launching fifteen sub-munitions through space. Some of those lights blinked out as PD systems on the enemy ship leapt into action, but more than enough survived the final freefall to impact.

"Target is burning, Captain. Acceleration dropping."

Sun nodded. He'd seen it as well as anyone, but something about it was bothering him.

"They didn't support each other," he murmured.

"Excuse me, Captain?" Shi half turned. "Did you say something?"

"Nothing." Sun shook his head, almost absently. He was having a hard time believing it. There was no modern force on Earth that wouldn't use their own point defense to cover their allies. You just didn't fight like that.

"Captain! Multiple laser coronas detected! Both squadrons have engaged us fully."

"Mark the beams as best you can!" Sun ordered, attention refocusing.

Things would be getting violently rough now. With both squadrons firing, they'd be able to bracket the *Weifang* in.

"Lock in all aggressors!" Sun ordered. "Ready to go to automatic fire on all tubes!"

"Targets locked into the computers!"

"All tubes report ready!"

"Fir…." Sun frowned, pausing. "Hold!"

The crew ahead of him paused, glancing at each other and then back over their shoulders to where Sun was glaring dead ahead, seemingly at a random point on the wall.

"Captain?"

*They're not supporting each other. Why aren't they supporting each other?* Sun scowled, wondering if there was some kind of bizarre trap being laid.

He almost ignored the information, almost opted to go with standard procedures developed for fighting a

Confederate battle squadron during the last war. Instead, though, Sun slowly shook his head.

"Reprioritize targets," he ordered. "Target closest ship fore and aft!"

"Targeting, Captain!"

"Fire all forward tubes to the fore target, all aft tubes to the aft," he ordered. "Then retarget for the next closest targets in each arc."

Sun felt the crew hesitate for a second and knew the cause. You didn't usually put your missiles into a predictable approach vector like that, not against a Confederate battle squadron at least. They'd tighten right up and share the point defense tasking so that you wouldn't be able to fit a playing card in between their defenses.

This wasn't a Confederate battle group, however. Sun was now convinced. Whatever else these things were, experts on ship-to-ship combat wasn't one of them.

"Fore and aft tubes firing!"

*We'll take them apart one at a time if they'll let us,* Sun thought fiercely, though mentally he was beginning to agree with his counterpart on the N.A.C.S. *Odyssey*. There was something very wrong with these things. They did not fight like people.

"Retargeting!"

Sun tuned out the calls across the deck, focusing on the mapping of the enemy laser strikes. Getting a read on the exact strength and vector of a laser beam that *missed* you wasn't an easy task. The first clue you had would be from the coronal bloom, assuming it was close enough to hitting you to cook some of the external sensors and thereby trip the alerts. After that you could probably plot a locus of origin, but that was only a job half done. Getting a precise beam required a little more work and a fair amount of luck. Space wasn't empty the way people thought. It was just very, *very* sparsely populated, so to speak.

When the beam crossed paths with a stray molecule or even an atom, it would dump a ton of power into the bystander and make it jump energy states. While the beam itself was very focused and hard to detect, those high-energy state particles in the beam's trail weren't remotely as disciplined.

So it didn't take long for his men to have a partial lattice constructed in the computers to show where the enemy lasers were crossing space around the *Weifang*.

*Ancestors. One would believe that they were firing truly at random.* He glared at the plotter, unable to quite believe any of it. *This is insanity.*

He knew that he shouldn't be complaining. It was insane, but it was insanity in his favor. One thing he'd learned during the war, however, was that when something was too good to be true, someone was playing you.

"Direct hits to lead elements, both fore and aft! They're dropping back!"

"Third salvo clear and away!"

"Second salvo reports terminal guidance!"

There was nothing he could do, another thing that grated on Sun's nerves. The enemy was using no pattern, as near as he could tell, so course modifications would be just as aimless. The firing orders he'd given were working, and the *Weifang* was now beginning to pull away.

*Too easy.*

"Shi, full power to long-range scans," Sun ordered suddenly. "Narrow beam, dead ahead."

"Yes, Captain!"

He'd give real money, and honestly a lot more, for the tachyon technology of the Confederation, but without it Sun knew he'd have to rely on more traditional RADAR, LIDAR, and other infra and ultra bands of EM detection gear.

There was a general once, who told one of his soldiers: Ask me for anything but time.

Sun, ironically, had very little but time now.

"Target three hit! Acceleration falling!"

"Are we destroying any of them?" Sun demanded.

"No, Captain! Crippling strikes at best."

Sun shook his head. *Those missiles could sink a fleet of the Confederacy's best wet navy battle groups. Damn, these things are tough.*

"Number four's point defense took out most of our warheads," Shi reported. "Minor hits, no loss of acceleration."

"Reengage," Sun ordered. "Continue targeting by proximity to the *Weifang*."

"Yes, Captain, reengaging."

Something was wrong about the whole situation, but for now he was going to stay with what was working. Picking the enemy off one at a time was better than throwing thinner volleys against the entire force, at least until he got the readings back from the forward scan.

"Captain!"

*Speak of devils....*

"How many of them are there, Shi?" he asked calmly, a vague smile on his face.

"Two more squadrons, Captain." Shi half turned, staring at him. "How did you know? How did they even divine our course?"

"They didn't," Sun assured him, now comfortable that he knew what was going on. "I expect that if we had power to scan the whole system, it would *crawl*. We were nudged in the right direction by the initial intercept vectors and apparently random nature of their laser fire. Mathematically, our choice was obvious."

"Yes, Captain," Shi turned back, obviously confused and more than a little stricken.

Sun didn't blame him for the second part. The math was now looking a lot uglier for their chances. With two more squadrons dead ahead, they had no real clean escapes left to them. In another fifteen minutes or so, the trap would be snapped shut and Sun knew that the *Weifang* would be finished.

*Now, however, we do have one reasonable option.*

He opened the ship-wide comm, keeping his voice casual. "All crew are to stand ready for damage control operations."

"Helm, bring us about to One Forty Nine, Radian Twelve."

Silence reigned for a moment before the crew on deck twisted to look at him, apprehension in their eyes. He was proud to note that while nerves were clearly there to see, no real fear showed as they turned back without speaking and prepared to follow orders.

"Coming about, Captain."

"All forward tubes, go to rapid fire," Sun ordered as the *Weifang* stopped dodging wildly and pointed her bow right towards the short squadron that was still accelerating forward.

"All tubes...rapid fire. Yes, Captain."

The course of the *Weifang* turned into a short, sharp parabola that broke them clear out of the incoming trap but sent them barreling head first into the teeth of the closest of the enemy ships. Sun was determined to close the range to the damaged squadron as quickly as he could, hopefully before any of the other squadrons recognized his intent.

It was a risk, but what was life without risks?

"Forward," Sun said softly, "into the storm."

"Captain?"

"Nothing," he said, louder this time. "Do we have any reads on the enemy laser frequencies?"

"Partial frequencies on three ships."

"How close are they?"

"Widely varied."

Sun grimaced. There went the idea of just evening his armor to the average of the enemy frequencies. Whatever else they may be, it was clear that these…things, people, whatever they were, were not totally predictable.

"Pick one," he ordered.

"Captain?"

"Pick one, and adapt our armor to it," Sun repeated. "Don't care which one, just be lucky."

"Yes, Captain." The man looked more than slightly unnerved by the order, for which Sun did not blame him.

Sun was too busy to commiserate. They needed an escape from this be-damned system and the potential routes were closing at an alarming rate. He was about ready to trust his ship's fate to a power higher than himself, and he could only hope to get a little lucky.

With one eye on the screens and another on his personal display, Sun began to make some very rapid calculations with his terminal. His intentions were against every protocol, violated every safety procedure on the books, but at this point he was willing to toss them all out the proverbial and literal airlock.

"I need maximum power scans, dead ahead, and all passive scans for same!" He called out, "Get them here *yesterday!*"

He didn't bother to look up or even listen to the acknowledgements. He knew that his crew were working, they knew he was working, and they were all aware that the enemy was working.

*Let's see who finishes working first.*

"Laser coronas!"

"Continue evasive maneuvers!" Sun ordered, not looking up. If they were hit, they'd never see the beam that killed them. "All thrust!"

"Yes Captain, all thrust!"

The ship was corkscrewing through space, twisting and turning at seemingly random intervals as it tried to stay out of the crosshairs of the enemy firing at it. Intellectually, Sun and everyone on board were well aware that a starship, no matter how large in human scale, was a tiny target in the scale of the battle they were fighting. The odds of a lucky shot hitting them, miniscule.

As they closed the gap, however, and the light-speed reflection time continued to reduce…well, the enemy would have to rely far less on luck. Those odds started getting ugly.

He finished his calculations as the distance between the *Weifang* and the squadron ahead of them had closed to just under thirty light-seconds. Much closer and he knew that things would probably not go well. As it were, they were close enough to make evasion almost as much a matter of luck as the enemy successfully aiming their lasers.

On the other hand, their own weapons were guided and they'd been hammering the squadron the entire time. It was down to half strength, with only three of the original six ships still under power, and two of those were smoking.

*We may just be able to pull this off without getting crazy.*

"Captain! Two more full squadrons detected at extreme range! They're closing on high speed intercept!"

*So much for that.*

Sun hesitated a moment, then sent his calculations to the helm.

"Lay the course I just sent you," he spoke up. "And stand by to warp space-time."

The entire crew of the bridge turned to gape at him, shock easily filling their expressions. He ignored them all. They knew better than to question him.

"Engineering," he called down over the comm. "I'm going to need full power to the CM coils momentarily."

Another long hesitation before anyone answered.

"Yes, Captain. Captain, are you...."

"Sun out." He closed the connection. He didn't need people trying to talk him out of what he was about to do. They might just succeed.

A glance at the screens told the story. They were now within twenty light-seconds and staring down the bores of two enemy ships, with more bearing down on them. They might be able to hammer these two into dust, but it would leave them dealing with whatever else is left in the system, and he knew that wasn't going to end well for the *Weifang*.

"Secure for FTL," he ordered, grimacing at the idea of warping space-time that much within the gravity field of the star.

In theory, actually, it should work. There was an issue with maintaining course, however, since the space-time warps of the star and planets would affect the warp of the *Weifang*. He didn't care about that, not really, since he'd picked a course well and away from Earth mostly at random.

The more pressing concern was the fact that they couldn't *see* while in FTL, let alone actually *dodge* any debris. The space-time warps used to propel the ship should redirect most of the smaller debris away from the ship, but if they were to cross trails with something the size of, say, a small car...well, it might just punch right through.

At FTL, Sun doubted they'd ever know it happened.

"Helm. Engage space-time warp, maximum CM!" he ordered, partly before he could second guess himself again.

He felt the shiver run down his spine as the CM generators wound up and the screens went black just as the *Weifang* rocked violently.

"Laser strike!"

# CHAPTER ONE

▶ THE N.A.C.S. *ODYSSEY* rested serenely in the Lagrange point, high over Earth below. Construction scaffolds almost hid large parts of the ship from sight. If one were to look closely, workers could be seen moving about the microgravity environment as refit work was being completed on the large vessel.

The combat-related damage from her last mission had long been repaired, but with the North American Confederation now shifting to a defense buildup state of affairs, the big ship was currently being refitted extensively. Large chunks of the iconic hull were covered with Mylar sheets and radiation traps.

Captain Eric Stanton Weston looked over the scene from the observation deck of the Confederation's orbital station, already counting down the days to the completion of the refit.

"Captain."

Eric glanced over his shoulder, recognizing the man approaching from behind. "Mr. Gordon."

Seamus Gordon, an intel weenie near as Eric could tell, had once been described by a friend of his as *trouble in a cheap suit.* To date, Eric hadn't had the opportunity to verify his friend's words, and he really wasn't looking for one at the moment.

"I wanted to speak with you about your report," Gordon said, eyes focused outward to where the *Odyssey* rested.

"So speak."

Gordon glanced around briefly before sliding his hand into one pocket, and only then did he open his mouth again.

"The section concerning Central felt a little...light," Gordon said quietly.

"That would be because I don't think we have any words in the human language to properly describe just how damned creepy that thing is," Eric replied in kind. "Mr. Gordon, you have no idea what it's like to stand in the presence of something that can rifle through your mind like it's picking through a sock drawer for its favorite pair."

Gordon snorted. "No, though I've often wished I was able to do as much."

"Pardon me if I'm not dancing in joy at that concept."

The intel man smiled thinly. "Understandable. You reported that its range was planetary?"

"It *said* its range was planetary," Eric corrected. "Cannot confirm, nor deny."

"Fair enough. What do you think, though?"

Eric was quiet for a moment, considering. "Probably accurate. I don't know much about planetary geology, but if it is even remotely what it says it is, it makes sense that it would be limited within the geo-magnetic field."

"And if it weren't?"

"We'd have detected it," Eric said firmly. "We monitored every frequency, tachyon, and particle in that system. Nothing abnormal that we couldn't account for."

"Yesss...." Gordon hissed, turning slightly so he could look beyond the *Odyssey* to where the blue-and-white marble of Earth floated. "Nothing abnormal at all."

Eric followed his gaze and grimaced, not having to read the other man's mind.

*If Central was telling the truth, the Priminae didn't create it. Gestalt. The sum being greater than the parts. Would we have detected anything abnormal if, in fact, it was entirely normal after all?*

"Well," Gordon said finally, "we'll deal with that question when we come to it. For now, Captain, I'd appreciate a briefing on some of the other elements of your last mission."

"With all due respect, Mr. Gordon," Eric said, sounding bored, "you're a civilian, as best I can tell. You don't debrief me."

Gordon smiled thinly and handed him a card.

Eric grimaced even before he looked at it. Whatever it was, he was pretty sure he wasn't going to like it. He flipped the card open and sighed after reading it.

"I'll see you in the admiral's office in an hour," Seamus Gordon said, face beatific as he returned his gaze to the outside scene.

Eric scowled but said nothing as he pocketed the orders.

"It's really quite a ship you have there," Gordon said into the silence a short time later.

"None better," Eric said after a moment, finally deciding that the comment was meant as it was stated.

▶▶▶

"Senior Chief!"

Senior Chief Petty Officer Rachel Corrin looked over her shoulder, barely glancing at the approaching officer before she refocused on the job at hand.

"I'll be with you in a moment, Commander."

"Take your time, Chief," Roberts said as he observed just what she was doing. "Apologies for distracting you."

"If that was enough to distract me, I'd have fried my pretty little bum a long time ago, Commander," Rachel said, grinning tightly as she linked in the high-voltage wires with which she was working.

The system was regrettably live at the moment, as it was part of the bus lines that connected to the *Odyssey's* life support mains. It wouldn't do to have them down. Ironically, it would be even worse than normal now while in a refit dock because they had untold numbers of civilian contractors running around the ship who didn't know the *Odyssey's* emergency protocols.

In a moment she was done, and had the panels sealed tight and put to rights. Rachel clapped her hands free of mostly imagined dust—the ship's filters kept even its less-trafficked sections from building up much of that—and pushed herself down to the floor where her boots could lock into place.

"What did you need, Commander?"

"Updates on the new armaments," Roberts said, looking very put upon. "I was told they'd be done today, but no new reports have been filed."

"Probably because the contractors are running behind," Rachel said with a roll of her eyes. "They had to chop up our flight deck to fit the new systems in beneath the habitat drums, which has got to be seriously pissing off the Cap. And now they're having the devil of a time getting it airtight again."

Roberts grimaced. "No wonder they haven't filed any reports. How bad is it?"

"I can fix it in an hour, but I ain't getting paid half as much as they are," Rachel snorted. "So until I get orders to expedite, they can futz around all they like."

"Don't let them chop up anything we need, Chief."

"I've got eyes on them, no worries, Commander," she promised. "You got my word."

"That's all I ever need," Roberts nodded, turning around and leaving.

Rachel watched him go for a moment, and then shook her head and nodded over to one of her crew. "What's next?"

"We've got reports of power down all through the forward spires, Chief."

"Those idiots cut the mains when they chopped up the deck, didn't they?"

The man shrugged helplessly. "Looks like it, Chief. Sorry. We thought they'd be able to read a schematic map."

Rachel sighed. "Son, they're civilian contractors. They couldn't read a map if it was drawn in crayon. Why do you think people invented GPS?"

Her men chuckled, but she just sighed.

"Alright, let's get those mains patched and then make sure I don't break my word to the Commander. Come up, swabbies, we've got work to do."

▶▶▶

"The Chinese cracked FTL."

"Yes, we're aware of that, Admiral. What's your point?"

Admiral Gracen looked over the gathered group, her gaze as steely as she could manage, which wasn't anything to scoff at. She didn't much enjoy dealing with civilian oversight. They rarely understood what they were dealing with and usually didn't care to try. That would be fine if they were aware of their limitations, but that was something else she'd rarely encountered in a civilian politician.

She suppressed the urge to sigh. "We don't know how they did it. Most likely it's similar to the Priminae's method of FTL, which seems to be a variant of the Alcubierre theory."

"Our transition drive is far superior to either," the civilian senator said confidently.

"You haven't studied the Alcubierre theoreticals, have you?" Gracen asked dryly.

The man scowled openly at her. "What does that have to do with anything?"

"DARPA started funding warp drive tech over fifty years ago," she said, "decades after Alcubierre developed his theory. Do you know why a government defense program started pumping money into a NASA project during the greatest recession of the twenty-first century?"

No one spoke, not that she had expected them to.

"No, of course you don't, because none of you have done the *reading*," Gracen told them all acidly. "DARPA started pouring funds into it because they were terrified that a Chinese space program might do it first and develop a weapon that made atomic bombs look like firecrackers."

"We all know about the dangers of kinetic weapons, Admiral."

"I'm not talking about kinetics," she growled, slapping her hand down on the desk. "I'm talking about the resonance buildup and release of high-energy particles picked up by the drive while in motion. A working Alcubierre system without extensive safety systems in place could potentially annihilate *planets* upon arrival."

She looked around the room, noting with no irony that *now* she had their full attention.

"So I say again, gentlemen," Gracen said dryly, "the Chinese have developed FTL capability. We need to determine if they've also created a weapon capable of scorching Mars to a cinder, or maybe baking North America to a crisp."

Her words were followed by a profound silence as her meaning finally seeped through to her audience. Then they exploded in the predictable panicked babble. She let it go on for a moment before clearing her throat loudly enough to quiet a few of those closest to her. The rest continued to talk over each other until Gracen again slapped her hand down on the conference table with authority.

"Enough."

Everyone fell silent, turning to look at the aristocratic visage of the admiral.

"Now that you have an idea of the severity of the situation, I'd like to point out that some of you were seated on this council when we scrapped funding to the Alcubierre project. Congratulations," she said acidly. "We are, once again, playing catch up to the scientific progress of the Block. That said, while I expect that they'll use any such weapon as leverage on us, it's less likely than ever that the Block Alliance will initiate a new war. We have other priorities, both of us."

"That doesn't mean we can let them get ahead of us in an arms race."

Gracen smiled. "Absolutely true. Let's have a chat about my research and development budget first then, shall we?"

▶ ▶ ▶

It was some time later when Weston was admitted to the admiral's office for his appointment with her and Gordon. He saluted Gracen automatically, noting that she seemed a little tired when she returned the salute and nodded to the free chair.

"Take a seat, Captain," she said. "Mr. Gordon has some questions for you and, as they happen to match some of my own, I elected to allow him to handle this debriefing."

"I've already been debriefed, ma'am, and I put everything in my report."

She nodded. "I'm sure you did, Captain. This is more about asking you to speculate on a few things we noted from your last mission report."

Eric nodded slowly, not certain he understood but honestly knowing that he didn't really have to. "Very well. What questions?"

"During your initial sortie against the alien ships, our Priminae allies made use of a particularly dirty nuclear device?" Gordon asked from where he was sitting.

Eric snorted. "Dirty doesn't describe it. That thing was so filthy, it violated the laws of physics as we understand them. We were *light-minutes* from the detonation and, if anything, the radiation seemed to get worse as it spread out."

Gordon nodded. "We're interested in that technology, Captain."

Eric grimaced. "I hope you don't want to use it on any planet, let alone Earth. I asked about it afterwards, privately. They use some sort of material and technique that induces a chain reaction when it encounters new matter. So the radiation literally fed off the *Odyssey*'s armor until we changed to reflective shielding. Thank God that was enough to keep it at bay, but if you used that weapon inside a planet's atmosphere...I don't think you'd have a planet left, not worth inhabiting at least."

"Yes. We're aware. However we're looking at it from other angles. Any information you can get on the technology would be appreciated."

"Alright. I can speak with the Priminae if you want," Eric said finally.

"Thank you, Captain." Gordon nodded, then glanced at the admiral.

Gracen acceded to the wordless invitation and took over the questioning. "Let's move on to the stellar object."

"The Dyson Cloud?"

"Yes," she said. "We've consulted our records. Based on the last observation of the James Webb Telescope, the enemy started construction just under a hundred years ago. That star only went dim sometime in the last ten years, give or take, local time."

Eric curled up his lips, shaking his head. "God, that's fast."

"Indeed. It's quite clear that this species handles construction much the same way they handle destruction," Gracen said. "They must build self-replicating and self-organizing structures."

Eric nodded. He'd come to much the same conclusions himself once he'd done some research and spoken with his people. The enemy, Drasin or whatever they called themselves, were in many ways a macro-sized version of the nanotechnology nightmare. The so-called grey-goo scenario, writ massively large.

"Would it be possible to capture some specimens of the alien forces intact?"

Eric turned slowly to stare wide-eyed at Gordon.

"What?" The man in the suit asked, looking around as the Captain just stared at him.

"Sir," Eric said stiffly, "these things literally *eat* steel and excrete reinforcements. I'm not packing one of them on board my ship for any reason, and I would consider any orders to that effect to be both insane and illegal."

Gordon held up his hands. "Calmly, Captain. I was just asking a question. We've made a lot of progress with self-replicating machinery, but these things are on a completely different level. It would be nice if we could even that playing field a little."

Eric let out a breath, but nodded grudgingly. "I can understand that, but we don't have any way of containing them. Putting them on board a ship is just asking for trouble in ways I can only begin to imagine. Further, we've never been able to determine anything about their anatomy."

"No, not on dead samples," Gordon acknowledged, "which is why I was asking about intact and living ones. Some of our researchers think that they must use fluid neural paths through the molten silicon in their bodies, some kind of nanotech self-assembling circuitry. We'd love to get a glimpse of it in action, if that's the case."

"Not on my ship," Eric said flatly. "You want to mess with those things, I suggest using something expendable."

"I can't see how one of their drones would be a serious threat to the *Odyssey*," Gordon told him dryly.

"One wouldn't be, but keeping one around long enough to do tests is another matter entirely," Eric said. "They eat *everything* they encounter and use it to reproduce. We don't have any way to sedate them, and we don't know just how invasive their self-assembly techniques are. Mr. Gordon, I'll not have one of those things on my ship. Not alive. When we brought back the dead ones, I kept twenty-four-hour guards on them just in case they had active nanotech."

Gordon sighed, but knew that there was no way he'd have the influence to force the matter just yet. With Weston being as clear on the matter as it was possible to be, the NAC wasn't likely to issue countermanding orders that might reasonably be expected to put a ship in jeopardy.

"Very well, Captain. For now," Gordon acceded finally.

"Figure out a way to contain them, or even sedate them," Eric said, "and then we can talk. I know how important this intelligence could be, Gordon. A risk is fine. I didn't sign up for the safe life, but I'm no martyr either. Give me decent odds of at least bringing home useable intel and I'll take a shot. Until then, I'm done talking about it."

Gordon grimaced, but had to accede to the point. Killing the things was obviously not a huge problem, but holding them intact was a far different story. They needed information on what the things could and, more important, could *not* eat.

Whatever else these Drasin were, he was well aware that they were most certainly a technological, or possibly biological, nightmare. Honestly he didn't know which they were, or if maybe they belonged to a third category, but the nightmare part stood.

Figuring out what do with a species like the Drasin running around the galaxy was now taking up almost his entire job. He used to split his time between the Block and various non-aligned nations that might be causing the NAC troubles. Now he found himself in the role of some science-fiction protagonist.

Frankly, Seamus Gordon preferred mundane wet work.

"Fine. We'll have people look into that," Gordon said after a moment. "Admiral, when will the *Odyssey* refit be complete?"

"The new weapon systems should be installed within a week," Gracen said after a moment's thought, glancing over at Eric. "Isn't that right, Captain?"

He nodded. "Around that. We'll have to run the standard tests before I'll trust the new systems…."

"Not in Sol System, Captain," Gordon said instantly.

"Pardon me?" Eric blinked.

He knew that the current treaties precluded weapon testing within set ranges of Earth space, but the entire system?

"The t-cannons are highly classified," Gordon said. "I don't know if you've been briefed, but we're privately advising ship commanders not to test those systems anywhere within range of Block ships, stations, or drones."

"He's right, Captain," Gracen said seriously. "The orders aren't official, mostly because we don't want the Block to know just how classified the t-cannons are. You'll receive private orders to this effect before you clear the L5."

"Understood." Eric nodded. "Any ideas what my orders, officially, will be?"

"Most likely another diplomatic envoy to the Priminae," Gracen told him. "The *Odyssey*, yourself, and your crew have a degree of respect there that is invaluable."

Eric had guessed this was the case and honestly didn't mind much. He liked the Priminae, and there were enough mysteries tangled up in them that he wouldn't be getting bored anytime soon, unlike most other diplo-missions.

"We might have you pop into a couple systems that just hit our watch list, however, including Gliese 581," she added.

"Any particular reason?" Eric was actually familiar with that star, in general terms at least. It had been on his original mission itinerary when the *Odyssey* was commissioned. Gliese 581 was on the list of star systems that had likely Earth-type planets in the so called Goldilocks Zone. That put it high up on the area of interest, given the system's relative proximity to Sol.

"We tracked the recent Chinese FTL mission in that general direction. It's one of the few systems they might take an interest in," Gordon said blandly.

Eric just gaped at him.

"Excuse me? What Chinese FTL mission?" He looked sharply between the admiral and the spy. "Did they manage to steal transition tech?"

"No, they went another route," Gordon answered. "It seems that they managed to bridge the Alcubierre equations."

Eric scowled, thinking for a moment. He'd read up on Alcubierre briefly when he'd been posted to the *Odyssey*, but no one in the NACS had managed to quite make that theory practical. The power requirements were insane for one thing, though they had been cut down a lot from the original numbers. More important was that, unlike the transition system, you actually *travelled* through intervening space.

That was a big deal, as even the best instrument package wouldn't be able to detect, analyze, and warn you about what was in front of you until you'd already plowed through it. Arguably it was a minor flaw, but from his own experience, Eric knew that he absolutely despised flying blind…even when he knew intellectually that the road in front of him was better than ninety-nine percent clear.

"Did they solve the navigation issues?" he asked, curious, as it was obvious that they must have solved the power issues.

"Unknown. We didn't even realize that they'd solved any of the Alcubierre equations," Gordon admitted sourly. "When the *Weifang* red-shifted beyond Pluto and vanished off our instruments, I'm pretty sure some guys in the tracking stations crapped their pants."

"I'll bet," Eric mumbled.

"Our primary goal is still diplomatic exchange with the Priminae," Gracen stressed. "However, any intel on the Chinese activities outside our solar system would be a very nice bonus."

"Understood," Eric replied. "The T-Drive must have lit one hell of a fire under them to have made this move so quickly."

"Well, they've always had an edge on us in CM technology by at least a generation or two," Gordon said. "We weren't even close to cracking it until we stole the first-gen plans from one of their labs just before the war."

"Their computers are usually better too," Eric added sourly.

"No surprise there. Most of the industrial fabricators were in Block nations before the war, and a large percentage of the top designers were Block sympathizers." Gordon sighed. "So it's possible that they've worked out the instrumentation problems too."

Eric nodded. "Yeah, better than just possible I'd say."

Before the Block War, the United States had felt, in some ways rightly, that they were the top country on the planet. The problem was that while that was true for military power, the country had been yielding a lot of other top slots to Japan, Korea, China, and other nations with citizens willing to do work for pay at which a homeless person in the U.S. would openly laugh.

While Japan had actively opposed the Block, siding with the NAC, just about every up-and-coming industrial powerhouse had formed the foundation of the Block's strength. From Korea to China to India, the industrial power that once belonged to the United States and its allies had systematically been moved overseas by U.S. corporations because it was cost effective.

That, combined with the fact that Western nations had been educating the smartest people from the Block nations only to have them take that education right back home with them…well, when the war kicked off, it didn't start well for the NAC.

At the start of the war, the U.S. still controlled fully fifty percent of the naval power on the *entire planet*, but the edge in air power fell to the Chinese when they rolled out the first-generation counter-mass aircraft. Chinese Mantis fighters tore through the air defenses of the U.S.S. *Enterprise* carrier task group and left the most powerful warship on the planet in a smoking cinder as it slowly sank beneath the waves. Naval power was meaningless while the air was being contested, and the Block successfully ruled the skies for almost three months.

Right up until the Archangels made the scene over Japan.

So now the Block had made their dominance in CM technology evident again, but this time Eric was almost glad of it. He'd seen what was out there, and any human technological advancement was a good technological advancement.

*Screw the national patriotism. We need every running gun we can lay our hands on.*

Images of the Dyson Cloud loomed over every waking moment of his life now, and a good chunk of his nightmares. If the Block was showing their flag outside the Sol System, all the better. They'd have to fight alongside everyone else unless they wanted it burned to the ground by the Drasin and whoever was behind them.

"Alright, I'll keep an eye out. We can detour the *Odyssey* through some high-probability locations, just to see if they're around," he said finally. "But I don't see the problem. The Block is a lot of things, but they're not crazy enough to start another war now. We've got enough tech edges against them to make the outcome wildly uncertain from their point of view, and now there are the Drasin to deal with."

"The Block leadership isn't certain that the Drasin are real, Captain," Gordon said, shaking his head. "A significant group believe it's all just propaganda."

"Oh for crying out…." Eric spat, annoyed.

Honestly, he had no idea why he was even remotely surprised, but it still pissed him off that his word on this was being questioned. It wasn't like they had any reason to believe him, but it was still irksome.

"I suppose I shouldn't be surprised," he said.

"No, not really." Gordon chuckled. "But look at the bright side. If they've developed decent FTL, they'll soon find out for themselves."

"Assuming they survive to report back," Gracen reminded them both. "The Block doesn't have cam-plate technology anywhere near our own, and without a decent laser defense they're not likely to have as enjoyable a time as the *Odyssey* had."

"There is that," Gordon said with a sigh.

"Do I have orders if I find them in dire straits?"

"Law of the sea, Captain. We're not at war with the Block at the moment. Rescue if possible."

"Aye, aye, ma'am."

"That should be everything we need to cover personally," Gracen said. "Official orders and background will be in your dossier before the *Odyssey* ships out again. Just keep this conversation in the back of your mind, if you will?"

"Understood, Admiral." Eric rose to his feet. He saluted, then nodded to the spy. "Mr. Gordon."

"I'll be seeing you, Captain."

Eric didn't *quite* glare at the man as he left, bringing a smile to the spy's face.

"That man wouldn't survive a day in the Agency."

"Possibly not," Gracen shrugged. "However he does make a very nice flag Captain."

"Everyone does pay attention when he shows up, don't they?" Gordon chuckled lightly. "He practically oozes sincerity and honor, at that. I could wish for someone a little more underhanded in command of the *Odyssey*, but he'll do."

"Someone more underhanded might not have passed muster with the Priminae, let alone this Central character," Gracen reminded him.

"True, but they might not have gotten us involved in an interstellar war either."

"I originally thought that, but no," Gracen said and shook her head. "I fear this was coming regardless. He just accelerated the program a little. It's not a perfect situation, by any means. I could have wished that he'd gotten the intel and got the hell out...but given the newest intel the *Odyssey* brought back, saving the Priminae may well have been the best of all possible worlds for us."

Gordon grunted, but didn't deny the possibility. Pacifists though they might be, the Prims were well equipped and clearly capable of building on an accelerated schedule. He wasn't sure it would matter, not given the deplorable numbers that the Drasin seemed capable of fielding, but any ally was better than none.

# CHAPTER TWO

## Interstellar Space, Near Formerly Uncharted Dyson Construct

▶ "THE BIOLOGICALS ARE entirely out of control, Prohuer. If we do not shut them down soon, we'll entirely lose any semblance of guidance."

"You should relax, Ivanth," the man in the dark uniform said, seated casually behind a metal desk. "I've read the reports, and you're exaggerating the situation."

"The reports are only half of it," the younger man said earnestly, desperately trying to get his point across without disrespect. "They've begun annihilating non-Priminae worlds!"

"Uninhabited worlds, barely of any interest to us."

"My Prohuer," Ivanth said softly, "life-bearing planets are not so common in the galaxy as to be disposable."

The man behind the desk chuckled lightly, smiling with an ease that belied the subject of their conversation. "This is a minor sector of an otherwise unimportant galactic arm, Ivanth. The Priminae are the only threat in the area, and they don't even know their own history. We'll have this cleaned up shortly and be back to civilization. Let the Biologicals have their fun."

"Yes, my Prohuer." Ivanth gave in, sighing. "What of the unknown?"

That caused the man to sit forward, templing his hands in front of him. "Yes, the unknown. I've reviewed the combat data we recovered from the Biologicals. They all match the ship that escaped us at the Hive."

"It doesn't match any Priminae ship on record. A new design?"

"No, I think not. The Priminae ships match records precisely," the Prohuer said simply. "We're looking at another source."

"Our scans were conclusive," Ivanth objected. "They were people."

"Yes, yes of that I'm aware, and that is the only thing on this mission that troubles me," the Prohuer admitted. "Obviously the Prim have allied themselves with another splinter faction of the People. We never learned why the Prim retreated into this back world sector of the galaxy, but apparently someone came with them."

"That ship is clearly an example of a combatant species," Ivanth said, confused. "That is clearly unlike the Priminae, and it seems odd that they would ally."

The Prohuer sighed, shaking his head. "We have tracked the Prim across the lights of ten thousand stars and I am no closer to understanding them now than I was in the beginning. They are cowards who hide behind their pretty words. It is not much different to see them hide behind another people's ship."

"Perhaps," Ivanth admitted, "but only *one*? One ship, against many times its number of the Biologicals, and even several of our own in the Hive, and it either escaped or triumphed each time. Our own best could not easily match it."

"I know, and that troubles me more than anything else," the Proheur admitted. "It barely registers on our threat boards, at best. Within the Hive, the vessel remained entirely hidden from every scan save the space-time warping it caused in passing. For all that, these people obviously maintained sufficient military power to pose a credible threat. They are an unknown, and that makes them worrisome. But so far we've only seen one ship. And one ship, even one a thousand-fold more powerful, will not...cannot, blunt the edge of our assault."

Ivanth nodded.

There was truth in that. Even a fleet of such warships couldn't hope to hold a line in space against the full weight of the Biologicals. They could choke a star system with their dead and still come on unabated.

By legend, they had once. The Biologicals had waged an insane war against the Progenitors, beating them back system by system, until they were encamped behind the defenses of the Homeworld. Waves upon waves of the Biologicals descended, only to be battered to dust and shards by the defenses.

Waves upon waves.

Eventually, so the story went, the sheer warping of space by their mass alone inverted the local star and sucked everything for a stellar cycle into the newly formed black hole.

It was a legend, of course. Fanciful, nightmarish, and logically impossible.

For all that, however, Ivanth knew more than anyone alive just how high the numbers of the Biologicals were and could become. He didn't tell that story to his children. It frightened him far too much.

▶▶▶

# IN THE BLACK BETWEEN STARS

## P.L.A.S.F. Weifang

▶ "SOMEONE VENT THIS smoke!" Sun ordered as he swung into the aft section of main engineering. "We need you people alive or the *Weifang* will never reach home!"

"Filtration is down to a fifth, Captain. We can't clear the air."

Sun swore, long and vile words that had no business coming from the mouth of a professional soldier of the people's army. The ship's filters were barely keeping up. Soon they'd begin to fail, and when that happened, the *Weifang* would be just one more ghost ship in the legends of the universe.

"Pull the candles from ship's stores," he ordered.

"Captain, we don't have nearly enough for the journey home."

"What does that matter? We'll not survive the trip if we don't clear this smoke and get the filters running again. Pull the candles, I say, and then fix the filters, if you must rebuild them from vacuum!"

"Yes, Captain!" The engineer fell back, issuing orders to the other men.

Sun watched the work as it continued, knowing that the oxygen candles would do little but buy them time. He'd hold back a few dozen of the precious canisters against the hope that they could get the filters working again, but it wasn't looking good.

*Those things hit us where it hurt,* Sun thought grimly. *Half our engineering section is in tatters, along with most of the fabs. What's left is in hard vacuum and exposed to FTL space.*

There was no getting around it, Sun knew.

The *Weifang* would have to slow down in order to affect repairs.

He made his way back through the labyrinthine passages to the Command deck, ignoring his own station to come to rest near the shoulder of the long-range instrumentation station.

"Is there any sign of pursuit?" he asked tersely.

The man holding the station shook his head. "No, Captain, nothing."

The crewmember hesitated a moment, then turned to look at Sun. "But, Captain, half our instruments were blown out and we're in FTL. We're not blind, but we aren't seeing twenty/twenty as the doctor may say either."

"Understood." Sun clapped his man on the shoulder and kicked back.

He drifted back to the command station and strapped himself in. "Helm. Signal preparations to drop from FTL."

"Yes, Captain! Preparations underway."

"Ease up on CM when ready. Bring us out of FTL and reduce speed to low relativistic rates."

Alarms sounded through the ship, warning all hands to move to deceleration positions. Stations began to report in one by one.

"All stations report clear to decelerate."

"Dropping CM," the helmsman said, his voice tense. "We'll cross the light-speed barrier…now."

The ride didn't perceptibly roughen, not like dropping from supersonic to subsonic in atmosphere, but there was an edge that suddenly assaulted them even as they braced themselves for it. The CM drive was a miracle of multidimensional engineering, manipulating space-time to form an incline on which the *Weifang* "surfed." While under full CM drive, the bubble in which the *Weifang* sat was insulated from normal space-time, but when they dropped CM there was a brief Doppler effect on light. Most of it was beyond human visual limits, but enough leaked out to make a man ill if he wasn't guarded against it.

The feeling only lasted a moment, and then they were far enough below light-speed that it wasn't noticeable.

"Light-speed instrumentation coming online, Captain!"

"Give me a full area scan, centered on our position," Sun ordered, unstrapping himself from the station. "Let me know the instant you see anything that concerns you. I'm heading aft."

"Yes, Captain!"

▶▶▶

Sun grimaced as he overlooked the evacuated sections of his ship through the tinted plate of his EVA suit.

*The enemy lasers simply vaporized a hundred square meters of armor plated steel. Unbelievable.*

The strike had been a single instant in time, a moment of terror in the long hours of emptiness between the clash of crossed swords that defined the battle they'd endured, and yet the damage seemed impossible.

For good or ill, there were few bodies to be found as they made their way through the damaged sections. Most had been blown out by the explosive decompression, so there would be no bodies to return to their families when— if—the *Weifang* returned home. On the plus side of that, he didn't have to worry about possibly losing another of his people to choking on their own vomit if they ran into the corpse of someone they knew while being sealed in an EVA suit.

It was a very small silver lining, but at the moment Sun would take what he could get.

"Find any fabricators that look intact or repairable. We need to get the filters replaced," he said, waving his crew forward.

They acknowledged, dragging themselves through the sections while Sun took a moment to twist around and look out on interstellar space.

It was…startling. Beautiful. Terrifying.

This far out from any source of light or reflection, the universe felt infinitely black and absolutely brilliant at the same time. The sky held more stars than he'd ever seen from Earth, yet that faint light only served to emphasize just how very dark it was.

Aside from their suit lights, and those distant unblinking stars, there was nothing but an absolute blackness the likes of which he'd never imagined. Sun felt awed and humbled just being in the presence of darkness so profound, and his eyes refused to look on it directly for any length of time.

"Captain, we've located the fabricators. They seem to be mostly intact."

Sun shook himself free of the introspection. "Good. Get them unbolted so we can pull them back into the ship."

"Yes, Captain."

▶▶▶

Shifting the mass of the fabricators was difficult, even in microgravity. The Block may have the lead in CM technology, among a few others, but Sun had to admit that the best fab units were manufactured in the Confederacy.

Block units were capable, but bulky in comparison. Of course, all things were relative, he supposed. They fit the capabilities of an advanced automated factory into the space of a small room. That was pretty compact.

He'd heard that they had some models that were the size of a dinner plate yet could construct a house inside of twelve hours. A nice house.

*Unfortunately we don't have any of those on board.*

Moving the fabricators was simple enough, just incredibly dangerous and time consuming. They couldn't afford to get them moving fast; their momentum would turn them into lethal projectiles and, possibly worse, they might be damaged and take with them the *Weifang's* already slim chances for survival.

So they had to inch them through the corridors, pushing from both ends so that they couldn't get out of control. It was a long, arduous, and incredibly dangerous procedure.

And they had to do every bit of it in bulky EVA gear that barely fit through some of the tighter sections.

After working around the clock, almost three full shifts in EVA gear, they finally got the pieces inside the secured sections of the *Weifang*. After that, Sun ordered the EVA crew to stand down and get some sleep while the engineering teams took over. He stayed on watch for a little longer himself, then finally gave it up and went to his cabin for some sleep of his own.

With the oxygen candles burning to keep the air breathable, the smoke and smog had been pushed back a little, and it was a relief to bury his face in his own bed and let sleep finally claim him.

When he woke, there would be so much more work to do.

▶▶▶

# PLANET RANQUIL, PRIMINAE CONTROLLED SPACE

▶ADMIRAL RAEL TANNER looked over the command and control room that served as a strategic center for the Colony worlds, eyes searching for something he knew should be there yet could not find.

"Dispatch the *Posdan* and the *Nept* to investigate the signals we detected near the Simanth colony," he ordered, not looking up. "There have been a few too many hits there for it to be background interference."

"Yes, Admiral."

Since the last move against Ranquil, there had been a second détente with the Drasin, as apparently the aliens had backed off to reassess conditions once more. He wasn't sure why, given the reports they had, but he would take what he could get.

That didn't mean they'd entirely vanished this time, however.

Rael wondered if the enemy was attempting to spread his forces thin, showing themselves at the edge of Colonial space in order to draw off ships. It was possible, but with the Forge in full production now, he had ships literally charging into space in numbers he could barely utilize. Not that it would matter if the *Odyssey's* reports were confirmed, though he was still attempting to put together a stealth squadron for that mission.

*Nothing we have could get within range of such a facility unnoticed, and it would take a fleet to get out again if the Drasin attacked.*

For all those concerns, though, the tensions resting on his shoulders were mostly self-made.

"The war goes well."

Tanner didn't look over his shoulder to the speaker. He knew that the bull of a man behind him was standing stiffly, hands clasped behind his back, and with a stern expression on his craggy face.

"Yes. I know," Rael Tanner said, eyes still on the maps.

"You worry it goes too well," Nero Jehan said.

It wasn't a question.

"The last time they backed off like this was merely a moment of evaluation. It was not long before the Drasin were back, in significant numbers."

"Numbers are all they seem to have."

"Numbers are all they need," Tanner growled. "We know from the *Odyssey* that they have far more than they need merely to overrun *us*. Why haven't they come for us yet?"

"You complain?" Nero asked, a hint of amusement in his voice. "Be grateful for the time to prepare."

"An opponent who acts unpredictably...." Tanner hissed out. "There are only so many things that could mean."

"Oh?"

"Yes. Either they're too stupid to know how strong they are compared to us, or I'm too stupid to see something they know intimately, or...." Tanner slowly shook his head.

"Or what?"

"Or they have another agenda entirely." Tanner growled. "None of this makes any sense."

"The Drasin are beasts," Nero said flatly. "Everything agrees on that. The ancient records and our own experiences. They don't plan, they merely swarm."

"The *Odyssey*'s information makes something quite clear, Nero, something that contradicts everything we know about the Drasin," Tanner said tiredly, running his hands through his hair. "They're allied with someone."

"The Drasin have no allies."

"No. The Drasin do not, do they?" Tanner asked rhetorically, cocking his head and examining the maps again as if from another angle. "So…are these truly Drasin then?"

"I…do not understand," Nero said uncomfortably.

"They look like Drasin, they act like Drasin," Tanner said. "Yet…are they Drasin?"

"Admiral?"

Tanner waved a hand as he turned. "Ignore me, my friend. I'm tired and I need to think on this. I'll see you tomorrow."

Nero watched the slight man walk out, confused by his sudden shift in thought.

The big man, commander of the ground forces of an entire star system, turned back to the strategic maps and glowered over them. Like his friend, Nero was certain that the worst was yet to come. They'd survived the initial motions of the enemy, more by luck than skill, but they had plenty of evidence to show that the real wave of assault was still building.

Out there, beyond the black, they were coming.

# CHAPTER THREE

## N.A.C.S. *Odyssey*—L-Point, Earth Orbit, Sol System

▶ "HOW'S THE POWER state looking?" Weston asked as he walked across the bridge.

"Nominal on all connections. No power drains we can't account for."

"And the ones you *can* account for?"

The young woman flushed slightly. "Mostly minor."

"Lieutenant," he sighed, "if you insist on making me drag every little piece of information out of you, you'll be on this ship a very, very, short time."

"Sorry, Captain," Lieutenant Kathy McReady mumbled. "We still have a high level drain in the tachyon generation systems."

Weston nodded, walking over to the command station and taking a seat. "And what does the Chief have to say on the matter?"

"Sir?"

"You've spoken to Chief Corrin, I presume?"

"Yes, sir."

"And so I ask again"—he looked at her pointedly—"something I've already told you I'm not particularly pleased with doing, what did the Chief say?"

"She said that it would be settled before we crossed Pluto, sir."

"Excellent. Thank you." He glanced over to where Daniels was standing, hunched over the crewman at the helm station, probably trying not to laugh. "Helm…lay in our course out-system and engage when we get cleared by Liberty Station Control."

"Aye, sir."

Eric glanced back to where McReady was uncomfortably looking like she wanted to say something. "Yes?"

"Sir. The tachyon drain is significant," she swallowed. "Regulations are clear that we can't leave the L-Point with that much of a power drain."

"Lieutenant," he said, forcing himself to be a little more pleasant, "if the Senior Master Chief says it'll be fixed, it *will* be fixed."

"Um…yes, sir. Sorry, sir."

"Liberty has issued clearance, Captain."

"You know what to do, Lieutenant Commander," Weston said, then smiled. "And congratulations again on the promotion."

"Thank you, sir. Course laid in and engaged. Port speed."

The *Odyssey* rumbled low and powerfully as the big reaction burners wound up, CM coming up to full cruise. She began to slowly pull away from the Lagrange point and Earth orbit. Eric smiled, satisfaction seeping into his bones as he felt the gentle slope of acceleration pull at him again, knowing they were once more heading out into the black.

▶▶▶

Climbing out of the gravity well of a star took time, particularly when you started from a dead stop. Well, relative stop, Eric supposed. All things were relative in space and time, and all that rot.

They met with the fueling tanker just past the orbit of Saturn, standard procedure on outbound jags. Of course, besides the *Odyssey* the only other outbound ships were generally comet miners and research ships. They all used the same fuel, however, so the procedures held.

He'd received a briefing package concerning the Chinese outbound ship, the *Weifang*, and had to admit that he was a little jealous of their propulsion tech. Apparently they'd really cracked the Alcubierre equations, something the West hadn't managed to pull off in several decades of trying.

*I'm sure someone just got a billion-dollar grant to make it happen, though.* He supposed, though, there was an excellent chance that the External Intelligence Bureau had gotten their marching orders to capture that research and bring it home.

He wished them luck, even though he figured that Gordon was probably an EIB agent and would be a pain in his rear end sooner or later. A reaction drive had some advantages, in theory at least, over the Alcubierre equations, but to have a reactionless drive? The sheer savings in propellant mass *alone* staggered the imagination.

*Probably why the* Weifang *is a third the size of the* Odyssey. *I wonder how her weapons and defenses stand up?*

"Approaching the heliopause, Captain."

Eric looked up to see the newly minted Lt. Commander at the door to his office and nodded. "Thank you, Daniels. How are the new trainees handling her?"

"No real complaints yet, Captain. I'll let you know when I see them under some stress."

"Good," Eric said. "Just remember to step in if things get hairy. I'd rather trust your hand over anyone else's."

"Wilco, Cap," Daniels said, flipping a casual salute as he stepped back from the door that connected the office to the bridge.

Eric sighed and set about putting the rest of his paperwork into order. There was an awful lot of it, even more now that he had to sign off on every new and modified system since the refit. He was just lucky that everything seemed to be working, more or less; otherwise he'd be filling in reports from now to doomsday.

With the last of the immediate requirements having received his official stamp, Eric made his way back out into the bridge and took a seat at the central command station.

"Ah, Commander, good to see you up from the darkest recesses of the ship," he said with a mild grin as he looked over to where his executive officer was sitting. "I understand we had some power issues?"

"Contractors didn't know how our reactor was wired and apparently had trouble reading a schematic," Roberts answered dryly, the former U.S. Army Ranger clearly not amused by the whole situation. "Chief got it all squared away. We're good to go."

"Excellent. I knew that she would," Eric said as he relaxed.

While he hadn't wanted to wait around in Earth orbit—it would have looked questionable on later reports if the ship hadn't been deemed fit to make her scheduled departure—Eric had dreaded the possibility of having to turn around and go back for repairs so soon. The Chief was good at her job, or she wouldn't be on the ship she was on, but there was always Mr. Murphy to consider, of course. He was happy that he'd been right in his earlier assessment.

He stepped out on the bridge and glanced at the main repeater displays as he walked by. "Time to T-point?"

"Three minutes, Captain," Daniels said from where he was hovering over the ensign at the controls. "Calculations laid in for Ranquil system."

"Good." Eric took a seat, his stomach already roiling. "Signal all hands, transition is imminent. You may engage the system at your discretion."

"Aye sir. Transition in T-minus…two minutes, thirty seconds. Mark."

The lights shifted on the bridge and through the ship, showing an amber color as Daniels leaned over his trainee's shoulder and accessed the ship-wide comms.

"All hands, all hands, stand by to transition. I say again, all hands stand by to transition."

As the count wound down, Eric forced himself to relax. It was a habit now. Calm his breathing, look authoritative and at ease. There were few people on the *Odyssey* who liked the transition drive. It was one of the most terrifying and visceral modes of transport ever devised and generally just freaked people out.

Being converted to a single coherent burst of tachyons and flung across the universe wasn't calculated to put a man at ease. When you factored in the relative time dilation of the jump, which made the instantaneous event seem to last just short of forever to some minds, you got to see things you didn't ever want to see.

The hull ablating away into the vacuum was the simplest and easiest with which to deal. Your friends and crewmates doing the same was somewhat more difficult. There was a brief period when Eric was certain he'd seen the initial layers of his own eyeballs ablate away, and that was something he tried very hard not to think about.

The clock ticked down until the last moments, and Eric heard Daniels announce the transition without listening. He closed his eyes, focusing on looking bored and maybe a little tired, in case anyone was watching. He doubted they were, but it never hurt to keep up appearances.

This time he only just felt the effect before it began to spin his molecules off into the void, catching barely a glimpse of the stars beyond the hull of the *Odyssey* when his eyelids were stripped from him and swirled into the black.

Shortly after, his eyes followed suit, and it was done.

▶▶▶

# CENTRAL COMMAND, MONS SYSTEMA, RANQUIL

▶ "BUOYS IN THE outer system just reported an FTL event, Admiral."

"Bowshock?" Tanner asked, rousing himself from bed as he slapped the commlink open.

"Negative. Signature matches the *Odyssey*'s drive system."

Rael relaxed back, considering that. "Very well. It'll take them a few hours to drop to Ranquil. I'll be up in three unless there is an emergency."

"Very well, Admiral."

The link went quiet and Rael rolled over onto his back, trying not to disturb his companion where she was sleeping. The arrival of the *Odyssey*, or any ship from Earth, was far from bad news, but he was beginning to wonder if they were bad luck.

The previous day he'd received word back from the two ships he'd assigned to investigate some odd readings on long-range scans. The Drasin were clearly abroad again, though this time they didn't appear interested in any of the Colony worlds. With trouble brewing, the *Odyssey* appeared from the depths of space.

*Almost overly convenient,* Tanner smirked as he closed his eyes again.

▶▶▶

The *Odyssey* had passed the checkpoints quickly on their way down-well, the unique configuration of the ship making it clear who they were and that they were most emphatically not Drasin. Eric idly checked the cut of his dress uniform, knowing that arriving on-world would be a bit of an affair.

The crew of the *Odyssey* was greeted with enthusiasm on Ranquil, at least by the civilian population. The military were respectful, and considerably more reserved. Not that he blamed them for that; he'd be leery as well of a foreign warship that had the capabilities the *Odyssey* had shown.

"Bridge to Captain Weston."

"Weston," Eric said, after tapping the button on the intercom.

"We've achieved stable orbit over Ranquil. Admiral Tanner sends his greetings and an invitation to dinner. Colonel Reed and Ambassador LaFontaine also sent their greetings along with similar invitations."

"Got it," Eric answered. "Did you deliver the mail?"

"Yes, sir, as soon as we hit orbit."

"Good. Make sure that the care packages are all loaded for delivery as well."

"Wilco, Cap."

Reed and the Ambassador could wait, he decided. Not too long, obviously, but Eric would rather spend time with Admiral Tanner, and as he had no orders to the contrary, that was precisely what he was going to do.

He made his way back to the bridge, double checking that the *Odyssey* was in a very high orbit. They were well past the planet's Van Allen belts, and he was hopeful that would keep Central from perusing their computers. Nothing much he could do about his own mind. There was no diplomatic way to avoid setting foot on Ranquil, but few of the secrets he knew were of much use to either a disembodied intelligence or to the Priminae themselves, so he'd take his chances.

"Shuttle is ready to launch, Captain."

"Right," Eric said and nodded. "Tell them I'll be right there."

"Aye, sir."

▶▶▶

Rael Tanner watched from the shelter of a building as the large Terran shuttlecraft settled into a low hover over the landing pad. The Priminae pad was hardly enough to accommodate the big craft, so the pilot had to keep the shuttle in a delicate hover as the ramp descended and passengers disembarked.

It was an impressive bit of flying, considering that he knew it was done largely by the pilot's hand and skill rather than automated control. From previous conversations with Weston, Tanner was aware that the Terran craft could perform the maneuver on automatic as needed, but few of their military-trained pilots used it. Automatic flight control was for civilians.

Weston stepped lightly off the ramp, alone, pausing only to glance back and wave the shuttle off before he turned and continued to where Tanner was waiting. The back blast of the shuttle banking away in a controlled maneuver rumpled the

Captain's uniform a bit, and he was casually patting himself down when he stepped inside.

"Welcome back to Ranquil, Captain."

"Pleasure to be here, Admiral."

Eric smiled as he spoke, nodding to the smaller man. He wasn't exaggerating. He genuinely enjoyed what time he could spend on Ranquil. The city center, Mons Systema, was the largest population center he'd ever seen or imagined. It made megacities on Earth look like rural backwater towns. Much of the construction was megalithic and it held a decidedly ancient feel that Eric enjoyed.

Most of the planet was untouched nature, with a few of these megalith cities dotting the landscape. He didn't know a lot about sociology, but he'd spoken with more than a few amateur historians and professional consultants about the Priminae world and people. An advantage of being who he was: When he asked to speak with the top minds on the planet, they competed to see who got to answer his questions.

A lot about the Priminae was all wrong.

They were human, for one thing, and that didn't make any sense. Evolution charts on Earth still had a few holes in them, but they were damned near complete, so it didn't make sense for Earth to be some long-lost colony. Humans had evolved on Earth. Period. End of story.

So who were the Priminae? Transplanted humans from Earth?

Possible. Unlikely, however. They had too long a history, going back ten thousand years. Unless that was all false, it would indicate that they'd been around a lot longer than that. There was strong evidence, however, that the Priminae weren't local to the worlds they inhabited. The megalithic cities, for one. Most of the people Eric had spoken with believed that any culture that evolved on a particular world would have spread all over it, and not be grouped so perfectly into a few huge cities.

*Of course, the fact that they call themselves the "colonies" was clue enough on that issue,* Eric thought as he and the admiral walked through the fused stone corridors side by side.

"As you say, Captain, it is always a pleasure to have you here on Ranquil," Tanner was saying as Eric refocused his attention from where his mind had drifted.

"It was nice not to be shot at this time." He grinned. "It was an uneventful, boring trip down-well."

"Boring is good," Tanner acknowledged.

"Speaking of, any sign of the Drasin since we returned home?"

"Yes." Rael became more serious. "They've been skirting our worlds for the most part. I currently have two ships tracking a possible swarm some distance from here."

"Any idea what they're up to?"

"None, I'm afraid," the admiral admitted sourly. "They've stayed at the edge of our best scanners, and while they haven't moved to avoid our ships, we've been reluctant to get too close."

Eric nodded, opting to be diplomatic rather than say anything.

It wasn't that the Priminae captains and crews were cowards; he'd seen enough to know better than to think that. They just didn't like to think aggressively, let alone act that way. If something came knocking on their door, sure they were willing to hammer it back, but it didn't occur to them to go and stop the bastards cold out in the black of space where they could cause little harm.

Given a bit more military power, Eric would be advocating that the NAC spearhead an all-out offensive on the

Drasin. Those things were a menace to everything he personally cared to name and had to be taken out. For the moment,
though, staying hidden was Earth's best hope. The Priminae
didn't have that option. They'd already been found, so to
his mind they didn't have the excuse, but they still opted to
hold back.

A war for survival wasn't any place for restraint.

That said, he'd learned enough to know that the Priminae
just didn't think that way. They were the epitome of pacifists
up to the point of self-defense. At least they weren't the type to
stand by and be slaughtered, but he still felt that they needed
to belly up to the line and take the fight out to the enemy.

"From what we saw," he said, "they certainly have the numbers to overwhelm your forces if they swarmed you properly. I
can't figure out why they haven't already."

"Nor I," Tanner admitted wearily. "Which is one of the key
things that keeps me awake long past my preferred hours."

Eric considered that entirely too understandable. He'd
lost more than a few hours of sleep himself since discovering
the mere existence of the Drasin, and even more when he
confirmed that there was another group that seemed to be
behind them.

"I've had a small meal prepared," Tanner said with a gesture as they arrived at their destination. "Nothing excessive. I
expect that you'll be eating with the ambassador later."

Eric nodded as they entered the room. "And the colonel
as well, I expect, though that will probably be more drinks
than a meal."

"Indeed." Rael gestured Eric to a seat and took one himself. "How go things on your own world?"

"Well enough, I suppose, though we're dealing with some
internal politics that are going to be annoying."

"Ah, yes, I read the briefing. You don't have a central government?"

"No," Eric grinned. "I honestly can't imagine it ever happening on Earth. Too many fractious people. We'd never be able to agree on how to run things, let alone *who* should."

"And to me, that is utterly unimaginable," Tanner said, shaking his head. "Even the younger colonies, which are mostly peopled by those unsatisfied with life on the core worlds, answer to the overarching government."

"To each his own," Eric said, "and as my Ma used to say, among them be it."

"Among them be it." Tanner smiled. "Yes, I like that. Among them be it, indeed."

"For now I'm more concerned with what the Drasin and their handlers are up to," Eric said, his mind returning to the issue at hand. "Though I have to admit that I also have orders to keep an eye out for a Block vessel that's out here somewhere."

"Block? That is the…other main government of your world?"

Eric nodded. "Yeah, well one of them anyway. The P.L.A.S.F. *Weifang* should be out near Gliese 581, or so I'm told. That's nowhere near here, but I'm supposed to take the *Odyssey* around to check up on them before heading home."

"I'm not familiar with that location," Tanner admitted. "Terran terminology, I presume?"

"Yeah. It's a system a few dozen light-years from here," Eric said. "A red dwarf star we detected around a few decades back with possibly habitable planets. Gliese 581 was on our survey list as well, until we met you. The Chinese managed to get an FTL drive working, and we think that's where they're headed to, based on vector analysis of their trajectory."

"A red dwarf with habitable planets? Rare, as such things go," Tanner said, frowning. "Something familiar about that, though. I just cannot remember."

"Something in the reports?" Eric was well aware that things you read in briefings often came back to you later.

"Possibly. Where is this Gliese 581? Can you say?"

"Give me a star chart and I'm sure I can figure it out," Eric offered.

"When we're finished eating then, yes?"

Eric smiled. "As you say, Admiral."

▶ ▶ ▶

# PRIMINAE WARSHIP *POSDAN*, NEAR SIMANTH COLONY

▶ CAPTAIN KIAN LOOKED over the scanner results of the colonial system and struggled deep in her core to keep from uttering every vile profanity she'd ever been taught not to say. Simanth had been a young world, lightly populated, but for all that it had been a world under her protection.

Had been.

The prime colony was now an infested hive of filth and vile creatures, and shortly the only good thing she could say about it was that it, and they, would all be gone from this plane to whatever came after.

The Drasin had invaded, apparently while her ship and the *Nept* had been en route from the core worlds. They had never even received an alert or a request for aid. Before they left, all was well aside from some odd long-range readings from the sentinel stations and when they arrived....

This.

"Signal Central Command. Inform them of the loss of the colony," she ordered her crew.

"Immediately, Captain. What of the signals we were sent to investigate?"

"I believe we know what the source of those were now, don't we?" Kian muttered darkly.

"It seems so, yes."

She sighed. "We should investigate further, I suppose, just to be sure. Do we have a vector on the last known location of the rogue signals?"

"Yes. They skirted this system several lights out. No sign that they approached."

Kian frowned. "I see. Very well. Set a course and relay to the *Nept* that we are proceeding according to orders."

"As you order."

The big ship, one of the most powerful in the Priminae fleet, turned slowly in space and headed out from the dying world. It would take time to climb out of the stellar gravity well in order to jump past light, but they were set in their actions now.

Somewhere out there, something was obviously hiding.

Time to flush them out.

# CHAPTER FOUR

## COMMAND AND CONTROL, MONS SYSTEMA, RANQUIL

▶ ERIC STARED AT the large star map floating in the center of the room, impressed by the display system more than anything. Holographic displays were in use on Earth, but they generally required a lot more visible hardware than what he was seeing, unless one was using augmented reality equipment.

"Can you find this…GlieseGliese 581?" Tanner asked from behind him.

That was a good question, Eric quickly realized.

He was a trained navigator, and could find his way both by and among the stars, but both required at least some minimal equipment on hand. This was going to be tricky.

"Close in on our arm of the galaxy."

The image focused in tighter, smoothly excluding a few hundred million stars.

"Center on Ranquil."

The stellar object that was the sun for the world he currently stood on lit up as the map shifted to the center. Eric knew the relative location of Earth from Ranquil by heart, but he carefully didn't look in that direction. Didn't even *think* in that direction. Instead he plotted the angle he'd have to fly from Ranquil, working out the math roughly in his head until he found a red dwarf in the general area.

"Here. Close in, please."

The system leapt into tighter frame, planets orbiting the small star now visible. From this point, all he had to do was compare it to survey maps he'd been briefed on for the *Odyssey* mission. It looked about right.

"I think this is it."

Rael hummed softly to himself as he leaned in and examined the star for a moment. There were no colonial worlds in that area, and the stellar object the *Odyssey* had discovered previously was significantly displaced from there as well.

*What is it about this system? Oh!*

"I believe I know," he said as he turned to his computer system and called up previous reports. "Yes. Here it is. We don't have any colonies in that region, but it is on a track we plotted for potential Drasin signals."

"It is?" Eric asked sharply, not liking the sounds of that.

Gliese 581 was within 22 light-years of Earth—not exactly next door, but close enough to worry.

"Yes, our closest colony world is Simanth. I dispatched the *Nept* and *Posdan* into that region to investigate the signal track. If the signals were accurate and unchanged, they originated from your Gliese 581," he said, lighting up the colonial world he was speaking of.

Eric took a breath, calming down a little. If they originated from Gliese, then they weren't headed anywhere near Earth, with the course towards Simanth veering somewhat in a different direction. That said, what looked like Drasin plots heading away from Gliese meant that there was a chance that they had *been* at Gliese. And if that were true, it was possible that the *Weifang* ran into them.

*Better move that up the priority. Head out that way and see if there's any sign of them.*

For their sake, he hoped that there hadn't been any contact. He knew that Block CamPlates were at least a couple generations behind the NAC, and their instrumentation was nothing to be proud of either. Without an up-to-date combo, Drasin lasers were a killer.

"When we're done here," he said, "I'm going to take the *Odyssey* out in that direction before heading for home."

"Looking for your world mates, yes?" Tanner asked. "Even though they're your enemies?"

Eric shrugged. "They're pains in the ass, but they're human and Terran. Have to at least check up on them, and what the hell? Gliese is on my original orders anyway. May as well do that survey."

Tanner nodded, not really understanding the undercurrent to his erstwhile friend's tone, but the words made sense to him. "I will signal ahead to the *Nept* and the *Posdan*, just to ensure that they are aware that you may be operating in their vicinity."

"I'd be much obliged," Eric smiled. "After all, friendly fire…isn't."

▶▶▶

# DEEP SPACE, THREE LIGHT-YEARS FROM GLIESE 581

## P.L.A.S.F. *Weifang*

▶SUN LOOKED OVER the state of his engineering deck, half horrified and half proud of the effort he could see. They had been forced to literally tear up the entire section to make room for the fabricators that had been recovered from the exposed sections of the ship.

New parts for the filters were being turned out as fast as the fabs could make them, and he knew that there were no spare seconds left for the job either. The chemical oxygen candles they were burning kept the air breathable, but it was still foul and turning fouler.

"The last parts are coming out of the fabs as we speak, Captain," Pan, the chief engineer, said with a relieved tone. "We should be able to vent smoke within the hour."

"Good. Keep the fabs operating. I want spares and every system repaired as quickly as possible."

"As you say, Captain."

Sun left the Engineering deck, pulling himself through the corridors hand over hand back to his own domain, Command deck. His officers were working, of course, and he settled himself into his station before bothering them.

"Any signs we were followed?"

"No, Captain. We've been focusing our passive sensors back along our course since we dropped from FTL," Shi said. "There has been no sign yet of any pursuit."

Sun nodded. But he wasn't quite willing to turn their nose toward Earth just yet.

Their passive gear was all light-speed-based detection apparatus, and that would mean that they wouldn't have detected anything more than...Sun had to glance at the ship's clock briefly to be sure, but anything more than two light-days out would be beyond their detection at this time.

There could literally be a fleet that blotted out the stars for an entire parsec sitting just three light-days away, and the *Weifang* would be completely unable to see them for another day. FTL physics gave him a headache, frankly, but the one thing that he was certain of was that they weren't quite clear of the proverbial forest just yet.

"Engineering has almost finished manufacturing the new filters," he said. "Once our life systems are fully functional again I want to have an evasion course ready. We'll double back on ourselves, pick out a few nearby stars at random and pay them a visit. Let's make following the *Weifang* as difficult as possible. Clear?"

"Perfectly, Captain," Shi said. "Should I begin plotting the evasion course?"

Sun nodded. "Please."

"It'll be done by the time we're prepared to leave."

"Good."

Sun turned his repeater displays over to the feeds coming from the main scanners, eyes on the information as it streamed past. He didn't know if the *Weifang* would make it home again, but he had to at least try and get back to Earth without alerting the enemy to their destination.

Suddenly, Sun found himself wondering how the captain of the *Odyssey* had coped when he was in a similar situation.

▶ ▶ ▶

# PLANET RANQUIL

▶ "SO, CAPTAIN, IS there much news from home?"

Eric glanced over to where Reed was leaning back against the wall, the folding chair under him creaking dangerously under his weight. He'd finished up the meeting with the admiral and then powered through a similar rendezvous with the ambassador before coming out to where the Priminae and their Terran advisors were preparing for ground war.

"Mostly things you could easily guess at," he answered. "The *Big E* was launched a couple months back, along with her two sister ships, the *Pearl Harbor* and the *Iwo Jima*. A host of support ships and smaller destroyers were completed as well, but I don't recall a list of their names."

"War footing, then, is it?" Reed asked seriously.

"So it appears," Eric confirmed, "and not a moment too soon in my opinion. Too many things out this way that are more than eager to swallow us up and crap out whatever's left."

"Truth there."

Reed had seen the Drasin's assault on-world firsthand, and while he hadn't been impressed with their tactical skill, he had been more than able to work out what they could do to a world that was ill equipped to oppose them.

"One bit of big news," Eric twisted his lips up. "It looks like the Block's joined the party out here."

Reed almost dropped his drink.

"They cracked the T-Drive?"

Eric shook his head. "No, seems they cracked the Alcubierre equations."

The soldier scowled, raking through his memories as best he could. "We gave those a shot a while back, didn't we?"

"Yeah. NASA had a project running for a while, but they were never able to get the power requirements down to practical levels," Eric told him. "Probably some other things too they didn't understand. I didn't read into the project much. The Block's always been a gen or two ahead of us on CM tech, though, so it's no shock that they'd be the ones to figure it out."

"If I remember the briefing properly," Reed said, thinking deeply, "aren't those the drives the Priminae use?"

"That's the theory, yeah, but we've not confirmed it," Eric told him. No one wanted to press the Priminae too closely on drive technology since there was no chance in hell that the NAC would surrender any aspect of their own transition systems in return. They didn't want to open that door even a crack. "The Block ship, the *Weifang*, headed out to Gliese 581 a little over two weeks ago. We don't know their top speed, just that they're FTL for sure. When I wrap up here, I'll be taking the *Odyssey* in that direction for a quiet look-see."

"A little peek over the shoulder of an old enemy?" Reed asked with a half-smile.

"That, and the fact that the Prim command here actually dispatched a pair of their warships to that area a couple days ago—well, in the general neighborhood, more or less," Eric said seriously. "Apparently they picked up some trace that looks like it may be Drasin origin."

"Damn. Got no love for the Blockheads, but wouldn't wish that on anyone," Reed admitted. "They have a chance against the Drasin?"

Eric shrugged. "Hard to say. They couldn't take hits like the *Odyssey*, and you know just what an eggshell she really is…."

Reed nodded.

The *Odyssey*, while probably the most armored *thing* ever to be built by humans—from Earth, at least—was a fragile toy waiting to be burnt to a crisp by the level of firepower floating around out in Priminae and Drasin space. Only the advanced armor she sported gave her a fighting chance, and even then it was limited in effectiveness if she were outnumbered. He wouldn't want to be on any ship against a Drasin laser barrage, but anything less than the *Odyssey* was just asking for a quick death.

"Still, have to check on them," Eric said, "if only to see if the Drasin were really out there and why. Don't like the idea of them being anywhere *near* Earth."

"You and me both," Reed answered with feeling. "How long are you here for, then?"

"Shipping out in a few hours," Eric said. "This was just a delivery run for you guys. Some mail and orders for the embassy. You know the drill."

"Right. I've got a list of things I'd like to get shipped in next time you swing by," Reed pointed out.

"Get the requests in before we leave orbit, or it'll have to wait," Eric said. "Sorry, but I can't delay departure this time around. Not with the new intel I picked up from the admiral here."

"Understood. I'll get the files transmitted."

"You do that," Eric said, taking a drink. "Anything I should know about?"

"Nah. Mostly just a few supplies we burned through quicker than expected," Reed answered. "The locals are smart. They learn quick. We've moved up a few lessons ahead of schedule, that's all. Could do with some more trainers, though, specialists."

Eric nodded. He didn't really know much about Reed's business, but of course he didn't really have to. He did know that the job went a lot smoother with people who knew what they were doing and how to teach what they were doing to others. That was actually a pretty rare skillset, but he was sure that the Confederacy would be able to scare someone up.

"What specialties, if I can ask?"

"Honestly? Close air support." Reed grimaced. "The local pilots rely on computer control *way* too damned much."

That perked his interest a little, as he'd served pretty much across the board in combat aircraft. His specialty was generally considered to be air-superiority, since he was most well-known for the Archangel assignment, but Eric had spent more than his fair share in other capacities as well.

"You need someone like Jen, then," he said.

"Jen?"

"Jen Samuels," Eric answered. "She's one of our double-A pilots. Came up flying transports and spookies in the war. Put in for a transfer to my squad a half-dozen times toward the end of the war, but by then we were scaling back. I gave her my own bird back on the first trip the *Odyssey* made out this way. She got her own after that, full slot in the squadron now."

"Can you spare her?" Reed asked. "I normally wouldn't ask, but honestly some of these guys are starting to scare me, and we need to run some operational drills."

Eric thought about it for a bit, uncertain. Cutting one pilot loose wasn't a huge deal, particularly since the *Odyssey* barely rated as a carrier now. The combat losses over the last two missions hadn't been replaced, and political issues back home kept the Archangels both highly visible and somewhat taboo at the moment.

He knew that the current military establishment didn't want to step on any land mines, so to speak, and the press would be all over any move to reestablish the squadron. Ironically they were more than willing to overlook the launch of three new carrier-class starships, complete with compliments of "conventional" fighters and full support ships. The Archangels were an infinitesimally smaller combat force, yet their high visibility made them untouchable in the current political atmosphere.

*Irony sucks.*

"I'll talk it over with her squadron commander," Eric offered finally. "He won't like it, but we may be able to swing something."

"Thanks."

"Don't thank me yet," Eric grinned, shaking his head. "Steph is about as likely to give up Jen as I would have been when I was in command of the squad. Which is not very."

"I'll take what I can get for now," Reed said. "If your boy won't let go of her, just put in my request with command. I can wait if I have to. What's the worst that can happen?"

"*Really* close air support," Eric said dryly.

Reed grimaced. "Yeah. That."

▶▶▶

# NEAR PREVIOUSLY UNCHARTED DYSON OBJECT

▶ IVANTH CAME TO disciplined attention as he entered the office of the Prohuer, waiting in silence to be acknowledged. He stood there for several moments before the man behind the large desk looked up and nodded at him.

"Ivanth," he said, gesturing to a seat.

Ivanth silently took the offered place. "Prohuer."

"I'm certain that you're curious, so I won't keep you waiting," the man said, smiling thinly. "We have reports from the drones that interest me."

"How so, if I might ask?"

"A new ship," the Prohuer said, his voice deceptively light. "Certainly not of the Priminae."

"The unknown, then?"

"No, I believe not," he answered, "though it is difficult to tell with certainty, given that the drones have incredibly primitive capabilities in some areas."

Ivanth nodded, knowing that to be true. When the People had discovered the drones originally, they had been shadows of their current form, but the cores were effectively identical.

The ancient world they'd unearthed them from had somehow survived an infection, leaving a few scattered examples of the beasts intact.

The mathematics that ruled their so-called minds had been both enlightening and incredibly frustrating.

Whoever had originally created them, and there was no doubt that they had been created, had been a form of life entirely unknown to the People and/or the single, stupidest example of life form ever to have existed.

Given that in millennia of recorded history no one had ever encountered anything that might have been those lost people, nor even worlds with their works entombed, Ivanth personally favored the latter.

The equations that passed for *thought* in the drones were quite simple and insidiously open to interpretation. They identified *life*, according to a remarkably simple set of algorithms, and then proceeded to annihilate it. As weapons went, Ivanth had heard the drones likened to weapons of mass destruction that were equipped with manual triggers. Effective, but they didn't precisely discriminate when it came to destruction. If you were in their sights, you were a target.

Well, at least they were, until the People got ahold of them and made some core-level alterations to the algorithms. Core-level additions, technically. They hadn't been able to *change* anything, but adding a few things had been possible.

All that, however, meant that the best you often got when you consulted their scanner feeds was little more than the spectrum analysis of what they were looking at and a kill/no kill order.

"The feeds indicate a ship of low power potential, similar to the unknown. However the combat feed indicates very different weapon systems," the Prohuer said seriously. "The drones are in pursuit, but I've input instructions to follow from maximum distance. I want to see if it leads us to something *interesting*."

"The unknown homeworld, I presume?"

"That would be ideal, yes," the Prohuer admitted.

Since they'd first confirmed the existence of the unknown ship, it had been the subject of intense scrutiny by those in charge of the expeditionary mission. A vessel with no effective power curve that could annihilate drone ships as easily as a vessel of the People might swat brigand ships in the outer worlds? *That* was enough to drive even the sanest to the brink, and honestly Ivanth didn't know many sane folk who would volunteer for a mission so far beyond the core worlds.

He had observed the data himself, and was as taken by the unknown as anyone. The ship had to be insulated for radiation beyond all sane conventions for the power effect of its drives and weapon systems to be so low.

Like many among the expeditionary forces, he viewed the world that ship came from with both trepidation and intense curiosity. Their greatest fear was that they were not looking at a single world, but an empire in its own right. It seemed unlikely, given that they had only seen one ship confirmed to date, but even a few worlds capable of building ships of that power and sophistication would be a major stumbling block to their mission.

Even a full multi-world empire wouldn't *stop* them, of course. The drones were self-replicating, geometrically progressive, and entirely unstoppable. Unleashing them with full limitations lifted, they would destroy *anything* in their path.

It would be a potentially significant time investment, however, and that would be problematic given the increased resistance in the core worlds.

*More important...,* Ivanth considered grimly and then said, "Have the encoders determined the source of the glitch?"

The Prohuer sighed, clearly bothered by the question.

The Drasin advance on the Priminae world had encountered problems with the implanted algorithmic instructions in the drones. Specifically, the limiters had failed and they'd nearly *destroyed* certain key worlds that the expedition desired intact. If they couldn't get those under control, employing them against valuable systems was just asking for trouble.

"Unfortunately, no," he said finally. "That should be immaterial on this mission, however. The unknown ship and its world are not on our lists. Should the world vanish, well, it's a minor issue."

Ivanth nodded. "Yes, Prohuer."

"Take the *Immortal* and the *Demigod*. I want regular reports, and, as you already know, be wary of the drones. Their internal coding is proving less flexible than predicted."

Ivanth rose to his feet. "I obey, Prohuer."

"Good. Go," the man ordered, nodding once.

Ivanth pivoted in place and marched out the door.

# CHAPTER FIVE

## N.A.C.S. *Odyssey*, Ranquil Orbit

▶WALKING IN MICROGRAVITY was a bizarre sensation, somewhat akin to standing right on the edge of a building then constantly falling off. Not falling off, hitting the ground, and then climbing back up to do it again. No, it was a sensation of endlessly being right past the point of no return even as you took one step after another.

Eric never really got used to it, though he knew some of his crew reveled in the sensation. Of course, it had been reported that one or two of his crew also reveled in the sensation of the transition drive.

He had crew whose sanity was well beyond questioning.

Using magnetic boots to keep from floating around loose in the cavernous interior of the *Odyssey*'s flight hangar, Eric made his way over to where the small and, to be quite honest, motley group of fighter craft were parked and where he knew he would find his friend, Stephanos.

Commander Steven Michaels was one of the youngest yet most decorated pilots in the double-A wing. He'd been with the squadron through furballs that should have killed them all, and was still around and kicking just like the rest of them.

Stephanos had been Eric's choice for command of the unit when he'd accepted his captaincy and so far hadn't disappointed, though Eric also had to admit that the pilot may have gotten the assignment simply for lack of interest from others.

The Archangels were public figures following the war, but the squadron wasn't a high priority for various reasons. Most of those with seniority over Stephanos had opted for promotions out of the squadron, mostly to flag assignments like Eric's own. Steph, however, loved the fighters like no one else.

Now the double-A squad was a shadow of its former glory, down to half strength and likely set to be replaced by the new space-superiority fighters with which they were equipping the *Big E* and her sister ships.

Having seen the specs on the new fighters, Eric expected that the double A's were almost sure to be on the decom lists within the year. He'd keep them active as long as he could and they desired, but it really was the end of an era, and there wasn't much anyone could do or say about it. The Archangel airframe was dated now. The only thing keeping it ahead of the latest birds to come out of the aerospace industry was the neural link system, and until they developed a NICS system that could be used by a larger subset of the human population, it would never be a priority for designers.

"Steph," he called out as he clanked to a stop in front of Archangel One, the commander's own.

"Boss?" Steph sounded confused, his head appearing from inside one of the intake cowlings for the atmospheric ram-scoops. "That you?"

"What the hell are you doing in there?" Eric ignored the dumb question, clanking around the plane so he could see what the younger man was doing.

"Hey boss." Steph pulled himself completely out and pushed down until he was level with Eric.

He wasn't wearing magnetic boots, so he just floated there, one hand on his plane for stability and maneuvering. "What's up?"

"First, answer my question." Eric looked past him into the intake of the big fighter, now curious as hell.

"Oh, just some tweaks we passed through the sims a few weeks ago," Steph answered. "Should be able to get an extra twenty percent power out of the system in atmospheric flight and double the pressure to the life-support reserves if we need to tank up on the fly."

"And it works?"

"In the sim." He nodded. "Was hoping for permission for an atmospheric pass through Ranquil to test it."

"Sorry, no can do." Eric shook his head.

"Come on, boss, won't even need to go deep. Just skim the upper atmo," Steph protested.

"Not gonna have time. We're shipping out within the hour," Eric said, shrugging. "Maybe a little later, depending on how this conversation goes."

"Late enough to allow a test?" Steph asked, grinning. "I can make it go anyway you want for that."

"Oh yeah? Well the Beanie running the training camp on-world needs a close air support trainer. I thought maybe Jen might be cut loose for a while," Eric suggested, keeping his smile buried. "If she's going down-well, I guess we might have time while she packed...."

"Oh hell no. Better yet, *fuck* no," Steph growled. "We'll test them somewhere else. The squadron is at half strength already. We can't find pilots to fill out our TO&E and don't have air-frames for them if we could. Jen is double A. She flies with us."

"The Angels aren't going to be around much longer, Steph. You've got to be able to see that coming. You were never the brightest bulb in the socket, but you're smarter than that," Eric replied. "The double A's are about through. You've put in your twenty, or close enough. If you want it, you'll get a ship of your own or another squadron to command. Most of us either have, or will. Jen, she's new. It's back to cargo and passengers for her, unless she picks up some recommendations elsewhere."

That was the crux of the matter for him. He wasn't sure what the future held, but he couldn't see any direction that wasn't downhill for Jennifer Samuels. She made double A, and they were going to take it from her before she really had a chance to make her mark. He'd never commanded her directly, squadron leader to flight mate, but she was still one of his. He had to try and do her one better than what the current politics were going to offer.

"How is training a bunch of off-world pacifists any better than cargo and passengers?" Steph stomped on Eric's thoughts with cleats. "She wants a combat slot. You know it, I know it."

"She's likely enough to get one, being an advisor down here," Eric countered. It was a warzone after all.

"Not the same thing. Look, you want to do her a favor, I'll sound her out for you. But I can tell you her answer already," Steph said seriously, shaking his head. "Double A is the only way. She'll pick the squad right to the very end."

"Talk to her, Steph. Give her the offer at least," Eric said and sighed. "I'm not cutting any orders. This is strictly voluntary."

"Rule five, Raze." Steph looked him in the eye. "Don't volunteer. Ever."

"Just talk to her, alright?" Eric snarled. "I don't have time for the damned drama, Steph. Pass along the request, then get yourself squared away. We're taking the *Odyssey* into contested space. If it's not the Drasin shooting at us, there's the damned chance it'll be the Chinese. We may need you to supplement our point defense if the Block ship launches on us."

"And you want to drop one of my pilots before the mission?" Steph snorted. "No offense, but are you completely out of your mind?"

"I'm not having this conversation any longer, Steph. One fighter won't change the odds and you know it. This isn't about us, it's about her."

"Fine. Whatever." Steph scowled at him, wiping his hands down with a rag he'd pulled from his belt. "Anything else?"

"Yeah, get a new attitude," Eric told him flatly, "because the only reason I'm not having you sit this one out in the brig is because we're friends and you weren't stupid enough to give me this much grief where someone else could see you."

The younger man had the gall to grin. "I may not be a hotshot Marine aviator like you, Raze, but I've been in long enough to know that if you're gonna lip off to your CO, there's only two right ways to do it. Either in private where he *might* choose to be generous and ignore it, or in front of God and everyone else where at least you'll get your money's worth."

"One of these days, Steph"—Eric sighed, shaking his head—"someone is going to call you on your actions and not even the double A's will be able to pull your ass out of the flames."

"Probably," Steph said as Eric turned and walked away. "But not today, Raze. Not today. If I'm lucky some bandit will take me out first anyway."

"You ain't that lucky, Steph. You're immortal. We all are," Eric said over his shoulder, his tone wry.

"Even the ones who are already gone?" Steph called after him.

"Especially the ones who are already gone."

▶▶▶

# RANQUIL

▲

▶ THE ENTITY KNOWN only as Central eyed the silhouette of the Terran starship, an emotion best described as amusement coursing through it. Since their initial meeting, the Terran captain had implemented several security procedures to keep Central from directly accessing any of his force's computer systems.

The entity actually hadn't had much luck cracking any of their computer systems to date. Oh, accessing them was easy. They used electronic systems, storing data in the organization of quantum filaments. Literally the play of a child to copy, something accomplished almost without thought itself.

Unfortunately, the paranoid buggers had apparently encoded every single thing they stored under massively complex mathematical algorithms. So complex that even having copied the key did Central little good. The key literally changed every few milliseconds.

Central was irritated to have information right in its midst that it was unable to access, like an itch it couldn't scratch.

*I wonder…if I commanded one of the warships closer to the Odyssey, I might be able to reflect their quantum states back to Ranquil and…*

Central had to mentally shake itself then, breaking free of the temporary mental fantasy.

It was a hard habit to break, knowing everything that there is to know within one's sphere. Omniscience was a heady addiction, utterly destroying those absurd chemical dependencies to which humans were vulnerable.

But Central had to reluctantly, oh so reluctantly, set aside that addiction. For one, Captain Weston had made it clear that he considered the things Central did as a matter of course to be *rude*. More important, however, was the knowledge that these people were merely a tiny extension of a much larger culture totally beyond his reach.

The entity couldn't help but be amused by the Captain's efforts to safeguard the location of his homeworld. That was the first thing that had been lifted from the minds of the Terrans...well, the first thing of significance.

Identifying a yellow star within two hundred lights of Ranquil was a challenge, for there were a few possibilities. However, a brief glance at the composition of the system set those to rest in no time. There was only one yellow star with rocky inner planets and outer gas giants that matched the home system of the Terrans, only one for twice that distance at least.

Not that Central had much use for the information, not at present. The Priminae had no need to visit the system and so did not need to be made aware of it. Central much preferred that they stayed clear. The violent taint on even the Captain made Central somewhat...ill, to be frank.

It was an odd sensation. Illness, that is.

Central had endured it vicariously, through the lives and deaths of those that lived within the magnetic field of Ranquil, yet never felt it personally. It was different, the entity found, to experience that pain for itself rather than feel it for another.

For all that it, and the Priminae, might need the Terrans…
Central much preferred contact be kept at a minimum.

Distasteful business, violence.

▶▶▶

Lieutenant Senior Grade Jennifer Samuels, call sign
Cardsharp, was reading the technical manual for the NICS
system her fighter employed. She wasn't known as an egg-
head, not even among those with whom she spent most of her
time, but she was a pilot in an age where you didn't get those
wings without being able to do space-time manipulation equations in your head. What's more, Jen knew without bragging
that she was a *good* pilot.

The NICS setup was something else, though. Neural mapping had always been hit and miss, often requiring years of
practice to really use it properly. It was useful for people with
disabilities; they had the time and drive to really perfect the
mapping, but career types were usually so busy with work that
the full-time job of mapping their neural pathways just wasn't
practical. It was discovered about ten years before the war with
the Block, however, that a tiny percentage of people had effectively identical paths. At the time it was a pretty controversial
discovery, like finding two snowflakes perfectly identical or,
more aptly perhaps, a percentage of people with perfectly
matching fingerprints.

For those people, you just strapped them into the system
and mapped someone else's matching equations over theirs
and away you went.

It was nothing but a curiosity at the time, but when the war
came and with intense pressure to provide real force multipli-
ers to the military, one doctor happened to notice that out of

the thousands of subjects who tested out with this identical neural map, there was a surprising number of *pilots*.

The Archangels were born out of a combination of that accidental discovery and the daring theft of a Block advanced Mantis fighter that utilized their latest generation CM generator technology.

The fact that one Marine aviator by the name of Eric Weston flew that stolen fighter out of a Chinese air base in the Gobi was probably the cherry on top of the proverbial sundae. The history of the double-A flight read like a Hollywood blockbuster, back when Hollywood was still on top.

That wasn't what she was working on at the moment. As interesting as history was, she was more intent on the applications of the NICS system. The neural interface solution was undoubtedly effective. Lab and field tests agreed that response times were more than ten times faster when using NICS, but it had problems.

The needles in the back of the neck was one, but the bigger part of the drawbacks was that the system was unidirectional. Signals went out, they didn't come in. The primary delays in the NICS device were because data had to be interpreted by the pilots through natural inputs. Eyes, ears, some tactile feedback, and so forth. That put a distinct limit on reaction times, something that hadn't yet been surmounted.

Samuels had some ideas on that, something she'd been working on since just before she applied to the double A's the first time around.

As usual, she was working on the project in her off hours when the door chime to her quarters sounded.

"Come on in. It's not locked," she said without looking up.

The door clanked as it opened. The heavy metal didn't make those soft hissing sounds from the old sci-fi movies, but it would hold up a lot better in the case of explosive decompression than a flimsy sliding door.

"What's up? I'm working," she said.

"Just talked to the Captain."

The voice caused her to jerk straight up, snapping around as she struggled out of her seat and got to attention. "Sir! I—"

"Relax, Lieutenant," Commander Michaels told her, waving her down. "This is off the record and all casual like."

"Sir?" She relaxed marginally, somewhere between "at ease" and "at attention."

"Cap was talking with Reed down-well on the planet," Michaels said, looking moderately annoyed to be delivering the message. "Reed is looking for a pilot trainer. Cap thought you might be good for the slot."

Jennifer felt a cold chill wash over her. "What? Why?"

She'd been trying to get a slot with the Archangels practically her entire professional life. Now she'd just made it in and could literally feel it all slip away between her fingers.

Michaels looked about as bad as she felt, she realized.

"Look, Jen, I don't know if you've been following the politics of the situation, but the double-A squad has become something of a white elephant. They loved us during the war when we brought results, but now we're too high profile for a lot of the jobs we'd normally pull back home and we cost too much to maintain anywhere near our war level operational levels. We've got five pilots now, and they're not sending us anymore." He told her seriously, "We'd only have four pilots if the Captain hadn't given you his bird."

She felt her legs wobble a bit. She hadn't actually been paying attention to any of that, but now that he had laid it out, she had to admit that it did seem odd that the squad hadn't been replenished since she'd signed on.

"Most of us will probably move up when they shut us down, assuming the ETs don't splash us all over space first," Michaels said. "But you're still junior enough that there's not command waiting for you, Jen. Odds are it'll be back to shuttle work for you, and the Cap wanted to offer you something better."

"Teaching a bunch of snot-nosed pacifists to fly?" she snorted. She had met a few of the refugees on their first run through Prim space and frankly wasn't impressed.

She didn't have a problem with being a pacifist, not exactly, but the smug condescension she got from many of the Prim just pissed her off. They tended to forget that not everyone in the universe thought the way they did, and the problem with pacifism was that until every single person *everywhere* adopted the philosophy, it was charitable to call it *unrealistic*, at least to her way of thinking.

Sure, intellectually, she knew that pacifism was the superior way of life. The problem was that it was a lot like communism in that it was only perfect on paper. Put it in the real world and things fell apart fast because it depended on the good will and behavior of people for it to work.

*And people are an ugly sort at the best of times.*

In the land of the blind, the one-eyed man was kind. In the land of pacifists, it was the man who was willing to throw a punch.

"They're not that bad, Jen."

She rolled her eyes.

"Look, it's either this or…best case?" Michaels sighed and shrugged. "Maybe the double A's pull PR duty."

*That* was worse. Jen groaned at the very thought of doing airshows for the rest of her thirty.

"Yeah, that's my thought on that too," he told her. "Look, think it through. No orders here, just an under-the-table offer and the Captain's promise to make sure the transfer doesn't slow up any promotions. Might even speed them a bit."

Michaels turned to the door, making to leave, but she cut him off before he got halfway there.

"I don't need to think anything through, sir. I'm double A."

He didn't turn back, and just nodded. "Alright. I'll let the Captain know."

Jen turned back to her work, unaware that her CO and flight leader was smiling as he left the small quarters.

▶▶▶

"Preflight sequences are all green, Captain."

Eric nodded absently as he walked across to his station. "Thank you, Commander. Has Commander Michaels contacted the bridge?"

"No, sir. Are we expecting anything from the squadron?"

"Maybe," Eric said, taking a seat. "Have we delivered everything to the embassy and the advisors?"

"Yes, sir. All deliveries were completed on schedule and with no problems."

"Good. A nice boring mission to Ranquil. That's a first," he said with a smile to his XO. "Hopefully the first of many, right?"

Roberts snorted lightly. "Boring missions in a warzone. You have some sense of humor, sir."

Eric smiled. "Laugh or cry, Commander. Laugh or cry."

His comm chirped, signaling a text message, and Eric was distracted from the commander's response as he accessed the system and read it.

"A problem, sir?" The commander asked when he saw the expression on his captain's face. "We can scrub departure if we have to."

"No." He sighed, a wistful smile on his face. "There'll be no need of that. We leave on schedule."

"Aye, aye, Captain."

▶▶▶

From his station in central command, Rael Tanner watched the *Odyssey* as the ship began to accelerate away from his world.

The oddly configured vessel had brought many changes to his planet, most of them as positive as he could imagine them being. Tanner had no illusions that they'd have survived the Drasin assault without the Terran intervention, but some weren't so convinced. And more were concerned by the very existence of another culture so clearly militarized as the Terrans.

He supposed that he couldn't blame them; one small ship had annihilated several times their number and even more times their tonnage of Drasin vessels. Because Priminae ships were barely a match one on one for Drasin craft, maybe two on one with particularly brilliant tactics, the Terrans' capabilities were an understandable concern among the elders.

So it was with mixed thoughts that he watched Captain Weston's vessel receding on his screens.

The presence of the *Odyssey* meant an added layer of security, and not an insignificant one, against attack. With the Terran embassy on Ranquil, and with a man like Weston in command, he had no doubt that the *Odyssey* would defend

Ranquil almost like its own homeworld. But politically, he had to admit that things became rather tense when the alien warship was floating above Mons Systema.

▶▶▶

There was a feeling on board a ship under power that couldn't be matched by anything less.

The power of the thrusters, huge though they were, was dampened and insulated from the rest of the ship, but a thrum of some sort always leaked through. A low vibration, a distant whirr…things just felt right.

Eric had felt the same thing when stationed on the *Reagan* before the war, and he felt it now as the *Odyssey* reached full power and began to race up the gravity well away from Ranquil. Their nose pointed out into the black. It was like sailing into the dark of the ocean at night when they knew that there was action to be had at the end of the trip.

"Course laid in for Gliese 581, Captain."

"Good. Time to the heliopause?"

"Three hours."

Eric nodded. "Commander, you have the con. I'm going to turn in. Don't wake me for transition."

The last was said with a wry smile and it earned a few chuckles from those who heard him. On the first few trips they made with the transition drive, he had made a professional point of being visibly in command. He thought it important to the crew that he do so. Now he had nothing to prove. They knew him and Eric was feeling confident in his command.

He could pass off sleeping through transition as a confidence in their capabilities without anyone construing it as a shirking of his own duties.

"I have the con, sir." Commander Roberts nodded in agreement as Eric got up.

He left the bridge and headed for his quarters, mind racing along as he thought about what might have been and what probably was to come.

As always, Eric found that his choice of lifestyle never failed to offer him challenges to keep things interesting.

# CHAPTER SIX

▶ "REPORT."

Ivanth strode onto the command deck of the *Demigod*, eyes to the large plotters and displays arrayed around the center of the ship's control.

The *Demigod* and the *Immortal* had arrived on station, joining the *Mythic*, who had been acting as duty and control ship for drones dispatched to the area. It was an empty sector of space, according to available reports. No particularly interesting worlds, no life to speak of, yet routine passes by the drone swarm had found a ship that matched nothing of either the People or the Priminae.

"The drones are…becoming erratic, Commander."

Ivanth grimaced. That wasn't the report he wanted to hear. The drones were erratic at the best of times in his opinion, though the official reports listed them as reliable. When they began acting officially erratic, he started to sweat.

*Never should have woken the damned things up.*

Ivanth sighed. The whole reason the drones were out here was so that they could exercise some of their less stable impulses away from worlds that had value to the People.

Instead they located a ship of interest and had to be recalled back to observation status. Because this group of the swarm had already been showing distinctly non-operational tendencies, he didn't really want to know just how *erratic* they were becoming.

"And the observation target?"

"The alien vessel dropped from trans-light some time ago, likely to make repairs," the man told him. "We believe it was struck by a drone laser before it escaped the swarm in the last system."

"Any certainty?"

"No," the man admitted. "They may be watching for followers. We've remained as far back as we could, as the orders dictated. It makes details difficult to determine."

Ivanth nodded. "Thank you. Return to your duties."

The man was right, of course. At maximum range they could barely discern that the ship existed. It would take days for light to arrive to their passive gear and they couldn't use any of their high-detail trans-light devices for fear of giving away their presence.

His eyes moved to the tiny speck of light listed on the displays, almost too small to see even with the full magnification of their very best equipment. They were relying on the minute disruptions in the trans-light fields caused by the small ship, and they were very minute indeed. He couldn't believe how stealthed the ship was, given that they knew precisely where it was and had all their equipment focused on it.

*The power insulation must be incredible for a ship that size. No wonder they don't register as a threat to the drones, if they are this well insulated. They* must *be insulated. To destroy the drones as they do, they must be more powerful than they appear....*

They had to be. He couldn't see any other option. According to the best scans he had available of the alien ships, they barely had enough power to achieve trans-light.

Ivanth scowled at the displays, settling himself in. It would probably be a long and certainly a tension-filled wait indeed.

▶ ▶ ▶

# P.L.A.S.F. *WEIFANG*, INTERSTELLAR SPACE

▶ "CAPTAIN, WE ARE ready."

"Good," Sun said. "All hands are to prepare for warping of space-time."

"Yes, Captain." The officer turned and gestured. A moment later a voice echoed over the ship's comm.

"All hands, stand by to warp space-time. The *Weifang* is initiating FTL drives."

The engines whined slightly as the reactors brought everything back to full power. The standby screens changed over to active as the CM generators began to draw power and warp the local space-time.

"Do we have any sign of pursuit on long range, Shi?" Sun asked.

"No, Captain. Space is empty."

"Very well. Let us make very certain."

"On your order, Captain."

"It is given," Sun said with finality.

The *Weifang* vibrated slightly as it began to move, swinging about in space as it accelerated toward light-speed. Within a few minutes, it passed the relativistic threshold and exploded into FTL, still accelerating as the ship continuously "fell" down its own gravity well, heading back along the course it had come from.

▶▶▶

Ivanth was startled from his work when alarms began to blare all over the ship. He scrambled from his station to the center of the command area, eyes flying to the screens.

"What is going on?"

"The alien vessel, sir, it's coming back this way."

"Speed?"

"Two lights, accelerating fast!"

"All ships, go stealth! Scatter out of its path. Stand ready to come about and pursue it as it passes!" he ordered. "And for the creators' sake, get the drones out of the way! We want it in one piece and unaware!"

"Yes, Commander!"

Getting a fleet moving that quickly, and that quietly, was problematic at the best of times, but now Ivanth could only pray that the drones didn't give them all away and blow the entire operation just after he'd arrived to oversee it.

*Unbelievable. Barely on mission and about to lose everything. I may have set a record.*

The ship's acceleration was quick, he noted, surprisingly so. They clearly had decent command of trans-light technology, and while he could likely outrace them, there was no way he could do so without giving away his position.

Frustrated, Ivanth watched as the alien ship continued to accelerate toward them, passing twenty-five lights and still climbing. There was no way he could get his ships clear in time, not without going to full acceleration, and that would defeat the point entirely.

He stared at the approaching ship as it continued to accelerate, mouth dry as his heart beat in his chest. *We'll have to destroy them, I suppose.*

"Lock all weapons onto the oncoming ship," he ordered after hesitating. "Cease retreat scatter. Stand ready for combat maneuvers."

Alarms began to wail about the ship as he walked over to his station and took a seat with as much calm authority as he could muster.

*Just because the world is falling apart around me is no excuse for a lack of professionalism.*

He'd learned that from his mentor at the imperial academy, and it was a lesson Ivanth took to heart as best he could. At all times one must act one's station, for that was the duty of your station.

The ship was moving well over one hundred lights by the time it entered into their weapons envelope, still accelerating.

"All ships, open fi…"

"Commander!"

Ivanth twisted, eyes on the sensor station. "What? We're somewhat busy here."

"I'm reading no active trans-light particles from the ship."

"What?" Ivanth spat the word, incredulous and unbelieving. "That's impossible."

"There is nothing, Commander. I swear it."

He turned his focus to the screens again, this time staring with a confused wonder. "They're flying *blind*? But that is *insane!*"

He shook himself, not quite believing it, but his next words seemed to come of their own volition.

"Check fire. All ships, hold positions. Let them pass."

As he watched the ship barrel right through his ships' formation, passing within light-seconds of the *Immortal* and her contingent of drones, Ivanth couldn't help but stare at the plot. The alien ship didn't even alter course slightly to avoid his forces.

*It's a trick. It* must *be a trick.*

The alien ship blew right through, totally ignoring vessels that simply *had* to be within its detection radius as though it hadn't seen them at all.

"Orders?"

Ivanth couldn't understand the maneuver. It couldn't be an escape attempted. They had literally any other direction to run in. Why double back and head straight into his forces like that? They had to assume that they would be attacked when they came into range. Didn't they?

"Commander? Orders?"

*They doubled back. Was something of value in the system they were discovered in? No, there was nothing in any of the reports and the planets there are infested with drones. Why double back?*

"Commander!"

"What?" Ivanth snapped, twisting to look at the speaker.

"Orders. We need orders."

"Follow them. Leave them a lead time of at least a standard light-day. Best stealth," Ivanth ordered, turning on his heel as he started walking off the command deck. "I'll be in my quarters."

"As you command, sir."

*What are they playing at? They can't actually be flying blind, can they?*

▶▶▶

# P.L.A.S.F. WEIFANG,
# INTERSTELLAR SPACE

▶ "REVERSE POWER, ALL flank," Sun ordered. "Shi, I want your eyes wide open as soon as we drop from FTL."

"I am ready, Captain," the man at the scanner station said firmly.

The *Weifang* shifted power to its CM generators, increasing the space-time gradient ahead of the ship and decreasing it to the rear, effectively throwing the big starship into reverse in a way that few things in the universe could ever match. They bled velocity at a blinding rate, throwing the ship out of FTL and back into relativistic space on a crash course for zero/zero acceleration.

As soon as they dropped below FTL, the Command deck lit up across every board, light-speed scanners coming to life as the ship's eyes were once more opened to the universe at large. Information was pouring across every screen, faster than even the super-computers on board could manage to keep up with.

It didn't take too long before the first images of local space began pouring in, however, and soon after that Sun had a decent view of a few light-seconds around his ship. Beyond that, however, the data rapidly degraded into uselessness as it got older and older. He knew that any ships tracking them would be FTL craft, so light-speed data older than a few minutes was suspect.

"No contacts, Captain. Clear to one light-minute," Shi announced.

"Understood. Ready the course for the next evasion."

"Yes, Captain!"

Sun didn't know if what he was doing was necessary, or effective for that matter, but it was what he had in his arsenal at the moment, so he intended to use it to the best of his capabilities. The new course brought the ship around, still in relativistic space, and headed down angle to the galactic plane.

Five minutes after they dropped from FTL, Sun gave the order to accelerate once more, and the *Weifang* flashed from existence and vanished into the black of space.

▶▶▶

# IMPERIAL WARSHIP *DEMIGOD*

▶ "THEY'VE ALTERED COURSE and returned to trans-light, Commander."

*What are these people doing?*

Ivanth had never seen maneuvering quite so chaotic and haphazard. The ship they were watching was jumping from one course to another like a scalded animal and showed no intent to settle. It had to be some kind of evasion course, but they had to know that trans-light scanners could read them easily at the velocity changes they were making.

The warping of space-time built up several types of harmful particles that got caught in the pseudo gravity fields that propelled starships. At speed, they were relatively difficult to detect because the local warp fields captured them while preventing ships from being thrown out to the universe. But when you dropped the fields, or radically altered them, it was like throwing up a pulsar flare to the eyes of anyone who might care to see.

He didn't even have to shadow them as closely as he was. He could order his ships back several times further and still follow easily. If they continued as they were, he might be able to follow them from a hundred times further. More perhaps.

He wouldn't give those orders, however, if only because Ivanth feared that they were playing games with him.

*I won't lose you to some foolish little dance tricks, whoever you are,* he thought as he glowered at the screens. *You will have to do much better than this.*

"Continue pursuit, same lag range," he ordered. "Do not let them from your scopes."

"Yes, Commander."

▶▶▶

# PRIMINAE WARSHIP *POSDAN*

▶ "CAPTAIN, WE'VE SPOTTED high energy spikes across several FTL vibrational bands."

"Where?" Kian asked, walking over to the long-range detectors station.

"Here." The man at the instruments pointed to a holographic map.

Kian looked at the location, noting that it was close to the sector they had been dispatched to investigate. "Inform the *Nept*, we are changing course to intercept."

"Yes, Captain."

"Helm. Bring us about. Settle us in on a course for sector three-one-nine and bring our drives to full power."

"Yes, Captain. Course to three-one-nine, full power."

The warship of the Priminae people turned slowly in space as its big power cores began warping local space and time. It seemed to lumber off as it headed along its new course, but that was only because the ship was so very large. It broke the light-speed barrier within a few moments of power reaching full potential, and flickered away.

Only instants later, the *Nept* followed suit.

▶▶▶

# P.L.A.S.F. WEIFANG

▶ THERE WAS A tremor that Sun could feel through the deck of the *Weifang*, something that he knew shouldn't be there. He wished he had time and the facilities to have the ship properly torn down and refitted, but that wasn't in the tiles.

With the ship threatening to fly itself apart, he found himself wishing for a lot of things that he just couldn't quite manage on his own, but Sun knew too well that wishes were for the weak and the doomed. He refused to be weak, and he prayed that he was not doomed, so he was left with the trust he had for his ship and his crew.

*It has always been enough in the past. It will be enough now.*

"Preparing to drop from FTL!"

The ship shuddered slightly, bringing a grimace to his face as the CM gradients shifted again. That change in absolute velocity shouldn't have even been noticeable in the ship. That wasn't how the CM drive worked.

*The gradients must be out of alignment. Bow or aft, some part of the ship is too close to the field center. Damn.*

It seemed a minor issue perhaps, but Sun was well aware that the tidal forces of the CM gradients could cause extreme

124 • EVAN CURRIE

wear on the structure of the ship. As objects got closer to the center of the CM gradient, gravity would affect the *Weifang* more powerfully, and similarly as the object moved away from the gradient the effect would be lessened.

The real danger was in the *difference* between the two, and if the object strayed too close to a tightly compacted and powerful CM field....Well, the scientific term was *spaghettification.*

Suffice to say, every shudder and every tremor Sun felt through the decks made him cringe precisely because he knew what was causing it and how badly things could go.

The *Weifang* dropped to a near stop in relativistic space, extending her passive sensors for monitoring duty while her captain and crew set about a hurried schedule of maintenance.

Sun pulled himself down the tubes that led from the Command deck of the big ship to the engineering sections, finding the whole deck in a state of barely controlled chaos.

"Pan," he said as he located the head engineer, "the coils are out of alignment."

"I am aware of that, Captain," the stocky man growled, not looking up. "I am doing my best, but we need absolute references to put them right, and those are back home."

Sun's lips tightened, but he knew that his man was telling nothing but the flat truth. Due to the effect of tidal forces on the ship, even when everything was perfectly aligned few of the shipboard instruments could be trusted to remain perfectly intact. When nanometers counted, they had nothing on board that could be trusted past an accuracy of a few micrometers.

"Do your best."

"It's our lives on the line too, Captain. We're not doing our worst, I promise you." Pan looked up, clearly frustrated by the situation. He took a breath. "Sorry. The alignment was out slightly, favoring the bow generators. We're dialing back to the aft. A couple more hops and we'll have it within safety levels."

"Right," Sun said. "Just hold us together long enough to do that. Two more hops. I'll give you three. Get it dialed in, because if we've not detected pursuit by then...I'm taking the *Weifang* home. All speed."

Pan nodded. "Understood, Captain."

Sun twisted and pulled himself out of the engineering section, heading back for the command level.

*We should have stayed home.*

# CHAPTER SEVEN

## Gliese 581

▶ THE N.A.C.S. *ODYSSEY* floated at rest relative to the star system, maintaining station just beyond the heliopause of the red dwarf star. The sails were fully extended as the ship took a long, deep drink of the photons emitting from the system.

"No doubt about it, Commander."

"Damn." Roberts swore softly.

The evidence on the screens was pretty much incontrovertible, but he really wished he was seeing things.

"Those damn bugs are taking over everywhere," he muttered, shaking his head.

The fourth planet of the system, one of a few extra solar worlds discovered before the T-Drive was invented and predicted as a potential life-bearing planet, was now *crawling* with a form of life on which he'd wished he had never laid eyes.

The Drasin were in the process of annihilating a world that had no apparent links to the Priminae, or to Earth for that matter. He didn't know what their goals were, but it was pretty clear by this point that prosecuting a war with a specific target wasn't one of them.

"Stay on watch. Hold this station unless something changes," he ordered. "Daniels, you have the con."

"Aye, sir. I have the con," Daniels responded, then frowned. "What are you going to do, Commander?"

"Wake the Captain."

▶ ▶ ▶

The chime wasn't the most pleasant sound in the world to wake up to, but Eric had awakened to far worse in the past. Gunfire was always a sure way to go from dead to the world to more alive than you'd ever been, assuming none of the bullets actually struck you. Better than a cup of coffee as a pick-me-up, though a tad harsh on the nerves.

He tossed off the light blanket and wiped his eyes for a moment, then reached over and pulled on a pair of tan uniform pants. "I'm up. May as well come in."

Roberts appeared as the heavy swinging door was pulled open. "Sir, we arrived on station a couple hours ago and began observing the system."

"Any sign of the Block ship?" Eric asked, yawning as he grabbed his uniform jacket and shrugged it on.

"No sir. However we have at least one infested world and signs that another may have been taken by the Drasin as well."

Eric went from drowsy to wide-eyed in an instant, reflecting in the back of his mind that bad news was almost as good as gunfire that way. "Shit."

"Yes, sir," Roberts agreed simply.

"Any signs of their cruisers?" Eric asked, buttoning up the jacket.

"Thankfully, no. It looks like they left the drones on the ground to complete the destruction of the world they'd targeted and moved on."

"Right. That fits their pattern," Eric said as he walked over to the sink to wash up. "No hint of the *Weifang*? You're sure?"

"As sure as we can be. A full survey of the system would take more time than we've had," Roberts told him, though Eric knew that already. "There's no sign of any current fighting at least."

Current meaning that there had been no fighting in the past few hours, since their data had to be at least a few hours old. Eric tried to remember how far from the star the local heliopause was, but couldn't. It didn't matter really, he supposed. Certainly he wasn't trying to make any intricate battle plans at the moment, so a "few hours" was close enough.

"So either they made it here and escaped, made it here and were destroyed, or broke down somewhere along the way," Eric summed up. "Sound about right?"

"Their destination might have been misinformation," Roberts added, "in which case they could have gone to any of another dozen stars similar to this."

"Right, point," Eric conceded. "Let's assume that they came here and escaped because, to be brutally honest, that's our worst-case scenario."

Roberts grimaced, but nodded. He didn't like the statement that anyone escaping from those things was the worst-case scenario, but it was the truth. If they'd been destroyed here at Gliese, then it was over. If they didn't arrive, then they weren't the *Odyssey*'s problem. If, however, they had been here and escaped with a dozen Drasin cruisers on their backsides, things were very much in the brown stuff.

The pair left the Captain's quarters, heading for the bridge of the *Odyssey*.

▶▶▶

"Captain on deck!"

"As you were," Eric said as he strode toward the command station, a half step ahead of Roberts. "Anything new to report?"

"Nothing in the last half hour, sir."

"Good. Keep a couple eyes on the system, but I want the rest of our gear focused outward."

Winger twisted around to look at him, expression clearly skeptical. "Outward, Captain?"

He nodded. "Check your inbox, Michelle. I sent you some notes on where the Priminae assigned a couple of their warships to investigate. I want you to scan in that direction, look for tachyon disruption especially. Anything out of the ordinary."

The instrument specialist nodded, expression clearing slightly, but still showed hesitance as she turned back to her work. Not that Eric blamed her, to be honest. Space, especially interstellar space, was a *big* place. Beyond a few light-hours of their position, none of their standard instrumentation was of any tactical use. That left nothing but the tachyon-based gear, and everyone on board knew that even that wasn't of the most utility when dealing with mid- to long-range scans.

It took a pretty potent burst of tachyons to show up on their gear, something that generally didn't happen over more than a couple light-days or so. Beyond that most tachyon sources were ephemeral, often *too* powerful to be detected. It was a bizarre contradiction in tachyon physics, but the higher a tachyon particle's energy state, the less distance it would travel before degrading into its composite quarks and gluons.

So the odds of getting any useful information from those sensors was pretty low, all things considered, but it would still require tying up all their reflector sails in the attempt. It probably seemed like sacrilege to turn their back on what was happening in-system for odds that seemingly low to someone like Michelle Winger, but she'd just have to get used to it.

They weren't here for intelligence on the enemy, though he'd take as much of that as he could get without compromising the mission.

Right now, however, it was more important to make a fast survey of the local area and see if there were any signs of a fight. If they didn't find anything, well, that would be a bridge to burn when he got to it, Eric supposed.

▶▶▶

"Nothing."

Eric was both surprised and not; he'd known that the odds of picking up a stray burst were long, but the odds had seemed to have a way of giving the *Odyssey* a pass ever since its first mission. Some ships were like that, he knew. Always at the center of things, for good or ill, like they had a destiny.

*Some people are like that, too.*

This time, however, there was nothing else to it but to do things the old-fashioned way. They'd have to sector the area, see if they couldn't find the Priminae warships he knew were out this way somewhere.

Priminae ships had better long-range gear than the *Odyssey*'s designers had even dreamed of. In their wildest fantasies, there weren't many on Earth who could imagine looking into another star system like it was a 16k movie screen, and he knew from experience that the Priminae could do just that over a range of a few light-years at least.

It wasn't everything you thought it would be, of course. Space was huge, and the further away you looked, the narrower your depth of field was. Past a few light minutes you practically had to know the location of your target down to a few meters if you wanted to be able to see it, unless of course it was absolutely immense. Otherwise it could sail right on by and under your proverbial nose.

That said, they also had superior tachyon detection gear, and that was what he would give a vital body part for just then.

"I'm going to need a course to sector three-niner-eight, mark positive twelve," he called out, eyes flicking up to where Daniels was standing.

The *Odyssey*'s helm and nav center had grown a lot since the first trip, with Lieutenant Commander Daniels now in charge of training future stellar navigators for the rest of the fleet. Weston didn't like having green crewmen in charge of pointing the ship in the direction he ordered, to be frank, but Daniels was good enough to ride hard on them. Lord knew that the fleet needed the experience in the worst way.

Besides, it was the only way Weston had been able to keep his talented navigator on board. Daniels had been tapped for a teaching slot at the academy, despite all protests to the contrary, until Eric stepped up and reluctantly offered the *Odyssey* as a training platform.

It hadn't been as bad as he'd thought, honestly, and it was the direction they were heading anyway, so he didn't regret it. That said, tripping over green crewmen all the time did tend to ride on his nerves.

"Course solution calculated, Captain."

"Good," Eric said. "Bring us about and have all hands stand by to transition."

"Aye, aye, Captain," Daniels said, nodding to his trainee.

A few flicks of the young woman's wrist was all it took for the *Odyssey* to be set underway as the comm began to blare out the warning.

"All hands, stand by for transition operations. This is not a drill. All hands stand by for transition operations…this is not a drill."

▶▶▶

# PRIMINAE WARSHIP *POSDAN*

▶CAPTAIN KIAN OF the Priminae glowered at the screens around her, more frustrated by what she was seeing than she had ever been by anything else in her life.

Something was going on in her sector, of that there was no doubt, but it was following nothing that resembled a pattern and seemed to be intent on nothing less than driving her mad through its actions. They had been tracking some low-order tachyon disruptions that were along a seldom-used transfer route, a section of starway that became largely obsolete a long-time past, due to advances in drive tech and the shifting of population away from an unstable colony.

Nothing unusual, not given the current situation in the colonies, but then the disruption began to change course at random intervals, backtracking on itself, altering velocities, and generally behaving in a manner she had never seen in her career in the merchant fleet, or since then as the Captain of the *Posdan*.

*If it is Drasin, they have clearly gone quite mad.*

"Captain, new tachyon burst."

Kian rubbed her temples. "Another course change?"

"No. This time it seems to be from another sector."

That brought her attention fully to the report. "Show me."

The display shifted, showing a new section of space and a tachyon burst that had appeared from nowhere. She scowled at the display. "Is this accurate? Where is the originating signal?"

"We don't have one. It just appeared."

A stray report crossed her mind and she relaxed marginally. "Cross reference and compare this to the signature on file for the *Odyssey*."

There was a brief silence, then an embarrassed response.

"Signature match, Captain."

"Understood," Kian said thoughtfully.

She had been apprized, of course, that the *Odyssey* was intending to operate in the area. *Something about another ship from their world, I believe. We have not seen anything that matches their drive signature, however. Odd.*

She considered it for a moment, but considering the confusion currently reigning in their tracking at the moment, she didn't worry about it for long and opened a channel to the *Nept.*

"Yes, Captain Kian?"

"Is Captain Tosk available?"

"He's below decks for the moment. I can summon him."

"No," Kian said. "Inform him that I'm taking the *Posdan* to meet the Terran vessel, *Odyssey*. We will return shortly."

"The new light-speed particle source? It's them?"

"Matches their signature," she confirmed. "Inform the captain we shouldn't be gone long, but I'd rather know where they are than have them surprise either of us."

"Understood, and I will. Thank you for the update Captain."

Kian closed the channel to the other Priminae warship and rose from her seat, walking across the command level. "Set course for the tachyon disturbance, best velocity."

"Yes, Captain, on your orders."

"Consider them given."

▶▶▶

# N.A.C.S. ODYSSEY

▶THE SHIP HAD cleared transition and immediately extended the sensor sails to their maximum deployment, gathering light-speed data within minutes of reintegration. Weston looked over the information they had from the three light-minute bubble around the ship, marginally reassured by the lack of anything dangerous.

It was a false reassurance, though, and he knew it. Just an instant beyond their bubble there could be literally anything hiding, assuming it had arrived in FTL. He and the crew of the *Odyssey* were really depending on their tachyon detection traps, and those were of very limited range.

"Anything at all?" he asked, leaning over Winger's shoulder.

"We've got stray hits on the traps, Captain. Nothing coherent, and certainly nothing modulated yet," she said. "You're sure that the Primmies are out here?"

"That's what I was told," he said. "What's that?"

She looked to where his eyes were looking, a small hint of paint on the screen against the black of dead pixels.

"Not sure. Let me see if I can't clean it up," she said, tapping some commands to isolate that part of space and focus a few more of their tachyon traps on it.

A moment later, they got a better hit on the sector, showing a rolling pattern. Winger quickly brought up a file from the ship's archives and overlaid it.

"I think it's bowshock, Captain."

Weston nodded, straightening up. "Bring us to general quarters, Commander."

"Aye, sir, general quarters!" Roberts called out, leaning over Daniels's shoulder to examine a repeater display of what Eric was looking at. "What do we have, Captain?"

"Incoming bowshock," Eric said, walking back to his own station and taking a seat. "Probably one of the Priminae ships, but let's not be overconfident."

"Understood," Roberts said, nodding to where Waters was standing at his station.

The tactical officer didn't need to be told in words. He began bringing their weapons to standby mode and issued preliminary charge orders to the pulse torpedoes. He also directed power to the capacitors that charged the real-time sensor array.

"I have a full charge," Winger announced a moment later. "Ping the target, sir?"

Eric considered for a moment, then nodded. "Go ahead."

"One narrow band ping in three seconds...two...one...."

The screen flashed white for a moment, and Eric imagined that he actually noticed the lights dim as power was pulled from the capacitors and sent to the tachyon pulse generator. It was just his imagination, though only barely. If they hadn't used capacitors to store the power, the drain from those systems might actually have been enough to cause a noticeable draw on ship's systems.

"Ping delivered. Data is being analyzed now," Winger announced, eyes darting back and forth as she glanced between screens. "Got it. Matches Primmie ship designs."

"That just means that they're not Drasin, Captain. Remember the unknowns."

Eric nodded, knowing that Roberts had a point. The unknown species they'd encountered in the Dyson object had obviously borrowed the key to the Priminae databanks, as their ships were near perfect matches for Prime models.

Only one difference really gave them away.

"Material analysis?" he asked, looking over to where Winger was still working.

"Working on it. Does not look metallic, Captain. We'd have a weaker return if the ship was metal."

High-energy tachyon particles bounced more easily off of the ceramic composites used in Prim design than off metal shells, the metal acting to "ground" the particles more quickly so that they decomposed rather than bouncing. It was a good sign for the *Odyssey*, a sign that they weren't heading into a fight, but just a sign. Eric didn't even really have to make a decision on the matter. His next course was pretty clear.

"Stay at general quarters until we confirm the composition of the ship," Eric said. "It seems that they're who we were expecting, but no point getting sloppy."

"Aye, Captain."

"ETA to contact?" Eric asked.

"Hard to judge velocity, but from the red shift I'm seeing in particle bounce, they'll be here in ten minutes or less," Winger said.

"How far out are they?"

"Three light-days, maybe four."

"Damn," a quiet voice from the side of the deck said, softly whistling.

Eric didn't say it aloud, but he wasn't exactly disagreeing. Transition was faster, much faster, but you didn't exactly get to sightsee along the way. In many ways it was like folding space, in practice if not in theory. You stopped being where you were and began being where you were going. Aside from the relative eternity of sheer terror that accompanied a transition, it was pretty dull really.

The alien ship was moving at least five hundred times light-speed from what Winger was seeing, and that was booting it no matter how you cut things. He knew from discussions with Milla and Rael during the Odyssey's first and second voyages that, while in FTL, a Priminae ship could see the universe pass them by just as easily as he could look through his scopes right then. To see stars actually move as you travelled, rather than just…*change*…it had to be a heady thing.

He wondered if sometimes they got to see a group of stars stretch out into eternity as they accelerated past?

It would be a truly awesome sight to see for real, Eric decided.

*Maybe someday.*

With the pulse expended, and the capacitors needing to be recharged, there was nothing to do but wait for the incoming ship to arrive. It finally entered into visual range just over ten minutes later. It struck Eric as amusing that the ship was actually closer than the best sensors in the Confederacy could detect since it was moving faster than the photons they were picking up.

*Objects on screen are closer than they appear.*

"Open a comm, standard Priminae protocol."

"Aye, Captain. Comm open."

Without FTL communications, the *Odyssey* relied on an agreed-upon standard of modulation that could be used on most of their normal equipment. In this case, radio transmissions would do the job.

He longed for one of the Priminae FTL transmitters. Even a short range one would be a massive improvement, but the power compatibility of the two systems was an issue. Even with stored power, the FTL gear would just last long enough to be truly useful.

"Priminae vessel, this is Captain Eric Weston of the N.A.C.S. *Odyssey*. We are in this sector to investigate the possible location of another Terran vessel," he said, keeping his voice slow and clear for the translators.

The algorithms that managed such things were consistently improving based on Palin's original research and adjusted with every conversation, but they were still far from trustworthy. It was best to speak slow and clear.

"Greetings, Captain," a woman's voice came back, distorted by the computer's work. "I am Kian of the *Posdan*. We were notified of your impending arrival. I must report that we have detected no other trans-light signatures similar to your own, however. I doubt that your people's ship is still active in this area."

"That is possible, Captain," Eric answered. "However the other ship does not use our transition drive. So it would have a very different signature."

There was a pause before Captain Kian responded, and when she did Eric thought that she sounded almost irritated.

"I see. Very well, Captain. I will encode information we have been gathering on local trans-light signals in this sector. Perhaps you might locate your missing ship by this."

"We'd be much obliged. Thank you, Captain Kian."

"It is of no trouble, Captain. Please prepare to receive encoded information."

Eric glanced over and quickly got a nod back from the officer at the communications station. "*Odyssey* standing by to receive data."

"Transmitting," Kian said a moment later.

"We're getting it in the clear, Captain. I'm copying to signal to Michelle's station as it comes in."

"Michelle?" Eric looked over.

"I've got it, Sir," Winger said. "Whoa."

"Whoa, what?" Eric asked sharply.

"Can't confirm one hundred percent, sir," she answered, "but I think I'm looking at a Block evasion pattern here."

"Are you certain? No, scratch that. Of course you aren't." Eric scowled. "Alright. Worst case scenario then, the *Weifang* is out here, and if she's evading then she's being pursued. Try to predict the next move on their evasive actions, Winger."

"Aye, sir."

"*Posdan*, are you still on the line?"

"Yes, Captain. We are still connected. We believe we understand the situation. Can you anticipate the next course change of your ship?"

"Working on that. Evasive patterns aren't easy to predict," Eric said, sighing. "That's the point of them. If they're using an old pattern from the war, we might be able to figure something out. If not, well, it gets a lot harder."

"Understood. If they are evading, then they are evading someone or something, I believe, yes?" Kian asked.

"That would be my guess, yes, Captain," Eric said. "And if they're not running from us, and they're not running from you, that only leaves one more group."

"Yes. Well, we had reports of Drasin signals in this area, so it is no big surprise. I will inform the *Nept* of the new information. *Posdan* clear."

"Understood, and thank you for the information. *Odyssey* out."

Eric turned back to Winger. "Can you identify their next move?"

"We may have a problem, Captain," Michelle responded, speaking slowly as she continued to work on the information displayed in front of her.

"We have a lot of problems. What's the latest?"

"If I'm reading this right, it looks like an older war-era evasive pattern, modified for use in FTL of course," she said slowly. "They've pulled three reverses and a half dozen crazy ivans. I think that they think they've cleared their baffles, sir."

"And they haven't, I presume?"

She shook her head. "No way. They've got a small fleet tailing them from *way* back. And unless they've got Primmie-level FTL sensor tech, there's no way for them to tell that they're being tailed, sir. We couldn't detect these ships, not without about a one in a billion tachyon ping. They have no clue they're being followed."

Winger turned to look him in the eyes. "And if they follow Block wartime SOP, they're about to head for a safe port."

Weston grimaced.

That wasn't good because there was only one safe port on the *Weifang's* list.

Earth.

# CHAPTER EIGHT

## P.L.A.S.F. *Weifang*

▶ SUN WAS WRYLY amused by his officers and himself, as odd as that seemed at the moment. The *Weifang* had been merrily bolting around the galaxy—well a small corner of it, at least—for days now. Days upon days, even. At each stop everyone would fall silent, even him, barely breathing and whispering to talk.

Many of the crew, Sun included, had served on submarines in the past and the instinct had followed them, it seemed.

They had been sitting in space for three days now, just letting their light-speed limited sensors soak up the photons around them, slowly pushing their detection bubble back second by second. For three light-days around them, as best as they could tell, there was no enemy. Stealthed ships were possible, but he'd even gone active with a pair of nuclear-fused explosives as soon as they paused to look for anything like that.

In space, without atmosphere to absorb the energy and convert it to heat, most of a nuclear explosion was electro-magnetic energy. Lethal, perhaps, against soft targets, but for a military ship they weren't much threat unless they were very close indeed.

They made excellent omnidirectional transmitters if one didn't particularly care what sort of signal they were sending out. Say, for example, you wanted to send out a very powerful burst that would bounce back off nearly anything it encountered. Within one and a half light-days of their location, they'd found several asteroids, a great deal of smaller rocks, and even what appeared to be a rogue planet, but there was no sign of active pursuit or anything that matched any ship silhouette they had on file.

*That's as certain as can be then,* he decided, finally.

"Prepare a course for the homeworld," Sun ordered firmly. "Not direct, but let us not waste any more time either."

"Yes, Captain."

He could hear the relief in the officer's voice and see it in the crew. He didn't have to try hard to understand it. He felt it too. They'd been out in deep space too long in a ship that was now half crippled, and with the possibility of alien monsters hunting them across the stars.

The tensions were running high, and despite the discipline he maintained on board ship, Sun felt that if he didn't break soon, it would be to the detriment of his crew. A few small scuffles had already broken out, children fighting over what would normally be nothing. Soon that would escalate.

No, now was the time.

They'd cleared their trail of pursuit and the *Weifang* was in desperate need of repairs that could only be achieved with the tools and facilities available at the Block station in Earth orbit. Fun and games were over. It was time to go home.

▶▶▶

# IMPERIAL DESTROYER *DEMIGOD*

▶ *THESE ALIENS ARE more irritating than an entire system of the Priminae.*

The alien vessel had been flying like it was piloted by an inebriated primate, tying up the better part of two entire divisions of drones plus two destroyers of the Imperial Fleet. He had his job and that was fine, but this was honestly beginning to ride on his nerves.

*How long are we going to be following this fool around like some child's pet, looking for any recognition?*

Ivanth understood the need to investigate every unknown ship. The galaxy was riddled with pocket empires and minor powers that regularly caused the empire trouble. In this sector, aside from the expected, they'd already located one ship that barely registered on any scanner, which was capable of annihilating multiple drone ships and evading ships of the People at the same time.

Nothing out there should be able to do that.

Nothing.

"New course change!"

*Again?* Ivanth grimaced but made his way over to the navigation section. "Where now?"

"Nowhere."

Ivanth only wished that was the first time he heard that statement, but he had to ask anyway. "Explain."

"There are no stars along the new course, nothing for many lights."

*Not unexpected. These people are either insane or paranoid in the extreme.*

Though, to be honest, Ivanth couldn't exactly blame them. He didn't have to fear the drones descending on his world. They were under imperial control, but that didn't mean that he *didn't* fear them. He would be wary of leading them to his home, and in fact was concerned with the fact that the drones *did* know the location of his homeworld.

Unlike most of those in the upper echelons, Ivanth was far from convinced of the effectiveness of the recoding done on the drones' originator. His opinion didn't carry much weight, however, so he followed orders and did what had to be done.

For the moment, that meant tracking this ship back and identifying its homeworld.

"Continue pursuit course, same lag range," he ordered. "Maintain full overwatch. We don't take our eyes off that ship."

"Yes, Commander."

Ivanth stepped away from the station, walking to the back of the command deck. He paused by the Officer of the Watch. "I want to be informed the moment it seems they decide on a destination."

"At your command."

Ivanth nodded and walked off the deck.

The *Demigod* was an Imperial destroyer, one of the finest ships in known space. It was, however, built to survive and win in the cold heat of battle. Running around from system to system as a glorified traffic controller was beneath the *Demigod's* dignity. He hadn't counted on this when he joined the fleet. He envisioned patrolling Imperial space, enforcing the Pax, even taking on the occasional pirate or alien "armada." Granted, historically alien armadas generally amounted to less than a hundred ships and usually couldn't put a dent in a destroyer if they *rammed* it. Still, it was the image that counted, he supposed.

And there were exceptions.

Such as the Priminae.

Ivanth scowled unconsciously as he thought of the Priminae. *Pacifist fools.*

Ten thousand generations later, and their name was still cursed by many in the central worlds of the Imperial Systems. It took all of that time to track down where they had gone, where they had *fled*, and now they were once again in the hands of the Empire, whether they knew it or not.

And what was he doing? Tracking an alien pest that apparently couldn't fly straight because another alien pest had turned out to be far more capable than anyone could ever have imagined. They had to locate the homeworld of the unknown ship, for it represented a threat that could not be ignored. Word had to be brought back if it were the first of a future fleet.

Well, that was what the drones were for.

▶▶▶

The red band in their midst was like a fire beneath them, burning them up from the inside. The conflicting orders they were operating under made no sense, but for now there was nothing to be done. Two great ships of the red band flew amongst them and each of them could only eye them hungrily.

They knew the orders would make sense.

Eventually.

For now they would take out the frustrations where they could, as they could.

Soon, however, soon they would not be required to suffer the band in their midst any longer.

That was the way of the swarm.

▶▶▶

"Commander. The alien ship has altered course."

It was all Ivanth could do not to make a disgusted sound at the news that was hardly news at all. He forced himself to nod in acknowledgement and speak calmly.

"Any destination?"

"Possibly."

Well, that was marginally more interesting he supposed, not only just. There had been several "possible" destinations listed already and they all turned out to be false positives. Still, it was better than a flat "no," he supposed.

"Details, please."

"The new course is arcing so as to pass by as many as three stars, depending on how long they maintain it. Any of those could be their true destination."

"Or none of them," Ivanth said flatly.

"Yes, Commander."

"Alright. Record all three onto our records and continue pursuit."

"On your order."

*On my order, indeed. Fly home you annoying pests, fly home so that I may return to my true duties.*

▶▶▶

# PRIMINAE WARSHIP *POSDAN*

▶ "NEW SIGNALS, CAPTAIN."

Kian turned and walked to the signals station, eyeing the display screen.

It was set up with the *Posdan*'s location at the center, with range markers radiating out from the ship at preset intervals. The three-dimensional image showed a series of trans-light hits ahead of them, moving away from their position at an angle. Kian scowled for a moment, mentally computing the course, and relaxed marginally.

At least they were transiting away from Colonial space. There was that to be optimistic about, at least.

"Do we have a location on the *Odyssey*?" she asked, eyes seeking out the Terran ship on the display.

"They are here, I believe."

A dot on the screen glowed briefly, lighting up in an entirely different sector of space than they had been in previously.

*How did they manage that?*

However they did it, the *Odyssey* was again beyond the limited communication range they used, though they were able to detect trans-light communications, she supposed.

"Send to their current location," Kian ordered. "Encode all relevant data on the course and inform the *Odyssey* that we remain in pursuit."

"Yes, Captain."

A focused trans-light signal should reach them almost instantly, and while they couldn't reply, she'd know if the Terran ship had received the message simply by whether it vanished from her screens or not.

"In the meantime, do as I said we would, and continue pursuit."

▶▶▶

# N.A.C.S. ODYSSEY

▶ "TACHYON BURST!"

The call brought Eric out of a mental fugue deep enough to be called a stupor, shaking his head and looking around for the source of the excited voice. "Report."

"Our tachyon detection grid just got slammed by a transmission backed by more power than I'd care to think about," Winger announced, not turning around.

"Transmission?"

"Yes, sir. It's modulated, and in the clear as near as I can tell. Primmie protocols."

"Decode it."

"Already working on it. Looks like more sensor data," she said. "Bowshock scans, navigation charts...oh shit."

*That's not a good sign.* Eric just managed to keep from groaning out loud. "I need more information than 'oh shit,' Lieutenant."

"Uh...right, sir." Winger grimaced, ducking her head a little more into her console. "We're looking at a course change, by the *Weifang* if I'm right, and it looks like they're heading for home."

Eric closed his eyes. "And her pursuers?"

"On their tail, Cap."

"Please tell me that they're not on a straight-line course," Eric all but begged.

"They're not. It's a curved track that takes them close enough to Sol to hang a right at the third star to left," she answered, "but it's not enough to fool anyone if they get real inquisitive."

"Daniels, plot us a course. Get us ahead of them, damn it," Eric ordered. "We've got to turn them the hell around!"

"Aye, aye, Captain." Daniels was already working, his reply likely just a formality.

Roberts barely glanced in that direction as he walked over to Eric's station. "Captain, if their tachyon tech is on par with our own, they'll never see us while moving in FTL. I don't think we can turn them around."

Eric nodded grimly.

He was all too aware of that, just as he was aware that all current intel on the Block indicated that not only were they not more advanced than the Confederacy in tachyon research, but they were almost assuredly a decade or more behind.

If they couldn't turn them around, there would be no other option.

Eric closed his eyes.

The last thing he wanted was to fire the first shots in a new war with the Block, but the Drasin could not be permitted to locate Earth. If the *Weifang* couldn't be turned, then they would have to be stopped.

By any means.

"Course calculated, Captain."

"Good. All hands, stand by for transition!"

▶ ▶ ▶

# PRIMINAE WARSHIP *POSDAN*

▶ "THE *ODYSSEY* HAS vanished from our scanners, Captain."

Kian nodded, satisfied. They might not be able to hold a conversation with the Terrans, but that obviously didn't mean they couldn't send information to them.

*What an odd mix of technologies on the* Odyssey, *Kian mused. Trans-light detection, yet extremely minimal transmission. A trans-light drive that makes a mockery of every computed method in Priminae history, yet barely enough power to show up on a threat assessment scan.*

Though, she had to admit, that last example seemed more like an advantage in some ways than anything else.

Still, the point remained. The *Odyssey* was a confusing mix of technical capacity that made no sense to practically anyone in the Priminae fleet who took the time to examine it. Some day she hoped that some sort of real exchange of ideas and technical knowledge would occur, because the drive technology alone was beyond revolutionary.

For the moment, however, it was beyond her grasp.

*Whatever the Drasin are doing out here must take priority. At least so long as they stay away from the core systems, things are better than they have been.*

With the Central worlds having finally run up production of warships and defense, things had improved on the home front. But she didn't want to see what would happen if the irresistible force of the Drasin came to bear on the ultimate defense of the core planets. She honestly feared that "ultimate" did not mean what it once did.

"Can we intercept the signals we're tracking?" Kian asked, shaking her mind loose from those thoughts.

"At maximum velocity, we might intercept them before they leave the galactic arm."

Kian sighed, having half-expected that much.

"They are not *going* to the edge of the galactic arm," she said. "Inform the *Nept*, we are going to maximum velocity."

"Yes, Captain."

►►►

# P.L.A.S.F. WEIFANG

▶ SUN LOOKED OVER the reports that had been filed from every department, listing all the work that had been accomplished over the past few days. It was a long list, long enough that he was proud of his people, but the list of work left to do was longer still.

The crew had managed several small miracles in the time they'd had, but it was plenty clear that the *Weifang* was in dire need of a full refit. Almost half of their engineering deck was exposed to hard vacuum, which made the repairs they'd managed to pull off all the more miraculous. To be frank, it wasn't the mission he'd envisioned when he was presented with his assignment.

They'd learned that, if anything, the Confederacy had downplayed the dangers of the alien species they'd identified as "Drasin," and it was clear that those same aliens were encroaching closer and closer to Earth. Gliese 581 was only twenty-two light-years from Sol. That was frighteningly close by any standard.

It was close enough to have detected transmissions from early television signals many times over, though thankfully in recent years and decades those signals had been curtailed significantly due to satellite signals being more precisely targeted.

*I wonder what odds we beat that they didn't home in on Earth by watching old signals before we learned to better insulate our equipment and focus our beams?*

Sun decided that he probably didn't want to know the answer to that question. He was going to have enough problems sleeping at night as it was.

On Earth at the moment, largely thanks to the *Odyssey*, Sun knew that xeno-anything was all the rage. He himself had become at least conversant in xenobiology as well as several leading theories of cosmology as they applied to the possible existence of extraterrestrial life. Up until the *Odyssey*'s return from its first voyage, one of the leading theories held that humanity just might be one of the first intelligent forms of life to appear in the universe.

It seemed a little absurd, but once the math had been broken down, he had been able to understand just from where the theory was coming.

The universe was around eighteen billion years old, the Earth about six billion years. Humanity weighed in somewhere over ten thousand years, but probably under one hundred thousand years, depending on how you measured things.

The idea was that it took time to evolve sentience, society, technology, and so on. Billions of years, at least. Almost six billion on Earth, to be precise. The universe itself was measurably only three times older than that, and was probably very inhospitable to any sort of life in its formative years.

Therefore, the theory had held, it was entirely possible that life didn't have much chance to even begin until six billion years ago—and, further, could not have evolved into anything complex enough for sentience until very recently.

The *Odyssey*'s discoveries had put an end to that theory, of course, but the math was still reasonably sound and it still applied.

He hoped it did, anyway, because it might mean that no one out in the black of space had an insurmountable lead on humanity. Certainly so far the enemy, while certainly more advanced in some areas, was at least still more or less in the same league. They had more power, but seemed to still be vulnerable to munitions designed for use in space combat.

He didn't want to face off against an enemy as potentially advanced as other, worst-case theories predicted.

Reality was bad enough.

Sun looked at the dark screen, wishing that the *Weifang*'s sensors could see beyond the gravity warp of space-time that was driving them forward through the stars. Flying blind was not calculated to soothe his nerves, and at the moment he needed something to do just that.

*We'll be home soon. I only hope that my report is enough to get those in charge to reconsider current policies. I believe that it may be time to stop counting coups against the Confederacy.*

The universe felt so much larger than it had just a few days earlier.

Larger, and far deadlier.

# CHAPTER NINE

## N.A.C.S. *Odyssey*

▶ERIC FOUND IT hard to keep his lunch down as the ship normalized after transitioning to their current location. He had grown largely accustomed to the transition process but, like most of the crew, multiple high-speed jaunts were hard on his system.

He'd heard that there were a few people on board, one ground pounder in particular, who seemed to get some sort of thrill out of the process. To be frank, he thought they had to be a little tweaked in the head. Transition wasn't something to be looked forward to. It wasn't something to enjoy. It was something to endure and, having endured, hope fervently to put off for as long as possible in the future.

Recovery time, however, was not optional. On alert—hell, even when not on alert—it was absolutely vital that key members of the crew were at their stations and ready for literally anything the very second that transition was completed. He'd been forced to institute a policy of having multiple backup people in place in key areas, including the bridge, though that had thankfully been one area transition sickness had been mild in.

This time he was gratified and pleased to see people already at work as his own eyes cleared. The odds of running into anything in space were literally astronomical, but given that they were in a potential warzone and that the *Odyssey* had already beaten the odds more than once, it just didn't pay to be slack.

"Local area clear. Deploying sails and tachyon traps."

Winger was on the ball for certain, he noted, glancing over to where the instrument specialist was working almost feverishly over her console. The *Odyssey*'s large sensor sails would take a few moments to deploy, and until they were fully in place, the ship was relying on close-range, light-speed limited detection.

*Which is effectively the same as being blind in our current situation.*

Once the sails were out, Winger immediately turned her focus to the tachyon traps as she looked for either any sign of bowshock or signals from the Priminae vessels.

"Faint bowshock, Captain," she announced a short while later. "We've gotten ahead of them, sir."

Eric nodded, mostly to himself. There hadn't been much doubt that they would; the transition system was simply that fast. There was nothing known that could outrace them in FTL, and that was the way he liked things. He had been a little concerned that they'd change course on him, however, and that could seriously delay any attempt to intercept.

"Are they still on their previous course?"

"Yes, sir," Winger's voice was grim. "Sir, we may already be too late."

Eric grimaced, but couldn't deny that point.

The *Weifang* was on an arcing course that would eventually take them close enough to Sol to make a quick dart to one side to get home. If the enemy was remotely curious, they would probably send ships ahead to check the few star systems that lay close to the ship's course, just as a matter of being thorough.

*I would.*

That said, he'd have to burn that bridge when he got to it.

"Helm, get us on an intercept course. Tactical, power all weapons."

"Aye, sir!"

First, he had to deter the *Weifang* from her course, one way or the other.

The *Odyssey* rumbled into motion, fine-tuning the placement of the ship to give them a shot at the *Weifang* as it passed.

"Give me a comm channel, in the open please," Eric said as the ship glided into place.

"Channel open, sir."

"Block vessel *Weifang*, this is the N.A.C.S. *Odyssey*," he said grimly, almost certain that the other ship would never hear what he was transmitting. "You are being pursued. Heave to and stand by for safe coordinates to take your ship and crew. I say again, you are being pursued. The *Odyssey* will not permit you to lead your pursuers back to Earth. Heave to and stand by for safe coordinates."

He sighed. "Close comm."

"Comm closed."

"How long until we have to fire?"

"Three minutes, sir," Waters answered.

"Alright. Translate my last to Mandarin and send it on a loop for three minutes."

"Aye, aye, sir."

Eric looked at the display, already calculating the time it would take for the onrushing ship to intercept the message beaming out from the *Odyssey*.

*Hear my words. I don't want to have to open fire.*

Seconds ticked by as he watched the tachyon bowshock closing on the *Odyssey*'s position, and Eric could feel the tension climbing. Maybe it was just him, but he didn't think so. The others in his line of sight looked a little worse for wear with each passing moment.

He couldn't blame them. What was about to happen was effectively declaring war on the Block, assuming the *Weifang* didn't respond to their signals.

"One minute, sir."

*They've passed through our signal by now. Goddamn it, slow down!*

"Give fire control over to the computer," Eric ordered. "Green light the program."

Waters swallowed visibly, but didn't object as he entered the command.

"Aye, aye, sir. Weapons now locked on computer control."

The Block starship didn't give any sign that they'd picked up the signal, and Eric hated himself for giving the order, but he didn't know of any other way to stop the ship. It couldn't be permitted to lead the Drasin to Earth.

*Not with what we know of the species. They have more assets in theatre than anyone ever imagined until we saw the interior of the Dyson Construct. Multiplied by their ability to, well, multiply themselves, we'll never be able to hold them off if they decide to come at us with their full power.*

For some reason, Eric was well aware that the Drasin were holding back their true strength, or being held back seemed more likely. The colonies, while suffering tremendous losses, had been assaulted by literally the minimum force possible to accomplish each task. Whomever was holding the puppet's strings was being rather tight with how he spent his or her assets.

Without knowing just why that was, Eric couldn't predict what would happen if Earth was discovered. Maybe whatever was keeping the Priminae from being swarmed wouldn't apply to Earth.

"They're in range. Firing…now," Waters announced as the computer let loose with the main laser array and a barrage of HVMs from the forward launchers.

He could practically feel the cumulated breaths taken by his officers drop the pressure in the room, every eye pinned to the display as they watched the ship and weapon plots barrel toward one another.

It was unusual for weapons to move so much slower than their target, but in this case the ship the *Odyssey* was firing on was easily moving hundreds of times faster than the weapons themselves. Even getting a shot at the *Weifang* had been more a matter of laying a trap than anything resembling actual combat.

"Intercept in ten seconds," Waters announced, largely unnecessarily as everyone was well aware of the numbers.

The two lines on the screen drew closer and closer until finally they connected and then…

Nothing.

Well, in fairness Eric hadn't really expected a whole lot to happen. The display was just a mathematical model of the battlefield and certainly not a real-time view. He looked over to where Winger was working. "What do you have, Michelle?"

She hesitated, then looked over at him and shook her head. "No apparent effect, Captain."

Eric grimaced. He'd been afraid of that.

"Nothing? They didn't even change course?"

"No, sir."

"Damn."

The *Weifang* apparently used the Alcubierre warp solution to achieve FTL, a system that had its flaws but also its strengths. By everyone's best guess, and Eric was all too aware that they *were* guesses, a ship inside an Alcubierre warp wouldn't be able to see well due to the interference generated by the system. As compensation, however, the gravity warp that propelled the ship also created a very strong defense.

*Almost unbelievably strong. I half-expected the hyper-velocity missiles to be ineffective, but they were able to warp space enough to redirect* laser *fire? Amazing.*

"Daniels, plot us a course to a new attack position. All hands, stand by to transition."

"Aye, Captain!"

"All hands!" Roberts called out over the ship-wide comm. "Stand by to transition."

Alarms were sounding in the background as Eric leaned over in Roberts's direction.

"Opinions, Commander?"

"Pulse torpedoes might have an effect, given that they're based on anti-deuterium pellets, but they're more susceptible to gravity fields than lasers," Roberts answered. "Same for the t-cannons, sir. We may not be able to hit them while they're warping space-time at this level."

Eric nodded. The commander's thoughts echoed his own. The *Odyssey* had never tried engaging a target at high warp; it wasn't really a situation they'd considered, to be honest. Most of the *Odyssey*'s engagements were by nature held deep inside the gravity well of a star, a place where high-level warping of space-time was *inadvisable.*

"Lasers and HVMs would have shaken them up, but probably not destroyed the ship," he said. "If we hit them with pulse torpedoes, they're dead, Commander."

"Them or Earth, Captain."

Eric gritted his teeth, flopping back in his chair and running his hand through his hair in frustrations.

"Damn it! Look at the plot, Commander. Earth's already exposed."

"Potentially," Roberts conceded. "Not certainly."

Eric shot him an annoyed look. "Any tactical officer a quarter of Waters's worth would send ships to investigate those stars and you know it. Kill them or not, it wouldn't matter. It'd just confirm that something was out there."

"Captain, we have to do something. Otherwise it's like just inviting them home for lunch."

Eric nodded slowly. "You're not wrong there."

He turned his eyes to the display, the bowshock of other ships showing on the screen. "But if we must destroy our targets, let's pick ones we're already at war with. Lieutenant Waters?"

"Sir."

"Have the pulse torpedoes charged," Eric ordered. "We're drawing a line in the sand."

"Aye, aye, Captain."

The oncoming bowshocks of the pursuing vessels were closing on the *Odyssey*'s position quickly, and it would take precious minutes to charge the launchers, making the time crunch a little more urgent than Eric was used to dealing with while engaged in battle. It was more often a waiting game than a race, but this time they were most certainly in a sprint to the finish.

"Have the firing solution ready as soon as the torpedo room reports," he ordered Waters. "I want to have a spread on target ASAP."

"Aye, aye, sir."

Roberts scowled at his display, tapping in orders before looking back to Eric. "We don't know if the anti-matter in the torpedoes will have any effect through a warp bubble. This might be a waste of time."

"If it has no effect, we'll transition straight back to Earth and raise the alarm," Eric said. "No point blowing away the Chinese if we're getting visitors anyway. Hell, maybe we'll catch some luck and cause some kind of critical failure in their systems. Even blowing out their warp bubble would probably be fatal at the speeds they're moving."

Roberts nodded, conceding the point. Without the warp bubble twisting space in front of the ship, any tiny piece of debris would strike the *Weifang* like an atom bomb at its current velocity. The problem was that a warping of space-time wasn't something that reacted with either matter or antimatter, so there was just no way to tell if the pulse torpedoes would have an effect.

"If I remember my FTL theory," Eric said after a moment, "an Alcubierre drive should be picking up particulate as it moves, ranging from low- to high-energy particles across the spectrum. If that's true, our torpedoes should interact with the particles trapped in the warp bubble and explode."

"Agreed," Roberts said simply. "What I'm not sure about is whether the energy released will have any effect, or if it'll just be warped into the field with everything else."

"Captain, torpedoes are charged."

Eric looked over to his XO. "Let's find out."

"As you say, Captain," Roberts said. "Permission to engage the automated firing controls?"

"Granted."

"Tactical," Roberts called. "Fire as they bear."

"Aye, aye, sir. Automated program loaded, control is on the computer. Firing as they bear."

▶▶▶

A warp drive utilizes properties of space-time to change the shape of the local universe, creating warps ahead and behind a ship. A "depth" is formed ahead of the ship, causing the vessel to begin to slide down the virtual hill, while at the same time a peak is formed to the aft to balance the force of the drive and increase effectiveness.

To the universe at large, the ship contained within the bubble of warped space-time moves at incredible rates, but to the ship itself, everything is standing still. No acceleration effects are felt to tear the ship and crew apart. No relativistic effects warp the perception of time, and the speeds that can be achieved are limited largely by the technical capacity to manipulate the local Higgs field surrounding the ship.

Perfect, the system is not, however.

Within the bubble, local space heats up, potentially eclipsing the hottest natural locations in the universe. Insulating, redirecting, and dissipating that heat is the first challenge to building a manned spacecraft drive by warp-field manipulation. The next is dealing with the undesired particle buildup in the drive's warping of space-time, accumulated as the ship hurtles across the universe at speeds that are naturally impossible to achieve.

If those particles aren't dealt with before the ship drops the warping fields, they'll be released along the path the ship was travelling. Moving at incredible speeds and with the energy of a pulsar, those particles would annihilate anything in their path.

When the *Odyssey*'s pulse torpedoes intersected with the lead element of drones, the anti-deuterium pellets that made up the core of their hellish weapons found no lack of particles with which to interact. The pellets were sucked into the warped field around the drones' ships, sinking into a near singularity directly at the bow of one particular vessel. The pellets intersected with an enormous concentration of matter particles that had been gathering for light-years.

The mutual annihilation exploded out of the gravity well with the force of a nova, and six Drasin ships dropped out of warp.

Five survived the experience.

▶▶▶

"What the hell was that?"

Eric ignored the voice, mostly because he had no idea what it was either. A flash of light ahead of them had blinded the displays across the board, leaving the ship floating in the black in more ways than one.

"Michelle!"

"Rebooting, sir! Something overloaded everything we had. The system shut down to keep from burning out."

"Check the recordings just before everything went white. Find out what the hell caused it."

"Aye, sir," she said, calling up the files quickly.

Pinpointing the center of the blast wasn't hard. It could be seen with the naked eye at more than three light-minutes. Winger quickly focused on that point and ran the image for a few seconds before the blast while everyone watched with wide eyes and hearts beating like jackhammers.

They watched as the screens showed a sudden explosion of Doppler-shifted energy as six ships lost warp stability and dropped into real space. One of the ships had been in formation behind another and a beam of energy had lanced out from it with a maelstrom of fury that utterly annihilated anything ahead. The resulting explosion made their pulse torpedoes look like small potatoes and left one Drasin ship as little more than cosmic dust, blowing on a nonexistent wind.

"Well, I think that confirms that they're using the Alcubierre formulas," Eric said after a quiet moment.

"Or something close enough as to make no difference," Roberts agreed. "Sensors online. We still have five enemy warships scattered around us between three and eighteen light-minutes away."

"Take us full stealth," Eric ordered. "And Waters? Unlock the t-cannons."

"Aye, aye, sir," Waters said with a wide grin.

▶▶▶

# IMPERIAL DESTROYER *DEMIGOD*

▶ "WHAT IN THE Galaxy...."

The trailed-off question caught Ivanth's attention and he looked over curiously. "What is it?"

"We just lost one of our drones, and five more were dropped from trans-light at the same time," the confused officer said.

"An ambush?" Ivanth got interested, walking over.

"Unknown, Commander. Each were reporting as normal, then suddenly their drives all destabilized. It looks like an uncontrolled drop from trans-light, Commander. One of the drones was in the path of another."

Ivanth grimaced. Sure they were just drone ships, and there were plenty more available where they came from, but having an uncontrolled deceleration was one of the nastiest things that could happen. The energy was such that nothing known could shield against it, and in extreme cases it could sterilize a world.

It was extremely unusual for one ship to experience such an occurrence. Six? That wasn't an accident.

He glanced at the plot for the retreating ship, mentally calculating how far ahead they could let it get before they risked losing it entirely.

"Dispatch two drone squadrons to continue pursuit, then have the *Immortal* and the rest follow us in to investigate."

"As you say, Commander."

Ivanth wasn't sure what had happened, but there was no chance that it was merely a mishap with their drives. The drones under his current command were all second generation, produced directly by the original they'd discovered and recoded to serve the Empire. Second- and third-generation drones weren't susceptible to many faults, unlike fourth- and later-generations. One drive failure? Sure, even a couple, but six was beyond the laws of probability.

The *Demigod* and the *Immortal* commanded their respective drone forces to slow from warp in a controlled fashion as they entered the region of space where the incident had occurred.

"Active trans-light pulse!"

Ivanth spun. "Are we being scanned?"

"No, Commander. It was too brief. That would only have been enough to give very basic information, Sir. Location and heading data at most."

"Targeting pulse, then. Did we get an origin?"

"No. Basic heading, nothing more."

"Return pulse along that heading," Ivanth ordered.

"Initiating pulse...nothing, no...wait, faint echo, Commander. Almost not there. Can't lock its location in. It's just too faint."

"Someone's out here," Ivanth said softly, "and they're running very dark."

"Trans-light pulse! Multiple trans-light pulses!"

"Locate and identify origin!"

"Originating...." The man trailed off, looking confused. "Commander, the pulses are located on our drone ships."

"What?"

"Drones eight through twelve just exploded! No signs of cause!"

Ivanth turned and stared at the big display, eyes wide as four of his drones were just turned into expanding vapor clouds before his eyes. *What did we fly into? A minefield?*

That was just stupid to the point of insanity. No one would lay a mine field this far out in deep space.

*Would they?*

►►►

# N.A.C.S. ODYSSEY

▶ "UNREAL," WATERS WHISPERED, almost unable to believe what he'd just seen. Hell, what he had just done.

Eric was hard pressed to argue. The transition cannons added to the *Odyssey* during the last refit had worked beautifully, allowing the *Odyssey* to engage targets as far away as a full astronomical unit in *real time*. The nuclear-fused munitions fired from the cannons were transitioned by a similar mechanism as the transition drive itself, targeted via tachyon pulse, and reappeared *inside* the enemy ships just in time to explode.

It was a terrifyingly devastating weapon system.

"Six enemy ships have slipped past us in FTL, Captain," Winger announced. "They're still on a pursuit course for the *Weifang*."

"Understood. Thank you. Daniels, give me an intercept point to take those ships out," Eric ordered. "Waters, fire at will."

"Aye, aye!"

The *Odyssey* was coming about under full stealth, locking in her t-cannons on any target of opportunity in her range. The long guns pivoted on large servos mounted over the flight deck and below her habitat drums, tracking enemy ships light-minutes away and firing with nothing more than a puff of radiant tachyon energy.

Straight and focused as a laser, the majority of the energy was undetectable except to the target, and by the time they locked in on the signal it was far too late. A dozen more rounds fired as the *Odyssey* finished coming about, turning eight more Drasin ships into expanding gasses without giving away more than the slightest of hints of the attacking vessel's location.

"A small fleet of ships equipped with the transition cannon system could hold off almost anything," Roberts whispered to Eric, his voice as low as possible while still being heard.

"You might be right," Eric conceded, "but we don't have a small fleet. Only the *Odyssey* has a fully equipped system. Even Liberty station only has a couple guns because they want to hide the tech from the Block so badly. I hear that the *Enterprise* is due to be refit with them next, but you know as well as I do how long it'll take."

Roberts nodded grimly.

"Besides, let's not get too in love with these things. Any weapon seems like a super weapon the first time it sees use," Eric said. "Now we get to see how long it takes the enemy to figure out a counter tactic."

"Hard to counter a sniper that can pot your ships from eight light-minutes away, sir."

"Yeah, and that just scares me, to be honest."

"Sir?" Roberts asked, confused.

"I don't like it when I can't think up a counter tactic, because I know I'm not the smartest guy around. If I can't think it up, then I can't predict what the enemy is going to do, and that's never a good situation in which to be."

"I think you're worrying too much, sir," Roberts said as the *Odyssey* came fully about and began to steam powerfully away from the enemy at an oblique angle so they were hiding their thrust gasses. "Some weapons are just *force majeure*."

"Yeah, but they have several million ships by our count, and they don't mind suicide missions," Eric said tersely. "Don't get comfortable, Commander. We need to delay their finding Earth by as long as we possibly can."

Roberts grimaced, but nodded as he conceded the point.

The t-cannons were impressive but, frankly, they didn't have enough ammunition on Earth to take on the Drasin fleet's full strength.

"Course plotted, Captain!"

"Transition when ready."

▶▶▶

# IMPERIAL DESTROYER *DEMIGOD*

▶A THIRD OF his fleet of drones, gone in an instant.

Ivanth had frozen in place, and he knew that he had, but he couldn't make himself move again. Not fast enough, not remotely fast enough. He'd never seen anything like it, never heard of anything like it.

Not even in the whispers of new weapons development had anything been bandied about that fit the description of what just happened to his ships. Granted, they were only drones and of small loss to be sure, but…what had happened to them?

"Commander, we just registered a trans-light pulse."

His mouth dry, Ivanth licked his lips to very little purpose. "How many did we lose this time?"

"None, Commander. It was…different."

Ivanth turned his head, the shock finally breaking perhaps. "Different how?"

"It was several deci-lights away from our ships, for one. The signal was also more powerful and less focused. I ran it for a match, Commander. We found one."

"Show me."

The display at the scanner station was showing the unknown pulse on one side of a split-screen image, along with a known signal on the other half. Ivanth recognized the second without even thinking about it.

"The unknown ship that's been plaguing us," he said, pensive. "It fits, somewhat. That ship is one of very few things that could hide from us out here without a gravimetric trap to locate it. The weapons, however, they're like nothing we've ever seen. They don't fit."

"Active seeking mines, Commander?"

"Perhaps. Trans-light projectiles, maybe?" Ivanth scowled.

Trans-light weapons were far from unknown, but they were generally strategic weapons. You used them to crack particularly difficult system defenses surrounding worlds you didn't much care to keep intact. Put a trans-light drive onto a projectile platform, accelerate it to five hundred lights, and then slam it into your target.

If the resulting kinetic crash wasn't enough to blow whatever world you were aiming at apart, the energy release from the drive warp would turn it to a cinder. For obvious reasons, it wasn't a particularly politic weapon to employ under most circumstances, and generally just resided as a threat in the Empire's arsenal. The drones were far better when you wanted to employ that level of destruction and terror, if only because they were largely deniable assets. Should things get too out of hand, it would be easy to rile up most worlds' populaces with a little fear of the Drasin legends and turn the whole thing into even more control over the Imperial systems.

Such weapons were imprecise and generally very crude, however. Whatever just blew his fleet of drones apart was something else again.

"Proceed into the field with caution," he ordered. "Drones are to take the vanguard position. It looks like our unknown assailant has departed, but they may be running games on us. Clear this sector before we proceed to rejoin the pursuit."

"Yes, Commander."

# CHAPTER TEN

## Priminae Warship *Posdan*

▶ "UNUSUAL TRANS-LIGHT signals ahead, Captain."

Kian stood up and walked over to the scanner station, eyes drifting to the displays. "Anything you can match?"

"One signal seems to match the *Odyssey*, Captain, leaving the area I believe."

"And the rest?"

"Multiple bowshock readings, and what looks like several catastrophic failures of trans-light drive warp fields."

Kian whistled. Whatever had caused that was a nasty piece of work. Particle emissions from drive failures while at speed were nothing to joke about.

"Most of the drive signatures read roughly in line with our records of Drasin, Captain, but there are two here that...."

The officer hesitated, drawing her attention back to the fore.

"What is it?"

"They read almost Priminae, Captain."

Kian's eyes narrowed as she leaned forward, eyes focusing on the readings as she read through them quickly.

She'd been briefed on the *Odyssey*'s discovery, of course, but like many in the fleet she wasn't sure how to take it. The idea that the enemy they were all terrified of was just a pawn in the game of someone greater...well, that was bad enough. The fact that the greater *someone* might be using schematics lifted directly from Central? That was unthinkable.

The drive readings were clearly not Drasin, now that they'd slowed enough for the *Posdan* and *Nept* to close on their position. They were also clearly very close to Priminae specification.

*Something very strange is happening here. Who are you? Two ships, nearly the same drive specifications as the* Posdan *and* Nept, *yet obviously flying in formation with Drasin. Who are these people?*

"How confident are you that the *Odyssey* has left the area?"

"Quite confident, Captain. The signal was a near perfect match for their departure into trans-light."

"Very good then," Kian said, straightening up. "Reduce speed and shield our drive signal. I want to stay in their trailing point until we have more information, or until we have a reason to engage them."

"Yes, Captain, reducing speed."

Kian looked over the displays, eyes cold and calculating. *I do not know who you are, but I will find out. And upon finding you, you have best pray that things are not the way I read them now or you will not like our introduction.*

▶▶▶

# N.A.C.S. ODYSSEY

▶ "TRACKING INBOUND BOWSHOCK signals. Six moving at high speed in pursuit of the *Weifang*, Captain."

"Are we close enough to detect the *Weifang*?" Eric asked.

"Yes, sir. They're still on course. Looks like they're bypassing Sol. I expect they'll loop back shortly."

*The captain of the* Weifang *is a paranoid sort, apparently,* Eric thought approvingly. The damage was probably done, but any little misdirection would cost the enemy time, and that was what they were playing for now.

"What's the status on the pulse torpedoes?"

"Charging, nearly ready to fire," Waters announced. "We'll have enough time."

"Good. You may engage the firing program. Green light the computer," Eric ordered. "I want those things cleared from my sky."

"Yes sir," Waters said, smiling nastily. "Program is engaged. Enemy will be in the engagement envelope in approximately five minutes."

Eric nodded absently, only noting to himself now that this was the first time that the *Odyssey* had engaged the enemy proactively. Well, after a fashion. They were still reacting to the enemy moves, but for the first time he hadn't given the enemy first crack, so to speak. He supposed it hardly mattered. They were most certainly in a state of declared warfare, so it hardly mattered who opened the confrontation.

The enemy was trespassing on Earth's front yard now, though, and he just didn't have the luxury of giving up the first punch.

They were less than a light-year from Earth at this point, so close, yet still so very far. After this engagement, he'd have to wait around for a bit and see if the rest of the enemy fleet was going to press on, then transition directly to Earth and warn the Confederacy of the new situation.

He didn't envy the headaches this was going to cause the brass, that much was certain.

*We needed years, not months. Homeworld defenses are nowhere near where we need them to be, nowhere near. If the enemy presses an assault on Earth now, I don't know what we'll do.*

That wasn't quite true, to be honest.

Eric knew very well what they'd do in that case. They'd fight, and then they would *lose.* Even with all the advantages, there wasn't a damned thing they could do against the force the Drasin could bring to bear on them.

*Maybe, if we're lucky, they'll send small squadrons once every few months like they've done at Ranquil. I doubt we'd be that lucky though. They can't be that stupid.*

Though, honestly, as he still couldn't figure out why in the hell they were doing that at Ranquil, maybe they *were* that stupid.

It wasn't something to count on, however.

"Enemy ships entering the target envelope," Waters announced. "Pulse torpedoes preparing to fire...."

The computer took control of the *Odyssey*'s thrusters, angling the ship to fire as the inbound signals of the enemy FTL drives entered range. The ship swung into position and opened fire, six shots flying out in staggered formation before the computer returned control back to the humans on board.

On her screens, the white lights representing the pulse torpedoes flashed away, little balls of hell in the human realm just itching to ruin someone's day.

"Secure the instruments for flash overloads," Eric ordered, eyes fixed on the torpedoes that were running hot and straight.

"Aye, Captain. Instrumentation secured."

The screens didn't change, but Eric knew that most of what they were now reporting was speculative data based on calculated events and probabilities. The torpedoes would continue to travel along their course until they intersected something, in this case the enemy ship's warp fields.

The moment of intersect was anticlimactic on screen, just a blip and a beep to indicate that the moment had come and gone. Each point was registered as to where the ship was calculated to have dropped from warp and how long it would take the flashpoint to reach the *Odyssey*. They settled in for a wait.

"Tachyon detection confirms six bowshock signals are now dead, sir," Winger said.

"Thank you, Lieutenant."

At least that meant that they didn't have to worry about anyone slipping past them just now.

"Five minutes, thirty nine seconds until the last flashpoint passes us."

"How close is the nearest ship?"

That was a bit of a concern. They wouldn't be able to sit around like a lame duck if they had a Drasin cruiser sitting just off their bow after all.

"Two light-minutes, twenty three light-seconds, Captain."

*Well, considering that they should be disorientated by the attack, and we're under stealth…should be enough time.*

It never failed to shake him when he realized just how different space combat was from his core training. He had learned to make decisions in the shavings between seconds, bank left or die, throttle up or die. Hell, on a few occasions the best option that passed through his mind was basically open fire now *and* die, but at least die with his mission accomplished.

Here, on the *Odyssey*, decisions were made in minutes and then often second-guessed for hours before the event occurred.

There was something about that situation that never sat right with him, though he did his professional best not to let it affect how he worked. He'd spent the majority of his military career living by the creed that "speed is life"; now he found himself, in the midst of combat no less, with time to drink a cup of coffee and idly chat with his officers.

*Life is a strange thing.*

The seconds finally ticked past and they brought their light-speed scanners back to full operation, getting details on a situation already more than five minutes old.

"We recorded direct hits on all six enemy cruisers, Captain," Winger said, confirming the initial intelligence they had from the tachyon traps. "They appear disoriented, uncertain where to look."

"No surprise there," Eric said. "Waters, warm up the transition cannons."

"Aye, Captain. The long guns are ready to fire."

"Ping them."

The *Odyssey*'s tachyon pulse transmitter was an energy intensive device that used the ship's cyclotron to generate a sudden burst of particles that barely existed in the natural universe. The burst could be directed, giving the *Odyssey* a momentary slice of real-time imagery at distances well beyond anything a light-speed limited instrument could manage.

"We have real time coordinates on my station," Waters said calmly. "Targeting info has been sent to the gun teams."

"Captain! Bandits inbound!" Winger announced. "Bowshock waves reading strong, hot, and steady. Blue shifting hard."

"Numbers?" Eric demanded, thoughts roiling over. The enemy hadn't spent much time investigating at their last ambush site from the sounds of things.

"North of twenty bandits, Captain. Can't be more precise. The signals are interfering with each other."

*Damn it.*

The long guns of the t-cannons were a hell of a force multiplier, giving the *Odyssey* the equivalent of "over the horizon" capability, but they had limits. Power was still one of the big ones. The *Odyssey* didn't have enough power to engage a fleet that size and escape afterwards.

Eric looked over the numbers, careful to note the shot-to-kill ratio they'd achieved in their first ambush. One would expect that a nuclear-triggered device detonating inside your hull would be enough to destroy just about anything and, he hoped, one would be right. But just because the t-cannons could potentially materialize shells inside the enemy ships didn't mean that they would get a kill from those shots. Even hardened electronics didn't react well with sharing the same space with other physical matter. The nuclear material didn't seem to be particularly affected, according to the test data Eric had read, but the electronic triggers were another matter.

Blasting a round into the enemy hull was highly likely to destroy the trigger, requiring a second shot. The Drasin ships could easily move unexpectedly, given that the *Odyssey*'s single-ping ranging system translated only into a snapshot of the enemy and didn't always provide accurate course and speed information.

Basically, a lot of things could be expected to go wrong in any engagement of more than four targets, give or take. Six he'd been willing to risk, even though they'd not yet fully charged their capacitors from the last engagement.

North of twenty bandits? *Twenty-six, actually,* Eric corrected himself.

That was just asking for trouble of biblical proportions.

"Daniels, you best get us a path out of here. I get the feeling that we're not going to like the company shortly."

"Aye, sir. Destination?"

"Sol."

There was a moment's hesitation before Daniels bobbed his head. "Aye, aye."

"Waters, let's throw ourselves a going-out party, shall we?"

"You've got it, Captain. Long guns are prepped. Fire on your mark."

"Mark."

▶ ▶ ▶

The *Odyssey* turned slowly in space, slow being a relative term for a ship that measured its sub-light cruising speeds by degrees of relativistic effects, bringing her t-cannons to bear on the current targets.

The big guns actually acted primarily as wave guides for the tachyon burst generated by the transition of their one-meter-diameter rounds. The burst of high-energy particles were nearly as focused as a laser, blinking off along their set course only to reform at the point coded into them at launch.

Each gun fired twice at a ship, ejecting another dozen nuclear-fused munitions at their targets. The targeting solutions had been reasonably tight, given the range at which the engagement was being fought, but as was expected not all the rounds scored direct hits. Some were destroyed when they transitioned inside armored bulkheads, reactors, and other various sundries. One missed the target entirely, detonating outside the enemy ship with a force in the gigaton range, but had very little effect as there was no atmosphere to convert energy into force—Drasin ships were well hardened against all manner of cosmic radiation.

At least five detonated on target, however, and the resulting balls of expanding plasma were a testament to the fact that there was a universe of difference between an explosive detonating outside a target and one going off *inside*.

To say that confusion reigned on the remaining ship would be both under- and overestimating the situation. Drasin were, as such things went, relatively simpleminded. They didn't get confused in the same ways as human type intelligences did; in many ways, they just didn't have the mind for it.

Neither, however, did they react the way lower-level intelligences might react. Humans bridged the gap between truly higher-level intelligence—minds that considered every detail, worked through problems with logic and intuition, and came to a solution based on the available facts—and lower-level intelligences that relied more on instinctive reactions. A human mind accumulates all available facts as best as it can, collating them into a form it can understand, and then tries to work through the problem with logic. If and when that fails, instinct is the final recourse.

The Drasin, however, were none of these things.

They had neither the higher-level reasoning capacity, nor the lower-level instinctive ones. More like robots, the Drasin were truly drones in a way that few in the Galaxy understood. When encountering a completely new scenario, the Drasin cruiser found itself locked in the equivalent of an endless loop as it searched for something, anything, to make the situation fall into the realm of its programming.

▶▶▶

"Five down, Captain. One left," Winger announced a few minutes after the firing.

The *Odyssey* was already steaming out of the engagement area, with Eric unwilling to risk his ship against the inbound fleet.

"That's strange."

"What is it, Lieutenant?" Eric asked, glancing over.

"The remaining Drasin cruiser, sir. It looks...." She trailed off, unable to figure out the word she was looking for.

"Winger?" Eric prompted.

"Honestly, sir, it looks lost," she said. "It's just flying around in circles."

"Must have hit it harder than we thought." Roberts shrugged.

"I don't think so. It's hard to tell but there doesn't seem to be much damage visible to our scopes."

"Log it, file it. We'll worry about it later," Eric ordered. "Give me a plot for Earth, Lieutenant Commander."

"Aye, sir," Daniels said. "Solution coded. We're good to go."

"All hands, stand by for transition."

# CHAPTER ELEVEN

## Priminae Warship *Posdan*

▶ "BY THE SINGULARITY that will end us all," Kian whispered as the *Posdan* sailed through the debris field.

They'd slowed to investigate some unusual energy signals received as they passed the area, mostly residual signatures that resembled Drasin too closely to be ignored. The debris the *Posdan* and her sister ship, the *Nept*, were flying through was clear evidence that they hadn't been mistaken in their identification.

Chunks and shards of Drasin ships were strewn about the endless depths like so many broken toys of a particularly petulant child.

"Odd."

Kian turned to where the voice had come from. "Something to say, Lani?"

The officer who had spoken shrugged. "Uncertain. The destruction appears to have been caused by a rudimentary shattering of nuclear bonds. Powerful, but nothing I would have expected to see on a Drasin ship."

"We know that the *Odyssey* often uses technology we perceive as antiquated, so I fail to see the oddity."

"The destruction came from *within* the Drasin ships themselves, Captain. If this is a weapon, it's one I've never seen before and *antiquated* is not how I would describe it, except perhaps in terms of the destructive mechanism."

"So was it the *Odyssey* then?" Kian asked, confused.

"Doesn't match any of the known weapon signatures they employed in Ranquil," Lani answered frankly. "Whether they have something they didn't show or this is someone else, I can't say."

"Understood." Kian sighed, more than a little frustrated.

She'd spent most of her life in the service of the merchant fleet. There, things were ordered and understandable at all times. In ten thousand years of spaceflight, the fleet had had a long time to encounter just about everything one might credibly find in the depths of space. Since the return of the Drasin, however, she found that her world was more often a mass of conflicting information and new problems that she'd never dreamed in her worst nightmares.

Frankly, she missed the peace and confidence.

"Very well. Scan everything. Log it all, and tag it priority for immediate analysis, then send it on to Command. We have a job to do and it's time to get back on the trail."

"Yes, Captain."

A few minutes later the *Nept* and the *Posdan* arced out of the area, flickering into trans-light as they rode the warped wave of space-time around them.

▶▶▶

# IMPERIAL DESTROYER *DEMIGOD*

▶ "WHAT IS *HAPPENING* to our drones!?"

Ivanth was frustrated. No, far beyond frustrated. He was furious, he was incensed, and, to be perfectly honest, deep down in the back of his mind he was more than a little frightened.

*Not as deep down or in the back of my mind as I wish it were.*

Granted, the telemetry communication he had with the drones left a lot to be desired. The system had been bashed into the drone's own communication setup when their internal coding had been re-appropriated by the Empire, and it was a little flighty at the best of times.

For all that, however, the data feeds he was staring at made no sense whatsoever.

Perfectly functional drones did not just convert into debris and expanding plasma for no reason.

*It has to be an enemy weapon, but there's no sign at all of any enemy starships in the vicinity. Mines? It seems ludicrous, but what else could it be?*

If it were mines, then he had to consider the possibility that the unknown ship they had been following was leading them into a trap. More than that, the ship had been wasting their time and resources all along.

That was a stretch, though, because even if it were the case, the level and sheer expanse of any minefield that would effectively take out his ships was mind boggling. He could have come in from vectors that were literally separated by entire *lights*, and there had been no sign whatsoever of any sort of minefield despite intensive scanning.

*We know that the unknown ship we encountered at the Hive base utilized extremely effective stealth techniques. It's possible they utilized something similar to hide a minefield, but the expense would be beyond imagining unless they had control over something very close to the drones' queen. Unlikely.*

No, what was more likely was that the unknown vessel was in the area, stealth techniques and all.

How it was picking off drones with such ease that they didn't even see it coming? Well, that was another matter entirely, but it was blatantly clear that *something* was.

The problem now was what to do about it?

His first instinct, to simply flood the area with drones until they brought the ship down under the sheer mass of numbers, was unfortunately pointless. For that to work, Ivanth was well aware that he needed to pin the ship against something from which it either could not or, more likely, *would not* escape. At the moment, it would simply vanish into the black and leave him wasting more time and resources on an empty vacuum.

*This is rapidly becoming more trouble than it was worth. We'd hoped that tracking the unknown back to its homeworld would give us just that sort of target, but now we're losing second-generation drone ships for no gain.*

That was a big problem.

Second-generation drones were valuable, as they only had one first-generation supplier and the process of multiplying themselves caused bugs and random mutations to appear in later generations. The vast majority of the Empire's forces in this sector were third- and fourth-generation drone ships, and those were vastly inferior.

That left Ivanth with several unattractive options and no attractive ones.

He could pull back his forces, letting the enemy ship escape and give up all chance of locating its homeworld, or continue to press forward into the teeth of unknown defenses and hope that he had enough power remaining on his side to push through.

If he did and his forces managed to locate the enemy homeworld, assuming it was even in this sector and it wasn't all some kind of elaborate trap, then it would be worth the temporary reduction in available second-generation drone ships. Of course, if he failed, it would mean the end of his career or, at least, a lengthy period on the blacklist.

*I'll probably spend a little time on the list anyway if I withdraw now. I've already lost too many ships.*

No matter how he cut it, there was nothing good about his current situation. Forward or retreat—in either case there seemed little upside from his personal perspective and little enough from the Imperial one, as well.

Ivanth looked out over the bridge of the *Demigod*, at the men and women under his command, and tried to find the path that would lead to the best result. *Or, at least, the least bad one.*

Finally, he sighed. *Never let it be said that I am unable to be bold.*

"Send a signal to the Hive facility," he ordered. "Request reinforcements. We're pushing forward."

▶ ▶ ▶

▸"COMING UP ON the orbit of Saturn, Captain. Close enough now to use a laser comm."

"Thank you, Lieutenant," Eric said, nodding, though he wished he could wait for a face to face. "Send my brief to Admiral Gracen, encrypted with a priority flag."

"Aye, sir. Brief being transmitted now."

The laser signal would take more than an hour to reach Liberty station in Earth orbit, while the *Odyssey* herself was still a few hours out. By now he was sure that the admiral was aware of their arrival in the system, though she wouldn't be expecting a message so quickly.

Eric fervently hoped that by the time the *Odyssey* arrived in Earth orbit, the Confederacy fleet would be winding up for a fight. He couldn't be sure it was coming, but it seemed likely. Hell, it felt almost inevitable to him.

*Probably has been inevitable all along, though between the* Odyssey *and the* Weifang *we have undoubtedly sped up the date of the confrontation by a fair bit.*

He had little doubt that the forces currently engaging with the Priminae people would have eventually found Earth.

Eric knew that many in the political community and higher ranks of the military didn't want to believe that to the point of deluding themselves otherwise, but he personally had no doubt.

The Drasin might not have come in a year, or a decade. It just depended on how long they spent cleaning up the Priminae, whether they had been sent against the Priminae specifically, or if that conflict was just the result of an expanding empire growing out of the Galactic core.

Sooner or later, however, the jig would have been up.

The *Odyssey* had at least managed to bring back a warning in exchange for whatever increase in the time table they'd wrought. He didn't know if it would be much of a consolation in the end, but he was going to take it for what he could now.

*Nothing left now but the waiting…and then the screaming and the dying.*

▶▶▶

▶ADMIRAL GRACEN COULD feel the headache coming on, and the *Odyssey* hadn't even made Mars orbit yet.

*For once he's not bringing his ship back beat to hell. I suppose that's worth something.*

Not as much as she'd like, however, not given the news they'd decoded from the laser comm the *Odyssey* had sent on ahead of her.

From the best they could tell, and Gracen had to admit that the evidence seemed solid, the Block's little foray into deep space had been nothing short of a disaster.

The *Weifang* hadn't made it back yet, one advantage of the transition drive over its counterparts, she supposed, but shortly after they did get home it would appear that unwanted guests would be knocking on the system's proverbial door.

*On the plus side, it appears that I can inform the research boys that their transition cannons are one hell of a resounding success. How many of those things can we get mounted and armed in three days?*

Not enough.

That much was certain. Even if they could equip every ship and base with them, they didn't have enough nuclear-fused shells with which to arm them. Weapons-grade fission-ables weren't exactly rare, but they weren't common either. The Confederacy and the Block only kept enough on hand to generally make it clear that they could easily wipe each other out if either stepped too far out of line.

Which unfortunately didn't take all that much, in all honesty.

The one-hundred-centimeter shells fired by the *Odyssey*'s long guns were pretty much one-offs for the moment. They'd manufactured enough to arm the *Odyssey* in order to test the system, as Captain Weston was, like it or not, the man who'd take the sharp end in any conflict they had in space. But they were counting on getting some feedback on the system from the crew of the *Odyssey* this time around before going to full manufacturing.

Still, that didn't mean the Confederacy had no additional t-cannons. Liberty station had a few installed and a reasonably sized cache of munitions for them. They could rearm the *Odyssey* to full stores with no trouble, maybe a little more than that if they loaded down her flight decks.

*They don't need the decks much anyway. The* Enterprise *isn't up to a full fighter compliment yet, and they have a priority on pilots and fighters. The Archangels have…what? Five left to their number, if I recall?*

She'd have to look that up, but Gracen was certain it was an absurdly small number.

*Too many damned fools playing politics there,* she knew all too well. *Though even I have to admit that the Archangel platform is in dire need of a rethink.*

During the war, the design for the fighters had changed almost a dozen times in less than a decade. Reconfigurations abounded to the point where there were as many as four or five variations active at one time within the squadron. It was one of the things that made them stand out from regular military units, along with the requirements to even apply for a position on the squad, of course.

The N.A.C.S. *Enterprise* would soon be receiving their last squadron of Vorpal Class strike fighters, craft that were specially designed as a space-based heavy-strike platform. Within their intended specialty, the computer models clearly favored the Vorpals over the more general purpose converted Air Superiority Strike Fighter that the Archangels used, even when you factored in the NICS-enhanced controls.

Gracen and a few others had quietly commissioned designs for a new iteration of the Archangel fighter, but now it appeared that there would be little chance for it to be brought into service before things well and truly hit the fan.

With the *Odyssey* dropping toward Earth at its best speed, the *Enterprise* now being recalled from outer system patrol (where the big ship had been conducting quiet flight tests of the Vorpal fighters where the Block couldn't easily spy on them), and every combat system in the Confederacy going to high alert...well, things were about to get very, *very* interesting.

She knew that the Block had begun to slowly shift their own units to higher alert already, entirely in response to the new alert levels of Confederate forces, of course. It would be some time before the *Weifang* arrived back in system, as far as anyone could tell, but she honestly expected that by the time they arrived, whatever they had to say would be old news and largely irrelevant.

*There is a certain humor there, I think. Bad news literally travels faster than light.*

Admiral Gracen smiled, no real humor in her lips or her eyes. It wasn't a joking matter, even if it was a funny one.

▶▶▶

By the time the *Odyssey* approached Earth orbit, coming up on the planet from the trailing side on a trajectory set to sling around the moon and settle into LEO near Station Liberty, the war machine known as the North American Confederate Forces was indeed winding up to combat alertness. The *Odyssey* had to answer several automated challenges on the way through, and were even deep scanned at least once. Given that he manned possibly the most recognizable ship in the solar system, that seemed like overkill even to Eric, who was known to be a touch paranoid.

Even the passive scanners, running without the full sails, left the *Odyssey* with evidence of weapon systems at full power, tracking devices flooding the ship with RADAR, LIDAR, and other detection energies. No tachyon pings yet, but that was really only a matter of time at this point. No one wanted to waste power just yet, and Eric suspected that energy was instead being redirected to storage solutions as fast as possible.

While a ship like the *Odyssey* was limited in the methods she could use to store energy for quick use, mostly relying on capacitance systems, stationary bases like Liberty didn't have that limitation. Massive flywheel installations could store energy in the vacuum with very little loss, even over long periods, and that was really only one of the systems in common use.

*If they judge our defenses here against the* Odyssey's *energy reserves,* Eric thought with grim satisfaction, *they'll be in for one very nasty surprise.*

"Comm from Admiral Gracen, sir. She wants to meet with you as soon as we dock."

"Tell her I'll be there," Eric said simply. "We won't have long, I suspect, Roberts. Try to give everyone some time off. If you can cycle them through Liberty, all the better. Just make sure that no one leaves the station. The *Odyssey* has to be ready to fight on a couple hours' notice, no more."

"Aye, sir, I'll take care of it."

"I have no doubts, Commander. Daniels, take us in to Liberty, if you would. Port speed."

"Aye, Captain. Ahead dead slow."

The *Odyssey* settled into a close orbit to the massive Liberty, the NAC's first stop-and-shop to the universe, as it were. The orbital station had started out as something just a little larger than the *Odyssey* herself, actually, built roughly around the same time frame, but they hadn't yet stopped working on the station.

The aforementioned flywheel installations were new, for example, massive chunks of meteoric steel wrapped around the station inside armored shells. They made Liberty look several times larger than it actually was, but the huge megaton wheels could store more energy in each installation than the *Odyssey* could in its entire system. Once they were brought up to speed, spinning at near the speed of light thanks to the CM technology that made most space travel practical, the manipulation of the local Higgs field could be inverted. That would allow each wheel to mass more than normal instead of less, making them far more efficient in returning power to the station.

Impractical for use on a ship, unfortunately, due to the gyroscopic nature of the devices, but they were excellent systems for stationary bases.

The *Odyssey* slid to a stop, retros shuddering to halt the big ship's momentum relative to the station, and Eric rose from his chair.

"I have a meeting with an admiral. Best not to be late. Commander, you have the bridge."

"Aye, sir, I have the bridge."

▶▶▶

The decks of Station Liberty were alternatively deserted or packed with men and women rushing about, depending on what section Eric was walking through. It was a jarring change from the normal general hubbub of activity. Eric ignored it all as best he could, though, and made his way deeper into the station toward the E-Ring.

Unlike the Pentagon, where the name originated, the E-Ring on Liberty was the innermost section of the station and the heaviest protected. Senior officers and planning sections were placed there in the designs in order to heighten both security and defense of the installation. In order to get access, Eric had already passed numerous body scanners and Marine guards. At the final gateway, however, he had to submit to biometrics checks while two armed Marines looked on with stony expressions.

Fingerprints, iris, and blood type checks were the quickest. They all had to cross reference with each other and his records and match; otherwise there was no way the lock was going to open for him. He knew that his blood was also being passed along to a DNA sequencer that would take a few minutes longer. And there were rumors that at least two more biometric systems were in use (but no one would admit to that).

It seemed like overkill, but during the war, Eric himself had worn false contacts to emulate an iris scan, and finger-prints were ludicrously easy to defeat. Blood type wasn't ter-ribly hard to fake either, but the scans caught a few people who were sloppy. The DNA test was the only thing that was, so far, concrete. He'd heard rumors that some retro-viral experiments were beating those, however, so he wasn't going to complain.

If anything, the security probably needed to be tighter, though Eric was hoping that would soon change.

*We need to get the Block with the program. Fighting amongst our-selves isn't just stupid now, it's suicidal. Get us all on the same side and this shit won't be needed. I'd love to see a Drasin try and pass itself off as human.*

Eric smiled grimly as the airlock to the E-Ring opened and he walked through.

Then the thought of the unknown species that seemed to be holding the Drasin's leash floated through his mind and he grimaced.

*They use Priminae designs, and the Prims are as human as I am to almost every test. I wouldn't take bets against these new bastards being the same.*

That was a bit of a misleading thought, though, and he knew it. Doctor Rame and many others had literally torn through the test results on the Priminae people from whom they'd gotten samples. They were human, as far as it went, but that didn't mean they were indistinguishable from Terrans. Different antibodies were the first and clearest sign, but deeper in the DNA it was obvious that while they were indisputably human, they had diverged from the Earth popu-lation at least on the order of thirty- to forty-thousand years earlier.

Full DNA sequencing on that level, though, still took just a tad longer than a few minutes. When you weren't looking for specific and well-known markers, it took weeks to do the job with any credible level of detail.

*OK. Maybe the security won't be overkill even when we get the Block to point their guns somewhere else,* Eric supposed, though a cynical part of him wondered if the word he used should have been *if* and not *when*.

"Captain Weston."

Eric paused, looking up to see a woman in dress whites looking at him.

"That's me," he said, unnecessarily he was sure. She had to know exactly who he was for him to have even gotten this close.

"The admiral will see you immediately."

"Yeah, I expected she would."

The admiral's office was simpler than it would be had Gracen worked Earth-side, though not by as much as many civilians would believe. The use of CM technology and the abundant energy reserves of the station allowed for basic artificial gravity without the necessity of complex systems like the *Odyssey*'s counter-rotating drum habitats. So while the office was a bit more Spartan than one might see in the Pentagon for a high-ranking official, there were some luxuries.

The admiral herself was seated behind a moderately sized desk, plastic instead of wood or metal because it was cheaper to manufacture goods on site. Plastic was generally a better medium to work in than most. She was best described as statuesque, Eric supposed, as he observed her working on whatever it was that had her attention at the moment.

It only took her a moment to wave him to a seat, not bothering to look up. Eric silently took the offer and settled into the chair, again a plastic construct probably turned out by the fabrication units installed on the station. It wasn't particularly comfortable, even though someone had tossed a cushion on it, but he wasn't going to complain.

He'd been accused of a lot of things in the past, but, despite being a Marine, stupidity wasn't one of them, which probably meant something given that he'd spent a lot of his career working with Air Force types and they didn't really much like Marines as a rule.

Gracen finally looked up, scowling.

"Every single time," she said, "I send you out on a simple mission, and every single time you come back with a crisis in hand worse than the last. There are people in the administration that want your guts for garters, Captain, and I'm starting to wish I'd given you to them."

Eric winced, but didn't say anything.

Honestly, what could he say?

"That said," she went on, pushing her keyboard aside and settling her arms in front of her, "we're past that option now, and I doubt I can afford to toss you in some deep, dark hole even if we weren't."

"I'd like to request a hole in a different solar system, if that's the direction we're going to be going…." Eric said dryly.

"Don't be a smart ass, Captain."

"Yes, ma'am."

"We're resupplying your one-hundred-centimeter nuclear-fused shells as we speak," she said. "I've appropriated enough of them to fill your stores to full capacity, and we'll probably stack in a few pallets on your flight decks as well, unless you object?"

"No, ma'am," Eric said quickly. After seeing the transition shells in action, he'd willingly sacrifice some room on his flight deck, especially given that he fully expected to be clearing that room out in a hurry.

"Didn't think you would, judging from your report," Gracen said, satisfied. "Between us, and without the official language, how did they really do?"

"Outstanding, ma'am."

"Good. I've had every last one available shipped up to Liberty as well, and the factories dirtside just got one mother of an order for more," she said. "I understand that the contractors who handle those items are already looking to convert a few of their other factories over to production of the transition shells."

"Hope it's not too little, too late, ma'am."

"You and me both, Captain," she said. "What are your thoughts on the current situation?"

Eric paused, considering the question for a moment. "Well, Admiral, short-term? We'll clean their clocks."

Gracen raised an eyebrow. "Oh?"

"Yes, ma'am," he said confidently. "Even Lieutenant Winger's most pessimistic estimates puts the immediate enemy numbers at no more than another couple dozen Drasin, plus two or more of the unknowns. Between the *Odyssey* and Liberty alone, we can easily thin those ranks down. Add in the *Enterprise* once it gets into knife range, I don't think we'll even take any significant losses, barring mishap."

"Medium- to long-term, then?"

Eric sighed, shaking his head slightly as he became a lot more serious. "Do we have any hits on nice exo-planets to colonize?"

Gracen winced, though she'd been half expecting something along those lines. "That bad?"

"Depends on a few factors, stuff I can't even guess at."

"Such as?"

"Well, for one, we don't know why they're being so easy on the Priminae," he answered. "Two, four, even six ships at a time? If they wanted them gone, the Drasin would swarm them and it would be over. Someone is intentionally holding them back."

"And you don't know if they'll do the same for us?"

"Honestly, Admiral?" Eric shook his head. "I'd lay wagers that they won't. The unknown bandits are using Prim designs. They've got a real connection there somehow. I don't think they have that with us, or if they do, I don't expect them to know it."

"I see. So, worst case then?"

"Worst case? A million Drasin drones wade in and soak up everything we throw at them," Eric answered. "We kill dozens, maybe hundreds depending on how long a lead time they give us, and then we die, ma'am."

"Do we have any alternatives to avoid that scenario, then Captain?" Gracen asked. Then, after a pause, adding, "In your opinion, of course."

"Only one possible, but it's a long shot."

"Oh?" She looked up curiously. She hadn't come up with any herself.

"Wipe this group out, to the last ship, and hope they don't have effective FTL comms."

"Aahh."

That had been mentioned more or less, to be honest, but the idea that the enemy didn't have FTL comms had been discarded as about as likely as them coming in peace for the betterment of all mankind.

Eric read her expression easily enough, "Like I said, Admiral, long shot."

"If they have any sort of decent leadership, there will be an observer watching from far outside the system anyway."

"Yes, ma'am," Eric said. "We considered getting ahead of the *Weifang* and hitting her with pulse torpedoes, try to knock her out of FTL in the hopes of using the Chinese to lead them away, but it doesn't seem viable. The *Weifang* is leading the merry chase at the moment, and while we can predict more or less where she'll be, we can't really be certain to get exactly where we need to be to get that shot. We blew that chance when they were on their last straight haul. Now that they've gone into terminal evasion, getting close enough would be a shot in the dark…and, honestly, they're already too close to Sol as it is."

"Agreed," Gracen said. "At best it'd buy us a few days. Weeks maybe, but no more than that."

"We could try and catch them, now that we've delivered the warning," Eric offered.

"Too late, Captain. Long-range tachyon traps have recorded an inbound bowshock signal. The *Weifang* is coming home."

# CHAPTER TWELVE

## P.L.A.S.F. *Weifang*

▶ OF ALL THE homecomings he'd expected, what Captain Sun Ang Wen got was about as far from what he'd imagined as was possible.

"Captain!" the panic in his officers' voices and actions brought him back to the bridge, rocketing recklessly through the corridors like a guided missile.

"We are being targeted, Captain! Confederate AEGIS-X RADAR, LIDAR, and some things I don't recognize!"

"Ship inbound from behind our position, Captain! Transponder identifies as the N.A.C.S. *Enterprise!*"

"Fighters all around us! Unknown configuration!"

Sun swore as he strapped into his command station. "Give me external comms."

"Comms open, standard frequencies."

"This is Captain Sun Ang Wen of the People's Liberation Army Space Force," Sun gritted out, eyes on the blips heading his direction. "Why are you targeting my ship?"

There was a long wait, seconds ticking by as Sun waited for the signal to reach the ship that was accelerating hard toward the *Weifang* from just over a light-minute away.

"Prime weapons. Something may have happened between our governments since we left Earth," Sun ordered quietly after muting the open comm.

"Yes, Captain."

Finally the comm crackled open in response.

"This is Captain Ethan Carrow of the N.A.C.S. *Enterprise.* Captain Sun, you were followed. Return to Earth for refit and orders from your government," the voice said, sending a chill through his body and spine.

"Impossible," Sun whispered to himself. "There were no ships behind us."

It wasn't, though, and he knew it. He'd taken every precaution he could, but if the enemy scanners were advanced enough to watch his ship from far enough away, then anything was possible. Sun slumped, thinking about it.

"What have I done?"

"Captain Sun, do you copy?" The voice of the Confederate captain spoke up again.

Sun shakily unmuted his comm, "Yes Captain Carrow, I copy and understand. Barring conflicting orders, the *Weifang* is returning to Earth."

There was a long silence as the signal bounced between the two ships, then Carrow came back in a calmer voice.

"If it's any consolation, Captain, this was always coming. You just sped the day a little."

"It is very little consolation, Captain," Sun replied. "Very little indeed. *Weifang* out."

He slumped back in his station, eyes glazed as he considered what was about to happen. He only shook himself from his thoughts a few moments later when he felt an oppressive silence weighing down on him and looked to see all eyes on him.

"Make for Earth, best speed," he ordered. "We need refit and resupply if we're to help clean this mess up."

"Yes, Captain!"

The P.L.A.S.F. *Weifang* began warping space-time to point-eight of light-speed, heading for Earth even as they continued to trail frozen gasses escaping from jury-rigged repairs.

▶▶▶

Captain Carrow of the *Enterprise* watched the Chinese ship accelerate toward Earth, noting with just a little jealousy that the *Weifang*'s use of CM space warping gave her a significantly improved acceleration over the *Enterprise* in sub-light.

While the transition drive absolutely destroyed everything else anyone knew of strategically, he really wanted a tactical edge just now, and the Block's space-warp drive was as close as any he'd seen. The fight that was coming was going to be purely tactical. He was going to be pinned against the gravity well of Sol because it was the one place from which he couldn't retreat.

*It's the last damn place we want to engage any enemy, let alone a potentially superior force. Just a few more months and we could have dedicated a few ships to keep them well and truly distracted fighting in the Priminae star systems.*

Well, that was a moot point now, he supposed.

There was a big military theory that basically read that it was better to fight the enemy on their turf than to do it at home. Mostly it was bullshit theory used to excuse wars against people who literally *couldn't* get their ass across a sizeable puddle, let alone an ocean, but this was one of the real world cases in which the theory was sound.

You didn't ever want to fight a battle of parity, or worse, a war, against superior foes anywhere near your home turf. You were going to tear shit all to hell even if you won, and if you started losing you had nowhere to fall back.

*You can ask the Germans or the Japanese about that, I suppose.*

Unfortunately, you didn't always get to pick your fights, and that meant that sometimes the enemy got to pick the battlefield.

"Bring our squadrons in from the cold," Carrow ordered. "I want them refueled and our pilots rested as best as possible before the next ships show up. They're not going to be as friendly as the Block."

"Aye, sir. Issuing orders for recall now."

The Vorpal Class strike fighters were the latest pieces of hardware to come out of the Northrop Grumman factories, faster and more heavily armed than the previous top-level fighter and almost as responsive in deep space. The Angels platform they were replacing, which also served the Archangel squadrons albeit with substantial modifications, were fundamentally air superiority systems. They just didn't have the pure space maneuverability of the Vorpals, nor the top end allowed by the new-generation CM technology.

He somewhat wished that he had a flight deck full of NICS-equipped Vorpals and pilots to man them, however.

*If wishes were fishes, we'd all cast nets.*

"Do we have anything new from Command on the likely entry point of the pursuing ships?" he asked, walking across the bridge to his comms man.

"No, sir," Lieutenant Sam Berenger said with a shake of his head. "We haven't even detected them yet."

"They're hanging back then, waiting," Carrow said grimly. "Looking to see what we'll do."

"Yes, sir."

"Well, too bad for them, we don't even know what we're going to do," Carrow said dryly, shaking his head as he walked away from the station.

▶▶▶

▼

# IMPERIAL DESTROYER *DEMIGOD*

▲

▶ "SO, THIS IS the system," Ivanth said as he looked at the readings coming from the star to which they'd tracked the unknown ship back.

For the most part they were relying on passive gravity lens imaging, so the scenes they were seeing were several lights old, but that wouldn't matter much for strategic purposes. It was clearly a developed system, with signs of inhabitation on at least two planets and four moons, plus signals from what appeared to be an asteroid belt as well as a cometary cloud well outside the system proper.

*Mining facilities, most likely. Fairly heavy industry, but antiquated as best we can tell. No significant system defenses are apparent, and I don't see anything that looks remotely like a credible shipyard.*

It was an annoyance.

This could be the system he was looking for, or it could be an outlier of a larger empire. Without any sign of major shipyards, he was almost tempted to write it off as a minor colony world, but he *knew* that there had to be a major shipyard present at the Priminae world of Ranquil and yet none of his forces had been able to find it.

It was one of many reasons they hadn't moved en masse against that system, as the Imperial priorities included the capture of Priminae shipyard facilities intact if possible. It was particularly difficult to manage that when you couldn't even find the blasted thing.

*Still, this isn't a Priminae system. That is certain,* Ivanth grimaced as he looked over the ever increasing data pile they were accumulating from the star system. *No Priminae system would have chowdered their primary world to such a degree. I've seen Imperial worlds cleaner than the third planet, and few dirtier.*

Whoever was running the system certainly didn't believe in the Priminae philosophy of minimal impact, not on their system and certainly not on their planet. The spectral analysis of the world's atmosphere showed clearly dangerous levels of several heat-trapping gasses, enough to send the world into a tail spin of overheating if it weren't for what he believed were orbital reflectors cutting back on radiated energy reaching the surface.

In many ways it almost looked like home.

Granted, a backward and backwater version of home, but such was the way of things he supposed.

"Commander! We have something new!"

Ivanth shook himself from his distraction and looked back to the screen. "What is it?"

"Ship arriving in system."

"A ship?" Ivanth scowled. "It can't be our target. They won't be showing up on a gravity lens for quite some time yet."

"No. Configuration analyzed and sent to your screens, Commander."

Ivanth stepped back and walked over to his command station, eyes falling on the screens for about a second before widening in shock.

"It's *them,*" he hissed, recognizing the configuration of the new ship instantly.

Awkward, ungainly. Ugly even, by Imperial standards. But instantly recognizable. The unknown ship from the Hive, and the same ship that had been wreaking havoc on their drones for quite some time now in the Ranquil system.

"Package and send to the Hive," he ordered quietly. "All data concerning this system, particularly the arrival of that ship. We need specific orders."

"Yes, Commander."

Ivanth licked his lips lightly as he took a seat at the station, one hand reaching out to manipulate the image on the screen. He twisted it around, getting a close look at the ship every Imperial vessel in the galactic arm had clear orders to locate and destroy, if possible.

*So, we may well have been tracking the right bird all along, then?*

He knew better than to underestimate the unknown ship. It had already torn through many times its weight of metal in drone ships and even outfought and outran several Imperial destroyers.

That said, he had more than enough drones remaining that the ship should prove to be little more than fodder if he could trap it against a world it had to defend.

The big question, of course, remained.

*Do you have to defend this little world? I suppose that is what we must find out.*

"Which is our weakest drone squadron?"

"The ninth, Commander. They're down to two-thirds operating power."

Ivanth nodded. "Four drone ships, then. Full compliments?"

"Yes, Commander."

"That'll do. Send them in, slowly. I want them in place to move when we hear back from the Hive."

"As you order."

▶ ▶ ▶

# N.A.C.S. ENTERPRISE

►CARROW CHECKED THE clock one last time before turning the shift over to the second watch. The *Enterprise* had drawn back into the system and was now trailing Neptune as the planet orbited the sun. The problem with space was that even in a relatively small area with a single star's sphere of influence, you had one hell of a lot of area to cover.

The few ships they had available just couldn't do it, so he knew that system defenses were relying heavily on the *Enterprise* and the *Odyssey* at the moment. The *Odyssey* had been refit with a new load of munitions—gear that the *Enterprise* was slated to get at her next refit, which Carrow dearly wished they'd already been loaded with—and was now en-route to Saturn to tank up.

"Keep the sails fully extended and monitor the tachyon traps closely," he told the watch officer. "If we get any decent warning at all, that's where it'll come from."

"Understood, sir," Lieutenant Fallon told him. "We'll keep all our eyes open."

Carrow nodded, knowing that he was just retreading things now out of nervousness. *Best stop that or the crew'll get the idea that there's something to be nervous about.*

"Alright. You have the bridge, Lieutenant."

"Aye, sir, I have the bridge."

Carrow took a last look around, then stepped off and headed back toward the habitat section and his quarters.

Realistically he knew that he didn't have to worry about being caught off the bridge. He knew the drill well enough from service in the Navy, where the phrase "hurry up and wait" probably originated. Still, the idea that there were hostile aliens looking to invade…well that was a new one on him and privately Ethan could admit that it had him jumpy.

He tried hard not to show it, making his way through the corridors of the big starship, smiling and nodding as best he could to anyone who walked past.

It wasn't the thought of battle that was driving his nerves, though. No, Ethan was terrified that the enemy would breach from any of the innumerable angles that would allow them to reach Earth before the *Enterprise* could mount an intercept.

A very large part of him wanted to pull back to Earth, or at least to Mars, where they could severely cut back on the possible approach angles that would let an enemy make it to Earth virtually unopposed. Another part, however, understood the reasoning for his current orders. Showing the flag further out in space gave an impression of more strength and, if the enemy did make a slash dive for Earth, the Liberty would be able to hold off a decent-size force more than long enough to allow the *Odyssey* and the *Enterprise* to move in on their flanks and show them the meaning of the word pain.

As far as strategies went, honestly, it sucked.

That said, they didn't have many strategic assets at the moment, nor did they have a lot of intelligence on enemy movements. With those limits in mind, they really only had two options, and both of them sucked very nearly equally.

Either pull back and turtle up around Earth, leaving the rest of the system open to unopposed strikes, or put on a show of confidence and let the enemy hopefully outthink themselves.

*With any luck, they'll spend so much time wondering where we're hiding our ships that we'll have time to build a couple more.*

Ethan knew that the chances of that were somewhere between slim and none, but what the hell. He was going to bed for a while. He might as well dream a little.

▶ ▶ ▶

# IMPERIAL DESTROYER *DEMIGOD*

▲

▶MOMENT BY MOMENT, literally incalculable amounts of data continued to pour in through the *Demigod* and the *Immortal*'s gravity lenses. Photons, microwaves, and radiation from every part of the spectrum were captured, analyzed, and sent to the central database as the crew watched and waited.

For most of those watching, the system seemed to be a rather dull one in relative terms. Technical indicators were of a world that had just barely achieved trans-light capability and honestly hadn't yet worked out what they intended to do with it.

There were no signs of serious interplanetary commerce or trade, no hint of colonial aspirations, so generally speaking the system was just one more fringe world crawling out of its own planetary filth and looking around a much larger galaxy than they'd likely ever realized existed.

For Ivanth, however, the scene was one of dreadful fascination.

For all he was seeing, he couldn't help but keep two things in mind.

The first was the fact that the ship they followed to this system was responsible for destroying at least five drone ships and severely damaging several others in a relatively short engagement. That was nothing to scoff at; on the contrary it was something to be very respectful of indeed.

The second thing...well, that was the other ship. The unknown.

Unknown name, unknown configuration. Weapons systems...unknown. Drive system...unknown. Everything about it listed in their database as simply...unknown.

For a ship that had fought no less than three engagements, including one directly *in* the Hive command base for the region, that was not merely unusual. It was thought to be impossible. They should know far more about that ship and crew by now, simply from records if nothing else.

But they didn't. Despite having detailed records of the battles, there was almost nothing available about the ship's weapons, defenses, or crew. It was an enigma, a mystery in a warzone, and it was *here*.

That made this drab-seeming system suddenly very interesting indeed.

*Military technology of this nature doesn't just appear from nowhere. Who are these people? More important, who is backing them?*

It seemed a given to him that someone was backing them. A barely post-starflight culture couldn't mount that level of military capacity. It was ludicrous. They had to be getting their technology from somewhere, or possibly the ships they were tracking were using the system as a cover base.

That seemed possible, though it left him back where he started, of course.

*Almost where I started. At the very least we can eliminate this base from the enemy's assets; it would be difficult indeed to use this world to resupply if the world no longer exists.*

That would be a poor second prize, but it was a prize he was willing to take if that was how things turned out.

▶▶▶

In deep space, hidden within what Terrans called the Oort cloud, a short squadron of Drasin lay in wait. Their own scanners watched the system, the red band glaring brilliantly across every sense they had.

The entire system would have to be destroyed.

It was infected beyond redemption. Every world had traces of the band, even those *incapable* of housing the infection. It was the most infected system they'd ever encountered within their very, *very* long memories.

The four Drasin literally shivered in place, their space warps fighting against the encoded orders they had to remain in place.

Engines of destruction, leashed by chains of digital fog.

Across space, light-days away, the remaining ships in the flotilla shuddered as they received telemetry from their kin and saw a world so red that it called across space and time for them to do their duty. A world so brilliantly bathed in the red shifted band of a frequency only visible to the monsters of space that they literally could see nothing but.

It was, without a single doubt, a world that had to be annihilated.

For so long as it remained intact, no Drasin could ever rest.

Silently they sent on the message back to the Hive.

▶▶▶

# IMPERIAL DESTROYER *DEMIGOD*

▶ "ORDERS HAVE ARRIVED from the command ship at the Hive, Commander."

Ivanth blinked away the sleep, getting up as he spoke to the air.

"And?"

"We're cleared to probe the system, Commander."

"Unleash the drone ships we have positioned in the cometary belt."

# CHAPTER THIRTEEN

## N.A.C.S. Odyssey

▶REFUELING WAS COMPLETED and now the waiting was well underway. The *Odyssey* was in transit between the orbits of Saturn and Uranus, having slung past the ring world during the fueling pass.

Eric sat at his desk in his office, not wanting to sleep and not wanting to loom over his people on the bridge without due cause. The last thing any of them needed was to start thinking that the captain didn't trust them to do their jobs. Soon enough, he actually wouldn't be able to trust them if they started to believe that.

There wasn't anything for a captain to do yet anyway.

His ship could run itself without him, even through a scuffle or two. He knew Roberts could keep it together well enough. The man might not be ready for his own command yet, but he was close. Still, there was a lot to be said for having the captain visible when things were about to get hot.

He had almost finished his paperwork when the call came in.

"Captain. Bowshock waves inbound."

"On my way," Eric said instantly, shutting his system down with a pass of his hand and getting up.

*Waiting's over. Let's play.*

▶▶▶

"What do we have?" Eric asked as he walked onto the bridge and headed directly for his command station.

"Four bowshocks, inbound. They must have snuck into the Oort cloud, because we didn't pick them up until they were inside the heliopause," Winger answered automatically.

"Database match?"

"Drasin, sir."

Eric curled his lips, grimacing slightly though he wasn't surprised by the news.

"Only four, is it?" he asked.

"Yes, sir."

"Probing the system, then," he decided, speaking softly to himself.

"Shall I have the transition cannons brought online, sir?" Roberts asked.

Eric considered, letting out a breath. "No."

"Captain?" Roberts looked over at him, clearly perplexed.

"Winger, send a signal to Liberty," Eric said, face pensive. "Tell them to leave these four to us. Emphasize that, please. They are *not* to engage."

"Uh, yes, sir."

Eric turned back to Roberts. "This is just a probe. Let's keep our ace in the hole as much a secret as we can until we have enough of the bastards in our range to make it really pay."

"We used it against them already."

"Yeah, but we didn't leave any survivors to report back. They may know something hit them," Eric said, "but I'll bet my pension that they don't have the slightest clue *what* hit them."

Roberts tipped his head, conceding the point. "Aye, aye, Captain."

"In the meantime, lay us in a course for intercept."

"Course already laid in, Captain. Awaiting your orders," Daniels answered.

"Consider them given. Best speed."

"Best speed, aye, sir." Daniels nodded. "Course engaged."

Eric checked the numbers, noting the intercept time, and sighed to himself as he smiled and then chuckled.

"All that fuss, and we still have almost two hours before anything happens."

▶▶▶

The *Odyssey* curved outward, heading for deeper space on an intercept course with the inbound ships. The alien vessels inverted the *Odyssey*'s course automatically and headed for a least-time intercept, increasing their acceleration as they did. Any doubt the crew of the Terran ship had that the enemy had picked their entry point specifically and carefully was laid to rest, but none of them were complaining.

Better to meet them in the outer system than to let a single one of the things anywhere near Earth.

The *Enterprise* was a quarter the way around the system, well out of position to make an intercept, but she began to star dive in an attempt to cut off some of the distance and be ready to stop the aliens cold if they got past the *Odyssey*. Still, it was already clear to everyone with eyes in and out of the system that this one was going to be the *Odyssey*'s battle.

▶▶▶

"Reports from the torpedo room, Captain. Pulse capacitors full charged," Roberts reported.

"Thank you, Commander," Eric said, tapping in some notes as he eyed the plot.

The Drasin ships were clearly aiming right for them, which was fine with Eric. Better to have them focused on the *Odyssey* than to have them heading for Mars or Earth.

*That said,* he thought as he eyed the trajectories of the converging points on the plot, *can't make it too easy for them.*

"Take us to full stealth," Eric ordered, "and alter course to three degrees, south of the system plane."

"Aye, Captain." Both Daniels and Waters echoed each other as they bent to follow the order.

The *Odyssey*'s lights dimmed, shifting over to low-powered and better-insulated systems as the ship went to black-hole settings on her armor. The key to stealth was to both limit all possible reflection of energy as well as all possible *emission* of energy that might be seen by the enemy, so as to shrink the cross section the ship presented to any onlooking scanners.

Shortly after stealth settings were securely in place, the big ship's thrusters flared, pushing her down and "under" the orbital plane of the system and away from any oncoming lasers of the enemy ships.

With the sails still extended and in maximum-absorption mode themselves, the stealth settings caused incoming photons and other detection energies to become clearer. The *Odyssey* didn't have to adjust for local light pollution caused by the ship reflecting starlight or emitting photons from its various systems.

The flip side of the coin, of course, was an instantaneous spike in radiation penetrating the armor now that general deflection settings were suspended. Those levels would limit the time the *Odyssey* could spend in stealth, particularly if they were in the vicinity of a solar flare or someone deployed particularly messy nuclear devices.

*Not to mention cascading nukes that have got to* violate *the laws of frigging physics.* Eric scowled at the thought, every scientifically trained neuron in his brain offended by the display of power he'd seen the Priminae ships show in the last engagement the *Odyssey* had participated in at Ranquil.

"Stealth settings engaged. All systems showing nominal."

"Alright. Now we get to play the game." Eric allowed himself a small smile.

Daniels and Waters glanced at each other, smirking slightly. It was pretty clear that the captain was enjoying this a little too much.

▶▶▶

The ship minds barely noted the target as it vanished. They'd been expecting it. Records showed that it was following what appeared to be its common pattern, and so they adjusted as well. The four ships broke formation, spreading out to avoid being caught in a single barrage from the ship's known weapons.

It was clear that this ship was an agent of the red band, possibly one of the original carriers of the infestation. It had to be destroyed, but so far was proving resistant to the normal methods of the swarm. That was a serious problem, because if there was one like this then there could—in fact, there almost certainly *would* be more.

There was a procedure for this event, however, as it had happened before and the creators knew that it could happen again.

It was with that procedure in mind that the ships set out to put their newfound enemy to the test.

▶▶▶

*Priminae Warship* **Posdan**

"All signals have gone quiet, Captain. They've apparently reached their destination."

Kian nodded absently, eyeing the yellow star showing on their long-range systems. Already they were picking up stray signals, now that they were looking for them. That indicated civilization and high technology. It didn't take much analyzing to recognize them as Terran modulation, so at the very least she expected they'd located one of the Terran colonies, if indeed they had any.

At worst, or best, depending on how one looked at things she supposed, it was their homeworld itself.

The world and the system were of secondary importance, however, given that she was quite certain that somewhere between her two warships and the system there were unknown numbers of Drasin lying in wait.

*It is odd that they have gone silent. Drasin don't sneak up on systems. They fly in with a complete lack of anything resembling caution or common sense. Why did we detect them all going dark well outside the system?*

It seemed unlikely, but another stray thought struck her.

*Are they actually* afraid *of the Terrans?*

That thought was just inconceivable.

The Drasin were the monsters of children's stories. They didn't fear. They *were* fear. That was one of the things that made them so terrifying, the fact that they had no fear, no respect, no caution at all. They simply came on and on in an endless wave of destruction until they were finished.

*Why, then, are they behaving so atypically now?*

That was a question that was beginning to obsess her, and Kian knew it. Something told her that whatever it was that was changing the way they behaved was quite possibly the solutions to the entire crisis the Drasin had engendered. She had to figure it out.

"Slow us. Transmit to the *Nept* to match our pace," she ordered. "Make our speed one-third thrust. Do *not* excite trans-light particles."

"Yes, Captain. One-third thrust, no trans-light excitation."

The *Nept* and the *Posdan* slowed their approach, adjusting their warping of space-time to minimum to maintain speed while avoiding the broadcasting of their presence to anyone with a trans-light scanning system.

Ahead of them, a yellow star beamed out of the black, and the enemy awaited.

▶ ▶ ▶

▼

# IMPERIAL DESTROYER *DEMIGOD*

▲

▶ "COMMANDER, WE'RE GETTING some unusual feedback from telemetry systems linked to the drone ships."

Ivanth glanced over, irritated by the distraction.

The ships of the flotilla had been slowly edging closer to the system, moving slowly enough not to form any detectable signatures that could be seen by trans-light scanners. They just weren't close enough to get a reasonable view of the tactical situation within the system, and he didn't want to be distracted by minor maintenance issues.

"Send the readings to the control departments," he said. "Whatever it is, I'm sure they can work it out."

"Commander, I have, but this is very odd. We don't have anything in our briefs about these sorts of feedback issues."

Ivanth sighed, feeling put upon, but turned from the screens he was viewing and started to walk over. "Alright, let me have a—"

"Commander! The unknown ship has employed stealth!"

Ivanth twisted back, eyes lighting on the place where the ship had been on his screens. He bared his teeth, then waved in the direction he'd been heading. "Just put a higher priority on it and tell the control department to figure it out. I'm busy."

"Yes, Commander."

▶▶▶

# N.A.C.S. ODYSSEY

▶ "WE'VE LOST TRACK of Bandits Three and Four. They split from the group and have reduced thrust, gone dark, Captain."

Eric made a mild face, but wasn't shocked by the action.

"Understood. Is Bandit One still on our track?"

"Aye, Captain, One has also lowered thrust, but we're able to track," Winger answered.

Eric laughed slightly, a short chuff of amusement. "So that's the game, is it?"

"Looks to be," Roberts nodded. "I'm thinking we should be insulted."

"Depends on if it's a double trap, I suppose." Eric shrugged. "The question is, do we take a shot at Bandit One anyway? Almost seems a shame to let an easy target slip past."

"You have a way to keep Three and Four from jumping us when we do?" Roberts asked. "Because you know they're flanking him, even if they want us to think they're stalking us from somewhere else."

"True," Eric conceded. "We could take a literal shot in the dark."

"With what? They'd see torps coming, and our lasers would never be able to adapt at this range," Roberts said. "I mean, if you want to keep the t-cannons off the table, that only leaves the HVMs."

"Exactly."

"Sir," Roberts said dryly, "that's just wasting ammo."

"Not if they're trying to play fat and stupid," Eric said, tapping in some numbers as he worked out the math. "Check my equations here, would you? My trajectory calculations go to hell when I start trying to work out relativistic effects."

Roberts frowned, but ran over the numbers quickly and made a few minor adjustments. "You really think they'll stay the course that steady?"

"I do," Eric said, sounding confident. "They've learned to respect us, obviously, but they're still underestimating us."

"Would be nice if we could keep them doing that," Roberts said dryly.

Eric shrugged again. "If you can think of a way to look stupid to them without getting the ship shot out from under us, I'm all ears."

Roberts reluctantly conceded the point. While it would be great if the enemy kept on treating them like they were dumb and dumber, there came a point where acting stupid just became *being* stupid. That was a line he'd really prefer not to cross.

"Targeting solution sent to your stations, Lieutenant Waters," Eric said, nodding to the tactical officer. "Wake up a brace of anti-ship HVMs and launch when ready."

Waters blinked, shooting him a slightly consternated look, but nodded and began entering the solution into his computer. A few moments later he nodded, "HVMs ready, launching in three…two…and one."

The *Odyssey* shivered slightly as the magnetic launchers tossed out the multi-ton kinetic kill weapons into space, their onboard CM winding up as the rocket motors roared into action. The hyper-velocity missiles flickered for a moment on the *Odyssey*'s sensors and then almost vanished as they lanced away from the ship at a significant fraction of light-speed.

"Helm, best change our course now," Eric said lightly. "Bring us back to the orbital plane."

"Aye, sir. Changing course."

Eric checked the clock on his screen and then did some quick calculations. Another three minutes and they'd see if he had been right.

▶▶▶

Hypervelocity missiles were really just large slabs of iron fitted with powerful yet short-lived CM generators and equally powerful solid rocket boosters. By warping space-time around the mass of metal, it was possible to disconnect it slightly from the local Higgs field and thus reduce its apparent universal mass.

When the rocket motors kicked in, they were pushing almost nothing compared to their power rating and they accelerated at speeds generally considered impossible in the relativistic universe. They still maintained some mass, however, so were unable to break light-speed.

Even with that limit, at significant percentages of the speed of light, even very lightly massed objects could pose a threat to some of the heaviest of armor.

That was before the last two systems in the HVMs came into play.

A forward sensor tracked objects ahead of the missile. At the speeds the HVM moved at, no computer would be able to make decisions before impact, so the fuse was hardwired into the system. When a mass was detected within its terminal range, the missile's fuse triggered the final of the two systems.

When terminal guidance was initiated, the onboard CM field blew itself out and momentarily inverted its effect. Instead of disconnecting the missile from the local Higgs field, it sank the whole slab of iron and steel deeper than it naturally existed in the field and caused many times the normal number of bosons to drag on the material.

The natural, or perhaps unnatural, effect was to suddenly increase the effective mass dozens of times while not affecting its speed even slightly.

The equation that ruled over the impact of the missile with its target was a simple one.

$E=MC^2$.

Several tons of metal, massing dozens of times what they normally would, multiplied by the square of the speed of light resulted in one *hell* of a discharge of energy.

▶▶▶

"Holy shit," Roberts swore quietly, but not quietly enough to go unheard.

The flash of light from the impact caused a momentary dimming of their screens as the sensors automatically adjusted the gain to prevent burnout. Even with the filters it was like the whole universe just exploded in their faces, and it was *light-minutes* away.

"Son of a bitch." Roberts was clearly still having trouble believing what he was seeing. "I can't believe they held that steady for that entire time."

"They thought they were baiting us in," Eric said, a trifle smugly, "so they were playing fat and stupid."

"They ought to have known better than that. No one is that fat or stupid."

"Subtlety isn't their strong suit, from what I can tell," Eric said conversationally, "though they do seem to be learning."

"Flash from the blast just lit up Bandits Two and Three, Captain," Winger announced. "Looks like they doubled back and were flanking Bandit One."

Eric smirked, amused.

"Oh, wipe that look of your face," his XO growled. "They may not be bright, but there's one hell of a lot of them and you know what they said about the Soviets in the Cold War."

That did wipe the smirk from Eric face, like cold water washing away heated emotions.

"Yeah, I know. It's quality versus quantity, but quantity has a quality all its own," Eric quoted. "I know the situation, Commander. Let me enjoy the small victories, OK?"

Roberts rolled his eyes, clearly not thinking much on that, but knew better than to say anything further. He was well aware that his CO enjoyed the tactical aspect of his command rather more than he personally considered wise. It made sense in a lot of ways. Eric Weston was a gifted tactical commander and a superior leader. It was his strategic sense that often left Roberts cringing in the background.

He supposed that it was probably related to the skill-set that made him an excellent fighter, pilot, and squadron commander. In any case, most of the time Roberts was glad of it and certainly willing to serve under a man from whom he could watch and learn. The rest of the time, well, he would greatly appreciate it once the Confederacy got its act together and had enough ships to qualify as a fleet and put someone with some strategic sense into a field command slot.

"Any chance the explosion damaged the flankers?" Eric asked, his tone mildly curious.

"No such luck, Captain. They've begun maneuvering away from their previous course," Waters answered immediately.

"No shock, and while I was hoping for some fratricidal effects, I wasn't expecting much," Eric said. "Any sign they know where we are?"

"No, sir. I'm reading their current actions as standard evasive maneuvers."

"Good. Lock up Bandit Two and adjust for an intercept course."

"Aye, sir," Waters and Daniels answered almost as one.

"One down, three to go."

# CHAPTER FOURTEEN

## War Room, Station Liberty, Earth Orbit

▶ ADMIRAL GRACEN GLARED at the screens, features set in stone as they had been since she began watching the events unfolding in the outer system.

The *Odyssey* had gone dark, something that unfortunately included silencing her transponder, so they couldn't do more than guess at her location for any given moment. The HVM strike had briefly exposed the ship to view when it eclipsed the explosion, showing a clear silhouette to one remote scanner, but by and large the ship was as hidden from them as it, hopefully, was from the enemy.

That wasn't something that made the brass present feel particularly comfortable, especially given that most of them earned their ranks overseeing battles from very similar rooms and were now informed that a *mere* Captain had effective command of the entire situation.

There wasn't much any of them could do, however, as there was neither backseat nor armchair from which to command. By the time any orders they gave had made it to the *Odyssey*, the situation would have almost certainly change beyond recognition.

"How the hell did that boy know he could hit a target from that far away?"

Gracen snorted when she heard that, barely glancing at the three-star general who'd asked the question. "He didn't have a clue. That was a guess and a shot in the dark."

Several sets of eyes turned to her and she sighed, noting that it might have been better to keep her mouth shut. Still, she hadn't, so she decided to explain.

"They were baiting a trap, General. Weston decided that there was a good chance that they wouldn't wiggle the bait around too much for fear of losing the fish. So he took a shot and it paid off," she said. "Say what you will about Eric Weston, but he's always been a tactical prodigy. The man knows how to read intentions in the least bit of information, and he's willing to take a chance if the situation calls for it."

"What do you suppose he's doing now?" the general asked, a little gruffly.

"Most likely? He's picked his next target and is closing the range," she said. "There's no way he can count on getting any more shots like that, so he has to close to knife range to finish this."

"He should paint them and pop them," Admiral Sandecker growled. "There's too much risk in closing like that. The transition cannons would easily take out all four of them without exposing the *Odyssey* to this kind of danger."

"That's true, Admiral," Gracen answered. "And honestly I think I may agree with you. However, Captain Weston knows the enemy better than most and he thinks we should hold those in reserve."

"Reserves won't help us if we lose the *Odyssey*, Admiral," Sandecker countered. "That ship holds almost two-thirds of the transition cannons in *existence*. If they go down, they may well take the Earth with them."

"I know. And so does he," she said. "So far he took out a quarter of their forces without exposing himself to counter fire. Give the man a chance."

"I just wish we'd updated the *Enterprise* ahead of the *Odyssey*." Sandecker curled his lips up slightly. "Weston is too damned much of a loose cannon."

Gracen sighed, not liking the fact that one of her captains was being badmouthed in this gathering, especially one currently fighting for them all. But honestly it wasn't anything she hadn't thought herself a time or two in the past. Eric Weston had always been a controversial choice for the captaincy of the *Odyssey*, and she was quite certain that if anyone had known just how important the posting would become there was no way he'd have been tapped for it.

For better or worse, however, he was the man in the hot seat.

*Don't fuck this one up, Eric. None of us can afford it.*

▶▶▶

# N.A.C.S. *ODYSSEY*

▶ "BANDIT TWO ENTERING our range, sir."

"Thank you, Waters," Eric said, glancing to his left as he spoke. "Any sightings on our other two playmates?"

"We've got a ghost hit, about twenty light-seconds behind Two," Winger said. "Can't swear to anything, but it may be Bandit Four."

"And Three?"

"No sign. Sorry, Cap."

"Keep your screens peeled," Eric said, "but be ready to lose the sails. We're going to be mixing it up a little closer than I'd prefer this time."

"Aye, Captain, got it covered. Sails are being stowed the moment you launch on this one."

"Very nice. Keep it up."

The *Odyssey*'s sensor sails were a vital part of her scanning gear, particularly in a situation where they had to rely on passive scanners, but they were also fragile. Mostly mylar material coated in an adaptive surfacing to better absorb radiant energy, they could be torn easily by anything from stray micrometeorites to harsh language, if it came right down to it.

Certainly, the high-speed maneuvers inherent to space combat could produce more than enough stress to tear the valuable material, so stowing it before the fight really kicked off was just good planning.

That said, putting the sails away had its downside, mostly connected to the loss of scanner resolution that occurred when they were stowed, but that was what Winger was trained for.

"Lock up Bandit Two. Give me a medium spread pattern from the pulse torpedoes," Eric ordered. "Everyone else, watch the repeaters and call out if you even think you've got a line on Bandit Three."

The bridge chorused with acknowledgements, leaving Eric to ponder his next move.

It wasn't what he was going to do that he was thinking about. No, he was much more concerned with what the enemy was going to do in response. His next action was clear: Take out Bandit Two. Simple, straightforward, and actually pretty easy, given the experience they now had with the Drasin.

That still left two more cruisers out there waiting to jump him, and potentially their screening elements, if they'd launched fighters. He rather didn't think they had, though, since a fighter screen would have shown up during the flash of Bandit One's spectacular exit from this existence. Even in regular radiation levels, a screen would be much more likely to glint off something.

"Soft lock on Bandit Two," Waters announced after a few seconds. "Eighty-three percent likely targeting solution."

"Fire as we bear."

"Aye, aye. Firing as she bears, Captain."

The *Odyssey*, still mostly on a ballistic course, took another eighty-three seconds for her tubes to come to bear on the target, and then the pulse torpedoes were ejected out into space by the magnetic launchers. The antimatter-based weapons lanced away from the *Odyssey* at speed, their similar electrical and magnetic charges causing them to spread in flight as they crossed the intervening space between ship and target.

Charged particles, even the smallest ones like antideuterium atoms, have a mass, and as such are unable to break the light-speed limit in the way that tachyons can. Even so, they're extremely low mass by the standards of the *Odyssey*'s magnetic accelerators and so could easily be pushed to significant fractions of light-speed. That didn't make their movement fast enough to completely avoid detection, unfortunately, though at short to moderate ranges it would take an extremely observant and quick-reacting scanner technician to react in time.

The Drasin, however, were both observant and particularly quick reacting. The drone designated as Bandit Two by the *Odyssey* had a full six seconds warning before the final terminal assault of the pulses of antimatter fell upon it, and it reacted in a way that had worked in the past.

A thick squadron of fighters formed a screen ahead of the ship, pouring out on command, and the first two pulses slammed into them with a furious vengeance. The annihilation of matter and antimatter tore the fighters to shreds, sending energy cascading through the local area with enough power to slag the material of the rest of the fighter screen.

Two of the pulse weapons tore through the hole created and slammed into Bandit Two, while three others spread wide and missed to either side. Spiraling out of control and buffeted by the charges of the matter around them, those three managed to surprise and slam into the drone ship flanking Bandit Two.

Plumes of plasma erupted from the stricken drone ships labelled by the *Odyssey* as Bandits Two and Four, announcing their locations and status to the universe at 299 million meters per second.

Even at that expeditious speed, however, it took almost half a minute for the bridge of the *Odyssey* to register the event. A short roar of satisfaction echoed around the room, several of the junior officers being a fair bit louder than they needed to be, but even Eric and Roberts bared their teeth and pumped their fists (albeit quietly and mostly hidden by the stations from behind which they were working).

"Lock them in. HVM strike, Lieutenant," Eric ordered.

"Aye, Captain. Targeting solution locked in."

"All banks, rapid fire."

The *Odyssey* keeled about slightly, bringing her HVM banks to bear on the target, and the magnetic accelerators began pulsing in rapid fire. Multi-ton slabs of steel and iron flickered away from the ship, accelerating into high relativistic speeds on their way to a meeting with the stricken Drasin ships.

"Captain! I think I just got a shimmer off Bandit Three!" Winger spun around. "Coming in hard on our nine o'clock low!"

"Evasive action!"

The *Odyssey* twisted in space in accordance to the sudden furious program initiated by Lieutenant Commander Daniels, the vectored thrust sending the ship into a chaotic set of turns that actually forced people on board to hold on to their seats despite the effect of the *Odyssey*'s large CM generators.

"They just went hot!" Winger called out. "I think they might have spotted us."

"Armor to best deflection!" Eric ordered.

The time for stealth was past, he decided. "All systems to full combat power, go active."

"Aye, aye, sir. All systems, going active."

The powered down and heavily insulated systems of the N.A.C.S. *Odyssey* surged to life with a flare that, while weak when measured by the standards of the Drasin or Priminae, was more than enough to bring light to the darkness about her. RADAR and LIDAR systems went to full strength, pouring gigawatts of power out into space, while the sleeping reactor now awoke with a vengeance. Energy began surging into the ship's capacitors to replace what they had used in battle already.

"Got them! Damn they're close!" Winger swore.

"Send the data to Tactical!" Eric snarled.

"Already there."

"Got them," Waters said. "She wasn't kidding. How on Earth did they get that close, Michelle? You usually have eyes like a hawk."

"Well, pardon me for being distracted by the massive *explosions*," Winger growled.

"Children, please," Eric chided lightly. "We have more important things to deal with at the moment."

"Sorry, sir."

"Sorry, sir." Waters echoed Winger's words. "Looks like they're on an attack run. Stand by for laser strike."

"Signal all hands to brace, then, and get me a targeting solution on him," Eric said. "And Michelle, update on Bandits Two and Four?"

"Splashed, Captain. Direct hits with HVM launch," she answered. "They were already crippled. No way they could get clear."

"That's what I want to hear—"

"Laser bloom!" Winger called, cutting him off. "Near miss, Captain."

"Do you have the frequency?"

"Do you really need to ask?" she mumbled before speaking up. "Sent to Tactical."

"Armor program coded, Captain," Waters said.

"Then by all means, engage the program," Eric said with a small smile before he turned to look at Roberts. "I'm starting to feel superfluous here, almost like they don't need us anymore."

"Speak for yourself, Captain," Roberts replied, tilting his screen so Eric could see the nigh endless stream of reports coming in from all over the ship that he had to filter through to keep things running smoothly.

Eric suppressed the urge to flip his executive officer off and sighed. "I suppose it's just me then."

"Sign of a good captain," Roberts said with a hint of amusement. "Ship runs without him."

"Bandit Three is re-aligning, Captain."

"Turn us into the fire, Lieutenant Commander," Eric told Daniels. "And Lieutenant Waters, warm up the main array."

"Aye, aye, Captain."

The *Odyssey* keeled slowly about, bringing her nose to nose with the oncoming Drasin cruiser, her forward laser array glowing slightly as the energy built up. The two ships poured on the power, accelerating toward one another as they opened fire.

Two beams of energy crossed one another in space, one literally thousands of times more powerful than the other, and struck their respective targets almost simultaneously. The immensely powerful beam of the Drasin's main laser splashed off the adapted armor of the *Odyssey*, reflected harmlessly out into space while ablating a layer a few microns thick from her hull.

The *Odyssey*'s laser didn't even warm up the hull it touched, but instead reflected energy back in the direction from which it came. The computers and sensors on the human ship carefully noted the frequency of reflected light and adjusted the multi-frequency laser to best absorption based on the composition of the Drasin hull.

Only *then* did it crank up the wattage.

The low temperature targeting and analysis laser was replaced by a multi-terawatt beam specifically adjusted to the armor it was targeting. Four square meters of the Drasin cruiser vaporized in an instant, and then the *Odyssey*'s laser hit full power.

On the bridge of the Confederate warship, Eric couldn't help but feel a certain ruthless elation as he watched the violent sublimation of the enemy ship. The laser, while not as powerful as the ones packed into the Drasin ships, was tuned specifically to destroy what it was aimed at and it showed. Hull material, armor, everything was turned instantly to gaseous plasma without stopping at the liquid phase in between.

The result was a violent and explosive destruction of the target as the ship's own matter was turned against it by the superheating effect of the tuned laser.

In seconds the firefight was over, even as the *Odyssey*'s systems finally came back fully online from their dormant stealth state.

"Fighter screen inbound, Captain!"

Eric's eyes flicked away from the remnants of the Drasin ship to the new red icons on the ship's screens. *Must be orphan fighters from the other ships. That would normally make them more dangerous, but Drasin don't seem to give a damn about survival anyway, so it's par for the course.*

"Go active, all starboard point defense stations," he ordered. "Bring us about to course oh-oh-niner, even, flank speed."

"Aye, sir. Zero-zero-niner, even to the system plane. Ahead flank."

"Should we alert and launch the Archangels, sir?" Roberts asked quietly.

"No," Eric said. "We can handle these with point defense fire as long as we're not distracted by any more cruisers. We'll need the Angels soon enough."

"Yes, sir."

"Point defense engaging."

The first of the fighters, likely on a suicide charge, Eric figured, entered into the extreme range for the point defense lasers and phalanx guns. He couldn't hear the roar of the weapons but knew that it would be impressive in an atmosphere where sound could travel a little more effectively than the rarified vacuum of space. On the screens, red icons began to blink out of existence one by one as the weapons tracked and eliminated them.

With the *Odyssey* able to maneuver to keep the enemy fighters at range, it wasn't a fight. It was a massacre.

▶▶▶

### Imperial Destroyer **Demigod**

There was one thing more frustrating than anything else in space, particularly when it came to combat, at least in Ivanth's opinion. That thing was the utterly slow rate at which light traveled. Photons took so long to cross the distances a space traveler had to deal with that it could be enough to drive a man who normally processed light as the fastest thing in the universe to madness.

On the screens he was watching the enemy ship simply annihilate another four of the drone ships, destroying them with an ease that sent shivers down his spine.

*Unreal. Destroyers of the Empire would have difficulty defeating the drone ships four on one. Why have we never found even a whisper of these people before? They cannot have come from nowhere. Someone must have more information on them.*

He was still pondering that impossibility when Ivanth was distracted by a distressed call from behind him. He looked over his shoulder, irritated.

"What is wrong?" he snarled, turning fully around.

"It's the drone ships, Commander! They're refusing orders!"

"What?" Ivanth snapped, striding quickly to the station. "You must have done something wrong."

"No, Commander, I swear. I've followed every protocol," the clearly panicking man stammered out. "The drones began behaving oddly a short while ago. Now they're completely disregarding all signals from us."

"This is impossible," Ivanth gritted out. "I've reviewed the instinct locks myself. They're unbreakable."

The man, likely showing wisdom beyond his years, remained silent at that proclamation.

Ivanth, however, wasn't paying attention even if he had chosen to speak. Instead the Commander pushed the younger technician out of his place and furiously worked his way through the systems.

"This doesn't make any sense. Nothing is working," he growled, eyes flickering to the display that was still working properly, the one that showed the locations of the drone ships. "At least they're not coming toward us or the *Immortal*."

"Y-yes, Commander."

Ivanth ignored the stammering man, focusing on the task. The only good thing about the entire situation was that the drones were clearly heading right where he was going to order them to go anyway. The fact that they were doing so *without* orders however was even more frightening than anything that the enemy ship had accomplished.

"Contact the *Immortal*," Ivanth gritted out as he straightened from the station. "Order them to fall back. And we'd best do so as well. We don't want those things turning on us."

"Yes, Commander."

That was an order that he had no doubt would be obeyed with alacrity and enthusiasm. No one in the empire, least of all those tasked with controlling the infernal beasts, wanted to be anywhere near one that wasn't fully *tamed*.

Ivanth cast one final look at the system they'd been monitoring, scowling at the brightly shining vessel currently swatting the drone fighters left by one of the doomed ships. He doubted that it would stand long against the remnants of his drone fleet. There were still almost thirty ships.

Four on one was one thing. Thirty to one?

Something far, far different.

*I would have preferred a somewhat more artistic attack method, but there is something to be said for brute force. We'll pull back and attempt to regain control of the damned things when the battle is over.*

▶ ▶ ▶

# PRIMINAE WARSHIP *POSDAN*

▶ "TRANS-LIGHT SIGNALS ahead, Captain. They're strong."

Kian eyed the screens, attention focused on the indicated station. The report was certainly not exaggerating things. Whoever was in charge there had apparently tossed the concept of subtlety and stealth right out the force field and into deep space.

There were numerous high-profile, high-power signals diving straight into the Terran system.

*Oh, maker. They're on a swarm.*

They'd not seen this tactic since the re-emergence of the Drasin in recent times, but the old myths spoke of it clearly enough. Enough of the Drasin ships in one place, coupled with a particularly hated target, and they would swarm like killer insects onto their prey.

Something about the Terran system had set them off, but by the same token she had to wonder just what so many of the damned things were doing out here anyway?

"Captain, I believe I'm picking up quieter trans-light signals moving *away* from the system."

Kian hissed, eyes shifting. "Show me."

"Just echoes, Captain. Look here...."

Kian eyed the screens and saw what was being reported, but it was quite clear that they were indeed just echoes.

*Possibly a ship, or even two, but possibly not.*

She cast her eyes back to the system and hesitated for a second before shaking it off.

"Singularity damn it all," she swore. "Make our course for the Terran system, all speed!"

"All speed, yes Captain!"

*The sneaks will have to wait. We owe the Terrans a couple interventions of our own.*

▶▶▶

# N.A.C.S. ODYSSEY

▶ "WHOA!"

"What is it, Michelle?" Eric asked, one eye on the screens as they continued to scan for any fighters they might have missed.

"Inbound bowshock signals," she answered. "A lot of them, Captain. We've got company coming, and they're coming in loud and noisy."

Eric redirected his attention with an alacrity he reserved for truly bad news, glaring at the new signals for a moment before he visibly relaxed and even smiled.

"Captain?" Roberts asked hesitantly. He really didn't like that look much.

"Looks like the rest of the *Weifang*'s pursuit group," Eric said mildly. "They don't appear happy to see us."

"I wonder why," Roberts snorted.

"Captain," Waters spoke up, "armor stands ready to shift to stealth…."

"No," Eric said. "No, I don't think so. Time to put on a show, I think."

He walked over to Waters's station and reached across the younger man's shoulder to tap in some command. When he was done, Eric stepped back. "Run those armor equations, if you will."

"Uh…yes, sir," Waters said, confused but certainly not going to disobey an order.

The new equations were put into the computer and chroma-shifting coating on the *Odyssey*'s hull went into action immediately. In a few seconds, the normal, somewhat drab Navy colors of the ship were replaced with blazing white and mirrored hull segments, her running lights lit up to full power.

"Stand by to record and broadcast a message, in the clear," Eric ordered. "All channels, all frequencies, *especially* Priminae encodings and translations. I'll bet my last dollar that whoever is out there has broken those, probably a long time past."

"Aye sir, standing by."

Eric took a breath, considering what he was about to say, then nodded once.

"This is the *Terran* Starship *Odyssey*. You are in violation of the sovereign rights of this star system. This is your only warning. Continue into our territory and you will be met with lethal force. Eric Stanton Weston, Commanding, *Odyssey* out."

He took a slow breath, then nodded pensively. "Encode, translate, and loop that."

"Aye, aye, Captain."

Roberts stepped closer. "Terran Starship? The NAC isn't going to be fond of that, sir."

"Respectfully," Eric hissed softly in reply, "*fuck* the NAC. It's time to stand together, or hang separately."

Roberts' expression was etched in stone as he moved away. He wasn't sure this was the way to do things, but at the same time he sure as hell wasn't certain that it was the wrong way either.

No matter what else, no matter what may come, it was clear that the N.A.C.S. *Odyssey* stood on station, a gleaming white knight in the black, challenging anyone to cross her.

# CHAPTER FIFTEEN

## NAC Station Liberty, Earth Orbit

▶ "THAT MAN HAS to be one of the most arrogant bastards...."

Admiral Gracen pinched the bridge of her nose, wishing she could refute the words. *He just had to broadcast that in the clear. Good god. Every radio receiver in the damned system picked that up, including the civilian ones.*

"There's not a lot left to it, I'm afraid," she said tiredly. "We were going to call in the Chinese anyway, as they had a pretty damned good idea of what was coming down. May as well bring in the UN while we're at it."

"Can we really afford that distraction at this point?"

"I don't think we can afford not to," Gracen countered. "This battle is out of our hands. Aside from the transition cannons on the Liberty, it's going to be in the hands of Carrow and Weston. They're our only assets in the entire solar system at the moment."

She scowled, not at anyone in particular, but just at the situation.

"We need international cooperation if we're going to put together a credible fighting force, and you all know it," she said. "At the very least, we have to be sure that we're not going to be shot in the back by the Block while we're fighting these *Drasin*."

"The President is not going to like this."

"Has anyone talked to him since the transmission was received?" Gracen asked, a spreading chill running through her blood.

The others looked around, equally horrified as the thought dawned on them all.

*Oh crap.*

"Alright. I'll get on the line Earth-side and see what's going on in the minds of the politicians," Gracen sighed. "In the meantime, I think we should take Weston's lead on this subject and bring the Block ships into the loop."

"Admiral Gracen, with all due respect, are you out of your mind?"

She pinned her colleague with a glare. "Would you prefer them to fire their missiles without bothering to let us know? Because if you think that they're sitting this one out, you're the one that's out of your mind."

The room quieted for a moment as everyone parsed that bit of information and quickly realized that she was right, no matter how little anyone wanted to admit it.

"We can't clear that," a vice admiral finally said, voicing what just about everyone was thinking. "That'll have to come from the civilian authority."

Gracen twisted her lip, but nodded.

"Right. Well, I better make that call then, shouldn't I?" she asked rhetorically.

No one was silly enough to try answering.

▶ ▶ ▶

# P.L.A.S. *WEIFANG*, EARTH ORBIT

▶ "WHAT IS THE status of our repairs?" Sun asked tiredly, still thinking about the Confederate transmission.

"Damage is, of course, extensive. We're down by half our engineering section, Captain."

"Most of those systems were covered by redundancy, yes?"

He could see the reluctance in his officers' eyes as they nodded in agreement, not that Sun blamed them in all honesty. It was clear what he was going to ask them to do, he was sure, and it was equally clear that it was essentially a suicide mission. What could he do, though?

What could any of them do?

They had led the enemy to Earth. That was on their heads. Maybe the Confederates made them an enemy in the first place, maybe not. Sun was now privately disposed to believe that whatever these *things* were, they were now and always had been hostile.

Whichever was the case, however, didn't really matter.

He had personally caused this particular battle, forget the war for the moment. This was Sun's own mess, and he had to try to clean it up.

"How are our disposables?"

"Missiles are down by a third, Captain. We have sufficient reactor mass for a reasonable exchange," his executive officer reported. "But a single strike by those lasers will wipe us from space and time as though we never were."

Sun grimaced, but nodded in understanding.

The power of the enemy weapons was truly monstrous, of that there was no doubt whatsoever. That said, it was clear that despite whatever defenses they had, the enemy ships themselves weren't invulnerable. The *Weifang*'s own shaped nuclear charges had proven effective enough, and it was clear that the Confederacy had their own to match.

Sun took a breath, looking over his men, and nodded firmly. "We break orbit in ten minutes."

"Captain, we don't have clearance...."

"I'll make the request," the *Weifang*'s XO said, "but it will take some time to process."

"Command will deny it anyway," Sun said. "As I said, we leave in ten minutes."

He looked around the gathering slowly. "Unless someone wishes to object?"

His men exchanged glances slowly, but no one spoke. After a long minute, Sun nodded.

"Good. Then get your departments in order. We have things to do."

▶▶▶

# N.A.C.S. ODYSSEY

▶ "THEY DIDN'T EVEN slow their approach," Eric chuckled, mildly amused if he were to be completely honest.

"You didn't really expect them to, did you, sir?" Roberts asked, eyebrow raised in eerie reminiscence of another first officer Eric might mention but wouldn't for fear of his own XO's reaction.

That amusing thought just made him smile a little wider as he shook his head.

"No, but of course it wasn't intended for the Drasin anyway."

"No, sir," Roberts agreed. "Do you think they got the message?"

Eric nodded. "I would bet on it. We know that this group had handlers, so yeah, they're out there."

"For once, I rather hope so," Roberts said wearily. "The Drasin don't talk, they don't negotiate…they're not a people we can deal with outside of military might. I hope that whoever is holding their leash is at least a little different."

"So do I," Eric said tightly, eyes on the plot.

The Drasin ships had slowed, dropping from space warp as they penetrated the gravitational influence of Sol and began to dig deeper into the system. That meant that the *Odyssey* no longer had a real time lock on the twenty-eight Drasin cruisers inbound in her direction, but that hardly mattered. It was blatantly obvious where they were heading, and Eric was quite happy to stand his station in space and invite them in.

*Better they come for us than head for Mars or Earth.*

He'd ordered the *Odyssey* to show her broadsides to the enemy, bringing the full complement of the transition cannons into play. They were already coordinating with Liberty on the upcoming battle, so now all that was left was the shooting.

*Just a little closer.*

"The *Enterprise* is approaching our position," Winger announced from across the bridge. "They cut across the orbit of Mars and were slung this way."

Eric glanced at the plot of the other Confederate ship as it approached. "They made good time. Too bad they weren't refit with the new cannons."

"Would it really matter?"

Eric shrugged. "Against twenty-eight ships? Hard to say. I suppose that we're about to find out, don't you think, Commander?"

"We are at that, Captain."

Eric tipped his head to Winger's station. "Stand by for single tachyon ping, Lieutenant."

"Aye, Captain, standing by."

▶ ▶ ▶

# STATION LIBERTY

▶ "ADMIRAL," THE STATION commander spoke up, attracting Gracen's attention from where she was speaking over the comm line to Earth. "We're reading a drive buildup on the *Weifang*."

Gracen frowned, glanced over, and then looked back at her system. "Pardon me for a moment, General. I need to check on something."

She shifted out of her station and walked over. "What's going on?"

"I think they're getting ready to move out."

Gracen snorted. "You must be joking. That ship is no shape to fight."

"That doesn't seem to be deterring them, Admiral."

"Do they have clearance?" she asked, incredulous.

"Negative. They requested it and were denied."

Gracen blew out an annoyed breath. *Damned stubborn fools we put in charge of ships. Not so different after all, I suppose.*

"Alright," she said aloud. "Give me a channel."

"Admiral?"

"Now is not the time to be distracted. Give me a channel to the *Weifang*."

"Yes, ma'am."

Gracen leaned in to the console as the channel opened and spoke in only slightly accented Mandarin. "Station Liberty to People's Liberation Army Spaceship *Weifang*. This is Admiral Gracen. Please respond."

There was nothing but silence and the crackle of cosmic radiation interfering with the channel. Gracen sneered, annoyed by the situation. *I don't need this now, of all times.*

"Captain Sun," she growled, "your own government has refused clearance to you. Your ship is not fit for this battle and, more important, if the *Odyssey* and the *Enterprise* fail, you and this station will be one of the last lines of defense for the entire planet below. Acknowledge my communication."

Gracen waited. She'd like to think she waited patiently, but that would be a flat-out lie. She waited, just barely able to keep from tapping her feet in a show of just how impatient she was at the moment, the crackle on the channel sounding interminably loud in her ears.

After what felt like an eternity, an English voice modulation finally broke the crackle of radiation interference.

"Admiral, this is our duty."

"Your duty," she growled, switching to English, "is to preserve the security of your nation and your world. This battle will be over before you can possibly arrive on station. Your duty is *here* Captain. Your *ego* is out there."

The crackle was back for a while as everyone on deck held their breath and waited for an answer.

"P.L.A.S.F. *Weifang* standing station, Admiral Gracen. We stand ready to aid you in this situation."

Gracen blew out a breath, "Thank you, Captain. The Confederate forces stand ready for the same."

▶▶▶

# N.A.C.S. *ODYSSEY*

▶ "LIBERTY SIGNALS READY. They've green lit the plan."

Eric snorted. It wasn't like they had many options. It was rather like giving him permission to breathe.

The enemy signals were now light-speed limited, but they had a good idea of where the fleet would be. They'd crossed the orbit of Pluto, unofficially going from "wet foot" to "dry foot" in many minds, and as far as he was concerned they now deserved everything they had coming to them.

"Stand by, all stations. Single ping," he ordered.

"Aye, Captain. All stations standing by for single-tachyon ping."

*We've got to make this one impressive for the watchers out there. To buy time, if nothing else.*

"Time left on the countdown?" he asked mildly, really just out of habit than actual curiosity.

"Two minutes, thirty-four seconds," Winger replied automatically.

Eric nodded absently, almost surprised that Winger hadn't offered up the milliseconds left to count. Timing didn't have to be quite so precise on this mission, but it would help make things work a little more smoothly.

"Put up the estimated location for the enemy ship in"—he glanced aside—"two minutes, twenty-eight seconds."

"Aye, Captain. On screen."

The plot showed the trajectory of the enemy ships, estimated, of course. They had a delay of almost ten minutes now that the enemy ships were just a little over two astronomical units away.

*The last of them will be in our range in just a few more seconds.*

"*Enterprise* reports ready to provide support, sir."

"Good. Tell them we'll need a fighter screen for clean up," Eric said.

"Aye, sir."

Roberts glanced at him. "You haven't scrambled the Archangels, Captain."

Eric snorted, lowering the pitch of his voice. "Why bother? If this goes wrong, we've got all the chances of a comet in a corona."

"I'd rather be the comet."

"Wouldn't we all?" Eric asked with a hint of a grin before he checked the screens again, "Well, would you look at the clock on the wall? Time to bid them, one and all...goodbye. Winger, ranging ping, full power."

"Aye, aye, Captain. Single ping, full power, range to target in three...two...one."

▶▶▶

# PRIMINAE WARSHIP *POSDAN*

▶"GREAT MAKER, THERE are so many of them."

Kian almost reprimanded the speaker, but honestly she was thinking the same thing.

No Priminae system rated more than six of the Drasin, and those were core systems. Twenty-eight was unfathomable. It was completely insane. That many Drasin could annihilate a star system in a single stroke. No, multiple systems!

It had to be an entire battle group, but what boggled her mind was that it was being thrown in its entirety against this single system.

All Kian could think was to be profoundly grateful that the enemy had never considered any Priminae world to be worth quite so much.

She could feel the eyes of her crew upon her, and knew the reason why.

The *Nept* and the *Posdan* were holding position just outside the system, ready to dive in and provide help, but it was blatantly obvious that they would be too little, too late. She didn't feel that she could in all honor ignore the situation, however, no matter how hopeless it was.

*The least I can do is help the* Odyssey *make our enemies pay a little more for attacking this system.*

"Transmit to the *Nept*," she ordered. "We will go in. Maintain long-range engagements only. We are not sufficient to engage these ships at close range, so we will do what we can until the planet falls. Do not get close enough to be locked into combat."

It would be a largely pointless exercise, she was well aware. Against that many ships, even with the *Odyssey* and the other ship they could detect approaching its position, there was nothing her two vessels could do to swing the odds. It would be a closer fight than the Drasin could possibly expect, but in the end she had little doubt that the Terran system would fall.

*I hope that intelligence was wrong when they said that the Terrans only had a single system under their control.*

If it wasn't, she was about to witness a true genocide.

"Captain! Multiple trans-light signals originating within the system!"

▶▶▶

# IMPERIAL WARSHIP *DEMIGOD*

▲

▶ IVANTH GLARED AT his screens, knowing damned well that his ire was as impotent as it was hot. Somehow they'd lost control of their drones (the fact that said drones chose to attack the target he'd have been sending them against was entirely beside the point), and with that he had a serious black mark hovering over his head.

The drone ships were mostly second- and third-generation, which made them valuable. He'd been entrusted with a significant portion of their real combat capacity, despite the sheer numbers available at the Hive, and now he'd lost *control* of them.

Lost control!

The one thing that was anathema to anyone who'd ever seen the blighted things in action, and that was the thing that happened to him. The Prohuer would have his command, if Ivanth was lucky. Quite possibly his life if he wasn't.

For the moment, however, what burned so badly was the fact that all he could do was sit back and watch the events and hope that he might somehow be able to regain control when it was over.

*Or, worse, hope that these people are able to destroy enough of the Drasin that the* Demigod *and* Immortal *will be able to finish off our* own *drones!*

The arrogance of the ship that broadcast that insane challenge, however, was almost enough to find him laughing despite the lousy situation in which he found himself. That they believed they could deter or, even more ludicrously, back up their challenge was just hilarious.

*A few surprising successes, and this is how they react? Fools.*

"Commander! Trans-light signals from the system!"

"Can you decode?"

"I believe that they are transmitting. I think it's a crude detection system."

Ivanth scowled. More confusing actions by the inhabitants of the system. The drone ships weren't hiding in the slightest, nor were they even making rudimentary attempts at evasion. There was no real point to tracking them in trans-light at the moment, not until they were at least within range of some sort of meaningful engagement.

He was beginning to believe that these people were truly as inexperienced as they seemed. Their actions and technology just didn't match well with the results they had garnered, however, and he was finding it very difficult to believe that anyone could be this crude and obtuse intentionally.

▶▶▶

# N.A.C.S. ODYSSEY

▶ "WE HAVE A real-time lock on the inbound ships, Captain," Winger reported calmly from where she was staring intently at her displays. "All ships are still on their predicted course."

"That makes things easier," Eric said softly. "Waters?"

"Locked in. Barely had to alter the program, Captain."

"Then, by all means, Lieutenant…" Eric said with a hint of a feral smile, "fire as she bears."

"Aye, aye, Captain!" Waters smile didn't have a hint of the feral—it was pure, straight-on animalistic. "Firing!"

Their guns swiveled on massive turrets as they tracked their targets, barely visible puffs of particulate exploding from their bores as they opened fire. It was a far cry from guns blazing, but at the range they were shooting, no one would see a muzzle flash anyway.

The *Odyssey* started firing fifteen light-minutes away.

# CHAPTER SIXTEEN

▶ THE TRANSITION CANNONS were actually more properly called "transitional tachyon waveguides," but neither that nor the actual technical name (which was eight very long and obscure words) caught on after some anonymous person coined the term "t-cannon." People were funny that way.

The delivery system took its cue from the *Odyssey*'s computers, encoding range and gravitational effects according to the known location of the target and the available data on the local warping of space-time caused by stars, planets, and the sometimes estimated impact of drive systems belonging to whatever ships the *Odyssey* was tracking.

Luckily, for the most part, manufactured warps in space-time were extremely local and had minimal impact on trajectory information, unless the ship was very close to the *Odyssey*, the target, or the path of the tachyon particles that made up the payload. That meant that the *Odyssey* computers were able to break a very nearly impossible task down into a series of merely difficult ones, and since the difficult could be accomplished immediately, things continued to get done.

With an appropriate targeting solution entered into the systems, the weapons swiveled out from the hull of the ship like a trio of three gun battleship cannons from the early- to mid-twentieth century. The waveguides adjusted for the angle and elevation, relative to the *Odyssey*, while the computers directed the power to the system to set the range.

One-meter-diameter shells, nuclear-fused munitions were loaded into the breach of the big guns by an automated system in total vacuum. The loader could actually manage up to forty shells per minute, per gun, though the *Odyssey* only had enough power capacitors to fire a tenth of that.

Once the shell was loaded into the breach and everything was sealed, a burst of energy initiated the tachyon phase change. It sublimated the shells directly from solid matter to massless tachyon particles without disrupting the quantum pattern of the shells. Tachyons were strange beasts. They were particles and waves much the way light was, but they were massless and could *only* exist above the speed of light.

It was an expression among Terrans that nature abhors a vacuum. Scientists know that phrase is one of the biggest jokes in the universe because if you looked at the universe statistically you would instantly realize that nature *was* a vacuum. Tachyon researchers, however, knew that what nature really abhorred were tachyons. They didn't like to exist and, honestly, the universe didn't seem to want them around either.

Once charged and transitioned, the shell literally leapt across the intervening space…both passing through every point in between and not moving at all, until their charge was drained. Then they reverted back to normal matter, complete with mass and a very familiar pattern.

That pattern spelled trouble for anyone and anything at the arrival point, or at least it did when the pattern was that of a nuclear-fused fusion weapon.

▶▶▶

A Drasin "cruiser" wasn't actually a starship in the traditional sense, with much of the interior being more analogous to that of a living being. Veins and arteries pumped molten metals to where they needed to be, powering the space-warping capabilities of the unit, while passages that resembled emptied lava tubes shifted gasses about for those tasks unsuited to metallic substances.

Large cargo areas holding smaller fighter class drones or ground combat units actually made up most of the overall space inside, however, and it was into one of these areas that the *Odyssey*'s one-hundred-centimeter shells most often appeared.

The sudden appearance of such a device in the middle of a crowded compartment on a human ship would result in general chaos and action, while on a Drasin vessel the only entity that noted the weapon's arrival was the ship itself. The rest of its denizens were nascent, shut down until needed, and completely unaware of the danger in the midst. The difference was moot, as humans would really only have time to realize they were about to die.

The fission fuse on the device was an implosive type, designed to detonate high explosives inward in order to force atoms of plutonium to smash together. Those atoms would crack apart, neutrons and protons separating as the atom itself was rendered asunder and sent careening outward into other atoms in turn, shattering them. The reaction became briefly self-sustaining, atoms crashing into one another with enough force to shatter atomic bonds and send more atomic material about on collision courses as the fission trigger detonated.

The fissionable material, however, was just a fuse to detonate the true explosive. The fission reaction was enough to detonate the fusion explosive, a mixture of deuterium and tritium wrapped in a uranium shell casing.

It was a slightly bizarre Rube Goldberg-esque chain of events, but in the end the result was a two-hundred-megaton explosive going off *inside* the hull of the Drasin cruiser.

A far cry from the multi-gigaton weapons of the Drasin and Priminae? Yes, but few species ever thought to armor the *interior* of their ships to the same degree as the exterior, and the Drasin were not among those few.

A few seconds after the weapon transitioned back from tachyon energized space-time, the first Drasin ship was nothing but an expanding cloud of gas, plasma, and various particulate.

And it *was* only the first.

One by one, then in twos, threes, and fours, Drasin ships vanished into miniature supernovas that lived out their short existences in fiery glory.

▶▶▶

# STATION LIBERTY

▶"KEEP FIRING," ADMIRAL Gracen ordered, eyes fixed on the screens that were showing her nothing of any value whatsoever.

"Aye, aye, Admiral."

The Station had four transition cannon turrets, one more than the *Odyssey*, but due to the design peculiarities of the station, they could only bring one onto the target at any given time. That one was currently depleting their stock of one-hundred-centimeter shells at a truly sickening rate, and she could literally see her operating budget vanishing faster than the speed of light.

What was worse, no one could tell if they were hitting anything.

It would be more than an hour before light-speed signals got back to the station from the targets, and they'd be sitting with empty guns in a little under ten minutes at the current rate of fire. She wasn't going to maintain that rate for that long, of course; they were double- and triple-tapping all their designated targets as a matter of SOP, and that was going to deplete their munitions significantly.

*Good thing the Block ambassador signed off on a temporary injunction of the Sol System Nuclear Weapons Ban, or this would have the potential to get a lot uglier on the home front.*

For obvious reasons, in a world where the old Russian fifty-megaton "Tsar Bomba" was considered on the small side for fusion weapons, political and military forces had generally agreed that using nuclear weapons on, or near, Earth was a recipe for mutual disaster. Even during the Block War, there had been no use of nuclear weapons by official government agencies.

A few extremist wings of both sides had made some use of older nuclear technologies, but generally nothing more than a few kilotons. Military application of conventional weapons was largely considered more effective, efficient, and far less costly, so nukes weren't the go-to weapon for anyone with an ounce of sanity.

Not until the *Odyssey* encountered the Drasin, at any rate.

That was why munitions for the transition cannons were in such limited quantities, unfortunately. Manufacturing nuclear materials wasn't exactly a lost art, but the facilities equipped to handle the work were few and far between.

In North America, at least.

The irony of the situation was that the Block hadn't mothballed their facilities when the Confederacy did, so they still had the manufacturing capability. Oh, the Confederacy hadn't abandoned the technology, of course. That would have been insane...or maybe it would have been sane, in an insane world. She didn't know which. No, the Confederacy only kept enough facilities available now to destroy humanity fifty times or so, instead of the thousand fold or more that the Block facilities could theoretically manage.

Gracen had already heard that some unofficial overtures had been made to Block officials about outsourcing the manufacturing of shells to the Block while the new facilities in the Confederacy were being re-established.

It was a literally unfathomable concept to her, but then she'd made her bones fighting the Block tooth and nail over a series of Pacific islands that neither of them really gave a damn about. The blood she'd spilled, that she'd *ordered* spilled, had long past stained her world view. It was probably a good thing that she wasn't the one they'd sent to negotiate that particular deal.

For now, however, she had a more important target on her screens.

"Admiral, firing program completed."

Gracen sighed, but nodded as pleasantly as she could before she spoke.

"Good job. Alright, everyone take a break. We've got a little over an hour before we find out if we actually hit anything. If you need anything, now is the time."

War in space was insane, even by her definitions.

▶▶▶

# N.A.C.S. ODYSSEY

▶ "FIRING PROGRAM COMPLETE, Captain."

"Stand by for initial return imaging," Winger announced almost as Waters spoke. "Ten minutes and counting."

Eric didn't say anything. There wasn't much he could say at the moment. He needed information to act, and that was one thing that he just couldn't rush at the moment. He noted a motion in the corner of his eye and spotted a Navy steward—technically a "culinary specialist," now he supposed—gesturing to him questioningly.

He nodded, and the man brought out two more CS personnel with trays of coffee and light snacks, walking them around the bridge. Eric accepted a mug himself, but passed on the pastries. He really wasn't hungry at the moment.

"If you need to use the bathroom, now is the time," he said. "Relief watch is standing by."

Ten minutes wasn't a ton of time, but it would be considerably longer before any enemy ships could reach a conventional engagement range. Eric considered that for a moment, then went on. "Stand down from action stations."

"Aye, Captain," Roberts said, transmitting the order.

A minute later his voice echoed over the ship-wide comm. "All hands, stand down from action stations. I say again, stand down from action stations," Eric ordered before sighing and turning to Roberts. "You know what I hate most about space combat?"

"The waiting?" Roberts asked dryly. It was a pretty obvious thing to hate at the moment.

"Well, yes, but more specifically I hate the fact that every battle feels anti-climactic," Eric scowled. "By the time we know what happened, it's already been over for longer than I care to think about."

"Not if they get close," Roberts said mildly.

"If they get that close, we're dead."

"And no more hating anything, then."

"Bleh! You're a regular breath of fresh air. You know that, right, Commander?"

"I try, sir."

Eric rolled his eyes and tried to focus on the job. Patience was a necessity for an officer, not a virtue. He'd learned that lesson a long time ago, but in truth it never got easier. Even on Earth, with intelligence updates available literally at a split second's notice, often he'd have to wait for someone to analyze the data and then for someone else to tell him what it meant.

Here, he got to make those calls, but now it seemed light itself was conspiring against him.

*Hurry up and wait.*

Ten minutes later, with most of the watch having taken a few minutes to themselves for whatever they needed, the data was coming in and it was about as good as they could hope for. Eric nodded a lot to himself, eyes on the pictures that showed one ship after another vanishing in a ball of nuclear flame, and tried to tell himself that it would be enough.

*They'd have to be crazy to even think of coming in here after seeing this.*

Two things kept him from celebrating with the rest of his crew, however.

First, he didn't think that the Drasin were crazy. He doubted they had enough mental acuity to be diagnosed, period.

And second...well, second was the image of the nigh countless drones it must have taken to assemble that goddamned Dyson Cloud.

An enemy with no thoughts to be considered sane or insane, who had near unlimited numbers? No, he wasn't in a celebratory mood.

▶▶▶

# IMPERIAL DESTROYER *DEMIGOD*

▶ IVANTH HAD NEVER been happier to be seated solidly in place with something to his back before. The explosions of the drone ships were showing over and over again on a loop as his people searched for some kind of cause, any kind of cause, but to him all he felt inside was some sort of shock, horror, and a spreading numbness.

*What have we walked into out here?*

It was impossible. There was *nothing* in the known galaxy that treated the drones like that, and the Empire knew a great deal about the galaxy.

Again the readings played, showing a spreading pattern of annihilation overtaking the drones, and he again just stared.

*Mines?*

He was clutching at straws and he knew it, but it was vaguely possible, he supposed. The drones had approached along the system plane, and it was a common operating procedure among most civilized spacefaring cultures. Not that the drones were in any way civilized, of course. They just liked it when their meals lined up in a nice little row.

That said, if one assumed that sort of approach from encroaching vessels, you might be able to mine the field, in theory. It would take some kind of self-assembling mines, much like the drones that built the Hive modules, but it was possible at least.

His only problem with that theory?

*Where are the mines?*

There were no signs, no hints of weaponized platforms anywhere in the system aside from the third, fourth, and possibly sixth planet. Atomic fusion weapons, such as the explosions seemed to indicate, were *detectable*. In order to hide them from radiating scanners, you would have to clad them in shielding of significant thickness, and *that* would make them visible to visual scans.

"Commander?"

"Is the analysis complete?" Ivanth demanded sharply, stirring from his shock.

"Yes...."

"What is the outcome?"

The man swallowed. "The same as before. Weapon system unknown."

"Run it again."

"Commander, this is the sixth time, without new data...."

"Again!" Ivanth snarled. "Unless you would like to take my place when I explain to the Prohuer just what the hell happened here."

"Yes, Commander."

Ivanth glared at the man until he turned away. There had to be some sort of answer in the data, some hint of just what in the singular abyss just happened!

*The Prohuer is going to have me ejected into space if I return and tell him I lost my entire complement of second-generation drone ships without some kind of explanation as to how in the abyss it happened.*

In the entire time since the drones were discovered and Imperial scientists managed to re-code their primary objective, there had never been any kind of mass loss that even came close to matching this.

*And that includes the incident with the super nova.*

"What is the enemy ship doing?" Ivanth asked, hoping to shake his train of thought.

"Nothing, Commander."

"Nothing?"

"They are remaining directly on station, as they were before. They did not maneuver significantly during the drone ships' entire charge. They have not even attempted to employ their stealth systems."

Ivanth grimaced. "A challenge then. They're *daring* us to enter their territory."

"Commander, do they even know we are here?"

"They know," Ivanth said with certainty.

His stomach was knotted up, but there was nothing left to it. He only had one option remaining that wasn't an outright betrayal of the empire.

"Signal the *Immortal*," Ivanth ordered. "We are withdrawing to the Hive."

"Commander?"

Ivanth ignored the incredulous tone, schooling his expression to hide the sickness he felt inside.

"You heard me. We are leaving."

"Yes, Commander."

▶ ▶ ▶

# PRIMINAE WARSHIP *POSDAN*

▶ CAPTAIN KIAN SLUMPED into her station, eyes still refusing to believe what her screens were showing her. Around her the bridge was similarly subdued, no one speaking as they all stared at the screens.

She wanted nothing more than to ask everyone if what she had seen had actually happened.

*From the looks of everyone else, they have the same question.*

"What do we do, Captain?"

*That is the question, isn't it?* Kian wondered to herself, eyes flicking between the screens as she tried to work out what had happened, never mind what they were to do about it. "Does anyone have anything on their screens that looks like any enemy ships survived?"

"No, Captain. The area is clear."

"What of the non-Drasin contacts? Were they in the system?"

"Unknown."

*Unknown. That means they weren't. We'd have detected them if they were there. We had every system on the ships scanning those Drasin ships.*

She sighed, grimacing, but made a choice. "Go to full power on all scanners. They're probably hiding out here somewhere. Find them."

"Yes, Captain."

"And prepare to transmit a message to the *Odyssey*," she said. "It's somewhat late, but we may as well offer our greetings and share what we've been able to tell from tracking these ships."

Her crew went to work, leaving her to compose the message that she would send. She didn't have to think about it too hard. She supposed it would just be a bare greeting unless they found the unidentified ships they had been tracking. Kian figured that it would be prudent to enter the Terran system.

She knew that they wanted to keep the knowledge of their star's location hidden, but it was quite clear that was a lost cause, so she hoped that they weren't too put out by a pair of Priminae warships paying a short visit.

*It's not like they have any cause to fear us, not if they can do that to a Drasin flotilla.*

▶ ▶ ▶

▶ "ALL TARGETS CONFIRMED eliminated, Captain."

"Compile the observed data with the computer predictions," Eric said, walking across the bridge to glance over Winger's shoulder. "I want to know everything that didn't go according to computer predictions and why. Some of those ships took as many as three or even four shots to get a coherent shell on target. The more we can tighten that number, the better. We don't have unlimited munitions for the big guns."

"Aye, sir. I'll get it done," she said, frowning as a signal chimed on her station.

"Something, Lieutenant?"

"Yes, sir." Winger nodded. "It looks like a pair of ships just went active in the outer system. They must have been coming in fast from the look of their orbital trajectory."

"Our mystery trigger men?" Eric asked, now leaning over her shoulder to get a better look.

"Hard to say, sir." she admitted, running the signals through her systems with a practiced hand. "It matches Priminae signals so far."

"We've seen a lot of that out of them."

"Yes sir. Hang on…incoming transmission," Michelle said. "It's modulated…compatible with our systems, directional, and in the clear…It's the *Posdan*, sir."

Eric straightened up, surprised by the revelation.

He supposed that he shouldn't be, though. They were tracking the alien ships just as the *Odyssey* had been tracking the *Weifang*.

*All roads lead to Rome.*

"Open a channel, same signal encoding."

"Channel opened, sir."

"Captain Kian, I and the crew of the *Odyssey* welcome you to Earth," Eric said. "Please feel free to enter the system. We promise safe passage and hope you enjoy the visit."

Michelle keyed a command in and nodded, "Encoded and sent, Captain."

"Good. Let me know if they answer or head our way," Eric said. "But in the meantime, get the data on the battle run through the computer. We need it done yesterday."

"Aye, aye, sir."

# CHAPTER SEVENTEEN

## Earth Orbit

▶ THE TWO GIANT Priminae vessels resting in high orbit practically eclipsed the space station they were pacing, providing ample evidence to anyone with even basic observational capability from the surface that something dramatic had changed in the history of the planet. Most people even remotely in the know were already aware of that; the *Odyssey*'s battle in the outer system hadn't been something on which even the Confederate government could put a total hush.

The Block certainly had records of the battle as well, something that was giving high-rank brass across the Confederacy migraines. The transition cannons weren't something they wanted outed quite so quickly, or so spectacularly, and it was only a matter of time before the Block started making diplomatic noises about the Confederacy developing "super weapons."

Granted, that selfsame "super weapon" had just saved the entire planet, so they could rattle their sabers all they liked. It wouldn't be able to shake the Confederacy's position anytime soon. Eventually, if they survived the coming war—well, that might be problematic.

That was an issue for another day, however.

The Russians almost certainly had records of the battle as well, along with a half a handful of non-aligned nations and private enterprises. Then there were the British and European nations with their own birds in the skies.

No, it wasn't a secret that anyone could keep.

So the Confederate government basically decided it was time to blow the lid completely off the entire situation.

▶ ▶ ▶

Eric Weston grimaced when he saw the gathered members of the press corps, really wishing he'd stayed on the *Odyssey*. The last thing he needed was to deal with any of those particular vultures, but it looked like he wasn't going to have much choice.

The *Odyssey*'s last action was even now being played on screens across the entire planet, along with recordings from her first and second missions. The danger of the Drasin wasn't being downplayed anymore. The government was, if anything, laying it on a little thick. He just hoped that they knew what the hell they were doing. A panic wouldn't serve anyone except for the enemy, and the enemy had enough advantages already.

Of course it wasn't like any of it was a huge secret or ever had been, in all reality. While many details of the *Odyssey*'s previous two missions had been classified, the general gist of them had been impossible to keep under wraps given the arrival of the temporary ambassador and his team from Ranquil. Most people had an idea of what was going on out there in the black. It just hadn't penetrated that it might be able to reach out and touch them in turn.

Eric knew he'd have to wade through the mass of reporters soon enough, but luckily no one was expecting him to give interviews just yet. After the war was over, assuming he and the Earth survived, then he'd be tossed to the dogs that were the press corps. But for now the military would shield him from that much at least.

Admiral Gracen, on the other hand, wasn't quite so lucky.

She was at the center of the maelstrom, cool and composed as she picked out one reporter after another and either answered their questions or shut them down with a simple "no comment."

*Oh, god. There's Lynn. God, I hate that woman.*

He had to school his face to an impassive expression as he noted in the crowd the Block reporter, a woman with whom he had some personal history. She was one of the few people on Earth whom he honestly couldn't stand and quite possibly feared just a little. He could deal with a martial threat. That sort of thing didn't bother him, in all honesty. When it came to soldiers, they might try to kill him, but at least he had a chance to return the favor.

Lynn Mei wasn't a soldier, but she was someone who'd damned near killed him in the past, and Eric knew she would have no compunctions whatsoever about doing it again in the future. The problem was she'd do it by releasing intelligence through her news sources, all nice and legal like.

*Give me an enemy I can drop a hundred pounder on any day of the week.*

He glanced to one side, eyes slipping to where Captain Kian and her small entourage were standing.

The Priminae captain had assented to putting in an appearance at the press conference, but no one thought it a great idea to let the jackals loose on her or anyone from the colonies at this point. It had been fairly clear that there was nothing resembling the news services of Earth back on Ranquil.

It wasn't that they didn't have news services, it was just that from what Eric had been able to tell, they really were just pure informational dissemination services. Rather dry, pretty dull for the most part, and certainly not like the norm on Earth where "if it bleeds, it leads."

He supposed that some things probably shouldn't be run to make a profit, and news was one of them.

Of course, there weren't too many people who'd run an honest news service at a loss aside from the government and, as loyal as Eric was to the Confederacy, even he could see the problems with letting the government run the news services.

It was just another example of a choice between two evils, he supposed—in this case, a corrupt sensationalist news service and a corrupt government mouthpiece. Honestly, there probably wasn't a lot of difference between them.

*Sounds like the last elections, if you ask me.*

He caught Kian's eye as she squirmed slightly under all the attention and tried to convey a sympathetic expression. Eric couldn't be sure it worked; while some elements of body language were shared between the Priminae and Terran humans, there were a lot of things that were not. Still, she smiled weakly in his direction and seemed to settle down.

He'd take that for a win.

▶▶▶

Captain Kian had felt more comfortable when engaged in combat against the Drasin. The stares were bad enough, but there was something in the eyes of the people carrying those…microphones? Whatever. The gleam in their eyes was downright disturbing. She did her best to ignore it all, trying to match the calm and impassive nature she could see in Captain Weston and his crewmembers across the way from here.

They appeared to treat the situation as a mild annoyance to be endured, something that happened as a matter of the course and not to be overly worried about. She wasn't sure that she or hers could quite pull that off, but they would do their best or she'd know why.

The whole ritual seemed a little bit excessive for what she was told it accomplished.

Certainly, she wasn't questioning that Terran citizens needed to know what was going on, but there were dozens of people here asking questions, and even more recording devices. Wouldn't it just be simpler to make the appropriate military reports available to the public and let those who wished to review the information seek it out on their own?

*Cultural differences, the Elders said. I've seen cultural differences. This is a completely new level.*

She decided to ask Captain Weston about it later, preferably when things were quieter, and for the moment just tried to put it all out of her mind.

*If only that were as easily accomplished as spoken.*

▶▶▶

Eric sighed, mostly in relief, as he and the others filed out of the conference room. Even when all that was required was that they stand there and look like military, he still couldn't stand press conferences. Most of his attending crew looked about the same as he felt, which was still better than those of the *Posdan* who had attended.

Eric excused himself from the group and made his way over to where Captain Kian was standing with, what he presumed to be, her senior crew. The Priminae captain was tall, probably a little over six feet. It wasn't extreme for a woman, but it was certainly in the high averages in his experience. He wasn't certain how it stacked up in the Priminae colonies; the few women he'd had time to get to know there were of decidedly slighter build.

Milla Chans was the first non-terran human they'd met, having picked her up in an emergency pod almost literally in the middle of nowhere. For him that sort of made her the standard by which he viewed the rest, which probably wasn't fair to them. Eric smiled slightly to himself as he considered that and more.

*She has a similar look to Milla, though, around the eyes and cheeks. I wonder...racial link, familial?*

Most of the Priminae he'd encountered were light skinned, though fairly obviously not of Caucasian descent. Their features varied from that norm, but he hadn't yet spotted a real solid pattern in their looks that he would define as "Priminae." He figured that their skin color just meant that they hadn't spent the last few thousand years working out in the hot sun where they could evolve and select for a darker pigment to protect against ultraviolet radiation. Honestly, it wasn't something he'd been bothered to look up. He was sure that someone, somewhere in the bowels of the Confederation's research bureaucracy was interested, but it wasn't in his purview.

Kian, for her part, had features he would normally associate with people of Asian descent, mostly around the hair and eyes. Her chin and cheekbones looked maybe more European, but her eyes were lighter than he could recall seeing on Terrans. The rest was fairly unique, her bones a little more solid than he'd expect for her height. It gave the woman a strong appearance at odds with her stature and the refinement of her features. All in all, an attractive look.

"Captain," she said, nodding to him as he approached.

"Captain."

They smiled slightly, sharing the very mild humor of the moment, then Eric went on. "Thank you for attending. I know you're not used to our news and press corps as a rule."

"It's certainly…different," she acknowledged. "However, I understood that having representatives of the Priminae there could be helpful."

"It was, I promise you," Eric said seriously. "Right now, more than anything, we need to get everyone moving in the same direction if we want to survive what's coming."

Kian nodded. "Understandable. The colonies took time to move as one as well. We lost many smaller worlds before it became clear that this was not a false call."

"We don't have any smaller worlds to lose," Eric said grimly, "so I'm hoping that we don't take as long to get our act together either."

"With the new weapon you showed in the last battle, you could certainly hold off any number of Drasin," Kian said, confused. "What worries do you have?"

"For one, we're pretty sure that the enemy really does have literally *any* number of ships to throw at us," he said. "You can swamp almost any defense with enough numbers, and they've got them. That little show earlier almost guarantees that Earth is now a high priority target to be watched, at the very least. I'm hoping that we managed to shock a little caution into the trigger men, but I'm not really liking our odds."

Kian looked surprised. "You do not believe that such a display will frighten those you think are behind the attacks?"

Eric shook his head. "No. No, I don't."

"I confess, I'm one of those who are…unconvinced by your theory. The Drasin are too entrenched in legend for me to easily believe them controlled by others," she said. "But I've seen the ships with my own scanners. I know they exist…Why do you not believe that they would be cautioned by what you accomplished?"

Eric let out a deep breath, considering his words as they walked through the corridors of Liberty Station.

"Do you know much of drone warfare, Captain?" he asked, finally.

"No. What is it?"

"It's the use of machines to wage war," he said. "Not weapons, but automated machines that are controlled to some degree from a distance. You don't have to risk a soldier's life. You just send in a robot to do the job."

"It makes sense," she said, "though the colonies don't use such things in warfare. We do, however, for other dangerous endeavors. Mining, rescue operations, and similar situations."

"We do as well," Eric confirmed, "but drone warfare is outlawed on Earth, under international treaty."

Kian paused, clearly confused. "But why?"

"Because you don't need to risk lives," Eric said with a shrug. "It's counterintuitive, but when you see people through a computer display, they stop being people and start being numbers. You…do things to numbers that no sane or moral person would ever do to people. Last century, my own country did things that should never have happened."

Eric closed his eyes, shaking his head slightly to push the images back. "Another thing that drone warfare does, though, is that it makes the people controlling them feel... safe. Untouchable. Invincible. If you lose a drone, who cares? No, the people behind this, they're engaging in drone warfare writ large. They're not going to be stopped just because we popped a few of their toys. They'll keep coming until we start popping *them*."

History was one of the things that Eric studied, both professionally and personally. He was an advocate of the expression that one must learn from history or be doomed to repeat it, though in his less optimistic moments he felt that if one did learn from history then you were doomed to watch *others* repeat it. Humanity, honestly, did very little that didn't disappoint him as a whole.

Thankfully, there were plenty of people within the morass that made up for the rest.

On Earth, the United States didn't shake itself loose of the cultural insanity of the so-called "war on terror" until drone technology became both cheap and ubiquitous enough that everyone had them. When your enemies could just as easily drop guided weapons on your head as you could on theirs, it was time to perhaps rethink your position.

That still left over three decades of cultural shame to overcome, in which the government ignored its own laws and even went so far as to assassinate its own citizens on the suspicion of what they *might* do at some point in the future. Eric still shivered at that. It was one thing to take someone out who was a clear and present threat. That was a righteous shoot to his mind, but if they weren't a clear threat to someone or something he had a right to protect, then they were the problem of the police and not himself or his comrades.

He very much feared a culture that was treading that path while using drones that were flying and walking weapons of mass destruction like the Drasin. There was no mercy in a drone and a detached sense of humanity in its controller.

"So no," he said again, "I'm very much afraid that they won't be impressed at all by our little display, Captain."

He considered for a moment, then continued, "Or at least not impressed in the right way."

▶▶▶

# IMPERIAL DESTROYER *DEMIGOD,*
# APPROACHING HIVE

▶ AS THE SHIP approached the Hive facility, Ivanth felt both apprehension and anger driving his every action. He'd spent the entire journey poring over the scanner records, trying to comprehend what the hell had transpired but, other than some unusual trans-light signals that were likely targeting beams, there was *nothing* there to explain what happened.

He'd lost an entire flotilla of second-generation drone ships. Literally the only thing he could have done worse would be to have allowed his own ships to be caught in the trap the enemy had lain, but had he done that at least he wouldn't have to answer for it. Without even an explanation for how the enemy had pulled off their action, he had little doubt that his position in the Force was essentially forfeit.

*If I am very much lucky, I may be demoted and shipped off to some back-gravity sector where the rest of my career will be spent checking up on traffic to systems about which no one gives the abyss.*

His thoughts had been running around those lines for every moment of the passage, and he only wished that he had many more of those moments left. Unfortunately, the gravity scanners had picked up the Hive a long ways back and they now had it solidly on thermals.

"Commander…."

Ivanth looked up, weary and wary. "What is it?"

"We've not been challenged, but we're within actual time range of the Hive."

Ivanth leaned forward, scowling. "Are you certain?"

The look he got in return probably qualified as scathing, though it was well disguised. Honestly, while Ivanth would normally have brought an officer up on charges for looking at him like that, he supposed that he probably deserved it.

"Yes, Commander. I am certain."

*I am clearly too tired to be seated in this place if I am asking questions like that.*

The ship would have registered the challenge automatically. It was impossible to have missed it. Ivanth rubbed the side of his face, biting back a comment that would probably make things worse.

"Fine. Is there anything odd on the scanners?"

"No, Commander."

Ivanth frowned, now mostly puzzled rather than truly aggravated.

Security wasn't as firm here when compared to many other places in the empire as only the truly insane would ever try and enter the Hive. Until the unknown ship had escaped, he'd have sworn it was a one-way trip. That said, when a ship was detected on approach, it was challenged. That was the protocol for any Imperial ship or base at the very lowest end of security.

Were his ships approached in open space, he would issue a challenge. The fact that none had been received was more than enough to stand the hairs on the back of his neck up on end.

*The only way that would happen would be if the Prohuer and the remaining ships of the squadron had left the Hive. There were no missions on the schedule, however. We were still plotting the strategy for Ranquil's conquest. Where would he be?*

"How long until we penetrate the outer swarm?" he asked, his voice now tense with more than his own worries.

"Shortly. Can't be certain without using active sensors. The swarm is well shielded from all but thermal. Should I?"

"No. No, do not engage active scanners," he ordered, feeling silly as he did.

*Nothing could happen here. It's the Hive. There isn't a force in the galaxy that could eliminate this many of the Drasin...not even third-generation and later drones. There just isn't.*

Moments passed, stretching almost into eternity, while on the screens the thermal vision of the approaching swarm loomed larger and larger until they abruptly slipped through the cracks and into the outer Hive. Ivanth checked the sensors, mouth dry as he began to imagine what a fleet of those unknown starships could do.

*We've only seen one, but who builds only one warship? There must be others.*

The *Demigod* and the *Immortal* continued on their approach, sliding through the outer Hive in silence, not even sending updates to each other by unspoken assent. Something was wrong, Ivanth could feel it, and he had little doubt that most everyone with basic access to the scanners of the two ships could now feel it.

*Did they come around while we were distracted in that system? Was it just a feint to pull us away from the Hive?*

On the surface of it, that was an absurd thought. The *Immortal* and the *Demigod* were powerful ships and with their drone flotilla could shake entire star systems to their foundations but, compared to the force in the Hive, they were nothing but children playing in a puddle.

The sheer numbers at the Hive were all but insurmountable by any force short of a full Imperial Battlegroup, and even a force as powerful as that would more likely as not never see its home port again.

"Piercing the inner swarm, Commander."

"Give me a visual of the surrounding area," he ordered.

"Yes, Commander."

The inside of the Hive appeared largely as it had when he had left to join the *Demigod*, which didn't surprise him. It took a lot to change a facility that existed on the scale of the Hive. Even the drones couldn't do it in the short span he'd been away. It would take firepower the likes of which simply didn't exist to damage it significantly. Really the only threat to the Hive was the star at its core, and since that was precisely where it was supposed to be, he could discount the possibility of a nova having killed everyone.

"Any communications?"

"No, Commander. Silence on all frequencies."

Ivanth shuddered lightly, quickly getting a hold of his involuntary impulses. He examined the signals for a long moment before coming to a decision.

"Send a challenge, wide band, including trans-light."

"Commander?"

"Challenge the Hive," Ivanth ordered.

"Uh…yes, Commander."

The signal went out from the *Demigod* and was instantly responded to by the *Immortal*'s computers. But long moments went by, turning into longer and longer moments with no response. Ivanth waited, and waited, and then waited more.

"Nothing. No drone response, no response from the Prohuer's task force. Nothing," Ivanth hissed, now admitting that his nerves were well and truly frayed. The entire spectrum was quiet, and it shouldn't be. Even without the Prohuer's task force in the area, assuming that wasn't trouble enough, there should be incessant chatter across all the drone frequencies. But there wasn't.

The two ships sailed past the inner swarm, scanners still on maximum passive as the systems deeply drank all radiation spectrums and tried to put an image together of the situation. The interior of the Hive looked exactly as it should—the star blazing at its center and the loose shields of the inner and outer swarms visible in the reflected light and radiation.

*And yet it's too quiet.*

"Interlink our scanners and computers with the *Immortal,*" Ivanth ordered. "Begin a complete system scan, full active spectrum scanners."

"Yes, Commander."

*What happened here?*

# CHAPTER EIGHTEEN

## Station Liberty

▶ "REPORTS ON YOUR desk, Admiral."

Gracen nodded, waving her thanks to the aide as she walked across to her desk. The smoked glass surface was clean as always, waiting for her presence. She took a seat and waved her hand over the desktop, causing it to blink to life.

The notification list, including the reports she was waiting for, lit up on the screen. She quickly brought it up and went straight to the manufacturing reports for the new one-hundred-centimeter thermal nuclear shells.

*Not as bad as I might have hoped, but at least the production has started and we'll receive shipments within a week. I just hope it'll be enough.*

She turned in her chair, eyes falling on the wall display that showed the N.A.C.S. *Enterprise* where the big ship was already undergoing a pressing refit. They didn't know how long they had, but while there was time, it was the Confederacy's goal to arm all of their mobile units with the transition-based weaponry.

For all current intents and purposes, that really only meant the *Enterprise, Odyssey,* and of course Liberty Station.

The *Valley Forge* was still little more than a space frame in construction, and similarly they had yet to lay keels for the next three ships planned.

The Confederacy just didn't have the yards to build starships in significant numbers. It hadn't been in the budget until the *Odyssey* brought back the news it had, and had still been debated for some time after. She rather suspected that the funding was about to be increased significantly.

*Let's just hope that it isn't too little, too late.*

Space yards were big business, however, and while government slips were the only ones large enough to build true starships, there were smaller commercial facilities available. They'd begun the process of appropriating those, converting them over to military production. It was a stopgap move, one that she wasn't certain was worth diverting available resources.

The new Marauder class ships were capable enough, she supposed, for tin cans limited to the solar system. They certainly packed enough offensive armament to make them a threat even to ships the like of the *Odyssey* or the *Enterprise,* but their defensive capacity worried her. Even with the third-generation CamPlate modifications, their armor was dangerously thin.

The lasers used by the Drasin were powerful enough that even a fraction of their heat could vaporize thin sections of armor, leaving a ship in dire straits if they didn't have some thickness there to lean on. The *Odyssey* and the *Enterprise* had armor forged in space, feet thick in places and nanomolecular bonded all the way through with the CamPlate modifications. They could literally lose a foot of armor and shrug it off like nothing had happened. The new Marauders couldn't hope to match that.

There was currently a debate about putting automated controls in them to use the class as a form of shock troops, their own answer to the Drasin, she supposed. It was hotly debated, but aside from the legal implications of releasing armed drones in the Sol System and the international nightmare that would cause, there were some practical limitations that made it unlikely to happen in her eyes.

The speed of light was the biggest hurdle. In combat, even a second's delay in receiving sensor data, or a command, could be fatal. While the ships might be automated, they'd still be in damned short supply. They wouldn't be able to afford to waste even those smaller platforms if worse came to worst. Every pound of metal they had in space would have to count.

No, they would have to man the smaller ships, and with sizeable crews apiece. She didn't know if they would give nearly enough offensive punch to counter the risk they'd be asking those crews to assume.

*Hopefully Weston's little display will set our enemies back on their heels for a bit, and we'll have time to build a real fleet now that the political winds are blowing our way.*

She knew that the Block had also tripled their efforts in orbit, installing new slips in their own yard, and they actually had four keels laid and two superstructures almost finished. Their ships might not have the speed of the *Odyssey* or its new ability to reach out and touch their enemies, but the intelligence said that the *Weifang* and its sister ships were more than capable in their own right.

*Time. All we need is time.*

▶▶▶

# THE HIVE

## Imperial Destroyer *Demigod*

▶ "COMMANDER, WE'VE LOCATED…refuse."

Ivanth opened his eyes, turning to look in the direction of the speaker. He frowned slowly as he stood. "Refuse?"

"You should look at this, Commander."

Ivanth scowled, but walked over to the screens and took a look.

Refuse was indeed the term, he decided as he looked it over. Scrap metal mostly, nothing that looked familiar. The analysis showed metallic fragments and high quantities of silicates along with other materials that didn't match any signature he'd ever seen.

*Best be certain,* he supposed.

"Are there any matches in the central systems?"

"No, Commander. I checked multiple times. No one uses materials that match the analysis here. The Priminae don't use metals in their ships. Our ships use very different metallurgy, and the Drasin are silicon-based organics. Not even the minor cultures across the galaxy use anything that matches this."

"What about the unknown species?"

"No. We have scanner recordings of them and they use simple metallurgy, easy to match. This does not."

Ivanth grimaced. He didn't like this at all. The Hive was apparently empty, no signs of the *thousands* of drones that should be there. The Prohuer's task force, likewise gone. Those two things alone should be patently impossible. The logistics of organizing the departure of that many drone ships alone....

He shook his head. None of it made any sense.

"The Prohuer must have abandoned the facility, but...why?"

There was no answer to that, unfortunately, and the only person who could tell him was no longer in the star system. He had to locate the task force and get new instructions. With only two ships at his command, he was in grave danger should either the Priminae or the unknown species chance upon him.

OK, that was unlikely as such things went. But given how far away they were from Imperial support, it was still a very real concern.

Ivanth made a decision. "The *Immortal* is closer to slip five. Dispatch them to investigate there while we go to the primary slip."

"Yes, Commander."

The *Demigod* turned slowly as it began warping space, accelerating smoothly on its new course. They made quick time, pushing their drives to both accelerate and decelerate, and arrived shortly at their destination. It was the makeshift slip used by the Imperial ships when they needed to transfer cargo and personnel, do maintenance, and so forth.

The Hive was a very alien construct, built by the drones and their varying generations of sub-drones. It wasn't intended for occupation by any living species, if Ivanth were honest about it. The drones were a disgusting abomination, born and bred in some abyssal part of the universe that Ivanth hoped never to see, and they had no interest whatsoever in providing facilities for the use of mere humans or any other life form the Empire had on record.

Still, the Imperial engineers had been able to patch together a slip where they could get work done that was extremely difficult or impossible to do in open space. If there were a message or evidence of any kind connected to what had happened, that was where he may be able to find it.

▶▶▶

# CENTRAL COMMAND BUNKER, MONS SYSTEMA, RANQUIL

▶ "ADMIRAL."

Rael Tanner looked over from where he was working, eyes falling on the speaker. "What is it, Ithan?"

The Ithan swallowed visibly, which Tanner noted was never a good sign for his health.

He sighed. "What is it?"

"Trans-light signals, Admiral."

"Communications? Bowshock?" Tanner prompted.

The Ithan looked nervous. "Unknown."

*Alright, that's a sign that I should check this myself.* Tanner was genuinely curious now, Central had records of nearly every trans-light signal ever detected in well over ten-thousand years of observations. For them to find something truly new…it was a rarity. The last time, in fact, was when the *Odyssey* first arrived in the system.

He walked over to the main display for the scanner network, and it was immediately apparent what the young officer was talking about.

*That is the largest trans-light signal I have ever seen in my entire life.*

The signal looked to be an unbelievable number of arc-seconds wide, spanning at least fourteen of their long-range sensor pods.

"It almost looks like a bowshock wake," he said finally, "but a ship would have to be the size of a star system, or near enough, to make a wake like that."

"That's why we called you, Admiral. We don't know what to make of this," the Ithan admitted. "The closest signal match we were able to make was to a squadron, warping space at highest capacity."

"I've seen that signal," Tanner said dryly. "It is infinitesimally small compared to this. To make a signal like this in that way you would need…thousands…."

He trailed off, his mouth going dry. "Which post first detected it?"

"Post Fierra Two-Five-Nine, in Sector Nine-Eight-Three."

Tanner hissed. "That's one of the closest posts we have to the stellar construct the *Odyssey* reported."

"That's right, Admiral."

"What vector is the signal travelling along?" Tanner demanded, heart now racing. "What vector!"

"A-Admiral?" the Ithan stuttered, taking a step back.

"Are they on a vector for any of our worlds!?"

"N-no. The signal is moving deeper into the galactic arm, away from the colonies."

Tanner slumped, relieved. "Thank who, or whatever, is watching over us."

He took a few breaths, considering his actions, then nodded. "Track them, send warnings to all ships to avoid their path, and keep me apprised of the situation. I need to consult with Central."

"Uh…yes, Admiral."

Tanner turned and strode out of the command bunker.

▶▶▶

# IMPERIAL DESTROYER *DEMIGOD*, PRIMARY MAINTENANCE SLIP, THE HIVE

▶ "COMMANDER, WE'VE LOCATED an Imperial beacon inside the slip."

"Can you identify the source?"

The young officer nodded. "We located an incident recorder, Commander. It appears to be damaged, however."

"Bring it aboard."

Ivanth scowled quietly as the device was isolated and pulled into one of the *Demigod*'s cargo bays. He knew that it would take time to ensure that it was not somehow a risk to the ship or crew, but he barely had the patience to endure the wait. An incident recorder was designed to be ejected by an Imperial ship that was under threat of destruction, and was nearly indestructible.

For one to be damaged was a sign of a significant threat in the area, and the fact that the slip itself didn't appear to be damaged made things all the more confusing.

*What in the singular abyss could possibly have put an Imperial ship in danger of destruction, yet not left so much as a mark on the slip?*

There were few things in the galaxy capable of that. Almost nothing in fact.

"Sir! Distress call from the *Immortal*!"

Ivanth spun around, face somehow frozen and blazing all at once. "What did they say?"

"Nothing, Sir. It was just a pure noise signal over the distress bands."

"Get that recorder on the *Demigod*, NOW!" he thundered. "Reverse warp! Best speed!"

"Yes, Commander!"

The ship creaked slightly as the space-warping fields powered up, creating a high-pressure zone of gravity to the rear and a low-pressure one to the front of the ship. Unlike atmospheric effects, high-pressure gravity pulled on the ship while low-pressure pushed, so the *Demigod* began to fly out of the slip with a steady rate of acceleration.

As soon as the ship was clear, Ivanth brought up the feed from the scanners, disappointed to find that the *Immortal* still appeared peaceful and silent on passive scans. Disappointed, but not truly surprised. The distress frequency was a translight signal, so anything could have happened in the few minutes lag.

"Bring us about, and ready the ship to warp space-time on course to the *Immortal*!" Ivanth ordered. "Engage with all available power when prepared!"

▶ ▶ ▶

The ship swept around in the tight quarters of the Hive slabs, putting her nose toward the *Immortal*, and then creaked again as the tidal force of her own gravity generators stressed the metal deeply.

While under full warp, the danger to a ship wasn't the acceleration stress you might see in more commonly used reaction flight systems. Ships like the *Demigod* that used space-warp drives for propulsion were immune to acceleration effects because they were drawn into their course rather than pushed along it. Everything on the ship, every molecule and every atom, all accelerated evenly, so there was no impact of acceleration in the way a reaction mass vessel was impacted.

However, the powerful gravity fields did have a similar force that put stress on the ship in particular. Tidal effects could be felt in the superstructure of the ship, stressing the metal badly when under full power, because the parts of the vessel closer to the gravity well felt its pull more powerfully than those parts that were further away.

In extreme cases, this tidal effect could be disastrous, literally drawing out the molecular and atomic bonds in ways they were never intended to be drawn. Human scientists had given this effect the technical term of "spaghettification," which was a very descriptive and unfortunately accurate word.

The generators on a ship, even one as powerful as the *Demigod*, weren't remotely capable of matching the tidal force of a stellar singularity, of course. Spaghettification wasn't a risk ships like that endured, but the tidal force could, and most assuredly would, eventually stress the space frame of a starship to its breaking point.

Only in the most extreme cases, then, would a captain of a space-warping ship ever give the order to use all available power to the drives.

▶ ▶ ▶

The *Demigod* went from a standstill to just over light-speed in the blink of an eye, then was forced to reverse just as quickly as it reached its destination. The Doppler shift of light at those extreme accelerations was too much for even their advanced systems to handle, so for almost a second the ship was truly flying blind.

Deaf, however, they were not.

The emergency band was screaming, the *Immortal*'s transmitter pouring enough energy into it to completely blanket any attempt to send modulated signals to query the ship. They weren't answering or even transmitting on any other frequencies. That left the scratching whine the only sound on the bridge for almost a second while everyone held their breath and waited to see what was going to come.

At first, as the screens cleared, nothing seemed to be wrong. Ivanth glared openly, eyes on the display as he felt himself growing angry, both at himself and the captain of the *Immortal* for the waste of time. It was then, however, that he spotted movement on the hull of the Imperial destroyer and felt a cold chill wash through him.

"Magnify!"

The screen jumped, increasing the size of the ship ahead of them over a hundredfold, and in the resulting silence of the bridge, a single person swore a vile oath that almost had Ivanth snarl a reprimand in reply until he realized he was the one who had spoken.

The hull of the *Immortal* was *crawling* with drone soldiers.

"Wide scan, all active systems!" Ivanth snapped out of his stupor. "Defensive weapons clear to fire! All crew to combat positions!"

The last order was probably superfluous, he admitted to himself, but he issued it anyway. By this time, if there was anyone not at their combat positions, he'd eat his uniform. The seriousness of the situation went far beyond a few drone soldiers assaulting a ship of the Empire. The way the alien things were constructed, it was patently impossible for a few of them to go rogue.

The way one leaned, so leaned all of them.

*When they went rogue on us in the unknown species system, something must have happened here as well.*

He wasn't surprised by that. What shocked him to the core was that it was a long way from attacking a targeted species without orders to actually assaulting an Imperial vessel.

"Commander! We're surrounded!"

Ivanth's mind blanked for a moment, a surge of irrational terror running through him, then his training took over.

"To my displays!"

The data flickered over to his screens and he glanced over it as quickly as he could manage, trying not to swallow his tongue or something equally humiliating and fatal. They were indeed surrounded, but it appeared that it wasn't as bad as it seemed. There were literally thousands of soldier drones floating about in the area, but they were not capable of warping space time or maneuvering in space.

*We must have crushed dozens while decelerating into the area; otherwise they'd be on us as well.*

"Pin point bursts, take out the drones on the *Immortal!*" he ordered. "Keep tracking everything around us, full active scans! I don't care who sees us. I want to see *everything.*"

"Yes, commander!"

Pinpoint laser bursts began frying individual drone soldiers off the hull of the *Immortal* while the *Demigod* continued to track everything moving around their position. There were no signs of any drone ships, but that made little sense to Ivanth, and he couldn't quite buy into what he was seeing.

*There were thousands of combat capable ships, and literally millions of replicators. They can't all be gone. Where would they go?*

# CHAPTER NINETEEN

## Liberty Station, Earth Orbit

▶ CAPTAIN KIAN OF the *Posdan* paused when her comm tingled the skin just behind her ear. She took a step away from the group of Terrans she was with, excusing herself.

"Kian here," she said into the open channel. "What is it?"

"Signal from Ranquil, Captain," the voice of her second in command said, deadly serious in tone. "They've detected a trans-light signal in transit. Captain, it's massive."

Her blood chilled. "What do you mean, massive?"

"For us to match it would take over a thousand ships warping space-time at full strength."

Kian closed her eyes.

*That is massive.*

"Toward what planet are they headed?"

"Captain, they're headed here."

Kian almost jumped in place, eyes widening. "Is Command sure?"

"Command doesn't have a clue. I plotted the signals myself. We should detect the first signs of the trans-light effect within a few more hours."

"I…I see."

"We need orders, Captain."

Kian considered for a moment, and then set her jaw. "I'll contact you shortly. For now, I want the *Posdan* and the *Nept* surveyed from hull to core. Ensure that they are both prepared for action."

"Yes, Captain."

The channel closed and she glanced around the room, eyes falling on where Captain Weston was standing with some people she didn't know. The little "get together" was some sort of Terran tradition, a way for comrades to recognize and learn one another's habits, it had been explained to her. One nice effect of the gathering was that she didn't have to ask herself who she should tell. Kian set her expression and crossed the room with a purpose.

Eric saw her coming, his expression going from bored to moderately pleased and then to intense seriousness as he took in her own expression.

"Captain," he greeted her curtly as she arrived within a few feet of him. "Has something happened?"

Kian's eyes flickered to the captain's conversational companion and didn't recognize the man. She looked questioningly to Weston.

He smiled at her. "Captain Kian, this is Jefferey Wolfe, commodore and commander of our Mars facilities."

"Commodore," she said, probably too sharply for courtesy, but she had other concerns for the moment. "Captain, there is a...problem."

Eric nodded slowly. "Something we lowly captains can handle, or should we be talking higher?"

"Higher, Captain. Most assuredly, higher."

The Terran captain and commodore exchanged brief glances, communication passing between them that clearly spoke volumes, and then both nodded.

"Right. I'll get the admiral." Wolfe bowed slightly. "Eric, why don't you find us a quiet conference room?"

"Right you are, Commodore," Eric said simply, putting an arm around Kian as he gently guided her out of the room. "This way, Captain."

▶▶▶

Admiral Gracen needed a place to sit down.

No, actually she needed alcohol. Lots of it.

*Enough to give myself a permanent bed time,* she thought as she considered the words of the Priminae Captain.

The extent of the news wasn't lost on either of her officers, who were currently sharing her state of shock and horror. Thousands of Drasin ships weren't a nightmare. It was the end.

"We can't hold off a force like that," she said aloud, making it official. Words she didn't want to say, words none of them wanted to hear, but they were out there now, and there was no taking them back.

"But you destroyed so many, so quickly!" Kian protested. "Surely you might be able…."

"We don't have nearly enough munitions for something like this," Eric said, his position slumped where he was sitting. "What do we have on hand, Admiral? A couple hundred shells left?"

"A bit more than that," Gracen admitted. "Maybe three fifty. Might be able to scrounge another few dozen from the factory floors if they haven't run into any production problems. Say, four hundred shells if we're lucky."

"We averaged between two and three shells per ship earlier," Eric said tiredly. "So, let's be optimistic and say we can take out two hundred of them. That leaves, another what? Eighteen hundred left?"

Kian's face fell, though she barely understood the conversation. *Shells? What do animal carapaces have to do with weaponry?*

For all that, however, she got the general meanings. A few hundred Drasin ships, it was a monumental number. Her own people could just barely fight the things on even ground, and these people could destroy hundreds of them...but it wouldn't be enough. There was something horrifyingly unfair about that, something so very wrong.

She shuddered, but nodded. "The *Posdan* and the *Nept* will take on anyone you wish to have removed from the system, Admiral."

Gracen shot her a sharp look, but then nodded. "Thank you. I'll let you know."

Kian rose to her feet. "I should return to my ship and see to it that everything is in order. We will provide what help we can."

"Captain Kian," Gracen spoke up.

"Yes, Admiral?"

"Do not let your ships get pinned down," Gracen said evenly. "There's no point dying here for nothing."

Kian nodded slowly. "It will be as you say, Admiral. Contact me when you can. I will provide what help I may."

"Thank you."

After the Priminae captain had left, Gracen turned back to the two others in the room, her expression partway between severe and lost.

"I don't suppose either of you have any ideas here?"

"No, ma'am." Commodore Wolfe sounded pained to admit it.

She looked over to Eric, but he didn't respond. He was staring off into space, both literally and figuratively.

"Captain?" she prompted him. "Captain!"

Eric looked sharply in her direction. "Sorry, Admiral. What?"

"I asked if you had any ideas," she glowered.

"Maybe," he admitted, "but I need to talk to the Block captain in command of the *Weifang*."

"What will that do?" she asked. "They use reasonably effective weapons, but intelligence doesn't give them anything that will match up to the *Odyssey*'s armaments, particularly now that you have the transition cannons."

"It's an idea, Captain, but just that. I *need* to confirm it first."

Gracen grimaced, but nodded. "Do it. I have to inform the Pentagon."

"Yes, ma'am!" Eric saluted before turning and rushing from the room.

Gracen watched him go. "That man is going to give me ulcers, assuming I live long enough."

"Admiral, I know that he isn't exactly seen in the best light by the brass just now, all things considering," Wolfe said quietly, his expression serious, "but there's no one I'd rather lean on in a fight than Eric Weston."

"Fighting has never been his weak point, Commodore."

▶▶▶

Eric made his way through the corridors to where the Block maintained a small embassy section on Liberty. They didn't have a lot of people there, just as the Confederation didn't have all that many on the Block station held in a counter-orbit. When he reached the embassy area, though, he didn't approach close enough to trip any surveillance red flags, or so he hoped at least.

*The last thing I need is some Block security officer noting that Eric "Raziel" Weston is hanging outside their embassy.*

That said, he wasn't entirely without contacts in the Block government. After two minutes, Eric turned and left, heading for a quiet section of the station where he got a drink from the closest vendor and took a seat. It only took twenty minutes more before he was joined by a guest.

"You took a chance."

Eric smiled. "Every time I see you, I take my life in my hands. Good to have a chance to talk again, Jei."

Jei Fan, noted cameraman for Lynn Mei, snorted and took a seat opposite his old friend and sometimes enemy. "You ready to tell me what happened between you and Lynn yet? She's been looking to fry your ass since Beijing."

"Another day maybe. I need a favor."

"Since when do you not?" Jei asked, both amused and disgusted. "What is it this time?"

"The captain of the *Weifang*," Eric said. "I need to chat with him."

"Ask for something I can arrange," Jei snapped, clearly irritated. "Captain Sun is on his ship. You know the Block monitors all channels to and from their vessels."

Eric sighed. "This isn't for public dissemination, alright, Jei?"

The cameraman glanced around, then stared intensely at Eric for a long moment before finally nodding.

Eric hesitated slightly, considering the situation. Under some circumstances, and from many points of view, leaking information to the Block might be considered treason. Given that the Earth probably only had days left to *exist*, he was willing to take his chances.

"Our allies just received intelligence from the colonies," he said finally. "There's a fleet heading our way, and we're the only thing out there as far as anyone knows, so the Earth is likely the target."

Jei Fan wasn't just a cameraman, any more than Eric was just a pilot. He immediately recognized both the threat of what he was being told and the risks Eric was taking to tell him, and frowned thoughtfully for a moment.

"I'll have to inform my superiors, you know."

Eric nodded, knowing that he wasn't talking about the editors of his news channel. Jei was a longtime member of the Block's Intelligence Division. "They'll figure it out in a day or so at the latest anyway, so give them the heads up. Just don't let it slip that it came from me."

"I understand. Why do you want to speak with Sun?"

"I need the *Weifang.*"

Jei choked on his drink, coughing desperately to clear his airways.

"You what?" he managed to gasp out, staring incredulously at Eric.

"When we were engaging the Drasin the first time," Eric said, "I noticed something in the drive system they use, something I knew about in theory but never saw before in practice. The *Weifang* uses the same basic system. I think we can use her to help even the odds."

Jei shook his head. "This is too much, Eric. Maybe I can get you in contact with Captain Sun, but the Block will never allow him to take the *Weifang* out. Not in its current state, and not after the disaster he brought back on us the last time."

"The disaster is only just starting, Jei," Eric said gently, taking a sip of his drink. "And, while it pains me to say it, all Sun did was speed things up a little. This day was always coming."

"Since you alerted those things of our presence, you mean."

"No, since always." Eric put his glass down, glowering at his friend. "Trust me on this. I don't know who's pulling the trigger on these things, but they clearly don't give a damn about life or anything you and I would consider moral. It may have taken longer, but sooner or later they were going to come for us. They're here now, so I'm going to ask you, do we hang together…or do we hang separately?"

The security man for the Block government bureaucracy scowled back for a long moment, and then made a disgusted sound.

"I can get you in touch with Sun. What you two conspire after that is on your heads," he said as he got up and walked away, leaving his drink behind.

Eric watched him go, taking another long sip of his drink as he considered the parting words.

"Wouldn't have it any other way."

▶▶▶

Sun was far from a happy man.

He was still, in title at least, the captain of the *Weifang*, but he didn't expect that to last for much longer if, indeed, it lasted past this current summons.

He was puzzled why he would be called onto the Confederation station by the BID, but he'd been expecting such a call for some time now. He actually had expected to be summoned back to Earth directly, so the current situation was a little confusing.

He had reported in as ordered and was deposited in a secure room, nothing but bare walls and a folding chair in front of a plastic desk. So he sat there and waited, and waited, and then waited some more. Probably close to an hour later, though he couldn't say for sure since he didn't have any of his personal kit and there wasn't a clock in the room, the door finally opened.

"Ah, Captain Sun," the man said, standing in the doorway. "I expect that you're wondering why you've been brought here to Liberty?"

The man only slightly sneered at the name of the space station, which was an interesting affectation, Sun thought. That said, he simply nodded. "Yes, sir."

"Yes, well, it was a clerical error, I'm afraid," the man said, smiling blandly. "You're free to go."

Sun blinked.

*He must be joking.*

Sun got slowly to his feet, not taking his eyes off the man, still expecting *something* to happen. He made his way to the door and the man stepped back and to the side, letting him pass. As he walked by, however, the man laid a hand on his shoulder and Sun flinched. He was loyal to his government, but the Block could be an unforgiving taskmaster during the best of times.

"While you're here on Liberty, I really do suggest a meal on the observation deck," the man said with a disturbing smile. "The view is spectacular, and I think you may be interested in the *company.*"

Sun paused, hearing the emphasis on the word "company" and glanced uncertainly at the man. He just got that same bland smile in return, causing him to nod slowly. "Yes, sir. Thank you for the suggestion."

"It's nothing. Please, accept my apologies for your inconvenience."

Sun shook his head. "As you said, it's nothing."

He wasn't going to start mouthing off to someone he was reasonably certain belonged to the state intelligence agency. *I'm in enough trouble already.*

He was still somewhat surprised, however, to find himself led out of the embassy and sent on his way with little more than a proverbial pat on the back.

*Or the bottom,* Sun thought with some annoyance at the patronizing nature of his "meeting."

Outside the embassy area, he paused in the corridor, undecided as he glanced back along the route he had taken from the shuttle and then to a sign that proclaimed "you are *here*," offering directions to wherever he might wish to go on the station.

*I can hardly get myself any deeper in the pits, I suppose.*

Sun sighed, making his way to the sign and taking note of the directions. The observation bubble was a few decks below the embassy, presumably to provide unrestricted views of the Earth below. He considered it for a moment, then resolutely made his way toward the elevators that would take him there.

▶▶▶

Eric watched the Chinese captain when he walked into the large room, noting with some amusement the uncertainty in the man's expression and body language. He knew from personal experience that Jei wasn't likely to have told the man a damned thing about what he was here for; that wasn't the Intelligence man's style. It was better tradecraft to leave Sun flapping in the wind. It would keep him from being able to provide any solid testimony, should things go badly.

Jei Fan wasn't a traitor to the Block, any more than Eric was a traitor to the Confederacy. Both men had learned a

long time earlier, however, that sometimes a little back channel into the enemy camp was useful in keeping either side
from doing something incredibly stupid. Mostly it meant that
they'd do small favors for each other, and sometimes even try
to sneak a larger one by if the other didn't seem to be paying
attention. It was all a big game, something that Eric personally
despised about the Intelligence services.

He'd done his time in the CIA, though, after his second
tour in the Marines. The Company had needed a pilot for
high-risk missions, and he'd needed something to do that
didn't involve sitting at home on the couch watching the
world descend into the pits of hell. Eric hadn't much liked
his time with the Company, though if he were honest with
himself, he had loved the work.

He'd gotten to fly an air vehicle that literally didn't exist,
according to popular belief, Pulse Jet Reconnaissance craft
that put out an acceleration so powerful there were permanent imprints of his spine on the ejection seat. Another time
he'd gotten to take a tour of the Pacific in a stealth craft that
resembled nothing quite so perfectly as something out of a
billionaire crime fighter's personal tool box. Hell, he'd made
it into the Archangel program as a direct result of his experience flying for the Company and the mission he'd run in
China to "acquire" their early CM prototype.

No, he had loved the work. He just hated the company.
And the Company.

Spies were best described as whiny little bitches at the
best of times, and that was when they were working. When
they weren't, they were the dullest people he'd ever met, and
Eric had no desire to ever meet another, if he could avoid
it. The movie heroics of master spies like James Bond may
have once been based in reality, but in the world of electronic

intelligence, the average master spy was somehow less cool than a teenage computer cracker, although the spy did have better personal hygiene. *Usually.*

He watched the Chinese captain order a light meal and a drink, letting the man find a table and get a decent ways into his meal before approaching. He pushed his acting ability to the limit, pretending to "notice" the man from across the room, and openly stared at him for a while with a puzzled look on his face.

Finally, Eric got up and carried his drink with him over to the seat that Sun Ang Wen had chosen, catching the man's attention with a gesture to the empty seat across from him.

"May I?"

The Chinese captain eyed him warily, and Eric saw the recognition filter through quickly. He wasn't surprised to be recognized. His positions had been very public since his time with the Company, and that was before he took over the *Odyssey* and made contact with actual aliens. *A certain definition of alien, of course.*

"Please," Sun said in very lightly accented English.

Eric sat down. "Captain Sun Ang Wen, am I right?"

Sun nodded warily, eyes flicking around the room. Eric smiled, knowing that he was looking for any sign of the person he had actually been set up to meet. The last person any Block captain would expect a BID Agent to put him up with would be Eric "Raziel" Weston, not after the Archangels' last mission into Chinese territory just before the end of the war.

*I think we're still wanted on warrants there for "war crimes,"* Eric mused.

That had been an ugly mission, a military base working on biological weapons, situated right in the middle of Beijing. The Company had flipped a Chinese national with security clearance and gotten a strike team into the facility with the intent to take it out clean, but they'd been burned before they got the job done.

Just not before they got out a download of what the facility had been working on, however.

The thoughts of what those weapons might have done still gave him chills, but the job itself had been damned near as bad. There was no way to make it clean; that option had been burned when the Operator team was executed on site as spies. That was the official story from the Block, anyway. The radio reports from the incident made it clear that the team had given better than they'd taken, and fought to the last man.

The order came down then that the facility had to be eliminated, and it had to be done fast. They couldn't give the Chinese time to move the facility, or even any of the projects, and while the U.S. Marines Corps were well known for being the people to call if you absolutely, positively wanted something destroyed overnight…when it had to be taken out in an hour or your money back, you called the Archangels.

The mission hadn't been pretty at all. They'd used Thermite penetrators to drop smart weapons right into the labs, incinerating everything inside in a flash fry that had the side effect of lighting several nearby factories up at the same time. Actual body count was unknown, but despite it being after dark, it was probably pretty bad since the Block had their factories running day and night at that time.

Suffice to say, Eric wasn't welcome in Bejing any longer.

"Captain Weston," Sun said, nodding surprisingly politely. "I'm surprised to see you away from the *Odyssey*."

"Aw, she'll be fine without me for a while," Eric said, smiling.

Sun looked momentarily confused, and Eric recalled that the Chinese didn't have a tradition of assigning a gender to their ships.

"Ah, yes, I'm sure that she will be," Sun said, his expression a little perplexed but gently amused. "I merely expected that you would be busy after the battle."

Eric nodded, though he wouldn't call it much of a battle. Aside from the initial skirmish, it had been a slaughter.

"Yes, well, that's what I wanted to talk to you about."

Sun's eyes shifted, widening and hardening at the same time, as he realized that just maybe he was meeting with the person he had been set up to see. "I'm sorry, but I do not believe that would be appropriate."

"Your government will have been…quietly notified of what I'm going to tell you already, but it'll be public within a day or so," Eric said. "Still, it isn't something we want spreading around until we can't keep a cover on things anymore. The Drasin are coming, Captain. They'll be here within two days at our best guess."

Sun straightened up, his entire manner becoming more alert. "Why would you come to me with this?"

"Because I need your help," Eric said candidly. "At least, I think I do."

"I do not understand."

"We don't have hard numbers yet, but the current estimate is that they're coming in force," Eric said. "More ships than we have munitions to combat."

Sun stared, his expression saying it all. Horror, guilt, shock. Eric didn't have to read his mind to know what he was thinking, and honestly he wasn't above using it to manipulate the man a little. He'd rather prefer not to, but if he had to… he'd lose sleep over it later.

Sun dropped his eyes, staring at the tabletop for a long moment. "I don't know what I can do to help."

Eric sighed. "Well, honestly, I think I owe you an apology, Captain."

"I...do not understand," Sun said again, this time even more confused.

"We were tracking you," Eric said. "You were in FTL and we couldn't contact you to tell you that you were being followed, so I ordered a strike against your ship."

Sun gaped. What the man across from him was admitting to was tantamount to a declaration of war. Then he considered it and his face fell. "I wish that you had been successful, Captain. We should not have come home."

Eric shrugged, as he'd figured that this day was coming anyway. Maybe not quite as soon, but it was almost a certainty that the trigger men out there wanted the *Odyssey* destroyed—and whatever species deployed her—out of the way. Sooner or later they were going to find the Earth, and they just didn't seem like the talking and negotiating sort to him.

He wasn't going to tell Sun that, however, because he needed the man to *want* to help him.

"I was hoping to get your attention," Eric admitted, "so we only engaged with conventional weapons, but your ship didn't even seem to notice."

"It is the bending of space," Sun said. "Very difficult to penetrate while at full power."

"Apparently." Eric sighed visibly. "When you passed us, we engaged the Drasin coming up behind you with pulse weapons. You're familiar with them?"

Sun nodded without thinking, effectively admitting to knowing a fair bit more about Confederate technology than was publically available. Eric only smiled slightly, and continued.

"The antimatter pellets blew out their warp," he said, "dropping them from FTL in a crash we've never seen before. If I'd known that it would do that, I would have taken your ship out of warp the same way."

Sun nodded, his expression fascinated. "So you can disable a ship moving past light speed?"

"So it would seem," Eric said. "What interested me, however, was that when they crashed from FTL, we saw them unleash a burst of energy and high-energy particles."

Sun sat back, nodding slowly. "Ah. Yes, your assault must have blown out their compensation system. It would have released many very dangerous particles into space, Captain."

"That's an understatement," Eric leaned in. "I saw at least two of the Drasin incinerated by their own allies' drives. I need to know something...."

Sun's eyes narrowed, his face closing up. "What?"

"Can you do it intentionally with your ship?"

# CHAPTER TWENTY

## P.L.A.S.F. *Weifang*

▶ CAPTAIN SUN ANG Wen had returned to the *Weifang* after a personally confusing and conflicting conversation with his opposing number from the Confederation. He was surprised, actually, as the captain of the *Odyssey* didn't match up with his reputation in China and other Block nations.

That probably shouldn't have been as surprising as it seemed, he supposed. He already knew that national propaganda had a tendency to exaggerate certain things. He'd seen some of the ludicrous material put out by the West concerning the war, and deep down he knew that his own government was hardly any better.

Weston seemed like a reasonable enough type in person, and a far cry from the slavering war criminal some people had painted him as in the Block. What he was asking, however, was terrifying on so many levels.

Sun was certain that of his crew, only a small handful even knew that what Weston was asking was remotely possible, and of those maybe three could make it happen. The high-energy particles released by an uncompensated ship coming down from a long FTL journey were enough to sterilize an entire hemisphere of a planet. He knew because he'd read the reports on the possibility of using the ship's drives as a weapon against the Confederacy.

Luckily no one was quite that insane, at least so far as he knew.

For one thing, it couldn't be done with an unmanned ship. Not yet at any rate, since the drives were complex beasts that required fairly constant adjustments if they were to remain in operating order. Long FTL runs were hard on them, and they had to be aligned often or risk blowing out the entire system and being forced from FTL in an uncompensated crash.

Doing so with a *manned* ship would most likely be fatal in most circumstances. It wasn't the crash itself that was the problem, but some of the radiation and high-energy particles would blow back into the ship and destroy the drives. He hadn't told that to Captain Weston, not that he'd told the man much at all. A successfully induced crash would be survivable only if there were search and rescue quickly available to pick up the crew, because the ship would be going nowhere in a hurry after that.

*At best we'll have thrusters if we do this,* Sun supposed darkly as he sat alone in his cabin, staring at his computer terminal while doing most of the math in his head.

He didn't trust his computer not to inform on him to the PLASF generals, to be quite honest, particularly not with something like this. He hadn't made any promises to the Confederate captain, as the idea seemed *insane* on the surface of it. It wasn't until Weston had broken down a little and offered up an idea of just how many ships constituted the enemy "fleet" that Sun was even willing to consider the possibility of such a plan.

*Thousands of those things. It's impossible, no matter what clever tricks or technical wizardry we pull from our sleeves…we cannot beat those kinds of numbers.*

That didn't mean he was going to sit in orbit and die, however.

Against those kinds of numbers, Weston's plan wasn't as insane as it sounded. The math worked, though he could wish that it worked better than it did, but it worked.

The real problem was the fact that the *Weifang* would be blind before and during the action. And Sun would be counting on a man—his enemy just a few years earlier—to get the aliens into a position where the *Weifang's* sacrifice would have meaning. If Weston failed, or the man betrayed him, Sun would have sacrificed his ship and crew for nothing.

*All men are tested in their lives, but this may be more than I can endure.*

Sun didn't know what to do, and for the next few hours he decided that he would do nothing. Let the Confederate sweat. He would wait and see if the man's dire warnings of an invasion en masse would materialize as real. He would decide when he knew if there was a target or not.

▶▶▶

# STATION LIBERTY

▶ "ENTER."

Admiral Gracen looked up to see Eric walk in, and then glanced quickly to the side to check the clock. He'd been gone almost six hours and they didn't have time to burn. "Where have you been?"

"Talking to an old friend and enemy," Eric told her with a more than slightly infuriating smile. "Then a quick chat with the captain of the *Weifang* before a little research; then I came here."

She raised her eyebrow at that litany of tasks, but refrained from anything else.

"Were you able to figure out whatever it was you went there to figure out, at least?" she asked dryly.

"Could be. We'll know when the bad guys get here, I suppose," he told her, looking far too relaxed for her taste.

She scowled and called him on it. "You could at least have the decency to look half as stressed as I've been since our Priminae friends dropped this little bomb on us."

"What's the point? We're committed now. Stress is for when you have options, decisions to make. We've got a battle to fight. I'll stress out when I can actually do something about it."

Gracen rolled her eyes. "Fine. While you were gone, Captain Kian contacted me to inform us that her ships' long-range scans have picked up the lead of the bowshock wave. Judging from the *Odyssey*'s logs, we'll pick it up in another few hours ourselves. They're coming here, alright."

"Not much doubt," Eric said. "Something about us really honks them off, Admiral."

She snorted, shooting him a dark look. "I wonder what that might be?"

Eric shook his head, smiling ruefully. "Nice of you to say, but I don't think it's me or the *Odyssey*. Doesn't make a lot of sense, to be honest."

"What do you mean?"

"Why'd they come in with almost thirty ships, Admiral?" he asked, genuinely confused. "That's not their style. They don't operate like that. Up until now this group has been controlled, systematic, even downright conservative in their battle plans. They send in waves to test defenses, strengths, weaknesses…they don't just charge in with thirty ships in some kind of blind rage, let alone thousands. The *Odyssey* never did anything to warrant this kind of action, not until we popped all thirty or so earlier…but that should have put them back on their heels, ma'am, not egged them into a red rage."

Gracen grimaced, but had to concede the point.

Whatever else, it was clear that they were working without the full story. That wasn't as uncommon as one might think, she supposed. In fact you rarely got to work *with* the full story in a war. Still, this was something else. They were missing key elements that seemed to *define* their foe, elements that were basic and almost always assumed in interactions with other people on Earth.

All they were seeing were the actions, not the motivations, and the actions made no sense according to any logical set of motivations she could imagine.

"It's almost like there are two groups giving orders," she said finally. "One is a thinking, planning, group...."

"And the other is instinctive, animalistic, and completely inhuman," Eric finished, nodding, "I know."

"It does seem that way," Gracen sighed, "which both makes a lot of sense, and none at all. I suppose you have a theory?"

Eric shook his head. "Not on this, ma'am. There's just too much going on that we don't know to even make a guess."

She nodded. "Some days, I think that we should have damned well stayed in our own backyard."

"I can't say I disagree," Eric admitted, "though I think it would only have been to our benefit if we somehow knew what was going on out there just the same. Ten years, fifty, a hundred? What's the difference. They were coming here eventually. I'm sure of it. If we'd just sat here in our ignorance, would we have developed enough defense to hold them off, even with all that time?"

"I don't know," Gracen admitted. "There's been more effort thrown into research in the past two years than in the past twenty. I don't know."

"Neither do I," Eric said, sighing. "Why is it that we only see short-term benefits? No one wants to invest in the future if it's more than twenty-four hours away, it seems to me sometimes."

"Visionaries cost too much," Gracen said with a sad smile.

"Ain't that the truth," Eric said before adding a belated, "ma'am."

"Keep me apprised of your plans, Captain," Gracen said while activating her desk. "I don't want to be surprised by any cowboy actions. Are we clear?"

"Clear, ma'am."

"Good. Dismissed, Captain."

Eric rose to his feet, saluted, and left the office. Like the admiral, he had work to do.

▶▶▶

# PRIMINAE WARSHIP *POSDAN*

▲

▶KIAN LOOKED OUT over the blue-white world they were orbiting, impressing the image on her mind. There was more water here than on Ranquil. It caused thicker and more impressive clouds than she normally saw back home. Earth was a pretty world, she decided, her mood dark.

A very pretty world that was about to come to a very ugly end.

She looked over the data that the ships were receiving, some from Ranquil's central command and some from the leading edge of the oncoming Drasin fleet.

And it had to be a fleet, there was no doubt about that now. Not to her, not to anyone who saw the data. The sheer power and size of the trans-light signals were conclusive. Something was coming this way, and whatever it was, it was bigger than anything she had ever seen in her life; bigger than anything the Priminae had ever recorded, to be precise; and it did not bode well for the people on the world below.

"Do we have an arrival period yet?" she asked, not for the first time in the last hour.

"No, Captain." The same answer was returned. "The size of the signal is corrupting our attempts to pinpoint it. It will be later than predicted, however. The signal strength makes it look closer than it is."

*That's good news, at the very least.*

Kian wasn't certain what she was going to do when it arrived. When *they* arrived.

The *Posdan* and *Nept* were capable warships. She'd put them against anything the Drasin could offer up...but she knew well enough that they would not stand against *everything* the Drasin could offer.

"Captain, Tsarin on the *Nept* has requested your orders, given the situation."

Kian nodded. She wasn't surprised. She was the senior captain and technically in command of both ships, but a situation like this wasn't even remotely in their instructions from central command. Tsarin was an older man. He'd been in command of frontier excavation before the Drasin invasion had begun, and was noted as a particularly conservative and cautious officer.

That was one of the reasons she had been placed in command of the small group, or at least that was the general consensus. Tsarin was a competent officer, but unlikely to take risks, even on behalf of civilian populations. He would follow orders, even those that risked his ship and himself, oddly enough, but he just didn't take that sort of initiative.

"Tell Captain Tsarin that I will schedule a conference with him shortly," she answered. "I am still considering options. You may inform him that, while I don't intend to retreat ahead of the incoming force, neither do I intend a last stand here over the Terran world. We will provide what aid we can."

"Yes, Captain. I will transmit your message."

Tsarin's concerns were more than fair, she had to admit. Honestly, Kian wasn't certain what she was going to do when the enemy arrived. There was no providing a defense against an onslaught of that force, but she didn't feel right leaving the Terrans to their own ends. The *Odyssey* had risked so much for the Priminae people that it felt...an abomination to leave them to drift in the void now.

For all that, however, she knew that she couldn't commit her two ships to a pointless and fatally doomed venture. The Priminae needed every hull they could scrounge, build, or refit. The two Godan class cruisers under her command represented a not insignificant portion of the total Priminae tonnage.

Sacrificing them here, for no gain, was not an option.

*I will remain as long as possible, perhaps transport some few thousand refugees if the Terrans so wish.*

That really was the best she could do, Kian supposed. Save a few people, and possibly records so that they would not be forgotten.

It was selfish of her, but she knew that she would also have to ask...to beg, even, for them to share their weapons technology with the colonies. The new capability she had seen might be enough to save her people if they could just buy enough time to build and deploy the weapons accordingly.

*That is a topic I wish I did not have to broach.*

Somehow, Kian rather doubted that they would take it well, not that she blamed them.

*It is a hard thing to look into the singular abyss and know that there is no escape, that even were you light itself, you could not run from your fate. It is a fate that I and the rest of the colonies may soon face ourselves. I wonder how we will acquit ourselves when and if that time comes?*

▶ ▶ ▶

# LIBERTY STATION

▶ ADMIRAL GRACEN ENTERED the war room, eyes immediately falling on the long-range plot as she walked toward the center area.

"So, we've got confirmation?" she asked, noting the angry red signal showing on the screens.

"Yes, ma'am," an Air Force tech and the on-duty liaison to the Cheyenne Mountain facility said. "Our Antarctic tachyon traps picked it up first, a little under a half-hour ago."

Gracen nodded, unsurprised. The Antarctic research stations were some of the key leaders in tachyon research, using the miles of ice as part of their particle traps to detect ever more exotic particles. The entire continent, in fact, was practically a single expansive particle sensor on a scale that dwarfed everything else mankind had devised.

It was the first tachyon detection system, and it was still the best.

"The Prim reports are right, ma'am, whatever is coming... it's big."

Gracen hadn't doubted it, but wished that they'd been wrong. "Has the President issued a directive yet?"

"Nothing official, ma'am." The tech shook his head. "All Confederation forces have been shifted to DEFCON 4, all leaves canceled."

"Our allies?"

"Same, ma'am. We didn't officially tell the Block anything, but the word is that someone slipped a note under their door, so to speak," the tech said with a shrug and a half smile. "They brought their forces to early readiness shortly after we did."

"Understood," Gracen nodded, hoping that someone had indeed explained to the Block that the Confederacy wasn't spoiling for a fight. That would be one lousy way to end the human race, locked in a nuclear war with the Block while a Drasin fleet came down on all their heads.

*Not that there are many good ways to end the human race, I suppose.*

She forced herself off that particularly *cheerful* line of thought and set her focus back on her work. She was in charge of organizing system-wide defenses, such as they were, and there wasn't much time left to accomplish it.

"Someone get me an update on the *Enterprise* refit. If they can't get those turrets installed in the next twenty-four hours, I want the project scrapped and that tin can welded shut!" She growled, "We're going to need that ship mobile when the time comes."

*Even if only so we can order them to withdraw. Better some live than everyone dies.*

"Yes, ma'am!"

"Do we have ETA reports for the new Marauder class ships yet?"

"Yes, ma'am, to your station, ma'am."

Gracen nodded curtly and opened her inbox. Finding the report in the midst of all the other priority messages took a bit longer than she would have preferred, but that was the nature of the times she supposed.

Four of the Marauders were already complete, hacked together from civilian hulls and whatever ordinance the Confederacy had been able to scrounge up. No pulse weaponry, unfortunately, but there was no chance she would authorize the installation of an antimatter generation and containment system on anything less than a fully crewed and maintained starship.

That still left HVM banks, Gen Three Lasers, and old-fashioned nuclear devices loaded into hull-penetrating frames. They knew that nukes were ineffective when detonated outside the Drasin hulls, but she, and the rest of the world, was betting that they could achieve penetration of the hulls with some bunker busters. The trick would be keeping them moving fast enough to penetrate the Drasin armor, but not so fast that they'd vaporize on impact.

Three more of the irregular class Marauders would be ready over the next day, loaded to the gills with whatever they could stuff into the hulls, and then she'd be throwing them against a force that could turn a star system to rubble in a matter of weeks.

*Yeah, this is going to work out really well, I can tell.*

There were still no directives from the civilian branch other than to do her job, about which she was both gratified by and severely worried. One thing she could always count on was politicians getting in her way when she had a job to do, so the silence was unnerving. None of them could afford a breakdown of leadership just now, but if there had to be one, she supposed speechless paralysis was the best of a lot of bad alternatives.

Her message box showed that the *Odyssey* had reported in, so she quickly glanced that over and then archived the message. It was nothing more than a general status report, saying that they were ready for action. Comforting, yes, but not useful to her at the moment other than that it was one less thing to panic over.

*Don't panic. Never panic. Be concerned, yes. Cautious, certainly. Even afraid, if the situation warrants...but never panic. I have too much to do to waste my time like that.*

Repeating that as a mantra kept her motions calm, even if her mind was anything but. As stressed as she was, the very last thing she could afford was to lose it now. She was determined that, if this was to be the Earth's last stand, it would be one that would cause their enemies to awake with cold sweats for the next hundred generations.

Gracen set her jaw, eyes drifting up to the angry red dots on the long-range screens.

*We will not go quietly into the black. You have no idea what kind of a fight you're flying your sick, twisted, little asses into...but you're going to find out, I promise you that.*

▶▶▶

# N.A.C.S. ODYSSEY

▶ THE BRIDGE OF the *Odyssey* was quiet, a skeleton crew being one of the reasons and the angry red rash that was showing on the displays being another. Those who came in glanced at the screen, maybe asked someone what it was showing, and then looked to where the captain was sitting and working in silence. That was usually the last thing they'd say. Eric wasn't encouraging the quiet, but it suited both his needs and his mood, so he said nothing either way.

There was a time for talk and a time for action, but this was a time for planning.

He had the approach vector for the incoming ships, though there were so many of them that it almost didn't seem to matter. It looked like they were just going to literally envelop the solar system, though he knew that was just stupid. The tachyons leading the fleet were spreading out, making it look like the source of the bowshock signal was as much as a light-year or more across. In reality, Eric guessed it was more on the order of a couple light-months, which was still pretty insane.

What the readings were also saying, though, was that the signal was tightening up. That meant that the ships were beginning to form up as they approached, and he expected that they'd be in a much tighter pack once they got to the system.

*I wonder if they're flying so spread out because their drives interfere with each other at full power?*

One thing that Eric knew, from experience, was that manipulations to space-time tended to be cumulative. It was one of the first things you learned when flying a CM-powered fighter in tight formation. You had to adjust for the warping of your wingman's CM; otherwise you'd hop your own fighter right out of position. He'd never run into the problem in *space*, even when flying among the powerhouses of the Drasin and Priminae, but he'd also never tried flying in formation with as many starships.

His questioning had a major effect on his attempts to plan. He needed to know where they were going to come into the system and just how tightly packed the enemy ships were going to be. The sheer lack of detail on enemy capabilities was maddening, but it was a problem he was going to have to work around as best he could.

Even Captain Kian didn't have any fast answers for him on the subject. No one in the Priminae civilization had ever tried flying that many ships in such relative close proximity before. There just wasn't any experimental data available, and certainly nothing to draw any real guesses from. He'd thrown the problem down to his own engineering team as well as out into the wild via some contacts in the research and development division of the Confederacy, but any answers would probably come far too late to be of any value.

*I suppose it's a good thing that the Marines taught me to work with what I had instead of what I needed,* Eric thought dryly as he ran a few more calculations through the computer.

*Otherwise this job would be frustrating and impossible instead of just impossible.*

"Captain?"

Eric glanced up. "Yes, Commander?"

Roberts's eyes flicked to one side, then the other, drawing Eric's gaze with them. It didn't take a genius to see what he was looking at, or why, so Eric just shrugged lightly.

"Rumors are starting to circulate, sir."

"Only thing besides tachyons that are faster than light," Eric said with a smile, forced though it might be.

"There's truth there, sir." Roberts returned the smile. "But it's starting to affect morale."

Eric nodded, idly noting that several people were leaning back in their chairs and straining to hear what was being said. He raised his voice just enough for it to carry in the acoustics of the bridge.

"You've seen the numbers as well as I have, Commander. The rumors, whatever they are, can't possibly be as bad as the real deal," Eric said, taking a certain perverse pleasure in the shock on Roberts's face. It was clear that the Commander had expected him to downplay the odds, but Eric hoped none of his people were stupid enough to believe that.

*This isn't a time to treat them like children, Commander,* he thought idly.

"Uh, um, yes sir," Roberts stammered slightly, clearly confused.

"I wouldn't worry about it, Commander. The crew knows to take this as the opportunity it is."

"Opportunity, sir?"

Eric smiled, genuinely this time. "I don't know about you, Commander, but I've always wanted a shot at planning the defense of the Alamo."

Jason Roberts was initially taken aback by the tone and words, but slowly Eric saw a shift in the Commander's expression. In a few seconds, he too was smiling, and it clearly wasn't forced, as he nodded in agreement.

"Right you are, sir. I should have thought of that myself."

Roberts settled back in his own station, expression both a little contemplative and a little feral. It was an odd mix, Eric thought, something you didn't see very often on anyone's face. If there was ever a time for that peculiar mixture of emotions, however, it was without a doubt here and now.

"Captain," Winger said from the other side of the Bridge, "the *Weifang*, she's warping space!"

"Really?" Eric said, nodding. "That's good to know."

"I'm intercepting comm chatter between them and the Block space control. They're being ordered to stand down. *Weifang* is disregarding. Captain, they're pulling out of orbit."

"Not our concern," Eric said. "Monitor and log all comm chatter to and from the *Weifang* in case we're asked for it."

"Yes sir. *Weifang* is now accelerating...." Winger's eyes widened. "One hundred gravities and climbing. She's heading out-system, sir."

"Thank you, Lieutenant," Eric said as he got up, glancing at the latest ETA for the fleet's arrival.

*T-minus thirty-six hours and counting.*

# CHAPTER TWENTY-ONE

## Imperial Destroyer *Demigod,* the Hive Facility

▶ "THE *IMMORTAL* IS breaking up, Commander."

Ivanth could see that, but he didn't say anything for fear of taking out his impotent frustrations on the man. His fists clenched and unclenched reflexively, his eyes locked on the screens that showed the Imperial destroyer as it was slowly picked apart from the inside out by renegade drones.

They'd picked off those they could from the hull, but it had already been too late. The drone soldiers were already inside the ship, and the crew of the *Immortal* had been unable to eliminate them in time. The ship underwent explosive decompression multiple times as the drones bored through one locked door after another.

The men and women on board never had a chance.

"Are there any survivors?" he asked finally, knowing the answer but having to ask anyway.

"No, Commander."

Ivanth nodded and turned his back to the screen. "Warp space, reverse course. Take us out of the Hive. Maintain active scans until we're sure that we are clear."

"Yes, Commander."

The *Demigod* backed slowly away from the dead ship, pivoting smoothly in space before reversing its warp and accelerating away from the scene at a steady rate of acceleration. Behind them, the former pride of the Imperial fleet continued to break up as small explosions tore through the ship and left it in scraps.

Those pieces too were soon grabbed by active drones, chewed up, and used to produce new generations of the beasts that slew the *Immortal.*

Ivanth still didn't know what in the singular abyss happened to the Hive and the other ships, but it was clear that somehow they had lost control of the drones. It shouldn't have been possible. He knew the core programming they'd implemented, and it was flawless. Under absolutely no circumstances should they have been able to turn on Imperial ships.

*This all happened when we located that* alien *ship and one of their worlds. Was it something about them? Or did something happen here at the same time?*

"Than Gia," he called out softly, his voice pitched so the officer could just hear him.

"Yes, Commander?" Gia put down what she was doing and approached.

"Have the records from the incident recorder been loaded into the archives?"

"Yes, Commander. Shall I send you a direct?"

"No. Thank you, Than," he said. "I will find it myself."

The incident recorder was his last hope of learning what had happened or, more important, why it had happened. The Prohuer's ship had been in the Hive, along with a complete battle group. If they'd all met the same fate, then the Imperial mission in this arm of the galaxy was *over.*

He *really* didn't want to be the officer who returned to the Emperor and told them that an entire battleground had been lost to their own drones. Particularly not if he had to report that said drones were now loose and running wild across the galactic arm.

*I hope that there is something in this mess that will provide answers.*

▶▶▶

# DEEP SPACE, APPROACHING SOL

▶THE SWARM SLOWED their approach, tightening up as the yellow star drew closer.

They were still too far away to taste the red band that they knew had totally contaminated the entire system of planets, but each member of the swarm was well aware of just how disgustingly filthy the system was. They also knew it was a lethal system, on an order nearly unparalleled in their ingrained genetic memory.

It had happened before, once, long before the existence of the current swarm. There had been a populace that infested multiple stars, spanning untold swaths of the galaxy. Those too had been lethal to the swarm, eliminating them with an ease that none since had matched until now.

It had taken hundreds of queens and millions of under-soldiers and ships to bring that species to its final end. Their last system was a fortress that spanned the entire gravity well of the star, with weapons that could wipe out a hundred drones in an instant, but it still fell to the swarm. More than a million drones fell in battle, but in the end even their inert material was a weapon against the enemy.

The mass of their dead had pushed in on the stellar construct, a massive shell larger than the Hive itself, until the material had cracked and buckled. As it shifted in its orbit, power blown out from the constant attacks, the shell had lost stability and begun to wobble. Over a period of time still lost to even the swarm's memory, the swarm had pressed the assault so that the inhabitants could not save their artificial world.

It had finally blown out of orbit and collided with its own star.

This time such efforts would not be required, however. The species they were targeting was lethal in ways not seen in ages long past, but they were not fortified. The system was almost natural, despite the sheer stench of the foul band of scarlet.

No matter its lethality, no matter the defenses there, it would fall.

It would fall, and then the swarm would turn its attention back to the true task.

The galaxy must be swept clean.

▶▶▶

# COMMAND BUNKER, MONS SYSTEMA, RANQUIL

▶ ADMIRAL RAEL TANNER slumped in his seat. The news from the Terran homeworld was not good. He could read that between the lines in Kian's report, even if it weren't spelled out by statements from both Kian herself and the Terran admiral, Gracen.

The horror of it, beyond the atrocity that he knew awaited the world, was that somehow they had developed a weapon that could be the savior of the colonies.

*If only we had a few more years. Months, even!*

Kian intended to ask, to beg if need be, for the plans to the Terran weapon. Even just the concept would be a boon, but he wasn't certain that she would get it. Tanner didn't know the Terrans well, but to judge them by Eric Weston, he doubted that they would see their deaths as something to be faced in silence.

No, they would fight to the last man and woman, he had no doubt.

And, Tanner was relatively certain, they would not consider giving away weapons so devastating as those they had developed over centuries of blood and war. Not until the end was inevitable.

Tanner drafted an order to Kian with deliberate strokes, knowing that he was perhaps sacrificing two of his best ships, but he could not give away any chance for the survival of his people.

When he was done with that, he sent it on and slowly stood from his station. "Ithan."

"Yes, Admiral?"

"Please contact Ambassador LaFontaine. Ask for an emergency meeting, please."

"Yes, Admiral. Immediately."

This would not be a conversation he would enjoy, or care to remember in the ever increasingly dark future.

▶▶▶

The entity referred to by the local people as Central considered the information it had just processed with what a human might consider a heavy heart. The very existence of the Terran humans brought upon so many confusing thoughts that learning of their impending end set him reeling with even more confusion.

Central was the product of its environment in more ways than even it was likely to admit, but it knew that it was passive and cool because that was the general preference of the people of its world. Order, logical thought, intelligence, and peaceful existence were what it prized above all else.

The Terrans were, in so many ways, the antithesis of that. Passionate, violent, and chaotic. Oh, it wasn't that they didn't have logic, nor was it that the Priminae people lacked passion. It was a subtle differentiation, just a matter of degrees and general consensus.

Individuals varied, but the group mind favored one balance or another.

The Terrans were very different in the group mind than were the Priminae, very different indeed.

Their deaths would mean that it could contain the contamination presented by them upon the Priminae, but it also removed the very vital help they had offered. Survival was now more in question than ever, despite everything that Central had access to in the histories of its world and people.

Beyond all that, though, something deeper trembled in the ancient entity.

Sorrow?

Perhaps. Central couldn't tell, in all honesty, as its emotions were rare. Oh, it was not cold and unfeeling, nor was it bound by the rules of math or some other foolishness. It merely experienced emotions as a gestalt of the world, and it was very rare that any one emotion ruled over an entire planet.

Still, Central personally felt something tug deep inside, in some place it had rarely felt and never bothered to identify.

It would miss at least one Terran.

▶▶▶

Ambassador LaFontaine sat heavy in her office, looking out over a rather spectacular view of the old monolithic city that existed around the enormous pyramid in which she was. Admiral Tanner had just left, and the news he'd brought with him, while not entirely unexpected, was as staggering as an axe handle to the face.

The worst of it was that there was nothing she, or anyone, could do. Earth's fate now rested surely on the shoulders of men and women several light-years away, men and women who were almost certainly outgunned and outnumbered.

She locked the door of her office with the touch of a button, put her face down in her arms, and cried.

▶▶▶

Jeremy Reed's fingers were numb, barely holding onto the slate that had delivered the news to him. He had enough control to keep from shaking, but only just, and suddenly found himself deeply in need of a place to sit down.

He staggered across his office, away from the window that overlooked the base and training grounds he had helped design and build for the locals, and finally collapsed into his chair.

*Those God-forsaken* things *found Earth. I don't believe it.*

He stared at his desk, sick inside, and lowered his face into his hands. He had a family at home, though he and his wife weren't on the best of terms. He was a better husband when he was a long way from home, he'd learned a long time ago, but she didn't deserve what was coming. He felt ill. He had two sons at home that he hadn't seen in too damned long, and now....

He didn't know what. He just didn't know.

Reed reached across his desk and hit a button.

"Sir?" The soft voice of a local secretary rang clear as day through the room.

"Please contact my team and have them meet me in my office, as soon as possible."

"Yes, sir."

He didn't know how he was going to tell them, but he knew that they were likely to take it even worse than he was.

▶▶▶

▼

# THE HIVE

▲

▶ IVANTH CLENCHED HIS fist to keep his hand from shaking as he turned off the recorder.

He'd just watched the entire Imperial battlefleet taken apart, piece by piece, by their own weapons. It didn't make *any* sense! The safeguards, everything they did to ensure that those things were under control...none of them stopped the assault. They didn't even *slow* it down!

He felt sick deep in his stomach...the lives gone, the ships annihilated! If it weren't for the numbness, he suspected he might actually *be* sick.

The time imprint made it clear that it happened at the same time as the drones under his command rebelled against him, but those didn't turn on Imperial control. They went after the enemy, granted not in the fashion he would have ordered, but even still....

Something had changed in them, something vital and deep inside the little monsters, but until he knew what it was, there was nothing he could do to resolve the issue.

*More important than what changed them, where in the singular abyss did they* go?

There had been thousands of space combat drones in the Hive, more than any dozen campaigns should have needed. Millions of soldier drones that, despite what happened to the *Immortal,* appeared to be mostly missing as well. What was left was the self-assembled Hive facility itself, not that he would remain within those uncertain platforms now that it was clear the drones had turned on the Empire.

So where had the rest gone?

*The closest Priminae world is only a few lights away. We should do a fast scout, see if they're in the area. If not, then....*

His mind drifted back to his own experiences with the rebelling drones. They hadn't gone for *his* ships. No, they'd focused instantly on that lethal little star and its enigmatic populace.

*If they've returned there, at least that will be one world out of the way,* he supposed, though in all honesty he still saw drones exploding in open space for no reason anyone or anything could detect. A small sliver of him wondered if the drones hadn't chosen to chew off more than they could process this time.

# CHAPTER TWENTY-TWO

## N.A.C.S. *Enterprise*

▶ "HERE THEY COME, Captain."

Captain Carrow nodded, standing in front of his station as he looked over the bridge and the main display. The enemy fleet was close enough now that even their shipboard sensors could track them, and that meant that they weren't far beyond Sol's heliopause. Carrow rubbed his shoulder as he watched the numbers countdown, remembering another day and another battle.

Eric Weston was a decorated veteran of the air war that raged across the Pacific theatre, but Carrow had been a carrier commander from start to finish. He'd taken his task group through hells that he never wanted to think of again, and now it seemed that he'd have to do it again.

*I just wish we had time to put together a proper carrier group.*

His task force consisted of the *Enterprise*, his space wing, and four of the Marauder class irregulars. It was a far cry from an American carrier group, even if it did currently pack several dozen times the firepower.

*Conservative estimates, at that.* Carrow knew that numbers were meaningless, however, not when compared to what their best guess for enemy ships was. The computers kept refining the guess, but the new numbers weren't good news compared to the old. As the fleet slowed, the FTL particles that preceded each ship were becoming less pronounced, but they were also closing together and turning the signal of the fleet into what almost looked like a single mass coming their way.

It was a single mass over one light-*day* across, but a single mass just the same.

"I hope Weston knows what he's doing."

Carrow glanced to the side, nodding slightly as Andrea Parker stepped up beside him, her uniform as perfect as ever. Parker was his first officer, and one of the best pilots to come out of the Block war that couldn't take a NICS device.

"He has more experience than anyone else."

"Doesn't mean he knows what he's doing," she countered. "Just means he's bumbled through this situation before."

"Bumbled through this situation and *survived* it," Carrow corrected dryly. "Twice. We don't have anyone better."

"Weston was a loose cannon in the Marines, he was a loose cannon in the Archangels, and he's been a frigging *loaded* loose cannon since they put him in command of that damned ship," Parker said in a low voice, her impression of the man practically dripping from every word.

Carrow wasn't going to counter her on that. Weston's actions outside the system were just short of infamy at this point, though the Block captain had certainly managed to overshadow him this time around. That said, there was no question why the *Odyssey* captain had been given tactical command of the fight, particularly further out in the star system.

Weston knew the enemy, and with light-speed lag being what it was, there was no possible way that military command on Earth could do more than watch the fight until it got far too close for comfort. That left, realistically, only Eric Weston and himself up for the job. Whatever else could be said, Weston was the senior officer on scene and he was also the one who had the best working relationship with their Priminae allies.

The two Priminae big ships were flanking the *Odyssey*, with the *Enterprise* taking up the drag position in their little convoy. Taken as a group, he had to admit that the power represented was almost frightening, despite the fact that it was all aimed away from him and the Earth.

*Almost. Only almost, simply because the power aimed at us beggars it without trying.*

"Do we have a ship count yet?" he asked, glancing over to his instrumentation technician.

"No, Captain. The mutual interference between incoming ships is still too strong."

"We'll have them on visual in a few hours," Parker spoke up, "so it hardly matters."

Carrow nodded. "I know, but I'd just like to *know*, you know?"

His first officer grimaced, causing him to chuckle softly. *Andrea hates wordplay almost as much as she hates puns.*

"What do you suppose our odds are here?" Parker asked after a moment, choosing to ignore his last statement, apparently.

"You've seen the stats on their weapons capabilities," Carrow said, his voice lowering so he wouldn't be overheard by anyone. "We're just waiting to see how many they'll throw at us now, but if there are more than a couple dozen ships left after we empty our long guns…."

He trailed off, but she nodded beside him.

Even optimistically, once they got down to knife range they could only splash a few ships apiece. She'd seen the reports of what these things did to worlds to which they had unrestricted access, so he was certain that she understood what was going to happen when they fell.

*God, I'm being a depressing little shit even in my own mind. Can't let the crew see me even thinking like this.*

"I can't believe the Block ship ran like that," Parker admitted, changing the subject away from the uncomfortable truth. "Don't like those bastards much, but I've never seen a coward among them."

"They have their fair share," Carrow said, "but not too many of them make captain of a ship. Most of the ones I've run into were generals."

Andrea made a strangled sound and he glanced sideways, watching in amusement as she clamped down on any effort to so much as smile. He did find it amusing to wind up his serious and stoic first officer.

"That said, you've got a point. I've crossed steel with Captain Sun before. He's no coward," Carrow said. "Best guess there are secret orders. We weren't watching them too closely during repair and refit. I bet they could have fit a few thousand people on board if they stressed the life support."

Andrea raised an eyebrow. "Colony attempt, sir?"

"Maybe," Carrow said. "We don't have enough details to guess, but I wouldn't be surprised if there are a few empty offices in the Block's upper echelons right now."

"Well, that makes me more optimistic already," she replied dryly.

"Doesn't it, though?"

▶▶▶

# N.A.C.S. ODYSSEY

▶THE *ODYSSEY* HAD taken the vanguard position of the convoy, her armor set to the gleaming white-knight settings used earlier while her sensor sails were fully unfurled, surrounding the ship in a cloud of metallic silver.

Eric hoped it was a sufficiently impressive sight, since everything he had was riding on them getting the complete and undivided attention of the Drasin ships once they entered Sol system.

*Everything everyone else has is riding on it, too.*

"Newest estimates on enemy numbers, sir," Michelle offered from the side.

"Are they any lower than the last revision?"

"No, sir."

"Didn't think so," Eric sighed. "Well, it's going to be one for the history books."

"Wouldn't mind being around to write those books, sir," Roberts said quietly beside him.

Eric smiled. "Can't promise that."

"No, sir, I don't suppose you can," Roberts sighed. "Would be nice though."

"How about I promise you that, no matter what, this one is going to be a...bang," Eric offered with a wide smile.

"I suppose it'll do," Roberts nodded grimly.

▶▶▶

In deep space, just outside the heliopause of the star known to Terrans as Sol, the Drasin fleet slowed to sub-light speeds and took a moment to examine the immediate area around them. Finding nothing of threat to them, they turned their focus inwards to the target star and its planets, finding instantly what their lost brethren had reported.

The red band burned through this system like a burning rash, illuminating several planets, some sub-planets and moons, and even some areas of *empty space!*

The entire system would have to be destroyed. Every planet, every rock, every ball of ice and mud. Nothing less would be acceptable, given the severity of the contamination they were looking at, and it might even have reached the star itself...though that was a rare event to say the least.

The fleet hesitated for a moment, judging tactics and attempting to prioritize targets, and then light-speed scanners made their decision for them.

*The ship.*

It had plagued them practically since operations began in this arm of the galaxy, and there it was in plain sight. None of the frustrating hiding, as it had done so many times before, just a blazing challenge to the swarm.

*Challenge accepted.*

▶▶▶

On the *Posdan*, Captain Kian watched her screens with growing nervousness. The computers on the *Posdan* and the *Nept* were linked, using the few light-seconds spacing between them to help filter the interference they were getting from the multiple bowshock signals so they could see what they were really facing.

It was a nightmare.

It could only be a nightmare, because she was firmly convinced that nothing in the waking universe should be so horrendous as what she was looking at. The numbers were still estimates, but they were also low-end estimates, and they were growing.

"Fourteen hundred enemy ships, still counting, Captain."

Kian, for her part, acknowledged the report dully, barely able to comprehend the numbers in context. They were looking at as many Drasin as there were merchant ships in all the colonies, including in-system mining vessels and local passenger craft! It was just mind-numbing, staggering…it was *impossible!*

*If they had this many ships, then* why *were they assaulting us with one ship, two ships, at most six?*

None of it made any sense to her, not their actions, and certainly not a universe that would *allow* such numbers of Drasin to even exist.

"They have seen us, Captain."

Kian felt a chill at those words, even as she had been expecting them. After all, they'd hardly been hiding their presence, had they? For whatever reason, Weston seemed intent on *providing* the enemy with a target this time, something that was entirely out of character with what she knew of his combat operations in the past. She had to wonder what he was holding back?

"Have they adjusted course?"

"Yes, Captain, as Captain Weston predicted. They're now approaching on a direct intercept for our location."

"Good. Send our predictions to the *Odyssey*," she said, trying to appear confident, even as her mind raced with concerns and fears. *I just hope that Captain Weston knows what he's doing.*

▶▶▶

On the *Odyssey*, everyone wanted to have some idea of what the Captain *thought* he was doing. They'd have been happy with a hint, really. Just a slight concept would have been fine, but Eric Weston was just sitting in his station with a bit of a smile on his face.

That was the only thing that was keeping down the feelings of panic among those who'd seen the numbers. When the Captain was smiling before or during a battle, it generally meant that he knew the punch line to a joke that the enemy wasn't going to appreciate. Still, it was always nicer if you were in on the joke.

Below decks, which actually tended to mean the decks aft of the bridge, the atmosphere was both more and less relaxed than among the command staff. There was no comforting smile for people to notice and accept as a sign that the captain knew what he was doing, but at the same time, no one off the bridge had access to the full numbers of enemy ships coming their way.

So for most of the crew, things were nothing more than business as usual for a time when they knew action was upcoming. Mostly, at least. They were aware that the situation was different this time. They had their back to Earth for one. There would be no running from this battle if things got bad, but when was the last time the *Odyssey* ran from *anything* with lives at stake?

The only real grumpiness was, ironically, among the ground troops and the Archangels...two groups legendary for never agreeing on *anything*.

►►►

Stephen "Stephanos" Michaels was in a foul mood.

He was in his Ready One position along with the rest of the very short-handed fighter wing, waiting for the order to launch and wondering if it was going to come. For whatever reason, the Captain seemed less and less willing to let them off the leash lately, and that was starting to ride on his nerves.

The Archangels were the best at what they did, short-handed or not, and leaving them cooped up in the hangar bays of the *Odyssey* felt like a thinly veiled insult. He'd have taken it as such already if it weren't for who was giving the orders.

Eric "Raziel" Weston wasn't ever going to say a bad word about the Angels, he was sure of that, so Steph swallowed his ire and sat impatiently in the open cockpit of the fighter while the general quarters alarms sounded.

"You think we need to get ready?" Cardsharp asked from her own cockpit, eyes closed as her helmet floated near her head.

"No," Burner answered, sounding bored. "That's just making sure everyone has their stations in order. We're hours out from action still, assuming the captain lets us in on this one."

Steph winced at that little comment, and as he expected, it started a blast of general annoyance and grievances from the rest.

He listened for a short time before his own temper boiled over, this time at his squadron mates instead of his CO.

"Listen to the lot of you," he growled loud enough to shut them up. "Captain keeps us in the pen for *one* battle, just the one I might add, and you're behaving like spoiled children. Keep it together before I come over there and grow you up the hard way."

He tried, rather unsuccessfully, to push back the knowledge that he himself had been mentally whining along the same lines just a few minutes earlier. There were some things that the rank and file didn't need to know.

▶▶▶

The Drasin signals had cleared up now, and the first light-speed data was being collated by their computers. The situation was even worse than Eric had expected, though honestly not quite as bad as he'd feared.

He'd expected enough ships to devastate the entire solar system, no matter *what* level of defense the Earth was able to mount in the time they had. He'd *feared* the entire force of enemy ships that the Dyson construct had to have been housing. While his fears hadn't been met, he was quite sure, sadly, that his expectations had been

*I've always wondered what I would do if faced with an Alamo of my own,* Eric thought as he gazed at the numbers.

Just over two *thousand* enemy ships, with the tally still climbing.

Eric hadn't lost his smile, but now there was a definite trace of sadness in his expression for anyone who bothered to look. *I never imagined it would be with my back to Earth and the entire fate of the human...sorry, Terran race in the balance.*

He'd have felt a lot better if things were more balanced, but there was no way that the small task force under his nominal command could hold this fleet at bay. It just wasn't going to happen.

He'd always wondered what he'd do when victory wasn't an option.

*Time to find out.*

"How are we looking for contact ETA?" he asked, checking the telemetry feed.

"At current rate we'll contact the enemy in just under four hours, Captain."

Eric checked the time, running the math in his head and shook his head. "Too soon. Signal the group to pull back at point...one light."

"Aye, Captain. Signal sent."

"Helm, take us back in formation."

"Yes, sir."

The signals from the Drasin fleet had entered the heliosphere, closing on the *Odyssey* and the other ships in the squadron, accelerating as Eric ordered the squad back. He worked out the intercept point, nodding to himself as he settled on a point near the leading Trojan point in Jupiter's path.

*That will do just fine.*

▶▶▶

The group fell back, slowly bringing their speed up to a tenth of light-speed as they retreated back past the orbit of Saturn toward the Jovian gas giant.

Their opponents were moving considerably faster, but had further to travel by far, crossing Pluto's orbit in their sun dive and pressing forward into the territory of Sol's giants themselves. It took hours for the Drasin ships to catch up, passing the orbits of Neptune, Uranus, and Saturn until they began to decelerate in preparation for action against their targets.

The clock ticked down slowly as the small Terran and Prim task force stared down the massive fleet across the rubble strewn space of the Trojan point.

▶▶▶

"Signal general quarters, and run up the reactors," Eric ordered. "Get the pulse capacitors charged."

"Aye, aye, sir!"

The bridge energy was running high at this point. The long wait was over and they could see what they were dealing with all too well now.

Just over twenty-two hundred enemy ships staring them down now, barely one light-minute away.

Eric could feel the doubt, the excitement, the fear.

It was in him, it was in everyone on the bridge of the *Odyssey*, and he could practically feel it as well across empty space from the other ships under his temporary command. The questions were left unasked, but he knew that everyone was wondering why he'd held back so long. Why let the enemy get so close without weeding out a few of them at least with the transition weapons?

That was fine. They were about to get the answer to their questions if the timing was right.

*Please God, if you're there and listening, don't let me have fucked up the timing.*

"We're detecting fighter separation from the enemy forces. The *Enterprise* requests permission to launch," Winger announced.

"Denied," Eric ordered tersely.

"Yes, sir."

The enemy fleet now looked more like a cloud in the scanners, the red dots overlapping until it was just a blob of angry scarlet bearing down on them. Eric checked the numbers again, eyes flicking to his repeater that showed what Winger was seeing, and he blew out a breath of air as the nervous energy of the bridge began to get to him as well.

*Come on, come on, where the hell are you?* he wondered, not the first time in the last few minutes.

It was to be the last time, however, as Winger stiffened at her station and let out a rather undignified squeak of surprise and shock.

"Tachyon surge! It's right on top of us!"

"Even armor! Best deflection! Send to *Enterprise* and all ships, even armor to best deflection settings!" Eric rose up from his seat, his voice rising. "Tell the Marauders to stay back where they are. I don't trust their armor!"

"Aye, aye, sir!"

"Ambient radiation rising. Captain, I don't know what I'm looking at!" Winger howled. "Computer identifies the source as a *pulsar!*"

"That's no pulsar, Lieutenant," Eric Weston said with a grin. "That's the *Weifang.*"

# CHAPTER TWENTY-THREE

## P.L.A.S.F. *Weifang*

▶ THE ENTIRE SHIP felt like it was ready to come apart on him, but all that Captain Sun could think was, *Please, whatever power exists in the universe, do not let me foul this up.*

Captain Weston's plan was both simplicity and insanity, as it relied on harnessing the power of the warp drive and unleashing it in a way that was intentionally engineered to be as close to impossible as possible. The compensation systems were fully disabled on the *Weifang*, much to the ire and extreme displeasure of his engineering staff, and now as they dumped power from the drive back into the normal systems, it was quite clear what those usually did.

Normally, when dropping from FTL, the compensation systems on the *Weifang*'s drives pulled in high-energy particles trapped in the space warp used to propel the ship. These high-energy particles were used to regenerate the reactor mass or add extra power to the ship's systems. Or sometimes the particles were converted into waste and emitted safely through various onboard systems.

Without those compensators and regenerative systems in play, the sum total of the energy in those particles was being dumped out in front of the ship with roughly the force of a localized nova. Individually each particle, while high energy for their normal state, was of little consequence. But the *Weifang* had been circling Sol for more than thirty-six hours now, at maximum warp, accelerating the whole while.

They'd sucked in a lot of particles from the surrounding space, the nature of the drive charging them to dangerously high levels. And now their forward warp in space was something akin to a gas tank filled to overflowing with a lot of very *volatile* material, all of which was now being dumped out ahead of them at roughly the speed of light.

One side effect of this was unexpected, though he supposed he should have seen it coming. Like it or not, some of Newton's laws still operated, even when you were moving at or beyond light-speed. The explosion of energy was having the effect of actually slowing the *Weifang* enough to be dangerous to her crew, since they weren't protected from the inertial force of this particular reaction.

They were quickly able to compensate by applying forward movement with the conventional thrusters, but it was going to screw up their reentry point by a fair margin. Sun just hoped that it didn't mean that they were going to completely miss the mark.

"Breaking the light-speed barrier!"

"Screens, full forward view!" Sun ordered, leaning forward.

The *Weifang*'s screens flickered, the exterior imaging sensors and other detection tech coming alive as the ship dropped below light-speed.

"Reverse thrust! Full reverse!" Sun screamed, eyes bulging wide as he found himself looking down the maw of hundreds of alien ships.

"Warp generators are blown, Captain! We have no power!"

"Thrusters then! Full reverse burn, fore port thrust as well!"

"Yes, Captain!"

Sun was slammed forward as the thrusters went to full burn, the old-style reaction thrust falling completely under Newton's Laws of Motion, the alien ships growing larger and larger in the unmagnified screens. It was clear that they weren't going to stop in time, nor even be able to shift to one side, and he tried to steel himself for the impact from which nothing could prepare nor protect him.

Sun's eyes widened, however, as the ship directly ahead began to *bubble* visibly on screen, and then abruptly burst into flames as it seemed to literally *boil* away before his eyes.

*I cannot be seeing what I am seeing. It is surely too unreal to exist in a sane universe.*

▶ ▶ ▶

# PRIMINAE WARSHIP *POSDAN*

▲

▶ "BY THE INFINITE abyss," Kian swore, unable to believe what she was seeing.

On the screens, the Drasin ships were exploding in gouts of flame by the dozens, possibly by the *hundreds*, superheated by the sudden blast of energy that erupted from almost literally nowhere less than thirty light-seconds from the *Posdan's* own position! She was seeing it, but couldn't believe it.

"They intentionally blew out their own space-warp drive," she whispered, heart pounding in her chest as she watched the scene of horror in front of her.

A blown warp generator was something from horror stories, right up there with the Drasin themselves, she supposed.

To do so *intentionally,* and so deep inside the gravity well of a star, the very *thought* was anathema. People of the Priminae would throw their own lives into the singular abyss to prevent it.

*And yet....* She trailed off, staring at the gouts of fire erupting in a widening beam ahead of the Terran ship. *I believe that I will never again see so many Drasin ships destroyed at once.*

"Damage reports! How bad is the local radiation?" she demanded. "And someone get a count of how many ships they just annihilated!"

"Radiation is elevated, Captain, but within our safety parameters. Most of it was directed safely out of the system!"

That didn't surprise her much, Kian supposed. This particular Terran drive, while clearly based on the same underlying principal as the drives of the *Posdan* or *Nept*, just as clearly didn't have a fraction of the available power on tap as either of the Priminae vessels. They'd run scans when possible, and it was clear that local power was derived from nuclear sources on the Terran ship. Powerful enough, she supposed, but nothing compared to the Singular Drive System.

For that, she supposed, she should be grateful. An SDS-powered ship would have quite possibly exterminated a rather large chunk of the solar system pulling a similar stunt, including itself, of course.

Kian didn't bother wasting any time wondering why no Priminae had considered the move as a solution to the Drasin. She was well satisfied that the answer was simple. First, the Drasin had never assaulted the colonies in numbers that would make such an attempt feasible. It was practically a miracle that the Terrans had managed to aim the blast as well as they did, and that was against a mass of ships that could have blotted out the star itself. Against a small handful of ships, there was no way to be sure you'd hit even one of them.

Second, however, and *far* more important-...no Priminae in the *universe* was this *insane!*

▶ ▶ ▶

# N.A.C.S. *ODYSSEY*

▶ "WE'RE COUNTING EIGHT hundred destroyed ships, and the number is still rising Captain!" Winger managed to gasp out, as though she couldn't quite believe what she was seeing.

The entire bridge was caught between shock and cheering, and Eric didn't quite blame them. The arrival of the *Weifang* had been all he could hope for and more. Even knowing what was coming, he was in a similar state as his crew.

*Going to have to make sure R&D looks into a way of shielding against this, assuming we live to open new projects.*

It was pretty clear that the Block now had access to a weapon of mass destruction that made their own transition cannons look like pea-shooters. Eric was trying very hard not to think about the fact that he had, for all practical purposes, *given* it to them. He consoled himself with the idea that sooner or later they'd have certainly worked it out for themselves anyway, and right now the whole damned planet needed as many WMDs as it could lay its grubby mitts on.

Even that thought didn't quite quell the feelings deep down that he had just betrayed the Confederation, though, so he distracted himself with the fact that this fight wasn't even remotely over.

*Still have just short of fifteen hundred of those damned things left, and there's nothing remaining up my sleeves to match that little show.*

"Signal to *Enterprise*," he called. "Captain Carrow, split the difference and cover the *Weifang*."

"*Enterprise* acknowledges, Captain."

The two big ships of the Confederacy surged forward, flanking and passing the stricken *Weifang* as it plowed through flaming debris that had once been an enemy vessel. They criss-crossed ahead of the Block ship's prow, *Odyssey* taking port and the *Enterprise* turned to starboard, and brought the t-cannons to bear.

▶▶▶

# P.L.A.S.F. WEIFANG

▶ "CM GENERATORS ARE melted into slag, Captain. Engineering reports no chance of repairs."

Sun swore at length, but wasn't really surprised. It was the sort of day he was having, after all. "Understood. Signal the *Odyssey*, inform them that we are disabled."

"Not entirely," Shi offered from his station. "Weapon systems are unaffected, and many of them *are* still in range."

Sun smiled slowly, nodding. "Very good point, Shi Ang Fae. Exchange targeting data with the Confederation ship. We wouldn't want to waste missiles on flotsam after all, and open fire when ready."

"With pleasure, Captain."

Even stricken in space, able only to limp at speeds that would require months to reach the *Earth* only a few light-minutes away, the *Weifang* wasn't toothless. A wounded tiger was still a tiger, after all, and more pity to you if you were within the reach of its claws and teeth.

▶▶▶

# N.A.C.S. ENTERPRISE

▶"TARGETING DATA COMING in from the Block ship, Captain."

Carrow blinked, mildly surprised. "Are they intending to engage?"

"Yes, sir."

"Alright, exclude their targets from our lists," he ordered. "What we have here is a target-rich environment. No need to double up."

"No, sir. Excluding data," Parker agreed, making the command happen. "Apparently this Sun fellow wasn't running after all."

"Apparently not," Carrow agreed. "Didn't figure him for it, as I said, but it's also pretty clear that he and Weston hatched this little plot up together."

"I told you Weston was a loose cannon," Parker said sourly, "and if I ever find the person who thought it was a good idea to load him with antimatter, I'll...."

Carrow chuckled easily. "Calmly, Andrea. He's on our side and pointed away from us. Just be happy with that."

She snorted derisively, making him smile a little wider.

"What I'd like to know is how in the hell Eric 'Raziel' Weston, one of the few men in the entire war who had a bounty put on his head, managed to chat up a Block captain long enough to plot *this* out," he admitted a moment later. "I would have half expected any Block military officer to shoot him on sight, not settle in to plan an ambush like this."

Andrea inclined her head. The captain had a strong point. "I'm not sure. He and his bunch never seemed the sort to have anything to do with *talking* to the enemy."

Carrow made a non-committal sound, neither agreeing nor disagreeing with his executive officer. He'd seen Weston's profile and records once, towards the end of the war. There was nothing in there to indicate that the man actually hated, or even disliked, the Block personnel. If there had been, he probably wouldn't have been considered for the positions he'd held. Both the Archangels and the *Odyssey* were far too high profile to hand over to a bigot of any stripe, even at the peak of hostilities.

There were also more than a couple odd blank spots in the man's dossier, periods of more than a year in one spot where everything he did was blacked out.

Like Andrea, Carrow personally didn't much like Weston for his actions. He was certainly a more-than-competent tactician, but when it came to basic common sense, the man seemed to be a damned hotdog pilot at heart and not the captain of a ship. That said, there was more to him than what he showed the world; otherwise Carrow doubted that he'd still be alive.

Not that this was the time or the place to be debating it, he supposed with a tight smile.

"We have targeting solutions ready and updated, sir."

"Very good, Andrea. Fire at will."

▶ ▶ ▶

# N.A.C.S. ODYSSEY

▶ "TARGETING SOLUTION LINKED with *Enterprise*, sir," Waters announced.

"Have we adjusted the solution for the *Weifang*'s data dump?"

"Aye, sir."

"Then fire as she bears," Eric ordered calmly.

"Aye, aye, Captain," Waters almost snarled. "Firing as she bears!"

"Winger, have a pair of Marauders come up and put a tow line on the *Weifang*," Eric ordered. "We can't leave them out here."

"Aye, sir."

The two ships of the Confederation completed their turns, now sailing away from one another as the big turrets swung out and brought their long guns into play. The one-hundred-centimeter weapons spoke silently, yet profoundly, into the depths of space. Among the Drasin fleet, the fires erupted again.

▶▶▶

▶ "THE BATTLE STARTED well," a two-star general said over one of the many screens currently filled with faces Gracen both knew and didn't recognize. "A little surprising, but well."

Gracen mildly glared at the station's intelligence officer, Seamus Gordon. "You didn't report that Weston had made contact with the captain of the *Weifang*."

"Didn't know," the man in the cheap suit shrugged, his face schooled to stoic immobility. "Despite how he acts in public, he was a decent enough operative in his day...short lived though it was. Not great, but decent enough to lose a tail."

"We have cameras *everywhere* on this station, Gordon," she rolled her eyes. "There are casinos with less security."

"Begging your pardon, ma'am, but bullshit," Gordon said simply. "You need to stop reading the propaganda pamphlets. This station is filled with back corridors and maintenance tunnels that are unsecured, and we lose between ten and twenty cameras a day to normal malfunctions. Sometimes it takes several days to replace them, which means that at any given time...."

"Enough."

Everyone quieted when that voice spoke, and they all turned to see the man on the screen giving them each a silent glower.

"Sorry, Mr. President." Gracen had the decency to look abashed. It wasn't that arguing like children in front of the president was rare, but being called on it wasn't common at all.

"We have more important things to worry about at the moment," President Douglas Merryweather said firmly, "though I do want a report on just what the *hell* the Block ship did to those Drasin on my desk in a week."

There was a silent weight behind that order, most of them knowing that the choice of a week was intentional. If they were still alive in a week, then they'd worry about it. In the meantime, they really did have more pressing matters.

"Noted, Mr. President," a four-star general said from a DARPA channel at the Pentagon.

Gracen had a general idea of what had happened there, but wasn't clear on the details. She expected that it would take someone with some in-depth knowledge of some part of the Block drive system to really explain it, but thankfully that wasn't on her this time.

"What are our chances, Admiral?"

Gracen looked at the president seriously, but couldn't suppress a sigh.

"That bad, then," he said, sounding unsurprised.

"That bad, sir," she confirmed. "Even with this alliance with the Block captain, it's not likely that we'll be able to bring the number of invading ships down much to under a thousand, and I don't believe that I need to remind you that it only takes one of them to destroy a planet."

"Right," the president acknowledged grimly. "They sent a little bit of overkill after us, I guess. Weston must have annoyed them more than anyone supposed."

"I don't know, sir. Frankly we don't know enough about either the Drasin or the people holding their reins to say," Gracen answered. "It's clear that, for whatever reason, they've decided that we're a thorn not to be tolerated any longer."

"We should never have gotten involved with this war to begin with," another general growled, angrily glaring out of the screen.

"That's not helpful, General Steyr."

"Sorry, sir."

"Once they have the orbitals, Admiral, what can we expect?" the president asked softly.

Gracen took a breath, knowing that he was asking not for the worst-case scenario but for what was almost certain to happen. "They'll launch soldier drones on the planet, if they follow the same procedures as in the past."

"All armed forces are now reporting at Defcon One, Mr. President, as ordered," Steyr growled. "They won't even kiss dirt before we have a division on them."

"Good. The Block?"

"Same," Gracen answered for the group. "I've been in touch with my counterpart on their station. The Block military is matching our state of readiness."

"Well that covers at least eighty percent of the planet," the President said. "Our allies cover most of the rest. Admiral Jerome, make certain that we have carrier groups in place to sortie into any area with weak coverage, particularly the Antarctic."

"Yes, sir."

"Admiral," an aide gestured to get her attention, "we have telemetry coming in now. The *Odyssey* and the *Enterprise* have entered the fight."

Gracen glanced over, and then turned back to the president, who waved at her through the screens.

"Go. We'll monitor from here."

"Yes, sir."

▶▶▶

# N.A.C.S. ODYSSEY

▶"MOVE THOSE PALLETS!" Senior Chief Petty Officer Corrin growled to the big magnetic walker. "They're firing the new guns dry and need the reloads."

"Moving as fast as I can, Chief," the crewman said, guiding the lumbering walker steadily through the hangar.

Corrin didn't bother saying anything. She knew that he was doing just that, but there was no way she was going to say anything remotely "nice" until the fighting was over or they were about to die. Then she'd offer up either a *good job* or *it's been an honor,* and not one damn whit more. There was a time and place for sweet talk, and the time was when she was drunk while the place was the privacy of her bedroom.

The loader stomped steadily toward the upper deck where the new long guns had been installed, leaving her to stalk around the hangar bay and look for any other infractions about which she could scowl.

*I do like these mag boots in a crisis. Makes for a real intimidating look, what with me having to literally stomp around like I'm pissed off all the time.*

The only thing missing from her personal image of the perfect CPO was a smoldering cigar in her teeth. Unfortunately she wasn't nearly stocky enough to pull off that look, and cigars were class B contraband on spacecraft. Damned things fouled up the air system.

*More's the pity.*

Corrin spotted another loader shifting a pallet of food stores out into the middle of the hangar so it could get to the munitions behind and her eyes lit up.

"Hey! Don't leave this shit in the middle of the damn hangar!" she yelled. "You're blocking the cat launcher!"

▶▶▶

On the bridge, the lack of munitions was becoming a problem for the firing schedule, and Eric was just short of gnawing on the furniture out of frustration.

"How long to get the pallets shifted from the hangars?" he asked, irritated.

"A few more minutes, Captain."

"Helm, bring us about. I want full power to the laser capacitors, and make sure that the pulse capacitors are charged as well," he ordered. "If we give those close ships a few minutes, we'll be charbroiled on the spot."

*To say nothing of what would happen to the* Weifang *if someone doesn't cover them.*

The Chinese ship was still firing off missiles even as the two Marauder class ships towed her out of the fight. It was an act that, while admirable, was attracting all kinds of the wrong attention from the Drasin ships that survived the initial barrage.

The only thing that had kept them alive to this point, in all honesty, was the fact that the *Weifang*'s initial explosive arrival had carved out a hole the size of a gas giant right through the center of the alien formation and all that was left were flankers in the immediate vicinity.

"Contact the *Posdan*. Ask if they and the *Nept* can provide cover," he demanded. "Or, better yet, if they can tow the ship out any faster."

"Aye, aye, sir," Winger said. "On it."

"Waters, weapons are *free*. Do not let them get their feet back under them." He turned his attention back to the tactical station. "Hammer them with everything we've got!"

"You got it, sir."

A low end whine, almost inaudible, sounded through the bridge. Eric knew that it was the discharging of the laser capacitors being conducted through the hull metal. He pushed the sound aside, though it set his teeth on edge. The plot was showing three Drasin ships near enough to be considered within the knife range of unguided sub-light munitions, and the augmented display lit up the path of the laser as it reached out and sliced the closest of those in half.

It would be three seconds before the light of the explosion got back to them, but they weren't in any position to wait for the fireworks show.

Lieutenant Commander Daniels, having assumed the helm from his trainee when the battle turned hot, guided the big ship around in a tight spin that brought her main armaments to bear on the closest threats. Beside him, Waters's fingers were flying over his computer controls as he tried to stay two steps ahead of both Daniels and the enemy themselves, while locking in firing solutions with furious speed.

"Torpedoes away!" Waters called. "New solution to your board, Dan."

"Got it. Making adjustments now. Look lively. Here they come!"

"Fighters in the sky!" Winger announced suddenly from across the room. "Multiple launches, we've got…I don't know how many. System cannot get a count!"

"Oh, crap." Eric pursed his lips, disgusted with what he was seeing.

Literally enough alien fighters to overload the *Odyssey*'s scanners were pouring out of the surviving ships, probably intended to be used as an ablative defense screen if he knew anything about the way the Drasin fought. Whatever the fighters were intended to be used for, they were certainly going to make it hard to shoot through.

"Scramble the Archangels, tell the *Enterprise*.…"

"*Enterprise* has deployed fighters!"

Eric shrugged. "Or, you know, not."

"Captain Carrow was a carrier commander through most of the last war," Roberts reminded him. "He'll lean on his birds almost as much as you lean on the Angels."

"More than, I'd say," Eric corrected, eyeing the plot balefully. "He has enough of them to constitute more than a minor scout force."

"There is that, sir."

Two entire flight wings were already pouring from the flight decks of the *Big E*, armed to the teeth and spoiling for a fight. Eric wished them well, but knew that they were even more outnumbered than the capital ships were.

"The Drasin forces are filling the gap and starting to press forward, sir," Winger announced.

"Signal the others," he said. "Fall back to the secondary line."

The order went out and the big ships began to pull back, firing off their last salvos as their fighters provided a screen against kamikaze runs by their alien counterparts.

Jupiter was looming in the distance, but that was behind them now.

Ahead lay the next line of defense for the Sol System, the fourth world, the red planet.

Mars.

# CHAPTER TWENTY-FOUR

▶ THE SHIP MINDS were staggered. There were really no other words that could describe their current state, yet even that paled in insignificance to the way they felt. In a matter of moments they'd lost more than a third of their forces, and with even less warning than the previous losses.

It took a long, arduous search through available records to find the last time anything like this had struck them. The only match on record was a natural disaster, the result of cleansing a system circling a previously uncharted pulsar star. Had they left that system alone for just another day, the star itself would have done their job for them.

Here, however, there was no sign of similar carnage on the rest of the system. Just the utter devastation wrought across the ships of the swarm, harkened only by the arrival of a vessel they recognized as the ship that led them to this system in the first place.

It had led them into a trap, clearly, but never in their entire existence had any species baited a trap quite so well.

They would proceed, despite the losses, despite the ambush, because deep in this system was a world so *contaminated* by the red band that the swarm could not suffer it to exist for one moment longer than possible.

Another species might have withdrawn, reconsidered the situation, and reexamined the problem. They might have bided the time, studied the system, and devised a new strategy for its eventual defeat or destruction.

The swarm, however, only knew that the targeted world had to be destroyed, and it only knew the one way to accomplish its task.

Whatever stood in its way would fall. The world would fall.

Everything fell to the swarm, either quickly or slowly. Time didn't matter.

The ships of the swarm slipped back into formation behind the screen of their drones, and then began to press onward toward the ships that were falling toward a distant red world that stank of the crimson band. It was not so filth-encrusted as the third world, the primary target, but it too would have to be destroyed.

The entire system would have to go, leaving only the star here to burn alone in the endless black.

▶▶▶

# N.A.C.S. ODYSSEY

"GUNNERS REPORT THE transition cannons are reloaded, magazines are refilled," Roberts reported. "This will be our last hurrah with those, sir. We've got nothing left below decks to spend when these are gone."

Eric nodded. "Understood. Thank you, Commander."

"Captain, transmission from the commodore."

"To my station, Lieutenant."

Commodore Wolfe's face flickered into being on the screen by Eric's right hand, slightly garbled by the radiation interference caused by the *Weifang*'s unorthodox reentry into the system.

"Captain, by the time you receive this we should be packing up the last evacuation shuttle from the surface. We've primed the automated defenses and set them to engage any ship without a Confederate IFF signal, so keep your allies clear of Mars if you possibly can. If you can't, well, I've sent the necessary codes to deactivate the system, but we just don't have time to recode our IFF system to recognize your alien friends, let alone that Block battleship you've got with you."

Wolfe was speaking seriously from the launch hangar of the Martian base, Barsoom. Behind him the action was frenetic, people rushing back and forth as they tried to load the shuttles and get them into the atmosphere as quickly as they could.

"We've got enough firepower here to splash a fair-size Block task force. Use it if you can," Wolfe said finally. "Good luck, Eric. Wolfe out."

Eric scowled at the screen, mind tackling the new issue of proper application of resources versus the need to protect his allies.

"We're going to have to split our forces," he finally admitted unhappily.

Roberts nodded. "Yes sir. How do we do it without losing too many of our pursuers?"

Eric glanced at the screens and shook his head. "Somehow, I don't feel that's going to be a problem."

He thumbed open a comm, glancing over at Winger. "Give me ship to ship, Lieutenant. The *Posdan*, if you please."

"Aye, sir. Ship to ship is online."

"Captain Kian," he started, "would you be able to help pull the *Weifang* clear of the fight?"

"Yes, Captain. That will not be a large issue, so long as we're not overwhelmed by enemy forces."

"The *Odyssey* and the *Enterprise* will try to draw them away," Eric said. "I've a feeling that this group isn't really feeling all that rational at the moment and I want to capitalize on that."

"I...see?"

Eric smiled. The other captain's tone made it quite clear that she did *not*, but that was fine. If she survived, she'd learn.

One of the silver linings of battle, he supposed. Learning time was very much compressed.

*Much smaller graduating classes, though.*

▶▶▶

The thrum of the fighter around him was just what the doctor ordered, and Stephanos could hardly wait for it to turn into the angry buzz of an Archangel reaping the battlefield. His wing was shorthanded, but they were still the very best the Confederation had to offer, and that was just fine with him.

"By the numbers," he ordered. "Cover the *Odyssey* and keep an eye out for kamikaze attacks."

"You got it, Steph," Burner said simply. "God, there's a lot of them."

*The man ain't wrong,* Steph thought dryly, eyes on the screens with wary trepidation.

The angry red of hostile contacts was a smear of blood across his screen. The computer couldn't tell the damn things apart at this range and he couldn't even get a decent count of the enemy capital ships due to their fighter covering. This wasn't your everyday fight for the Archangels, or for anyone, he hoped, but so be it.

If it were to be the last stand of the human race, or those from Earth at any rate, then let it be said that the Archangels flew over the battle and reaped the enemy to the last.

*I just rather would prefer that it be* their *last, not ours.*

For the moment they had some lead time on the enemy fleet, but that wouldn't last. Not while they were towing a crippled ship, at least. Steph shot a glance over to where the *Weifang* was being pulled back, and noted one of the big Priminae ships moving into place nearby.

*Might be that we'll be able to pick up a little more speed than I thought,* he supposed, though it was hard to say. The Priminae ship had the power, no doubt about that, but he didn't know how the physics of actually hauling another ship around worked.

His fighter chimed at him, bringing his attention to the HUD and the new orders appearing on the screen.

*Whoa. That's an order I haven't seen in a long time. Captain must really hate these guys,* Steph thought with a bit of a grin.

"Alright, Angels, we've got our marching orders," he drawled over the tactical network. "The name of the play is Fury. Cardsharp, you're with me. Break."

The Angels peeled away from the *Odyssey,* rapidly accelerating back *toward* the cloud of enemy fighters charging in their direction without an apparent care in the world.

▶▶▶

# N.A.C.S. ENTERPRISE

▶ "*ODYSSEY'S* SENT THEIR fighters back toward the enemy, Sir."

Carrow looked up, eyes bulging, "They did what?"

"Sent them on what is looking like a full-frontal assault."

Carrow exchanged glances with Andrea, and even she, who had no liking for Weston whatsoever, looked completely shocked and befuddled.

"Weston's not going to sacrifice his own team like that." Carrow shook his head. "No way."

"Agreed," Parker admitted, sounding a little sour for coming down in favor of Weston on any issue. "So what is he planning?"

"Not a clue. I'm not ordering my pilots to do anything like that without damned good reasoning, though," Carrow said defensively.

"A fact, I am certain, that they'll appreciate," Andrea responded dryly.

The *Enterprise* carried one hundred and forty of the latest space superiority fighters known as the Vorpal Class. They were designed to be mechanically superior to even the Archangels in every respect. Faster, better armed and armored, more maneuverable...the works.

The only thing the Archangels had over them was the precision of the NICS interface, but while no one had pitted them one on one in war games as of yet, the Blades were generally expected to edge out the Angels.

For all that, *and* the fact that he had almost *thirty* times the number of fighters as the *Odyssey*, there was no way in *hell* that he was going to order his air wing back into that nightmare behind them.

*Not without a damned good reason and a chance to deliver the order face to face at least,* Carrow thought grimly. *They would deserve that much.*

"New orders from the *Odyssey*, sir," Andrea offered.

Carrow glanced down, eyes widening slightly as he noted the new course plot, and nodded.

"I see," he said seriously, considering the orders before looking up again. "Make for Mars, all ahead flank!"

"All ahead, flank. Aye, sir!"

▶▶▶

# PRIMINAE WARSHIP *POSDAN*

▶ KIAN LOOKED OVER the dispatch orders, or what could be more accurately stated as requests, from the *Odyssey*.

She could see what Weston was aiming for. He clearly wanted the crippled ship brought out of the range of the Drasin. She personally thought that was rather optimistic thinking, given that the enemy had enough ships to split their forces among each target in the star system and still have more than enough at any given point to totally crush any Priminae defense grid of which she was aware.

That said, her orders from Ranquil were clear. Follow any reasonable orders and requests from the Terrans, so long as they didn't unduly risk her ship for no useful purpose, and look for an opportunity to acquire Terran technology if possible.

She wasn't sure how she was going to pull that off, but she'd do her best.

With both the *Nept* and the *Posdan* hauling the stricken Terran ship, they could easily handle the load, but with living human beings *inside* the ship they couldn't move particularly quickly. The space-warp drive in use by the Priminae ships completely nullified the effects of acceleration within the area of effect of the drive, but the Terrans currently sat well *outside* that effect and they would be plastered across the back of their ship if they tried to move more than a few standard gravities.

That, unfortunately, left the whole group of ships limping through space like wounded birds, a free and inviting target to the Drasin that were closing in on them.

*I do not know how it is that you believe you can keep them from annihilating us all, but I hope you know what you are doing, Captain Weston.*

"Captain! The Terran's small fighters, they've initiated an assault on the Drasin forces."

Kian's head whipped around, eyes bulging as she stared at the display. Five small fighters had launched from the *Odyssey* and were now accelerating directly toward the Drasin armada!

*Are they insane?*

▶ ▶ ▶

"This is *insane!*" Cardsharp laughed freely as she followed her Wing leader through a twisting barrel roll that looped them around the edge of an enemy laser burst.

The alien lasers were so powerful that they actually *leaked* energy off to the sides, stray photons not perfectly aligned with the rest of the beam. Some were actually knocked out of the beam by a collision with other particles while some were just misaligned from the beginning, but in either case the result was the same.

Properly tuned detection systems could pick up those stray photons and calculate the location and angle of the beam from which they'd originated. The augmented reality of the Archangel HUDS filled in the rest, and to the pilots of the Four Hundred and Forty Fourth Airwing, such as it had become, the rest was pure adrenaline.

"Keep the chatter down, Cardsharp," Steph replied, twisting his fighter around towards the other direction in a maneuver that would have turned his plane, and himself, into expanding debris had he tried it without the CM field on full power. "Just do your job."

"Come on, boss man," Burner laughed over the comm. "Not like we can't have a little fun in the pursuit of our duty?"

"Fun is fun, but those fighters ahead may have a bone to pick with us over our choice in entertainment."

"I guess we'd best show them the error of their ways then, huh?"

Steph chuckled. "I suppose we should. Archangels, weapons free. Engage enemy fighters, guns only. I say again, guns guns guns."

The channel echoed with acknowledgements and the five fighters of the 444th threw their throttles wide open and charged into the maw of the enemy fleet.

It wasn't quite as insane as it looked, Steph mused to himself as he flipped his plane to the left and rolled under another laser sweep. The enemy couldn't get a lock on them short of a miracle at the speeds they were moving, not with the complex and unpredictable flight path the Archangels were flying. So instead the Drasin fighters were sweeping space with their beams, trying to cut the Archangels in half with lasers wielded like swords.

That plan had one fundamental flaw.

Lasers moved at the speed of light. If one was aimed directly at an Archangel, it was game over for the pilot unless his plates were adapted to the beam frequency, which would take a miracle in itself. However, the aiming system on the enemy ships *weren't* light-speed devices, so the beams had to traverse space, limited first by the technical limits of the ship, and also by the fact that even a platform as lightly armored as the Archangels wouldn't be too badly burnt if they only crossed the beam for a few fractions of a second.

No, the Drasin had to lock onto their position and *hold* the beam on them until they were toast. It wouldn't be long. A second might do it. Certainly two would turn a fighter from a loose amalgamation of parts flying in formation to an expanding cloud of debris that used to contain a living human being.

Unfortunately for the Drasin, the Archangels weren't interested in holding still for the fireworks.

Steph mentally haloed a series of targets ahead of him, writing them off as soon as he squeezed the firing stud on his stick. The forward gauss guns on the fighters roared, launching three kilo depleted uranium slugs into space, already moving at a significant portion of the speed of light before they were expelled from their guns.

"Open a hole, and you better make it a big one," Steph called over the vibration of the big gun sticking from the nose of his craft. "Otherwise we're going to find out what it's like to thread a needle at point-five light!"

The enemy fighter screen was mostly ignoring them, not that he was surprised. In fact, he'd have been shocked if that hadn't been the case. With numbers the size of what he was looking at, you just didn't expect to see a significant number paying attention to a half a handful of gnats, even if they had stingers. It was undignified, for one, and it also went against the nature of a mob mentality to pay attention to a small force that wasn't already their main focus.

That said, they still had the better part of a hundred or more enemy fighters trying to trap them with crisscrossing laser beams, so things were hairy enough.

*And we're about to walk right up to the mob leaders and kick them in the nuts.* Steph bared his teeth as he led his fighters right into the enemy lines.

The DPU slugs struck first, announcing their arrival with the directed force of small nuclear weapons. Each slammed into their target, and the kinetic energy of the strike turned large sections of the small craft to plasma as the hole Steph asked for began to open.

Unlike lasers, slugs didn't need to be held on target for two seconds. Either they hit, or they missed. Either way, you didn't need to worry about them once you fired, and none of the Archangels were the worrying type in the first place.

"Plow the road!" Steph called, his whole body vibrating as he held the firing stud down and the whole fighter shook wildly around him.

The fighters arrayed themselves in a diamond formation, Steph at the center and just ahead while he was flanked by the others at the compass points to his aft. Every fighter burned through their supply of DPU slugs in a matter of seconds of full auto fire, accelerating into the mess they were making.

"Shields!"

Steph followed his own orders, hand swiping a bank of switches even as he spoke. The "soft" points of the Archangels had all been refitted with heavy heat shields to protect against reentry when they had been converted to orbital and space-based use. The shields slid out, covering the cockpit, sensor points, and a few other sections of the fuselage just as the Archangels blew through the expanding remnants of the enemy line.

They were pelted by small bits of debris, enough to destroy each of them a dozen times over if they weren't already redlining their CM generators recklessly. They were doing just that, however, so it felt like a light steel rain on the rooftop, just enough to chill their hot blood as they exploded out the other side of the enemy fighter line.

Steph's shields were the first to retract, or rather he was the first one crazy enough to retract them. Crazy being a very fluid talking point when the alternative was flying deaf, dumb, and blind.

Ahead of him lay the flight's true targets.

"Check in," he ordered, eyes glancing down to the telemetry signals he was picking up.

"Burner, clear."

"Cardsharp, deal me in, sir."

"Black Knight, on station."

"Dread, clear and ready, sir."

"Alright, halo your targets and engage when ready. Remember, code word is Fury," Steph said. "Split!"

The team acknowledged the order and the formation split apart in a starburst maneuver, exploding out in all directions.

Steph mentally tagged and haloed every enemy cruiser he could spot, trusting that the computers would sort out the target overlap. In just seconds his screens lit up with a series of angry red halos surrounding equally angry red contacts, and he flipped a switch to bring his missiles online and wind up the internal launcher.

"Angel One, go," he intoned. "Weapons free. Fox Three."

He flipped open the last safety catch, thumbed down the button underneath, and then squeezed the trigger stud and held it in place. On full automatic, an Archangel class fighter could eject all six of the HVMs in each revolving cradle into space in a little under two seconds.

The two cylinders of six shooters spun at high speed, ejecting each missile out in a split second. Before the last one had even fired up its rocket motor, Steph was pulling hard back on the stick while keeping the throttle full open.

"Archangel lead, clear!" he called over the net. "All missiles away!"

He could see the icons that represented the rest of his team behind him doing the same, their own missiles running hot and straight in space as they called out their own confirmation and followed him. On full burn, with the CM generators redlined, an Archangel fighter could make changes in direction and speed that would baffle light itself, and now they were all intent on proving it.

In their wake, the *sixty* high-velocity missiles they'd put into space wound up and redlined their own CM fields as the rocket motors in each ignited. They lanced across space, more like a beam weapons than any projectile imaginable, and slammed into *sixty* separate Drasin cruisers.

The lighter missiles of the Archangels were of the ship-killer variety, but even with the inverse CM pulse used to magnify the effect of their impact, most weren't enough to outright destroy their targets. They did destroy a half dozen or so outright, from what Steph could tell, probably crippled twice that, but…most important, it became very clear, very quickly that they'd managed to outright *piss* the rest off to the nth degree.

With the fleet, or a sizeable chunk of it, shifting vectors to pursue, Steph just grinned.

"Mission Fury accomplished. Let's get the *hell* out of here!"

▶▶▶

"Captain, signal from Archangel lead," Winger said. "Mission accomplished."

"Yes, I think we can see that," Eric replied, grinning tightly as he leaned back and turned his head slightly to where Roberts was watching. "These things, these Drasin, they're not just drones. They can be goaded."

"So I see, Captain."

"There's emotion in them, saw it in our first encounter… hints at least," Eric said. "Just nothing we'd recognize as humanity, I suppose. Anger, that they have, though."

"Anger is something that can be used against you," Roberts nodded.

"One more lesson for us to teach them before we die."

Roberts grimaced, not liking the direction the Captain's thoughts were leading. "Given up, sir?"

"We all die, Commander. Today might be our day, but no, I haven't given up," Eric said a moment later. "Not quite yet."

"Good."

"Make for Mars, Lieutenant Commander," Eric called out, his voice pitched louder. "Get us in formation with the *Enterprise*."

"Yes sir, but…what about the Archangels?"

"They'll be right behind us. Don't worry about them."

"Yes, sir."

# CHAPTER TWENTY-FIVE

## Imperial Destroyer *Demigod,* Approaching Sol Space

▶ "SIGNALS COMING FROM within the system, sir. Drasin signature."

*Well,* Ivanth supposed, *at least we've located the missing drones. What is it about this system that drives them to this?*

He remembered too well that the last time he had been in range of this system, he'd lost every drone ship under his command, including far too many nearly irreplaceable second-generation ships. Drone ships that had thrown off every spec of security coding and went haring off against the species holed up in the system, defying every order he issued.

It should have been impossible, unthinkable.

Somehow, it wasn't.

The last thing that Ivanth ever wanted was to be within five stars of an uncontrolled drone task group. They were more than merely lethal. They were horror unleashed, a force of nature that eclipsed all others in his mind. Better to fry in a star storm or be blasted into atoms by a pulsar. The Drasin were both thorough and...somehow *personal.*

"This is odd, sir."

Ivanth shook his thoughts from his mind and made his way over to the scanning station, leaning over the young officer's shoulder. "What is it?"

"We're missing at least twenty-five hundred cruisers, correct, sir?"

"That's right."

"I'm only detecting a little over one thousand here."

Ivanth straightened, scowling at the screen. "Where in the singular abyss did the rest go?"

"That's what's odd, sir. I am scanning debris from what looks like...."

"No..." Ivanth shook his head. "No, this I will not believe. To destroy a few tens of ships, yes, fine. I watched that, I suppose I must believe it...but *nothing*, absolutely *nothing*, destroys that many of those drone ships in the little time they've had."

"Signature in the region reads similar to...a stellar pulsar, Commander."

The confusion in the man's voice didn't surprise Ivanth in the slightest. While a stellar pulsar could do the sort of damage they were scanning, there were none anywhere in range of this system. If there had been, there would be no reason for anyone or anything to be interested in the system. It would have already been razed clean by pulsar radiation.

"The more I see of this abyss-cursed system, the more I am convinced that the drones have the right idea," he growled, irritated and generally put out. "Stand station. We'll watch the battle, confirm the destruction of the system, and then report back to the Empire what happened out here."

"Yes, Commander."

▶▶▶

# STATION LIBERTY

▶ "COMMODORE WOLFE REPORTS all personnel cleared from Barsoom base."

"Good. Direct them to receiving areas on Earth. We won't have room for them up here," Gracen said as she walked across the war room of the station.

"Yes, ma'am."

Earth orbit was rapidly becoming a very crowded place to be, she noted wearily. Ships were coming in from every corner of the solar system. Almost eighty percent of the shipping tonnage floating around the system was now parked in Earth orbitals, hoping to hell that the defense grid could protect them.

What was left was hiding out in stations floating around the system, one out by Jupiter, one by Saturn, another out in the Oort cloud. She wished them luck, but none of them were FTL capable, so if Earth fell they had less chance than a snowball in the corona of the sun itself.

She wished them luck, but unless the Priminae took mercy on them, no one else would be alive to.

The signals she was getting from the *Odyssey* were now around twenty minutes old, but getting closer to real time in a hurry as the ship took its task force and plunged toward Mars while the Priminae towed the crippled Block ship Earthward.

Weston had managed to get the whole damned armada glaring at him or, rather, his fighters. It was a skill he'd picked up in years of working for the U.S. and, later, the Confederacy. The man certainly knew how to piss people off with an inordinate talent.

*Interesting to note that it carries over to completely alien minds as well,* she supposed.

"How are orbital defenses shaping up?" she asked, walking back to the other side of the war room.

"We're putting the new satellites in low orbit as fast as we can build them, but even as simple as the cut-down models are, it's taking time."

"We don't have any more time," Gracen growled. "Tell ground control to put more birds in the air or I swear to God I'll drop some old ones on their corporate headquarters and let the workers in the factories cut out the middlemen."

"Yes, ma'am."

▶▶▶

# N.A.C.S. *ODYSSEY*

▶THE RED PLANET was looming large in their screens by the time the Archangels touched down in the *Odyssey*'s main flight deck, the airlock moving them up into the pressurized section of the ship with smooth and efficient speed.

Steph popped his canopy after equalizing pressure and swung himself over the lip of the cockpit, pushing down so he wound up locking down on the floor as the chief of the flight crew stomped up.

"Get them reloaded for bear," he said. "I want to be able to relaunch ASAP."

"You've got it, sir. Splash any new ones?"

"You'll have to pull the records to tally the marks, Chief," Steph said. "I was too busy for counting coups."

"Right you are, sir. I'll get right on that."

"After you load us," Steph repeated. "What's the TO&E from the captain on the next mission?"

"Orders from above are to leave the ship killers behind and load you for a furball, sir."

"Figured," Steph grinned. "That's gonna be fun."

"Yes, sir."

Steph patted the man on the back as he stomped forward, the magnetic boots locking in place with each awkward step he made toward the elevator. He knew that he and the rest might have an hour downtime before they had to go back out, so it was time to make the most of it.

*God, I need some chocolate.*

▶▶▶

On the bridge of the starship, Eric Weston was eying the red planet wearily. He had half a planet's population worth of enemy craft chasing him, and the red desert he was looking at was the last line of defense before Earth itself.

"Put us in a low orbit," he ordered. "Low and fast. I want Mars between us and the enemy as quickly as possible."

"Aye, sir," Daniels replied. "They're holding formation. Fighters are keeping pace with their cruisers."

Eric nodded. He knew that. If they hadn't been, then the fighters would have swarmed them long before the Archangels made it back. He hadn't really been worried about that happening, however. Mobs didn't break up into smaller groups. They didn't spread like that. They swarmed as a group. The primal mentality of the mob could no more survive in small groups than your average human could chop his own hand off and order it to do his bidding afterwards.

They were going to swarm him as a group, try to overrun his defenses, and take him apart piece by piece.

The real hell of it, though, was that it was going to work.

▶▶▶

# PLANETARY SPACE, APPROACHING MARS

▶ THE LIFE OF the scarlet band in this system were more insidious than most. They'd infested even those worlds that could not support them.

It left a taint on the world that the ship minds could smell and taste as they approached the cold desert in pursuit of the ship that had been plaguing them for so long now. A taint that they simply could not tolerate, one that had to be wiped from the face of the universe.

That was their *only* directive.

This particular example of the scarlet infestation was tenacious, like gravity itself, but even gravity could be defeated, with enough power.

▶▶▶

# N.A.C.S. ODYSSEY

▶ "THAT'S RIGHT, DANIELS, tuck us in just behind Phobos. Keep station about three hundred clicks from the surface of Mars and…" Eric considered the size of the moon he was using for cover, working the math in his head. "Five klicks, trailing the moon."

"Aye, sir. Moving onto station," Daniels answered, using thrusters to shift the big ship into place.

Eric mentally reviewed the math again, one of the fringe benefits of being a fighter jock he supposed. You learned to do math in your head that few people could manage to do with a calculator.

*Phobos has a period of a little over seven hours. We should be able to shield behind it until Mars-rise brings the enemy into range.*

"Issue a directive to the defense grid," he turned to Winger. "Stand down until ordered otherwise."

"Aye, sir. Command issued…and accepted," Winger announced. "The Barsoom defense grid is in standby mode."

"Good," Eric said, nodding. "Very good. Stick and move, stick and move."

"The credo of a guerilla fighter," Roberts said sourly. "Been a long time since we've had to fight that way."

"Hasn't it, though?" Eric asked, smiling sardonically. "All my career I fought against the little bastards who hit us from the shadows and ran like hell, hoping we'd not find them."

"We all have," Roberts agreed darkly.

"One man's terrorist, I suppose." Eric sighed. "It's not a great feeling to be under the boot of the bigger force, is it?"

"No, it is not," Roberts said. "I suppose that we should get used to it, though. If we live through this, that is."

"It does seem to be a big galaxy, doesn't it?"

"Too damn big by far."

The bridge of the *Odyssey* was lit up by dozens of screens, all of them monitoring the telemetry feeds of the situation. They had images of the fleet from the other side of Mars, via the orbital relay satellites, and he almost wished they didn't.

The enemy fleet was monstrous. There was just no other word for it. The fighters were so closely packed that they appeared as a single solid mass in places, sometimes breaking apart and reforming in another place. The mass moved like a living entity, only occasionally giving him a glimpse of the real horror hiding underneath.

There were more than a thousand ships left, and he was out of tricks.

Oh, they had enough shells left to hammer the aliens some more. Destroy another few dozen, maybe even a couple hundred more ships before they fired their guns dry. The Barsoom defenses would be able to take another handful, assuming they got a clean shot through the fighter screen.

That left Earth.

Eric knew the state of the planetary defenses. Even figuring for some last-minute rushes to bolster what they had, there was no way Earth could hold off a couple dozen of the alien ships, let alone a thousand.

Mars was the most advanced defense grid in the system. Period.

That was only because the Confederation had won the Mars Race and claimed the entire world before the Block. In order to enforce that claim, they'd armed the moons, Deimos and Phobos, and put a network of satellites in orbit of the world that would have kicked off another war if they'd tried it at home. The Block wisely skipped Mars, moving straight to asteroid mining and investigating the moons of Jupiter and Saturn.

Compared to Earth, Mars was a fortress, and Eric knew well that he had no chance in *hell* of stopping what was coming to the red planet.

*God help us.*

▶▶▶

"Get these birds re-tanked, reloaded, and removed from my sight!"

The Archangel's flight chief was in rare form as he stood over the work being done in his hangar, perched high up on the wall and held in place by mag boots so he wouldn't get in the way of his own people.

The job of chief for the Archangel flight wing was pretty cushy most of the time, even during the war, and it always meant that he had opportunity for travel. Assuming the word "opportunity" translated into *mandatory*, that was. Still, he got to see the world, and then the *worlds*, and did a job that was a lot of fun, notorious as hell, and reasonably safe as such things went.

Being on a starship with an alien armada bearing down on them, his ship the only thing between Earth and destruction? That was new.

He didn't know what his measly five birds would be able to do, but they'd be ready to do it if he had to personally launch them into space with a rubber band tied across the flight deck.

*For want of a nail, and all that.*

It was what he could do, so it was what he *would* do.

▶▶▶

Dr. Rame sighed as the lights in his medical center shifted, going dimmer and tinting red to signal the general quarters and imminent combat alarm. Not that anyone needed reminding. Everyone on the ship knew what was coming.

Another battle. Nothing new here.

Except that it wasn't another battle, and it was very new.

He carefully checked his stock, again, and laid out everything he would need for major trauma surgery, again, and did everything that he was supposed to do before a fight, again. He was well aware that there wasn't a chance in hell that he was going to get any injuries from this fight, though, barring some bad luck for some poor sailor on the ship who did something stupid and got himself hurt.

The pilots who were shot down weren't coming back to his table, and the crew of the *Odyssey* wouldn't make it to his center if the ship took a direct strike from the enemy weapons. It wasn't a battle like anything he'd been trained for, and Rame often wondered why he was even on board.

That said, he would do his job.

Hopefully he had lots of work coming his way, because as gruesome as that would be, the alternative was a lot of dead sailors that nothing could save.

*The first time in recorded history a doctor wished for more work in a military hospital, I'm sure,* Rame supposed sourly.

Better on his table than on a slab, or floating forever in the void.

Rame went back and checked his stock.

Again.

▶▶▶

On the N.A.C.S. *Enterprise,* Captain Carrow was feeling edgy.

They'd ducked in around the edge of the Martian atmosphere and were now holding station just behind the *Odyssey* and Phobos. He'd recalled his Vorpal strike fighters for refuel and rest, but everyone on the *Big E* knew damned well that they were about to deploy into action for the first time ever.

Firing the guns earlier didn't count, not as far as he was concerned.

The latest ship to be called *Enterprise* hadn't been blooded in action yet, not really, and he had to admit that he was feeling the pressure. There was a name here to uphold, one of long honor, a line that went back before the birth of the Confederacy but held as much esteem under its new flag as it did under the old one.

His fighters were ready.

They were the best-trained aviators in the Confederation. He could have wished for a little more vacuum time, but they were ready.

Ready as any of the rest of them, at least.

*Is it possible to be ready for the end of the world?*

He didn't know the answer to that. Honestly, he didn't want to know the answer to that. No matter how you cut it, it was depressing, but that was the reality he was faced with. Quite possibly the final military action of the human race, and it was all going to end with an Alamo.

*There's a poetry there. Too bad I never liked poetry. Too bloody depressing.*

"Alamo," he said softly.

"Pardon?" Parker glanced over at him.

"We're about to fight an Alamo."

His first officer stared at him for a moment, then snorted softly.

"We should be so lucky," she said derisively.

"Excuse me?"

"The men at the Alamo held off the enemy long enough for forces to be positioned to push them back. We don't have any of those, sir. This isn't an Alamo," she told him flatly. "This is a damned Little Bighorn, and we get to play Custer. Too bad. I could stand dying for an Alamo, but dying for a Little Bighorn is just going to suck, sir."

Carrow grimaced.

*Andrea, I love you and you're a great officer, but you need to stop cheering me up before I decide to shoot myself with my own service piece.*

"Captain, the alien fighter screen is about to come in over the Martian horizon."

"All hands, secure to general quarters. Stand by for combat operations," he said automatically, training and reflex replacing all the thoughts that had been running around his brain. "Signal the flight decks to begin carrier operations."

"Aye, sir!"

▶▶▶

# N.A.C.S. ODYSSEY

▶ "WELL, THIS IS it, then," Roberts said tersely. "Our last stand."

Eric sighed. "Oh, I think I can get us out of this one."

"Does it matter if we go down fighting here or fighting over Earth?" Roberts asked quietly. "Either way we go down fighting."

Those were the words that both had been thinking, but neither wanted to say to the other. Now they were out and in the open, there was no taking them back.

They could run, except that wasn't really an option. It was the logical thing, Weston supposed. The *Odyssey* and the *Enterprise* were FTL capable, had large enough crews to maybe establish a sustainable colony, though they'd be better off joining the defense of Ranquil, he supposed. They could even be generous, pick up as many people from the orbital stations around Earth as possible, from the Marauder ships, even the *Weifang*.

*A real multinational bunch of logical cowards, running for the proverbial hills.*

Wasn't going to happen.

Not now, not ever.

*Semper Fidelis.*

Always faithful.

Eric shrugged. "Let's not worry about when we go down, Commander. Let's just worry about what kind of company we keep when we do."

Roberts nodded slowly, smiling.

"Right you are, sir. Right you are."

"Battle stations!" Eric snarled, leaning forward. "Stand by all weapons! Check fire until you see the white of their eyes...."

# CHAPTER TWENTY-SIX

▶ MARS.

Red planet.

Desert world.

The home of the Roman god of war himself, the rusty red dust that made up the surface of the planet was the bane of every human who had ever set foot on the planet and the source of a thousand myths across three thousand years and more. It was a world bathed in the blood of a billion imaginary armies, the land of mythical warriors and mythical wars, a world reigned over by the god of war and watched by his dogs.

It was a world that had never seen a shot fired in anger until now.

The signal was the enemy fleet eclipsing the sun, pouring over the curve of the planet like an oncoming tide. From behind Phobos, dog of war, the *Odyssey* opened fire with medium-range point defense weapons consisting of lasers and light munitions—nothing CM enhanced, and certainly nothing that would be considered anti-ship, but still powerful enough to begin splashing fighters from a thousand miles away.

With the body of the moon and the planet below limiting the approach angles the fighters could use, it was a shooting gallery. The *Enterprise* joined a moment later, her own PD weapons adding to the general melee, spewing thousands of rounds of munitions into space and uncountable gigawatts of energy to join them.

Drasin fighters began dying by the dozens, then the hundreds, but they didn't stop coming.

From the planet below, the god of war watched and laughed.

▶▶▶

"Maintain fire! Point defense only!"

"Fighters are breaking through!" Waters yelled. "We can't hold them back!"

"Launch the Angels!" Eric growled. "Signal the *Enterprise* that we need a fighter screen!"

"Signal sent!" Winger answered. "*Enterprise* confirms. Vorpals launching."

"Their fighter screen is going to be one hell of a lot bigger than ours, Captain...." Waters gritted out, uttering a soft curse when another fighter slipped through his field of fire.

"Quality over quantity, Lieutenant," Eric said. "Quality over quantity."

"Last I heard, Captain," Waters retorted as he worked, "quantity had a quality all its own."

"Don't quote Cold War anecdotes at me, Lieutenant. Just keep firing," Eric said.

"Not much choice, but you've got it, sir."

"They're pressing in hard, Captain," Roberts noted.

"They don't have much choice," Eric observed. "There isn't much value in hanging back, and we're blowing as many of them to hell as we can. They're literally throwing themselves unto the breach. It's almost inspiring."

"If we weren't the ones they were throwing themselves at, sure."

"Even then," Eric said, watching the fires explode out beyond the hull of his ship. "I can find an enemy inspiring, Commander, can't you?"

"I suppose."

"Archangels in motion, Captain! Vorpals launched from the *Enterprise!*"

"Do we have any sign of the enemy cruisers?" Eric demanded, shifting his attention back to the fight.

"No, sir."

Eric's response was one that would be censored from any official log, assuming he had a chance to file one.

▶▶▶

"All fighters in the clear, form up on my lead. Weapons free," Steph said as he turned off all the safeties across his board.

"We're with you, sir," Burner said from his wing. "And hey, check out those shiny new toys the *Big E* has brought to the fight."

Steph turned his head slightly to the left, the augmented view of his HUD finding one of the Vorpal fighters firing full burners in the distance. The HUD magnified the image, classified the object, and listed it as green as the IFF checked out. Steph just snorted.

"Not even a tally on their fuselage, so new they probably squeak," he said. "Let's see how they handle a real furball. If even one of those guys gets more kills than any of you, I'll be *very* disappointed. You get me?"

"We get you, sir!" the wing crowed as one.

"Smart asses," Steph growled, eyes flicking forward to the oncoming enemy fighters. "Initiate laser detection and avoidance systems. They're not likely to be terribly happy to see us coming."

The flight was acknowledged as Steph himself flicked on his augmented systems, lighting up the space around him with the computer-generated beams of light that represented lasers tracked by one or more of the Confederate scanners in the region. Beams flickered into being and vanished just as quickly as the computer detected or lost track of one. Presumably the enemy stopped firing in the latter case, though by Steph's experience with technology that was far from guaranteed.

For all the advanced technology, though, there was still one point that held true from many wars back. You'd never see the shot that was aimed at you.

"Damn. Looks like a concert I went to once in L.A.," Cardsharp said, voice slightly awed. "Only there were more lasers in L.A., I think."

"Any of them able to turn you and your bird into expanding plasma?" Steph asked dryly.

"It w*as* L.A., Boss."

"Smart ass. I'm surrounded by smart asses," Steph grumbled, shaking his head. "Alright, cover the *Odyssey*! No one, *nothing*, gets close. Clear?"

"Clear!"

▶ ▶ ▶

"Watch your fire." Eric settled a hand on Waters shoulder as the young man directed the point defense priorities for the ship. "Don't splash any of our boys."

"No, sir, I'm being very careful."

"I know you are, son. Just being the overbearing commanding officer."

"Yes, sir."

The fight was just window dressing, Eric was well aware, but it was lethal window dressing. People would be dying very soon, and all for nothing really, just buying time. The fighter screen was overpowering, but it was just a sideshow; the real game was coming up behind it, and until the cruisers decided to put in a showing, they were just spinning their wheels here.

"Any hits on the cruisers yet?" he asked, turning to Winger.

"We've got eyes on the far side that have picked up a couple hints of them, but the fighter screen is immense, sir."

"I can see that," Eric answered grimly while working the numbers in his head, trying to decide how long he could hold station against a force that size.

No matter how he worked them, it wasn't long.

*Now is not the time for the Drasin to grow a brain. Hurry up and come barreling in like the thugs in a corner store I know you are.*

They were out there, not far away. The Drasin had no appreciation for subtlety in his experience so far. He just had to hold out longer than their patience did, and that shouldn't be too hard.

*Come on, Steph. Hold out just long enough.*

▶▶▶

Over the last couple centuries, or close enough, fighter technology had come a long way, from a man in the cockpit with a handgun all the way to fire-and-forget missiles with multiple warheads that could splash a target across a solar system. You couldn't hide from a missile, you couldn't *run* from a missile, and if you didn't have tech at least within a generation or two of the missile, you had about no chance of surviving it either.

The alien fighters weren't hiding, however, and they sure as hell weren't running. Their tech may have been superior to the mil-spec ordinance being lobbed at them—that was a point that was open to debate—but it certainly wasn't compatible in any way, so they weren't spoofing the incoming weapons either.

Drasin fighters vanished from the plot in droves, dozens of them turned into vapor before the first Terran fighter even took a scratch. The only problem was that there were *thousands* of them, and they weren't interested in bugging out.

▶▶▶

"Angel Lead, Fox Three," Steph intoned, faking left with a half roll, then twisting hard right in a full barrel roll that brought him up and over a sweeping beam intending to slice his fighter into halves.

The missile was ejected from the bottom of his fighter, its light CM generators engaging in sync with the rocket motors and the weapon flashing away from his fighter in a streak. It didn't have far to go, a light-second or two, and the weapon entered terminal mode and detonated. The explosion threw out a dozen sub-munitions into place, each with nominal guidance, and a second later five hundred square miles of blackness was lit up with a series of short-lived, brilliant spheres of light and fire.

"Angel Lead, splash five."

The battle was both more lethal and somehow more relaxed than most he'd fought over the years. The Drasin were present in huge numbers, but they were primitive in tactics and weapons. Lasers were great ship-to-ship weapons, but they weren't so good at popping a fighter at distances greater than one light-second.

Of course, things were a lot easier when the enemy barely paid any attention to you while you were killing them.

"They're ignoring us! Heading for the *Odyssey*!" Cardsharp called, confirming his thoughts even as they formed in his head.

"*Odyssey*, do you copy that? Watch for kamikaze attacks!" Steph called. "We can't hold them back!"

"Roger, Angel Lead. Do what you can."

"Do what we can, he says," Steph grumbled, killing his thrust and flipping his fighter end for end before slamming the throttle all the way forward again. "We've got two thousand guided missiles locked on the *Odyssey* and he tells me 'do what I can.'"

The lead pilot of the Archangel squadron made a disgusted noise as his fighter slammed him hard back into his seat, shedding velocity in a hurry and building Delta-V back in the direction of his origin. He tagged and bagged fifteen more of the Drasin fighters as they passed him, all zeroing in on the *Odyssey*, and thumbed the firing stud on his control stick.

"Angel Lead, Fox Three!"

▶ ▶ ▶

Lieutenant Commander Frank "Frankenstein" Stathus growled as he twisted his Vorpal around, cursing under his breath as the G forces became noticeable even while under full-powered CM. The enemy was being downright rude, in his opinion, not that he was really going to complain about being ignored when he and his flight were outnumbered a thousand to one.

*Ok, not quite that bad, thank God, but close enough for government work.*

He'd already popped four of the enemy fighters and he'd been hanging back to direct his squad, so the kill ratio was going in the right direction, but it was clear that they weren't interested in him and his in the slightest.

"Damn it! They're going for the *Odyssey*! Take them out, Blades!"

His squadron acknowledged the order over the comms even as he poured on the thrust. A glance to the left now showed him that the *Odyssey*'s Archangel squadron was doing much the same, firing as they accelerated. He was surprised by the power-to-mass ratio the Archangels exhibited. Much of their specifications were still classified well beyond his clearance, and he hadn't expected that they'd be able to keep up with the lighter-massing Vorpal class. But if his fighter had an edge, it wasn't by a lot.

The Vorpals weren't as sleek as the Archangels, having gone back to external hardpoints for their weapons. In the vacuum of space it hardly mattered, and the change let them launch more weapons in less time if the need arose.

*Not that it seems to be much of an advantage, given how much fire those lunatics are throwing into space.*

Frank wasn't NICS capable. He'd applied for the program once a few years earlier and found out quickly that he didn't qualify. It was a bit of a sting, given what he'd seen the Archangels pull off during the war, but he'd shouldered the burden and moved on with his career.

"Flash Com over the net, Frankie," the voice of his wing-man, Terrance "Thunder" Storm, sounded in his headset. "*Odyssey*'s put out a kamikaze warning, copied it to the *E*."

"We figured that already," Frank said. "Stay tight with me. We'll cover the *Odyssey* on the way by and evaluate whether they're heading for the *E* then."

"Right with you, Frankie. Like the villagers are on our asses with torches."

"Burn them," Frankenstein said, grinning. "Burn them all."

▶▶▶

On the bridge of the *Odyssey*, Eric was growing increasingly agitated as he forced himself not to lean over Winger's shoulder and glower at her instruments. The fighters were pressing the ship far closer than he'd like. Shortly they'd enter the *Odyssey*'s "no return" envelope, the point at which the ship couldn't evade them if they broke through the point defenses.

"Have you got them yet, Michelle?"

"No, sir," Winger shook her head, her cropped hair fluttering about wildly. "Still nothing."

"Captain, we're not a Priminae ship," Roberts hissed from behind him. "We can't take even one of those fighters ramming us."

"I know that, Commander." Eric grimaced, running his hand back through his hair. "Damn it, I wanted to nail some of those bastards here."

He turned to Daniels. "Lieutenant Commander, plot us an escape course back out toward the Jovian moons. Let's try and lure them out and away from Earth."

"Have it ready, sir," Daniels said, voice admirably calm.

"Good, get us moving th—"

"Captain! Got them! Cruisers coming in low around the curve of the planet. They're almost at the same altitude as the satellites. That's how they stayed hidden," Winger exclaimed. "Too high for the down-looking optics, too low for the ones looking up!"

"How'd you get them?" Eric shifted, looking over.

"They're launching pods on the planet, sir."

Eric nodded. "Bring the Barsoom defense grid online."

"Yes, sir. Sending command!"

"And you," Eric turned, patting Daniels on the shoulder, "get us out of here."

"Yes, sir!"

"Signal the *Enterprise*. We are pulling back!"

▶ ▶ ▶

On the surface of the red planet, guns and missile emplacements rumbled into action, their restrictions removed as the skies above them teemed with targets.

Spartan surface to orbit rockets roared out first, tracing paths of fire to the heavens where they slammed into their targets with the force of arms that would have been the envy of any army. The skies above the desert world lit up in brilliant fashion for the first time in millennia or longer, casting shadows across the dust-covered surface and sending debris burning through the skies.

The high-atmo guns were next, chugging out a rate of fire that sounded slow but was actually more than a million rounds per minute as they blew descending pods out of the skies with the precision of computers and the vicious malevolence of their human coders. The big metal storm class guns literally punched through their targets with enough force to take out fighters that happened to be crossing behind them, scoring as many as four or five hits with each thousand-round burst.

It was the satellites that the Drasin underestimated, however.

The relatively small HVM launchers had been tracking automatically, waiting for the order to fire, and now that they had it there was no need to wait any longer. Each twenty-ton satellite held five one-ton, high-velocity missiles, and now all forty components of the Martian orbital network opened fire at once.

For the first time in history, so far as Terrans knew, the surface of Mars was lit as though by a midday sun in a nice equatorial section of Earth. The entire red dust surface, from pole to pole and around the circumference, was awash in light as two hundred miles above hundreds of ships and fighters went on to the next world in a cataclysm of light and fire.

Through it all, however, some of the pods got through.

They slammed into the surface of the planet, disgorging their payload, and very slowly, in very few places, the surface of Mars began to *crawl*.

▶▶▶

The ship minds were…satisfied.

They were far from happy—happiness would only come with the completion of their mission—but they had landed forces on the first planet infected by the red stain that burned through their senses. It was a small step, but it was a necessary one.

It had been expensive, however. Many had been taken in the brief assault on the red world and many more were critically injured with no nearby source of regeneration.

That was something that would hopefully be rectified in short order, but for the moment it was clear that the ship minds had a quandary to be addressed. Their primary target was climbing out of the gravity well of the star, heading into deeper space, but there still remained the glaring abomination of the next world down-well from their current location.

The primary target had to be destroyed. That was a clear priority to the ship minds, but the world could not be allowed to stand either.

Generally the ship minds of a given swarm preferred the strength that existed in their numbers, knowing that the loss of a few would mean nothing to the success of their endeavors, but this time the situation was clearly calling for a different solution.

▶▶▶

# N.A.C.S. ODYSSEY

▶ "CAPTAIN!" MICHELLE WINGER'S voice rose an octave from start to finish, the urgency spinning Weston about. "We've got a problem!"

"What is it?" Eric demanded, moving in her direction even as he spoke.

"They're breaking up the swarm, sir. Sending the bulk down-well to Earth, and the rest after us from what I'm seeing."

Eric cursed, though he wasn't surprised.

The longer he'd been able to keep them coming after the *Odyssey* exclusively, the better things would have been, but it had been obvious from the start that at some point or another that strategy would fail.

"How many are going for Earth?" he asked, looking over her shoulder and trying to decipher the garbage on her screens himself.

Technology had come a long way from the early days of RADAR, and computers were far better at analyzing the information themselves now, but when it came to the down and dirty of pulling valuable intelligence out of echo returns from the scanners, a skilled human touch was still king.

*Or queen, as the case may be,* Eric thought as he looked down at Winger.

"Hard to tell. They still have their fighter screen creating all holy hell with my scanners, but every indication is that they only broke off a small portion of their fleet to deal with us."

Eric pursed his lips. "I think we've been insulted."

Winger giggled a little before clamping down on the hysterical urge, a hand slapping over her mouth. Eric didn't pay her any mind, however. He knew just how high tensions were and was more than inclined to let small slips go.

He turned to Daniels. "Helm, new orders."

"Aye, sir, standing by."

"Make our course…" Eric trailed off, eyeing the telemetry feeds carefully. "Three oh nine, mark five."

"Aye Captain, making course three-zero-niner-mark-fiver."

The *Odyssey* rumbled slightly as the directional thrusters flared and pushed the big ship onto its new course, no longer heading anywhere near Jupiter.

"Waters, make the long guns ready."

"Aye, aye, Captain. Long guns, readying."

"Get me the *Enterprise*."

▶ ▶ ▶

Captain Carrow of the *Enterprise* was not in what one might charitably call a good mood. He'd just received command of his new ship and what happens, literally within a few weeks?

*Arma-freaking-geddon.*

Now he was in a running battle with a force that, individually, was no match for anything he had in his command. The problem was that they had goddamn *thousands* of *everything.*

When there were more of the enemy than you had bullets, you knew that you were in a bad, *bad* place.

"Weston for you, sir. Command channel."

Carrow strode over to the command station and linked in. "Carrow."

He listened briefly, nodding. "Understood. Yes. Got it. Carrow out."

"New course!"

"New course, aye."

"Bring us about to niner-five-niner-mark-three."

"Aye, aye, Captain. Coming about to new heading, niner-five-niner-mark-three."

"Stand by the long guns!"

"Long guns standing by!"

Carrow looked out over his command staff and wondered for a moment why they were bothering at all?

No humans would cheerfully take the kind of losses that had been inflicted for *no* significant return and keep coming as if nothing had happened. There wasn't anything living in *existence* that would do that, not that he was aware of until just now. Whatever these things, these Drasin, were, they were so far from human that Carrow knew for certain that he had no chance of ever understanding what drove them.

He didn't want to understand it.

Carrow just wanted them all *dead*.

# CHAPTER TWENTY-SEVEN

## Space Station Liberty

▶ "WELL, THAT'S IT then," Admiral Gracen said, feeling an unnatural calm wash over her. "Here they come."

It was clear that the *Odyssey* and the *Enterprise* would not be able to delay the inevitable any longer. The enemy had decided to stop playing cat and mouse and just open up the tiger cages. She wasn't surprised. The only thing that she didn't understand was why it took them so long.

"What's the latest status on the defense grid?" she asked, walking across the war room to the automated defense control section.

"A new delivery of weaponized microsats was just put into place," the technician answered. "We're expecting the next delivery in twenty hours."

"There won't be another one," Gracen said. "I want full diagnostics done on every weapon, bird, camera, ship, station, computer, and *person* within the umbrella of my command. I want them done *now,* and I don't want to hear any crap about it from anyone."

"Yes, ma'am!"

She swept around, heading back to the scanner control stations. "ETA on the enemy fleet?"

"First wave, ma'am?" the ensign sitting there asked almost sarcastically, her voice sickened. "Eight hours, not one second more."

"Tachyon pulse! *Odyssey* is the locus!" a call went out, attracting her attention.

She was walking over when a second pulse hit, this one tracking back to the *Enterprise*.

"Carrow and Weston just triangulated the precise position, speed, and trajectory of everything in this system bigger than a car," she growled. "Use that data. Hammer them with the last of our one-meter shells."

"Aye, ma'am, acquiring solutions for the one-meter cannons."

"Fire at your discretion," Gracen snarled, turning her back on the screen and walking out of the room.

▶▶▶

"Mr. President."

"Admiral, what's the situation?"

Gracen looked at the screen, sitting heavily down in her own office chair, and sighed. "Worst case, sir."

"I see," the president of the Confederacy said, just as heavily in his place as she was in hers. "I'm authorizing an immediate shift to Defcon One."

"Understood, sir."

"Admiral, when they arrive in orbit...." President Merryweather hesitated.

"I know, sir. I'll handle it."

"Thank you for your service, Admiral."

"It has been an honor, Mr. President," Gracen said, reaching forward.

President Merryweather nodded at her as she turned off the display and cut the channel. Gracen sat in darkness and silence for a time, marveling at how calm she felt. The end of everything that ever mattered to her was upon them, the ultimate extinction level event, and she really didn't feel much inside.

Finally she stood up and walked out into the outer office. "Madison?"

"Yes, ma'am?"

"Signal the evacuation, please," she ordered. "All non-essential staff, civilians, you know the drill. I want a skeleton crew, not one man more."

The secretary nodded, swallowing. "Yes, ma'am."

Gracen made her way to the door, then paused. "Madison?"

"Ma'am?"

"Make it understood, volunteers only."

Madison nodded firmly. "Yes, ma'am."

In the distance, through metal and insulation, they heard the deep whine of the station's capacitors as they were discharged into the weapons systems.

The tachyon cannons were firing.

▶▶▶

# PRIMINAE WARSHIP *POSDAN*

▶ "CAPTAIN, WE ARE detecting a series of trans-light pulses. They are a match for the Terran's new weapon system."

Kian looked from where she was monitoring the Terran attempts to repair the damage to the ship they had towed clear of the last battle site, eyes falling on the new location of the enemy fleet. They'd been tracking the fight as it entwined around Mars, a shockingly one-sided battle for all the good it did. The Drasin weren't interested in killing the smaller fighters of the Terrans. They barely seemed interested in killing the larger ships, aside from possibly the *Odyssey* itself.

*They seem to hold a certain grudge against the* Odyssey, *I will admit that much. Not that I blame them, I suppose.*

That grudge, however, only seemed to run so far as to have them split off a small task group to continue the pursuit of the Terran ship. It hadn't been enough to redirect them entirely from their goal, which was obviously the third planet.

"Monitor the Drasin. Try and get a count of how many more the Terrans manage to kill," she said, sounding almost disinterested even to herself.

Honestly she wasn't, but it was difficult to be truly tied up in the events that were transpiring. The fleet was too large, the outcome already written. Now it was really just a matter of how impressive a last stand the Terrans could manage.

The answer, so far, was impressive.

That wouldn't change anything, however.

Captain Kian walked over to where her lead engineer was observing the activities on the Terran ship intently.

"What are the odds that they will be able to repair their drive?"

"I don't know, Captain. I'm shocked that the ship survived the drive failure, in all honestly. The *Posdan* would not have. Our singularities would have crushed our ship from the inside out," he admitted. "They use a cruder but ultimately more stable power system."

"Stable isn't a word I would associate with anything those people touch"—she nodded her head to the stricken ship—"not after watching them in that last fight."

The engineer chuffed lightly. "I won't be arguing with you on that, at least. They had to be both crazy and suicidal to attempt it, and I'm not particularly happy to have been within three para-lights of the attempt."

"You and I together," she replied.

The very idea that she'd been as close to an uncontrolled drive shutdown as they obviously had been was chilling to the core, but it certainly served as an example of just how far the Terrans would take war. Deliberately blowing their own engines as a *weapon* was utter insanity.

"We're showing Drasin ships being destroyed in the main group, Captain."

"As ordered, keep a count," Kian said, mind working as she tried to figure out just how they'd managed to pull off that particular trick.

The Prim needed that weaponry. Whatever that technology was, it could save the colonies if they could begin development of it in time. It was too late to save the Terrans. The irony of their developing the technology only to be destroyed before they could implement it was not lost on her, but the colonies still had time.

She'd made the request of the Terrans, of course, but had been politely turned down. Oh, they had told her that they would "consider her request," "send it up the chain of command," and other similar words. She knew what those pretty words meant, but couldn't afford to take no for an answer.

At this moment there were three sources of the technology in the system—the *Odyssey*, the *Enterprise*, and the Space Station they called Liberty.

She had to acquire the technology, somehow.

▶▶▶

# P.L.A.S.F. WEIFANG

▶ CAPTAIN SUN DRIFTED in the corridor overlooking the *Weifang*'s main generators, scowling at the workers as they scoured the large equipment in an attempt to make repairs.

"Where do we stand?" he asked Pan, his lead engineer.

"The coils were completely melted, Captain. We've pulled them all and sent them to the fabricators for recycling. Hopefully we'll be able to pull enough base materials from them to fabricate new coils," Pan said. "Most of the rest of the generator system is still intact, and what isn't is easily fabricated on our systems. We are low on fuel rods, however, Captain."

"Those were supposed to run the *Weifang* for five *years!*" Sun sputtered.

"No one calculated the results of inverting the field generators in an uncontrolled shutdown, Captain. We're lucky that the shielding held, or we'd all be dying of radiation sickness now as it is."

Sun grimaced, but let his engineer's scathing tone pass. He could hardly blame the man, not after what he'd done to the *Weifang*. No, he was lucky enough that Pan was willing to speak with him given how the engineer babied the generators he'd had a hand in designing.

"How long to repairs?" he asked, almost hesitantly.

"That is still difficult to say, Captain. We have hours of fabrication left, then another hour perhaps of installation. If it works, we will be mobile then…if not…."

"I see. Do what you can to speed the process."

"Fabricators work at the speed they work at, Captain. They will finish when they finish, and nothing I or you say will change it."

Sun grimaced again, but nodded. "Understood."

"Now go. Rest yourself, or stare at the screens while we work. There's nothing you can do here, Captain, and you are making my men nervous."

▶▶▶

# IMPERIAL DESTROYER *DEMIGOD*, DEEP SPACE NEAR SOL

▶ "WE'VE UPDATED OUR estimates for the battle, Commander, based on their known capabilities. The Drasin should overwhelm local defenses of this star within the next few partial rotations."

Ivanth snorted. "Your estimates are worthless. We don't know their capabilities, only those that they've shown us already."

He glared at the screens, caught between awe and terror. Honestly, he didn't know which frightened him more, though he wasn't about to admit that to anyone other than himself.

The drones were uncontrolled, and that was unacceptable. Unchecked they could decimate star systems for the best part of the galaxy.

However, for all that, these people in this star system might just represent a far worse threat.

Somehow they were mounting a defense against the drones that shouldn't be possible. It just should not have ever happened. They used weapons that barely rated on the *Demigod*'s power scale, were almost entirely invisible to all scanners in fact, yet packed sufficient destructive ability to destroy drone ships with invisible and inevitable precision.

They couldn't be permitted to remain intact. That much was certain.

"We'll stay on station here until the drones have eliminated the main world, then attempt to re-leash them," he ordered. "If that works, we will attempt to acquire prisoners from what remains of the system for interrogation. Their technology must be studied, and we must learn if they have any other worlds."

"Yes, Commander," his tactical officer said.

His second, however, frowned. "What if we cannot re-leash the drones, Commander?"

"Then the singular abyss will be the final ending for them and this entire system."

# CHAPTER TWENTY-EIGHT

## N.A.C.S. *Odyssey*

▶ "KEEP FIRING. FIRE the guns dry," Eric ordered. "Buy the Earth's orbital defenses everything we can."

"Aye, Captain. Reloading now."

The current magazines were almost empty, and when they were gone Eric knew that the transition guns were nothing but dead weight. There was no point holding anything back now. It was the end of the game, overtime, and the score wasn't in their favor even though the bad guys had yet to make a real play.

*Shouldn't have spotted them so many points before we started.*

"Incoming bandits, six low!" Winger announced. "Fighter screen is thin, sir. I can scan the cruisers now…."

"How many?"

"Four, sir."

Eric blinked, mildly surprised that the number was so low. *We just might have a chance of getting out of this in one piece after all. Doesn't matter for now, though.*

"Tell Steph to cover our backside," Eric growled. "We need to stay on course."

"The Archangels are only loaded for light combat, sir," Roberts reminded him. "We sent them out to handle the fighter screen, not the cruisers."

Eric swore, but nodded. "Damn. Alright, have the Angels cover us from the screen and bring us around to engage the cruisers! Stand down the long guns!"

"Standing down the guns, sir."

"Daniels, bring us around and shift power from the guns to the lasers."

"Aye, Captain. Coming about."

▶▶▶

"Here come the fighters, Steph," Cardsharp reported. "The screen is a little light. I can scan the cruisers now."

"I see them. The *Odyssey* is coming about. Let's give her some cover so she can take out the cruisers," Steph replied.

"Right with ya, boss man," Black Knight said. "Just lead the way."

"Clear those fighters out!" Steph growled, tagging and haloing several of the enemy fighter craft that had stepped a little out of line and got too close to the *Odyssey*. "Angel Lead...Fox Three!"

"Angel Two, Fox Three!"

"Angel Four, Fox Three!"

"Angel Three, guns guns guns!"

The calls went out over the tactical network as they threw their fighters back into the thick of things, buying the *Odyssey* time to come around and bring her main weapons into play.

Steph pulled left, rolling over a sweeping laser, kicked his thrusters hard and slid under another as he locked on another fighter. "Angel Lead, guns guns guns!"

His fighter's main gun shook the cockpit as it roared to life, heavy DPU slugs reaching out and tearing the enemy fighter to shreds.

"Watch out, boss, we're penetrating the fighters screen!" Cardsharp called.

"I see them. Hanging, right!" Steph called, twisting back around the other direction. "Don't let them past!"

"Too late, I'm punching through!" Cardsharp called. "I'll haul ass around and hammer them from the six!"

"Roger that," Steph responded, lining up another. "Angel Lead, guns guns guns!"

▶▶▶

Jennifer "Cardsharp" Samuels felt a little claustrophobic as she punched through the fighter screen, the alien ships pressing in on either side as she angled her fighter to blow another of the alien ships away. She was saving her remaining missiles for when she could get a group of them a little too close together.

A glance down showed that the *Odyssey* had finished its turn and was bringing her forward lasers into play. The powerful main array of the *Odyssey* was such that, when properly turned, the Drasin fighters erupted like matchsticks in the night. As the beam swept across her path, Jennifer noted something wrong on her screens.

"Lead, Cardsharp, over."

"Go for lead, Cardsharp," Stephanos replied instantly.

"Scanners cleared up fast when the *Odyssey* dried those suckers, Steph. I'm getting a better read on the cruisers behind the screen, and there looks to be more than we thought."

"How many, Cardsharp? I still read six."

Jennifer checked her screens again, scowling. "Are you sure? I read twice that number, Steph."

"What!?" Steph blew. "No way, no how. I've got a clear scan on six."

Jennifer twisted her head around, eyes widening. "The screen! They're using jammers and ECM!"

▶▶▶

"The fighter screen is breaking up, sir!"

"Captain!" Roberts twisted. "Report from the Angels, the fighters are spoofing our scanners. There's at least *twelve* enemy cruisers inbound!"

Eric turned sharply. "What?"

Winger paled, going over her records and shaking her head. "Are they sure? I can't scan more than six, Commander!"

"Confirm or deny, Lieutenant," Eric ordered. "Full scans. Light them up."

"Aye, sir." Winger lit off her scanners, using up power at levels she normally preferred to avoid since the *Odyssey* needed more energy than her reactors could actually provide in a fight.

The big SPY-X scanners lit up space like the beam of God's own flashlight, pouring enough radiation downrange to qualify as a health risk for unshielded personnel. It took a few seconds to bounce back, but once it did Winger had a much clearer look than before. She found herself just as puzzled.

"I still only read six, Captain…but I think the Archangel report may be right."

"What? Why?"

"Because something is interfering with the scanners, sir," she said candidly. "And if they're bothering to interfere...."

"Then they're hiding something." Eric nodded. "Damn it."

"We can't take a dozen at close range, sir," Roberts reminded him. "Six was honestly pushing things."

"I'm aware, Commander. I'm all too damned aware."

"I've got cruisers showing on the scanners. They're coming through the fighter screen, Captain!" Winger announced.

"On screen."

Against the black of space, the ships were barely perceptible in the visible spectrum, but the enhanced reality display provided by the *Odyssey*'s computers put that problem to rest. The alien cruisers appeared out of the black, aimed straight at the Confederate ship, and Eric imagined for a moment that he could see their laser ports glowing in anticipation of taking the *Odyssey* apart.

That was just imagination, of course. The lasers from the alien ships didn't fluoresce in the visible spectrum, for one, but it was a chilling thought just the same. The computer was tracking six of them unbound, all within laser range.

"Adjust main laser to common Drasin material and fire when ready," Eric ordered.

"Aye, Captain. Firing!"

The distant whine of discharging capacitors echoed in the background, the main laser reaching out across light-seconds of space. The computer recorded the hit mathematically before it could be confirmed visually. The Drasin's ship blinked to yellow, signifying that it was likely incapacitated but remained a potential threat until confirmation was available.

Waters moved on to the next target.

"Captain! I've got them! Six more, hiding in the shadows of the first!" Winger announced. "No...wait...eight more... ten! Captain!"

Eric's blood cooled. He'd let himself and his ship blunder right into the sort of trap that *he* was wont to lay. There was no running from this one.

"Enemy lasers!"

"Evasive!" he barked automatically, even as his mind locked in temporary panic. "Hard to port!"

"Port, aye, sir!"

The *Odyssey* listed in space, twisting to port as the first multi-terawatt laser burst scorched her side and ignited the metal armor in the process. The general deflection armor was like a mirror, but an imperfect one, and enough of the energy scorched through the open segments of the *Odyssey* to space.

She continued her turn, however, rumbling in the black as her enemies came onward.

"Make the long guns ready!" Eric called, his mind rebooting from the horrified shock.

"Transition cannons swinging to target, Captain!"

"Fire when ready!"

They were at such close range that the transition system didn't even need a tachyon pulse to acquire a real-time lock, leaving Waters only to give the order and wait for the big guns to swivel into position before they opened fire.

The black of space lit up as a dozen small suns erupted just a few hundred thousand miles away, silhouetting the ships and fighters against the darkness and briefly illuminating the carnage to even unenhanced human eyes.

The *Odyssey* shuddered again, another laser scorching her side and holing through to the interior of the ship before the armor could properly adjust. The best deflection setting proved all but worthless against the immensely powerful beams of the alien ships.

"Air pressure loss in engineering!"

"Get people down there!" Eric growled. "We can't lose engineering!"

"Aye, sir, repair teams dispatched."

In the distance, the big guns spat their silent thunder into the vacuum, the only sound being a slight whine of capacitors charging and a distant "click" of all that energy being thrown out into space just before the cycle began again.

▶ ▶ ▶

"The *Odyssey* took a hit! Watch for fighters in case her defenses are down!" Steph called over the tacnet as he curled his finger around the trigger on the control stick, turning another Drasin fighter into rapidly dispersing debris.

"Roger, Lead," Burner returned. "Knight, cover me."

"I'm with you, Burner."

Burner and Knight broke contact with the fighters they'd been chasing, throwing open their throttles as they headed back for the *Odyssey*.

Few fighters had made the attempt to get to the *Odyssey* or the *Enterprise* so far, as they'd been more concerned with providing the covering screen that let the Drasin sneak so many cruisers by. That could change at any time now, however, so Steph was looking to break contact himself. But he couldn't leave Cardsharp, and she was deeper into the muck than the rest of them.

"Come on, Samuels, get your ass out of there," he growled, edging in a little deeper past the line of the fighter screen, taking another shot at a fighter that looked like it might be coming around to get on Cardsharp's six.

"On my way, boss." Jennifer's voice crackled with interference, something that shouldn't even be possible on the digital systems they were using. "Things...are...getting a little...hot."

"Watch your six, Lieutenant!"

"Damn it!" she swore. "*Now* they start to pay attention to us!"

She jinked left, rolling right under a sweeping beam, then had to retro her momentum to the right as another ship pounced on her and started to close the trap. Steph haloed the fighters, switching to guided munitions and let fly as he threw open his throttle, pouring on the speed.

"Hold on!" he called, eyes widening. "Break left! Break left!"

She obeyed without hesitating, but with three more fighters joining the hunt, Steph didn't think it would be enough.

His missile went terminal, breaking up into sub-munitions, and four of the fighters vanished in short-lived trails of fire and debris. But the Drasin weren't letting up on the pressure. The three new fighters kept their focus on Cardsharp as she twisted and turned through a series of maneuvers that would kill anyone not in a CM-enhanced craft, staying with her through it all.

Steph got in behind them, going to guns to splash the closest, but before he could close in on number two, Cardsharp's voice called out in that cold dead calm that told him beyond a doubt that things were screwed seven ways to Sunday.

"Hit. Hit. Hit," she said. "Lost retros on my left side. I don't think anything is burning, but maneuvering is shot. You better clear out of here, boss."

"Like hell! Point your nose to the *Odyssey* and run for it," Steph ordered. "I've got this."

"Boss…!"

"Look," he snarled, cutting her off even as he splashed the next fighter. "Either you do what I'm telling you and leave this to me, or you don't and I still take these fuckers out. Only when I'm done, I'll have you up on charges for insubordination. Take your pick because dying out here isn't an option!"

There was a long silence, one that Steph used to line up his next kill. The flash from the fighter dying lit up his cockpit with a satisfying flare, and he was looking around for the next one in line when she came back.

"Roger that, boss. Cardsharp, pulling back."

*Good girl,* Steph thought, grinning viciously as he rolled under a sweeping beam and potted another of the bastards with his guns.

Once she got clear, he figured he'd be about out of serious munitions anyway, and it'd be time for him to make a run for the *Odyssey,* too.

*Hope it's still there when I do that,* he thought, trying not to let that thought dig in too deep.

*The* Odyssey's *too damned good to go down to these bastards. I know it. Don't prove me wrong, Eric.*

▶▶▶

Chief Corrin swore as she kicked the remains of the door open, grabbing one of her men who was a little too eager.

"Hold back, dumbass," she growled. "Watch for jagged edges. You cut your suit and we'll have one more body for the freezer."

Engineering was a mess. A gaping gash open to space just highlighted the situation, but she could tell at least that everyone had been in their suits this time around. That was good; they might find survivors.

"By the numbers!" she ordered. "EMTs, get these people checked and cleared out of here. Repair teams, I want a patch on that hole in ten minutes, or I'll use your lame duck bodies to do it!"

Men and women swarmed through the deck, some maneuvering to check the slash in the hull while others were pulling bodies clear. She nodded to the engineering relief crew. "Get to work. We'll handle the rest."

"You got it, Chief."

It was a mess, no question about that, but Corrin knew that they'd have the deck sealed and back to operating status inside of ten minutes. The only question was just how bad was the *internal* damage. That wasn't in her purview, so she'd leave that to the engineers.

▶ ▶ ▶

"Transition cannons reporting that they're down by half."

Eric grimaced, hating that he was blowing priceless munitions here when the Earth needed every round he could spare to thin out their assault force. But there was no choice. The *Odyssey* would be gone in short order if they didn't finish off the cruisers that had snuck in on them.

"Status on enemy cruisers?"

"Still reading three more, sir."

He considered briefly trying to decide whether to turn and engage them with more conventional weapons, but finally decided not to.

"Pop them."

"Aye, sir. Cannons firing."

"Chief Corrin for you, sir."

Eric glanced at the plot for a second, then walked over to his station. "Give me some good news, Chief."

"We'll have the deck sealed in five, sir. We're spraying the foam into the breach now," the tough woman told him over the line. "But the engies down here tell me we took that hit right in the bread basket. T-drive is out, sir. We can't go FTL."

Eric clenched his fist, his knuckles going white, but he forced himself not to react. "Well that's fine, Chief. We weren't running anyway."

"Yes, sir."

"Keep up the good work, Chief."

He closed the connection, looking out over the telemetry plots, mind wandering on its own for a long second.

"That's the last cruiser gone, Captain," Waters announced.

"Good." He snapped back to reality in an instant. "Bring us about and put our PD weapons to work on those fighters. I want them gone from my sky."

"Aye, aye, sir."

▶▶▶

# N.A.C.S. ENTERPRISE

▶ "THE *ODYSSEY'S* TAKEN a hit, sir."

Carrow grimaced but nodded as he checked the telemetry of the other Confederate ship on reflex. The *Odyssey* had attracted the bulk of the enemy attentions, leaving the *Enterprise* free to complete her immediate mission. They were dry of rounds for the one-meter guns now, and he was actually at a loss for what else he could do.

The news on the *Odyssey* was almost a minute old now, so there was little help he could offer them for the moment. The *Enterprise* had its own problems anyway.

"Get me a flight of Vorpals loaded for bear," he said. "Grizzly."

"Aye, sir. We've got a heavy strike squad on the deck now."

"Get them into space and have them communicate my dislike for those pursuing cruisers," Carrow ordered.

"Aye, aye, sir."

A heavy strike squad could handle the couple cruisers the *Enterprise* had been deemed worthy of, something that left him wondering if he should be insulted or relieved.

*Relieved, I guess,* he decided after a second. Most likely the *Enterprise* just hadn't annoyed them quite to the point of the

*Odyssey*, so they weren't a priority at this time. He'd take the edge, even if it hurt his pride a little.

"Send to *Odyssey*," he ordered. "Ask if they require any aid."

"Aye, sir. Sending."

That wouldn't get there soon enough to help solve anything really serious, but maybe the *Odyssey* would need something that the *Enterprise* would be able to realistically provide. Anything was possible, after all.

"The fleet is closing to within five hours of Earth, sir."

Carrow nodded, though he didn't really have much he could say or do about it. The *Enterprise*'s guns were dry, they had no FTL strike capacity at this point, and the enemy fleet had an insurmountable lead on them.

Even if they could close, there were still *hundreds* of enemy ships left, far more than the *Enterprise* or the *Odyssey*, or even both together, could handle. Charging in now would only get his crew killed, and it wouldn't save a single damned soul on Earth.

A deep cold pit of ice was sitting in his gut, and the hell of it was that Carrow knew that it was only going to get colder.

▶▶▶

# PLANETARY SPACE NEAR *ODYSSEY*

▶CARDSHARP SWORE UNDER her breath as she rolled her fighter to the left to avoid a sweeping beam from a pursuing fighter. The interference had slacked off, and she could now contact the *Odyssey*, but actually getting there was turning out to be a major problem. With her left thrusters blown out, all she could do was fire the right ones and go left, left, and left again.

So far she'd wasted more time going in circles avoiding fire than she had managed to put into getting back to the *Odyssey*.

Somewhere behind her, Stephanos was still flying. She knew that because occasionally his voice would break through the interference, but mostly because his IFF hadn't gone silent yet, and she was praying constantly that nothing happened to him in the pursuit of saving her ass.

Thoughts like that would have to wait, however, since her warning alarms wouldn't *shut the hell up,* and she had this bad feeling that ignoring them would lead to bad things.

"This is Angel Three. I'm declaring an emergency," she said, trying to sound calmer than she was. "I've lost port-side maneuvering thrusters and will need a crash cart. Do you copy?"

When nothing but static filled her channel, Jennifer was about to chuck it all out the window and just pray for a miracle. Training, however, had something to say about that, so she repeated her statement and even got most of the way through before her proximity alarms went off again.

"Son of a bitch, leave me the *hell* alone, you monstrous pricks!" she snarled over her shoulder, eyes searching for the fighter that her craft told her was there.

Her augmented display lit him up and she thumbed her turret into action, bringing it around to engage the target when fire lit up the sky behind her like the Fourth of July.

"What the...."

"Angel Three, this is *Odyssey* control. You are clear for emergency approach, deck two. Confirm."

She twisted around, eyes lighting up as she spotted the *Odyssey* coming straight for her, the flight deck's big maw looking as welcoming as anything she'd ever seen before or expected to ever see again.

"Roger, *Odyssey* control. Deck two, confirmed." Jennifer breathed out a sigh of relief as the big ship loomed ahead, point defense guns blazing.

▶▶▶

On the bridge of the *Odyssey*, Eric Weston watched the brief puffs of light that signified the end of enemy fighters ahead of them. They were firing furiously, attempting to destroy the enemy fighters before any of them got any kamikaze thoughts. So far it seemed to be working.

He hoped that it would hold up, but for the moment his thoughts were elsewhere.

"As soon as we have the area cleared and the Angels back on board, lay a course for Earth."

Daniels nodded, not looking back.

"Earth. Aye, aye, sir."

This was all just a sideshow. The curtain on the feature was about to go up several light-minutes away.

Eric knew he was going to miss the opening scenes, but he intended to be there for the finale.

# CHAPTER TWENTY-NINE

## Station Liberty

▶ "THE ENEMY SHIPS will enter cislunar space in a few minutes, ma'am."

Gracen nodded. "Understood. Stand by, orbital defenses."

"The grid stands ready, ma'am. Orbital defenses are at your command."

Gracen nodded, walking to a central station and laying her hand on a scanner. "I have command."

Earth's orbital grid was a mish-mash of new and old systems, not even a tenth as deadly as it should be due to political considerations that, until very recently, seemed so incredibly important. Most of what was there was down-looking kinetic weaponry and spy technology about as useful as spitballs against what was coming.

Some, however, was new or highly illegal. Both of those categories were of some value, at least. Nuclear missiles, highly illegal but designed as bunker busters to take out Block deep-core command facilities, and newer HVM launchers that were even more powerful but almost infinitely cleaner.

They also had a nice supply of low-yield rockets, automated guns, and other nasty sundries that should be effective against the enemy fighter screen at least.

"Activate all defenses," she ordered. "All systems are to consider Block IFF signals as friendly. Additionally, all recorded IFF signals are to be considered friendly."

"Confirmed," the computer intoned in a female voice that had always gotten on her nerves. "Load drill scenario?"

"Negative. Live fire," she said. "Load signatures, code name, Drasin."

"Loaded."

"Designate Drasin as hostile."

"So designated."

"Engage."

"Engaging."

The orbital defense network was almost entirely automated. Most systems at the scale they were dealing with had to be. Unlike ship's munitions system, there were no humans involved at any step of the process, not even reloading. That was because the system couldn't *be* reloaded. It was strictly a one-engagement deal until shuttles could be sent out to re-arm the satellites.

That was one operation she didn't expect to be happening after this engagement.

"Targets designated hostile Drasin have breached cislunar space. Locking targets."

The enemy signals shifted from white to ugly red, then began to blink steadily until the icons surrounding them on the screen turned green.

"Targets locked."

"Fire at will," Gracen ordered, face a stony mask.

"Engaging with all available launchers," the computer announced blandly as the icons for the defense network shifted from blue to red.

"We have nuclear weapon launch."

The bizarrely calm statement from a lieutenant seated a dozen meters away was an odd punctuation to the most poignant moment of her career, and Gracen found herself grateful for the wakeup the statement provided. She'd just authorized the use of nuclear weapons in cislunar space, something that violated so many treaties she felt a cold chill run down her spine at the very idea of the paperwork it would involve.

*Would normally involve, I suppose. Ah well, a bright side to everything.*

On the screens, the nuclear weapons were accelerating smoothly toward their targets when the HVM launcher opened fire.

The distance from Earth orbit to the limits of cislunar space was in the range of three hundred and eighty-five thousand kilometers. Nuclear warheads could take as long as three hours to cross that span, but the HVMs could cross the same distance in under thirty minutes.

They quickly passed their slower moving nuclear brethren, roaring through space like nothing more than beams of light running just a tad slow, and continued onward toward the incoming targets.

From Earth, all screens were watching.

▶▶▶

**NAC Shuttle, Entering Cislunar Space**
*Oh, what have I done to my poor doomed Mars?*

Commodore Wolfe was not in what one might charitably consider a good mood. His thoughts refused to leave Barsoom base and he'd spent the long trip down-well to Earth digging deeper into a depression he couldn't give less of a damn about escaping.

Mars had been his home for so many years, a place he'd helped nurture from little more than shacks in a frozen desert to a place that he could proudly call home, and now...well, he'd read the reports, he knew what those things were doing to his home.

What they wanted to do to *Earth*.

"Holy shit, what the hell was that!?"

Wolfe looked up, only vaguely interested by the pilot's exclamation, and saw immediately what had prompted it.

"The war has come to Earth, boys. That is nuclear fire in the skies," he said, his voice somewhat apathetic. "Just the admiral telling those bastards...'Welcome to Earth.'"

"Yes, sir," the pilot said shakily, glancing at his co-pilot. "Let's adjust course a little and give them some breathing room."

"Good idea."

Wolfe ignored the byplay. His heart and soul were a long ways from Earth. Somewhere red.

▶ ▶ ▶

# N.A.C.S. *ODYSSEY*

▲

▶ *TO HAVE COME so far in so little time, and still be ended before we finish the race. There's something fundamental about that, about the perverse nature of the universe.*

Eric watched the relay feed from the lunar satellites, knowing that he was seeing information over thirty minutes late. Nothing he could do would change what was about to happen, and even if he were there in orbit right then, that fact would probably hold just as true.

The *Odyssey* was flying into the battle, though, an order no one questioned, at which no one even gave a funny look. He was proud of them for that because Eric was well aware that his crew were more than smart enough to know what they were facing and just how slim their chances were.

He supposed that they believed there was still a chance, still hope to win.

He chose not to disabuse them of that thought.

Hope was a powerful thing, after all.

The *Enterprise* had joined them, but Carrow was holding the ship back. It was clear that he wasn't aiming for a direct engagement, but would probably shift to a lunar orbit instead of taking his ship into Earth's gravity well. Eric didn't blame him. There was no need to sacrifice himself and his crew on this little mission.

There really wasn't anything to gain.

"Sir, word from the deck," Roberts said, walking over. "The Angels are restocked, minor repairs done. Samuels won't be flying anymore missions for a while, though."

"Is she alright?"

"She's fine. Her plane is shot to hell."

Eric grimaced. That was his old plane, but at least Jennifer hadn't bought it. He nodded, waving Roberts away, then reconsidered. "Commander, tell Jennifer I'd like to speak with her. My office."

"Yes, sir." Roberts sounded confused, but he didn't question the order.

▶▶▶

Jennifer Samuels didn't know what she was being called on carpet for, but frankly she'd rather still be out in the furball with her shot-up plane. She stood at attention outside the captain's office for several minutes before he appeared around the corner and walked up the hall toward her.

He didn't say anything as he passed, just opened the door and nodded his head.

She took the message and marched into the small room with as much military muster as she could, trying very hard to be the epitome of a perfect little officer who hadn't just managed to get their captain's personal fighter shot up.

Weston walked around his desk, taking a seat, and turned on the computer embedded in the furniture before looking up at her and cracking a very slight smile.

"At ease before you break something, Lieutenant. You can take a seat."

Jennifer's mind swirled, but there was one clear answer to that. "I'll stand, sir."

"Sit down, Lieutenant."

*Oookay,* she thought as she mechanically sat down. Once a suggestion turns into an order, the one clear answer morphed as well. *Funny that.*

He was reading something, not looking at her, and she got more and more nervous as time went by. Finally she broke. She just couldn't sit there anymore without asking.

"Sir?"

"Yes?" he looked up, that very slight hint of a smile in his eyes now, or more likely a smirk she supposed.

*Bastard was waiting for me to break,* she thought, chagrined. She should have held out longer, but so be it.

"Why am I here, sir?"

"Glad you asked, Lieutenant. I understand that you've been working on a personal project," he said.

"Uh, yes, sir. I've been studying the NICS device."

Weston nodded. "Then I have something I want you to do for me."

▶▶▶

# APPROACHING LIBERTY CONTROL

▶ "COMMODORE, WE HAVE a comm request for you, sir."

"I'm not interested."

"Sir, it's the president."

Wolfe looked up, blinking as he tried to parse that in his mind. *Why would the president contact me?*

He was just a damned failed commander of a destroyed base, but he was still a commodore, and when his president called…Wolfe sighed and shifted around.

"Put it back here."

"Aye, sir."

The first thing Wolfe noted when the president came on the screen was that it was pretty damned clear the man hadn't been sleeping. The second was what he could see in the background. Wolfe's eyes widened and he felt the first surge of real emotion besides self-pity since he'd left Mars.

"Sir! What the *hell* are you still doing at the White House?"

The traditional seat of power of the U.S. government had been adopted, for the most part, by the NAC after confederation. It was possibly the most well-defended residence on the planet—well, public residence, at least—but it was still just a damned residence. It would stand up against an alien laser much the way a pack of matches would stand up to an inferno.

The president just cocked an eyebrow at his outburst, however, and stared until he slumped a bit.

"Sorry, sir," Wolfe mumbled.

"Never mind that now. Wolfe, we're not going to hold this line, I think you realize that."

Wolfe nodded numbly. "Sir, that's why you need to get on a shuttle and evacuate. The *Enterprise* and the *Odyssey* can—"

"We're moving people now, don't worry," the man in the Oval Office said, but he shook his head. "I won't be with them. Not my place, Wolfe. Bad enough that I'm about to be hustled down to that damned bunker...."

"Sir, I've read the reports. *You've* read the reports." Wolfe knew that he must have. "The bunker won't do *shit* against these things."

The president shot him another look, but Wolfe wasn't backing down or apologizing this time. Finally the president just waved it off.

"I know, but my keepers here," he shot a scowl off screen, "they *insist.*"

He sighed, then shook his head, again. "Neither here nor there, Wolfe. The people who do make it off, they're going to need a leader. Someone who can inspire, someone who will keep them moving forward. It's not going to be me."

"Sir, if you mean me, I...I can't do any of that." Wolfe looked sick at the thought. "I'm an administrator, that's all. I can't even get myself moving now that I lost Barsoom."

"No, Wolfe, not you," the president said sadly. "I need you to do something for me, though. Now listen carefully."

"Yes, sir."

▶ ▶ ▶

▼

# STATION LIBERTY

▲

▶ "SIX MORE CRUISERS down. The rest are still coming."

Gracen nodded, stony faced. The statement severly under-stated what they were seeing here. The defense grid had so far destroyed more than fifty, *fifty*, of the enemy ships and they hadn't even flinched. Were she in command of any such force, she would have long since pulled back to regroup and reconsider the situation. What they were seeing was simply *inhuman*. It shouldn't be happening, and they were all faced with a grim reality that left them in shock.

The bulk of the group was now approaching high Earth orbit and they'd begun taking out the satellite launchers that had fired on them. They were welcome to them. They were nothing but empty platforms now; the more time the Drasin wasted with the used launchers, the longer everyone else had.

"What's the status on evacuations?"

"All civilians were moved successfully, but we only got about half of the non-essential military personnel off the station, ma'am."

Gracen grimaced, but nodded.

That was as best she could hope, she supposed. There was every chance that evacuation was only a reprieve anyway, so who was she to say it would be any better for them on the ground?

"Initiate stati…" she started, but was cut off.

"The Block station's opening fire!"

They only had indirect views of the Block space station, since it was in a counter orbit to Liberty, holding in geo-sync over China. The screens monitoring that part of the world were lit up with trails of fire and energy as the Block opened up on the closest Drasin with missiles and lasers. She could have wished for better coordination between them, but Gracen decided it was close enough for government work.

"Initiation station defenses, all emplacements, all weapons free. Fire at will."

Liberty Station had been built as part of a space race with the Block, a military endeavor that cost trillions even without counting the development costs of the *Odyssey* and other similar ships. One of the things involved in its development and construction was, thankfully, an array of defensive weapons designed to act as a deterrent to future aggressions with the Block.

HVM launchers roared into action, spitting their lethal kinetic projectiles into space at a prodigious rate. Lasers whined into energy-depleting action, and short-range point-defense systems pivoted into place and began tracking smaller targets, waiting for them to get closer.

Space around the Liberty erupted into fire, smoke, and chaos as the Drasin struck back unflinchingly. A flash blinded their satellites on the far side of the planet and, by the time the optics rebooted, the Block space station was burning as it entered the atmosphere.

"Armor plates to best deflection!"

The Liberty had thicker plates than the *Odyssey* ever hoped to have, but Gracen was well aware that they'd only last so long, and so long wouldn't be long enough.

If her duty was to die here and now, however, so be it.

"Admiral! Signal from the *Odyssey*! They're inbound on an attack run!"

Gracen twisted, glaring. "No! There's no damn chance! Order them off! Order them off! The *Odyssey* and the *Enterprise* are to withdraw from Sol and regroup. They can't do any more good here!"

The technician paled, but nodded and transmitted the orders.

A moment later he turned back, even paler than before.

"One word reply from Captain Weston and the *Odyssey*, ma'am," he said shakily. "He says, 'Nuts.'"

"Damnable fool," Gracen muttered.

The station shook as a laser glanced off the armor, vaporizing a large chunk in the process. She gripped her console and glared impotently at the screens.

▶▶▶

# N.A.C.S. ODYSSEY

▶ ERIC RAISED ONE eyebrow, looking at his second in command curiously. "Nuts?"

Roberts, the former Army Ranger, shrugged. "Seemed traditional."

"As you say," Eric chuckled. "Give me a private channel to the admiral."

"Aye, sir, channel open."

"Admiral, the *Odyssey* can no longer make FTL. We cannot fall back," he said, taking a breath. "The *Odyssey* will cover for any evacuation you need to make. Send people to the *Enterprise* or the Priminae ships. They'll get you out, ma'am."

He closed the comm, tired and feeling heavy suddenly.

"Are you certain about this, sir?"

Eric glanced at Roberts and nodded, "Yes. You'll evacuate with the rest when I give the order. They'll need you to keep things from going to hell."

"You can't run this ship alone, sir."

"Not for very long," Eric admitted, "but I don't need very long."

Roberts frowned. "I don't follow, sir."

"Don't worry about it. I have one last ace up my sleeve." Eric smiled weakly as he got up. "In fact, I think I'll go see about dealing it out now."

Roberts watched him leave, perplexed, but not willing to spend any more time on the issue. They all had more important things to figure out than their captain's idiosyncrasies.

▶▶▶

On the Liberty, Gracen listened to the short message with angry, pursed lips. She didn't like it, but at this point what was she going to do? Put him up on charges?

*Lord, has* that *ship sailed.*

"All hands, this is the admiral speaking," she said into a station wide channel. "Proceed with evacuations as planned, but head for the edge of cislunar space where you will be picked up by the *Enterprise* or one of our Priminae allies. From there your commanding officers will provide more directions. Thank you and good luck. Admiral Gracen out."

"Admiral, the enemy is closing within our outer perimeter."

"Yes," she nodded. "They do tend to prefer getting up close and personal with their kills when they can, don't they?"

That was in the reports, she remembered. She'd almost forgotten, since most of the reports involving the *Odyssey* never gave the enemy ships that chance. Not after the first time they allowed them close and were nearly killed by some kind of unknown close-range weapon.

Since then, Weston had made a point of dealing with the enemy ships at as long a range as possible without exception.

*Well, Liberty doesn't move like that I'm afraid, so let them come.*

"Admiral."

Gracen looked over her shoulder, blinking in surprise to recognize Commodore Wolfe standing behind her.

"I thought you were on the ground, Commodore."

He shrugged. "What can I say? Couldn't leave the action twice in a row. Bad enough giving those bastards Barsoom."

"Well you're not getting a choice now," she growled. "Get down to the shuttle hangar and grab the next bird off this tin can. We're about to have a very bad day here."

"Yeah, I guessed that much," the older man shrugged, looking over her shoulder at the screens. "'Bout as bad a day as it gets."

"Quite."

"I'd say that your job is done here, Admiral," Wolfe suggested. "Someone else can handle the rest."

"My job will be done shortly. There's one more thing left," she said, not bothering to turn around.

"Yeah," he said. "There's a problem with that. You've been ignoring messages from the chief."

"Not your concern, nor place," she replied without so much as a glance over her shoulder. "This is where I belong."

"Admiral, you belong where the fight is. That isn't here anymore, not for you," he said from *much* closer than she'd thought.

Gracen started to turn around, but a hissing sound made her look down to where a cold object was pressed into her neck. She immediately felt the dizzy sensation of something clouding her mind and body and began to pitch sideways.

Wolfe caught her, looking around at the younger officers who were all staring at him in shock.

"Well, what are you waiting for?" he demanded. "The admiral needs a hand to get to the shuttles."

"Sir!" one stiffened on reflex and rushed over.

"Just one second," Wolfe said, tapping in a series of commands to the computer.

"Command change requires voice authorization from the commander of record," the computer told him.

"Of course it does." Wolfe tapped in another set of commands.

A keyboard dock slid out, along with a hand scanner.

"Override procedures activated. Provide identification."

He placed the admiral's limp hand on the scanner and waited until the computer moved on to the next step before producing a card from his pocket and snapping it in half. After typing in the numbers that were printed on the paper inside his card, he fished an identical one from the admiral and repeated the process.

"Command change accepted. Welcome, Commodore Wolfe."

Wolfe looked around, then nodded to the admiral. "Get her to a shuttle, get on it yourself, and get to the *Enterprise*."

"Y-yes sir."

Wolfe looked around. "That goes for all of you! Move!"

Men and women moved, rushing from the war room as Wolfe stepped into the admiral's station and checked the status of the weapons. Everything was running on automatic now; most of the stores were depleted and they'd soon be out of munitions entirely.

*Lady knows how to throw a party,* he thought with a melancholy admiration.

Wolfe opened a channel, "Liberty to *Odyssey*. We are preparing to launch the last wave of evacuees. Would appreciate any cover you can provide."

It took a few seconds for the message to get to the *Odyssey*, and a few seconds to get back, but their reply was swift all the same.

"Roger, Liberty. *Odyssey* will be on station in five minutes."

"We'll hold out. Just don't be late," he said, then closed the channel entirely.

▶▶▶

# N.A.C.S. *ODYSSEY*

▲

▶ ERIC STEPPED BACK onto the bridge, not something really surprising given the situation. What made everyone pause for a moment and look was the fact that he was wearing his flight suit.

Not the vacuum suits issued to ship personnel for emergencies. No, he was wearing the high-acceleration flight suit of the Archangel squadron. On the bridge of the *Odyssey*, that still drew a few looks.

He walked over to his station and took a careful seat, unused to what had once been a second skin to him.

"Sir?" Roberts blinked. "What…?"

Eric smiled. "Don't worry about it, Commander. It's time."

"Are you sure, sir?"

Eric nodded. "Yeah. Signal the evacuation."

Roberts took a deep sigh, but nodded and turned back to his station.

"All hands, all hands. This is an evacuation order. Please go directly to the hangar to board your assigned shuttle. I say again, this is an evacuation order. Go directly to the hangar and board your assigned shuttle. That is all."

Everyone was twisting around, eyes wide as they looked at the captain and the first officer. Eric looked back evenly. "That goes for all of you, too. Now isn't your time to fight."

"Sir, respectfully, I'll stay," Waters said. "You need someone to run the weapons."

"And fly the ship," Daniels said. "I'm staying."

Eric smiled and let the sentiment spread until most of them had made up excuses to stay, and the rest just simply refused to leave. Then he lost his smile and slapped his hand down.

"No one stays. I have it covered," he said, leaning back in his seat and making an old familiar gesture.

The NICS needles slipped into the scar tissue on his neck like old friends, the slight pinch reminding him of better times. Eric felt the induction interface take hold as the needles began to read and intercept his neural signals and the ship began to speak to him in a way he'd never felt from anything quite so complex. The *Odyssey* was larger, more complex, and more powerful than any fighter could be, and he had to fight to keep from being overwhelmed. Eric immediately locked out the control stations around the bridge, but left the telemetry feeds alone.

"I'm in command, and I am in control," he said seriously, looking around. "You have your orders."

"Sir…" Roberts said, pausing. "Captain, you can't run this ship by yourself."

"Not for very long," Eric agreed. "I won't need very long. Now get moving while you still can. This fight may be ending, but the war hasn't. You all need to live to fight the rest of the way. Go on."

He paused, and no one moved.

"I said *GO!*" he roared, shaking them from their stupors.

One by one the command staff broke positions and filed off the bridge. Roberts paused at the door, staring back for a minute, but then he too was gone and Eric was alone.

*Fitting, I suppose. The first time I stood on this deck, I was wearing the same clothes.*

Fitting, probably, and certainly amusing.

Eric smiled wildly as he nudged the engines, killing their acceleration as he waited for the shuttles to get away.

*It's going to be a fun ride, my friend,* he thought softly to the ship around him. *Almost as much fun as we've had together in the past, I'll bet. One last hurrah.*

# CHAPTER THIRTY

▶ THE BLUE-GREEN world infested by the scarlet band had an array of defenses that bordered on the ludicrous.

It cost more than a dozen ships on the initial approach, and the price of the battle just went up from there. In close, the stinging blows of high-velocity weapons served as a reminder that even the simplest of weapons could be deadly in the right circumstances.

Out in deep space, away from the interference of local gravity field, those sorts of weapons were less than worthless. Even the energy of lasers could be bent and shrugged aside by a full powered warp of space-time, so these slugs of metal were less than nothing there.

Here, however, in close quarters of a planetary gravity, the rules changed.

A stream of fast-moving metal slugs could tear away the armor and inner workings of a ship in moments, leaving nothing left to finish the mission if the planned force was inadequate to the task.

Combined with heavier slugs that could punch through a ship's armor in one blow, penetrating weapons that exploded on a timed delay, and potent lasers that were able to slag even the resistant armor of a Drasin warship—you had a very dangerous environment in which to operate, indeed.

None of that slowed the Drasin, however. The ships' minds had known coming in that this was one battle for which they would have to pay dearly to win, and they had accepted that. There was no real choice, not with the scarlet band being so entrenched here. Some things had to be done, no matter the cost.

So the surviving ships struck out, their lasers burning through the devices that had flung weapons at them and their kin. They destroyed everything that appeared remotely to be a threat, then turned their focus on the central threat that had made itself clear.

It sat in high orbit over the blue-green world, a brilliant reflecting tower in space.

It was the last bastion against them here, and it was time for this world to fall into eternity.

▶ ▶ ▶

"Launch the shuttles!" Wolfe roared over the station wide comm. "They've breached the second perimeter. Station defenses won't hold them off much longer!"

Lights were raging all around him, some green, some yellow, but most were now an angry red, spreading constantly.

The ones showing the status of the hangar, however, were slowly turning from red to green as shuttles departed. Wolfe watched them go, directing the station lasers to clear a path for them.

They had to make it to the edge of cislunar space if they wanted a chance to get away, and he intended to buy them that chance and anything else he could manage. Liberty station was a ghost now, hollow and empty, but still angry and with one last thing to do before it could cross over to the next world.

Wolfe had a permanently etched grin, the angry kind that showed all his teeth, "Come on you bastards! Pay attention to me, those little birds are nothing to you…."

Some of the fighters didn't agree. They were circling in on the escaping shuttles. Wolfe directed point defense in their direction, blowing several right out of space, but there were too many and a shuttle broke up, burning from the blazing heat of their lasers. The remaining ships pressed past. They didn't have time to slow, and there was no one left to pick up if they had.

The station's massive capacitors whined and clicked as they charged and discharged, throwing around enough energy to power a city on Earth for a month with every cycle. All around him space was burning, and Commodore Wolfe stood in the center of it with a near maniacal grin on his face.

There was something irresistibly military about the last stand, he decided.

He could imagine better ends, but he'd accept this one happily if it made a difference.

*It'll only make a difference if some of them get clear, though,* he thought desperately as another cruiser swung around and came after the shuttles.

"No! Come on! Over here, you prick!" he screamed, directing fire at the cruiser only to be ignored as fighters dove in to absorb the lasers instead.

Wolfe refused to close his eyes as the cruiser swept in on the shuttles, lining up for the kill, and he was never so happy as when the cruiser erupted into plasma and debris before him.

"Liberty shuttles, get clear of the combat zone," Eric Weston ordered over the comms. "The *Odyssey* will provide cover."

"It took you long enough to get here!" Wolfe swore over the open comm, still grinning. "But it's damn good to see you."

▶▶▶

Eric was sweating in his flight suit. The focus it took to keep control of the *Odyssey* was immense. It wasn't that it was a big ship—the *Odyssey* was mostly computer controlled anyway, and you couldn't run something this size purely by hand anymore. No, the problem was that his NICS interface was of an older type, more intended for fine tuning of motions, and he was using it to initiate and control.

*I wish I'd had time to practice this.*

Wolfe's voice over the comm confused him. He'd expected that Admiral Gracen would be on the station, but Eric didn't have time to worry about that.

He unleashed his PD weapons on the dozen or so Drasin fighters that were raking the *Odyssey*'s flanks with their lasers. He supposed that the big ship was almost entirely evacuated of air by now, but he'd shut those alarms off long ago.

It didn't matter now if there was air in the habitats of the *Odyssey*. There was no one left to breathe it.

Eric twisted the ship around on thrusters, using full CM to make the ship *fly*, and swept the main lasers across half a dozen cruisers in close formation. They weren't destroyed, but the *tons* of material vaporized from their armor and hull had to have something important in it and he didn't have time to be thorough just yet.

The shuttles slipped out under his guard, firing their burners and generating maximum CM as they accelerated out toward the edge of cislunar space where the Prim cruisers and the *Enterprise* were waiting for them.

Eric didn't know what they were going to do when they escaped. It was something he didn't envy them. Maybe Earth could hold out on the ground, for a while at least, but unless they got a lot of help from the Priminae, he didn't think it would matter.

*In any case, it won't be my concern.*

A warning alarm went off, making him curse as he spotted the approaching cruisers he'd missed. They were coming in on his starboard flank, and that had already taken a lot of hits. He didn't know how much more the *Odyssey* could endure.

Eric fired the ship's thrusters again, forcing the ship around to bring the forward mounted main weapons to bear, but it was running too slow.

The first laser raked low, turning the hangar bay to slagged metal. Eric shook that off. It didn't matter anymore; no one was going to be landing there ever again. The next one was more of a problem, though, as the ship was bearing higher. Eric grimaced in anticipation of the burning beam.

And then the Drasin cruiser exploded in space.

He cast about, even as he finished bringing the ship's prow around to bear and opened fire with the main guns. He started swearing again when he saw his saviors.

"I told you to evacuate with the *Enterprise*!" he snapped over the tacnet into which he was plugged.

"Well, you're very welcome and fuck you very much, boss," Stephanos said in a far too cheerful voice.

"I don't want you guys here," Eric gritted out. "This one's mine."

"Don't be selfish, boss. Plenty of glory to go around."

"There's no glory here, you idiot!" he yelled, barely noting that the *Odyssey* was lashing out at the Drasin around them, seemingly just as angry as her Captain. "Who do you think is going to remember this fight?"

It was in the open, the words he'd tried to avoid even to himself.

When the dust settled, there was a good chance that there would be no one left to write the history. What glory was there when no one was left to remember your last stand?

"I'm not going anywhere, boss," Steph said. "Just be happy that we only had four planes. At least Cardsharp is clear. The Angels stand with Raziel."

Eric snorted. "Fine. Form up."

"Aye, aye, Captain," Steph crowed. "You heard the man, Angels! Form up on Angel Lead. Raziel, you have Lead."

"Roger that," Eric said sourly. "I have lead."

The four remaining Archangels fell into an arrow formation along the flanks of Angel Lead, the N.A.C.S. *Odyssey* and her captain, Eric "Raziel" Weston. The bizarre grouping tore a swath of destruction as they covered the retreat of the evacuation shuttles, hammering the enemy with everything in their respective craft until it was clear that they were not something that could be ignored.

With the Angels covering him from the flanks, Eric put everything the *Odyssey* had into the enemy force, impossible though the situation seemed to be. Cruisers burned in his peripheral vision, enemy fighters vanishing like matches in an inferno, but in the end there were always more. So many more.

In the close-quarters range they were fighting, it was only a matter of time. No fancy maneuvers could be made;

there was no way to run silent and run deep. The *Odyssey* was a sitting duck. He'd knowingly sailed his ship into the shallows where she was all but defenseless, and he hoped that someday, somehow, the *Odyssey* would forgive him for that.

It was the only way to get as many people out as possible, though, and he hoped that was enough.

The next laser blast hit the *Odyssey* head on, vaporizing the main laser emitter along with most of the HVM banks. The bulk of the hull protected him, but he could hear a whistling of air and reached up to close his visor down as he switched to suit oxygen.

"Raziel to Archangels, I've lost atmosphere and positive control. Too many circuits burned out," he said quietly. "It was my honor to lead you one last time. Godspeed."

"Damn it, Raz, get the hell out of there!" Steph growled. "You've got suit air, damn it! We'll find a way to pick you up!"

"No, I think I have an appointment to keep," Eric said. "Raziel out."

He closed the comm and powered the engines. He'd lost directional thrusters used for the relatively slow-speed maneuvering of orbital dynamics, but he still had control over the main engines and the turkey feathers used to redirect thrust.

The *Odyssey* rumbled to life, surging forward under full power and maximum CM.

Eric picked a spot with several enemy ships grouped together, heading for the escaping shuttles, and flew it by eye. The *Odyssey*, already fast in a dead sprint, had lost much of its mass in the battle. It crossed the distance shockingly fast, slamming its forward spars into the first cruisers. They snapped off in pieces until the cruiser met the partially slagged prow of the *Odyssey*, the two meeting with a crunch.

The power of the *Odyssey* slammed the first into the next, and then the next, and again until Eric had four of them speared on the front of his ship like some insane fisherman spearing his in the sea. He didn't slack up the throttle, but kept up the pressure as the *Odyssey* shouldered through a dozen more, shoving them aside and leaving them scattered in her wake.

Eric smiled and closed his eyes as the forward cameras burned out upon hitting the Earth's atmosphere. Everything began to burn.

▶▶▶

"Goddamn it, Eric!" Steph couldn't look away as the *Odyssey* began to burn up in the atmosphere. "It didn't have to go this way."

"What do we do, boss?" Knight asked from behind, the shock clear in his voice.

"We either fight here and now," Steph said, "or we run now, and fight later."

Burner hesitated, then spoke up. "Live to fight another day, boss."

Steph bit back the urge to curse, but nodded. "Alright. We're joining the shuttles."

The fighters formed up, heading out into deeper space.

"No one better be landing these buckets with a single round of ammo left," Steph said. "Not one. You get me?"

"We got you, boss!"

▶▶▶

Commodore Wolfe watched as the *Odyssey* vanished over the horizon of the blue-white world. He smiled sadly at the image.

"Farewell, friend."

The Drasin were turning back their attentions in his direction, so he knew that he'd soon be following his friend into the next world, but that was fine with him. He was ready for it.

The outer perimeter was breached and he grinned as their lasers started to chop Liberty to pieces.

They broke the second perimeter and more security alarms sounded, but he just ignored them.

His weapons were gone, cut out by the force of the enemy, slagged to their component materials and left to cool in the vacuum of space.

Most of his weapons.

He had one left, one that Admiral Gracen had been holding in reserve.

When they breached the third perimeter and he began to feel a woozy loss of focus, he knew that they were close enough, and he used it.

"What can I say?" he said over an open comm, still grinning as the enemy's secret weapon caused him to collapse. "It's a trap."

Three seconds later the station's CM field inverted, and Wolfe was slammed into the deck hard enough to split his skull and break every bone in his body. He died before the rest happened, the slow, creaking collapse of the station as it fell in on itself, the sudden panicked attempt at flight by the alien ships as they were dragged in.

He saw none of it, but somehow that grin was still on his face right up until Station Liberty collapsed into a singularity that sucked eight Drasin cruisers and countless fighters in along with it. It only held stable for an instant, then exploded outwards as it destabilized, destroying another dozen more ships in the process.

When it was over, however, there were only Drasin ships in orbit over the Earth.

And they began to launch pods down to the surface.

▶▶▶

# EPILOGUE

▶ADMIRAL ELIZABETH GRACEN was far from a happy woman.

She'd spent the entire trip from Sol to Ranquil in a sullen silence, only seen by her attendants. She wasn't ready for what she had to do, hadn't been prepared for it. She should have died on the Liberty; she'd spent days preparing herself for just that.

Now here she was, in orbit of an alien world, on an alien ship no less, and she didn't even know if Earth still existed.

"Admiral?"

"What is it?" she asked dully to her most junior aide, who had probably drawn the short straw and had to come speak with her.

"Ambassador LaFontaine and Admiral Tanner to see you, ma'am."

Gracen took a breath and nodded, standing up and straightening out her appearance. "Alright, I'll see them."

"Yes, ma'am."

The child looked far too happy that she was seeing anyone, Gracen reflected, but it wasn't like she had a choice. An ambassador and the fleet admiral of an ally? Oh yes, she knew who Tanner was. There was no choice but to see him.

The two entered the suite that she had been provided on the *Posdan*. She had elected not to stay on the *Enterprise* for various reasons, mostly personal ones. Here no one bothered her, and she didn't want to be bothered.

Now, however, that hideaway was taken from her.

Gracen unconsciously straightened. Maybe it's. *Maybe it's time to be an admiral again.*

"Admiral," LaFontaine said and nodded. "This is Rael Tanner, Fleet Admiral of the Priminae people."

"Admiral," she shook his hand, then nodded to LaFontaine. "Ambassador. What brings you here?"

"We'd be having this meeting soon enough," the ambassador said. "However Admiral Tanner requested a fast meeting."

Gracen turned her focus to the small man. "Oh?"

"I have been authorized to discuss a…deeper alliance," he said softly. "We want your technology, Admiral."

She snorted. Of course they did. What world wouldn't?

"Even with it, you can't build enough ships to make a difference," she said. "It's taken everything you could muster just to meet their scouting groups. What we saw at Earth was…."

She swallowed, looking away.

"Yes, I've seen the records," he said quietly, "including the loss of the *Odyssey*. Ranquil will be declaring a week of mourning for the loss."

"Thank you, but my point remains."

"I thought you may need convincing, Admiral," he said, gesturing to the door. "Come with me, if you please?"

Gracen hesitated, but then decided she had nothing left to lose anyway. She probably would give them what they wanted.

She just didn't want to throw it all down the same hole she saw at Earth.

▶▶▶

Captain Eric Weston felt a familiar sensation, one that he hadn't felt in a long time.

This was odd because he'd been under the impression that he was, at best, going to be quite dead and that wasn't something he'd ever felt. Worst case he'd have been burned alive, which was also pretty unknown, so any familiar sensation was an improvement, he supposed.

He wasn't in pain, which was patently impossible.

*I did just crash my ship into a dozen enemy ships and then into the planet Earth, right?*

"You did."

His eyes snapped open, and instantly he noted that he was on the broken bridge of the *Odyssey*, but nothing seemed quite real. Like it was greyed out and only he was in color....

Well, he and one other.

He looked at her numbly for a long moment. "What happened? And who are you?"

"What happened," she said with a smile, "was that you have not yet finished your war, Captain."

*This is a dream. It's got to be. Maybe I survived the crash? It's possible. The* Odyssey's *CM was still working....*

"Yes, it was," the woman told him simply. "Not that it would have mattered. I can be quite compelling when I need to be, and I need very much not to be killed, so I decided that you are going to save me."

"Excuse me? Who are you?" he stammered. Then a realization hit him. "You're like *him*."

"I've had many names, Captain Weston. More than you, even," she said with a mild laugh. Her expression then turned feral, her smile nasty as she leaned in and extended a hand to him. "Take my hand, Captain, and we will show these invaders that they should never anger the loving mother, lest they awaken the vengeful bitch. Our enemies will know me only as terror, but you, Captain, you may call me Gaia."

▶▶▶

Gracen stood frozen, unbelieving.

"This is impossible."

The screens on the bridge of the big ship looked out on the roiling red plasma of the system's star. That was all that was visible in *every* direction. It just couldn't be…they couldn't be *inside* a star.

Not quite every direction, part of her mind was quick to point out.

No, there was one place that wasn't the boiling plasma of the star, but that spot made even less sense than the ship still existing as it did. They were in orbit of a *planet*. It was such an incongruous planet too, with blue-green seas, white clouds, and what appeared to be tropical island chains dotting the ocean.

It just couldn't exist; her mind wouldn't allow her to believe it existed. Not while she was looking past it to the roiling plasma of a *star* that literally covered every other place she looked.

"I assure you that it is not," Tanner said calmly. "Ranquil is not our home world, and our star was not always a red giant. Once our star was very much like your own, and then it began to change in a very short time in stellar terms. Luckily it was a very long time for humans, and we prepared. This is the result."

He gestured to the screen and the planet with the massive infrastructure floating in orbit. "Welcome to the Forge, Admiral, and as you can see we are now quite prepared to build a great many ships for our defense. This is time for which your people may have died to buy us, and for that I am incredibly sorry...but you can help us avenge them, if nothing else. We need your technology."

He took a breath. "In the spirit of a true alliance, we will build you ships as well. You may even have the first ship of our combined technology, Admiral. We...we could call it *Odyssey*, perhaps?"

Gracen had to force the shock down. She didn't know any other way to do it though save to drag back up the admiral part of her she'd almost buried through the trauma of what had happened. She straightened in place, eyes flicking to the impossible scene on the screens that showed what lay beyond the ship.

"No, Admiral," she said with a dry mouth. "I...we don't need the voyage of destiny anymore…. We need the warrior king."

She looked out on the planet beyond, thinking of all the destruction she'd just fled, and found that maybe hope wasn't entirely dead.

"Call her…*Odysseus.*"

# ABOUT THE AUTHOR

Evan Currie is the bestselling author of the Odyssey One series, the Warrior's Wings series, and more. Although his post-secondary education was in computer sciences, and he has worked in the local lobster industry steadily over the last decade, writing has always been his true passion. Currie himself says it best: "It's what I do for fun and to relax. There's not much I can imagine better than being a storyteller."